ONWARDS & OUTWARDS

Jack Caseros

Published by Kaleidoscope Reality.

ISBN-13: 978-0-9878969-1-9

Find more information on Jack Caseros and Kaleidoscope Reality at:

www.jackcaseros.webs.com or
www.jackcaseros.wordpress.com

Or follow the sporadic aphorisms of @JackCaseros on Twitter.

~~FOREWORD~~ FOREWARN

Dear Reader,

Onwards & Outwards began with a single short story. Truth is that it was the middle of winter and I was feeling especially nostalgic. So I wrote about Atlas & Henryk, two best friends who take a trip through the urban wilderness. Half way through the story I felt it—a complete gestalt. That first trippy short story was the inaugural adventure for the Homeboys.

The stories began as random scraps of the Homeboys' lives. Generally, I wanted to capture the quizzical essence of life, with its synchronicities, sufferings, and little awakenings. But the more I wrote, the more complete their story became (yeah, at this point I was just a stand-in typist for Atlas Sangman, Henryk Zdicz, Martin O'Neill, and Simon Arcan). This book is a fraction of their lives, just like any piece of art is a fraction of the multitudinous Truth it attempts to reveal. Despairingly, I cut out more stories than I wanted to, but the Homeboys had whittled the random occurrences of life into something like a plot—the very thing I was coyly avoiding.

Somehow, that original short story was lost.

The story is told in haibun vignettes. I wished that meant vegetable puppets too, but it is actually a blend of Japanese haibun and the post-modern vignette. They captured what I wanted to convey: (mostly) short koanic moments, when everything down to the smallest detail conspires to *mean* something to you. The little awakenings, as mentioned above, which underlie all of life's synchronicities and sufferings.

You can avoid the haikus. In fact, if you're not a fan of them, don't read them at all. They are supplementary to the prose. Compose your own haiku and ignore mine.

And, yes, this book is self-published.

Call it vanity, call it foolishness, call it impatience or pride—it won't matter. It won't change the fact that the idealized industry of the printed word has been so idolized that best-seller status (i.e. quantity) has surpassed the essential benefit (i.e. quality) of literature. Publishing houses have become ivory towers, where a handful of editors become holy sentinels, deciding which books are accessible to the public. And those dejected writers who have toiled over their stories feel like if they can't impress these gatekeepers their work is worthless. Understandably, these editors are trying to make money, which is unfortunate, because that means they need to adopt a corporate consciousness, which dictates that net profit is the goal of any published work.

The point being that just like any behaviour, art should be so engrained in our lives that we are all producing it everyday to the pleasure of our friends, family, community, or society. Whatever your medium, it is not just something you do but a way of living. Story-telling at the bar isn't pre-approved by an editor, so why should novels be?

On another note, you may or may not have an opinion on capitalism, imperialism, neo-colonialism, exploitationism, etc, but what we still probably share in common is a dread for money. Even if you like money, you only enjoy the things money buys you, which exist whether or not money does (money only lubricates their production). Money itself sucks. In many ways, money is like the airbags in this societal vehicle—it kills more than it saves lives. So why put more people in the way of money when art should be as accessible as a conversation or an anonymous dance in a packed nightclub.

I could save my ranting for political rallies or protests, but we both know those are useless. The only way that modern, mainstream North American society shows you respect is when you are the underdog who chooses their lifestyle with defiant courage (that's also how they profile you easiest when they need to assassinate you). I'm no hero, but I am defiant—that's why this book is self-published.

If you have any compassion you'd want to know this took me 1.5 yrs to write, but I don't care whether you want to know or not. In fact, let's make this a one night stand—you read what I write, and we won't call each other in the morning.

So stay corrupted & in love, dear Reader.

With sincere regret,

Jack Caseros

P.S. Om manipadme hum[1]

P.P.S. Also, to maintain the purity of the narrative and dialogue, there is an element of multilingualism. I

---

[1] ***Om manipadme hum*** — (*Sanskrit*) Buddhist mantra; usually associated with compassion

trust that you have the capacity to learn the variety of languages I used, but since I'm a good little Echo Boomer, I'll take for granted that you're as lazy as I am and won't bother looking them up (e.g. the mantra in the above postscript). Therefore, please refer to the linked translations.

All goes onward and outward, nothing collapses,
And to die is different from what any one supposed,
and luckier.

Walt Whitman

THE FIRST MOVEMENT

IT FELT LIKE AN ECSTATIC ENERGY IN THE SUBURBS

THE ANSWER
[Atlas Sangman]

The third final exam essay question, 'Modern Views of Politics' PS104-B.

Q: What was the long-lasting effect of the Age of Enlightenment?

A: ~~The long-lasting~~ The long-lasting ~~sha~~ effect of the Enlightenment was ~~a longing for liber~~ the long shadow it cast. Ah, fuck this.

RADIATE
[Martin O'Neill]

"Here's how it goes. Simple as this: all we are is a transfer of energy. Energy is mass, and we are mass, so we can infer that we are energy."

"Simon, my friend," Henryk grabbed Simon's shoulder. "How could you bust out quantum physics right now? As I recall, you weren't even in any science classes beyond the minimum requirement in highschool."

"Nope. Who the fuck would?" Simon said.

"I did," Henryk retorted.

"So what do you know about quantum physics, Dr. Hawking?"

"Well don't be such a prick, tell us about Dr. Hawking," I said.

It might have sounded angry, but I could only be so candid with these guys: the Homeboys. My Homeboys.

"Do you want to explain, Doctor Zdicz?" Simon teased Henryk.

"Simon's got some solid logic about it," Atlas piped in disjointedly.

"Well I still don't get it," I admitted.

"It's bigger than what I know. Very esoteric and complicated," Henryk said, "But what I can tell you is Simon's making Einstein's relativity theory assume social factors that it doesn't."

"Oh right, relativity theory."

I rolled my eyes, but hid it behind a drag on my cigarette.

"We can look it up on the internet," Henryk said.

"Using quantum physics?"

"Man, I just think we're all going to trip out on something worth nothing," Atlas shrugged.

"Hold the fuck up," Simon said, loading the pipe, "This isn't worth nothing. Atlas, you got your weird telepathic Claire thing, Henryk's got his nature thing, and Martin's got his eye thing. I got my energy thing. I've listened to your shit, and now I'm feeling my own thing."

"But you disregarded and criticized our things with the most inane points."

Though Henryk and Simon were technically arguing, they were laughing the whole time. In fact, everyone was laughing. It made sense at the time. The River riffled beside us. It was spring. We had had a serious downpour in the fall and blizzards all winter. It was brutal, and even the rivers were choked up with its departure. Nothing passed easily.

I watched Simon with intent as he lit the pipe and passed it on. I smoked my turn on the rotation and passed it back to the man himself.

"Check out all the stars, guy. There are none. I see nine airplanes," he said.

"Yeah, and two satellites. What a shame."

"The moon's out," I pointed to where it floated.

"That last time we were on acid I remember feeling like I was stuck on the earth, but not enough to hold me down," Simon said, "Like, I could've flung off if I moved my weight too far off the surface."

"I believe it's called gravity," I said.

"Gravity. *Grav-i-ty*," Henryk repeated to Simon, as if those three syllables explained what he was saying.

"My energy thing is tight. Fit tempo, guy. Gravity is a prime example of how we can actually feel ourselves attached to everybody and everything."

"Hey, check it out, that's Venus."

We all looked to where Atlas pointed with squinted eyes.

"Or is it a plane flying directly towards us?" I asked.

"Just a transfer of energy," said Simon. "It doesn't matter if we're here or there, we're still facing the basic human predicament: the impending inevitable loss of that energy. So it goes, I suppose."

"Sy, I'll read up on it and get back to you."

"I think it's a cool concept," I said.

I nodded to Simon, who was watching us while we watched the airplanes.

"Damn right. Martin's got the vision. He has the glass doors. Glass doors you can see through and be seen through, and that energy is as open to you as you are open to it. Give and take and give and take, and soon you're on a one way mission to Mars."

"Sy, man, you better get on that ship."

"Damn right, I'll be there. There'll be a volunteer seat for civilians like ourselves. My ass'll be on that seat, guy."

"I think I'm burning out," Atlas said after a few moments of silence.

"We should go," Henryk said, "I have to work in the morning."

We drove back home to the inner suburbs. Mississauga was one of Toronto's satellite cities, where cookie-cutter streets housed the culturally mosaic'd families whose lifestyles revolved around work and consumerism.

In the backseat I squinted from the streetlights. The music pulsed. The lights streamed by, faithful as ever. I counted them in between songs. Orange and blue, orange and blue. The colour I had known most intimately my whole life. Orange and blue, orange and blue.

I remember a time in my life when all I could remember was orange and blue, orange and blue: those late night benders out with my homeboys, when we first challenged the night, then society, and then the world, so to speak.

Atlas pulled the red Sunfire into Simon's parents' driveway. I snapped out of my trip and shook the man's hand. He opened the door, then looked back at us.

"If you guys get tired tonight, find my energy, bros, and you can feed off it. I'm gonna sleep and emanate. Just *emanate*. Peace in and out and all around."

We all responded with our peace. Atlas backed into the street and kept rolling on. Henryk fast-forwarded the tape to a song he was looking for.

My eyelids slipped over the lights, over the orange and blue, blue and orange.

When you are down, brother,
feed off my energy—
for our space theatre.

FENG SHUI OR NOT, HERE WE GO
[Atlas Sangman]

"Is Celina on shift?" I asked the hostess.

"Yeah, I think so. Did you need to see her?"

"No, not really. We just wanted to know. We're friends of hers. Actually, tell her Atlas and Henryk and all are here."

"Uh, okay."

She sat us at a table by the window and poured us water. She left and came back to tell me that Celina was busy, but that she'd be out when she was free. She also said our meal would be on the house (to cheers from the table).

Although I worked as a sous-chef at a restaurant (a real decent one too) *Fondue Pour Vous²* was the best thing worth driving to the outskirts of Mississauga for. It was an inconspicuous place, one picked up by the younger crowd who loved it because there was live music in the evenings, and it became more chic than sushi or sheesha because it was more niche. Celina—our mutual friend, who had Latino roots like Simon and I—had really made it for herself. I thought it would be cool to have a restaurant, but...well, maybe I didn't have a reason.

Simon rapped the table with his knuckles while Henryk flipped through the menu methodically, calling out the dishes he thought we'd appreciate.

"*Soupe à loupe³*. The *Sinner's Kiss*. Wow. She's made it about more than the fondue."

"I don't even know if I'm hungry, man," I said.

"It's not about eating, it's about taste," Henryk clarified.

"I am fucking starved," Simon protested. "This working man needs dem belly full."

"I want to get my fondue fill before I leave for school again," Lukasz said.

---

² *Fondue Pour Vous* — (*French*) Fondue for you

³ *Soupe à loupe* — (*French*) Wolf soup (does not actually contain wolf; refers to a hearty soup)

We were quiet while it sunk in that Lukasz Skarbek would be leaving us again for university. He had just returned for Reading Week, and after a couple more months in Waterloo he would be back for a handful of months before leaving again in September. Simon rubbed his eyes and explored the rest of the dining room with his gaze. He watched groups of people, even when we started talking about some article Henryk had read on the chemical effects of chocolate. Simon was tired; you could tell because his leg didn't twitch. That thing usually kept a quick ticking rhythm.

Martin joined us again, distracting all of us. The stale cigarette smell settled when he sat down. He leaned forward on his elbows with a wide smile.

"What is up with you?" Simon asked.

"Guess who just got that 'zine job? They just called. Just now," Martin said.

"That's awesome."

"Right on, bro. When do you start?"

"What magazine?" Lukasz asked.

"*Glossolalia*[4]," Martin answered, "It's a mag downtown. They're kind of new, but pretty established. I'm stoked. I feel relieved for the first time in months."

---

[4] ***Glossolalia*** — (*Greek*) Original iteration of the term "speaking in tongues"

Martin rarely talked that much about himself at once. But he was happy—I was jealous because he could understand such a thing.

"So let's get us some fucking fondue," Martin rubbed his hands together.

We ordered off the menu from the cute waitress who Simon shamelessly flirted with. She leaned in when she took our orders; she played hard for her tip. Too bad she didn't know that we were too broke and frugal to give a tip. Although I'm sure Simon would pay for head. So maybe that was her angle.

We ate a cheese fondue with Chilean red wine, matched as per the sommelier suggestions on the menu. None of us had ever had such expensive wine paired with cheese that fancy—so we giggled as we ate because it seemed like we were sneaking some taboo food. Simon perked up after the meal. He got the twitch back in his knee. He started joking about how he was going to quit his job and run a gypsy restaurant. I would be his chef, he said, with Henryk as the driver, Martin as the advertiser, and himself as the siren.

"I got a job now, I'm not going to be a gypsy if I don't have to," Martin said.

"Yeah, dude, and I only have one more year of university, then I'm done," Lukasz said. "I can't just stop."

"Why not? I did," I said.

"I'm thinking of starting school just so I can have something not to quit. You know, other than smoking," Henryk said.

The chocolate fondue came to the table and we poured another round of red wine. Celina finally came to the table and gave everyone hugs. We kissed cheeks, and she asked me how I was. I told her that she knew how things go: mostly shitty, sometimes cool.

"Thank you so much for coming out, you guys," she said, "I'm thinking of shutting the place down one night and having a big party for everyone."

"Make it tonight," Simon said.

"I wish I could."

"We're loving it, man."

"Oh Atlas, that's great to hear from you."

She told us how she had made the chocolate blend, and she offered to make us a batch if we really loved it.

"Word. We'll take it, *chica*[5]," Simon said. "I would fuck this chocolate. Straight up. It would be my sweet gooey lover."

---

[5] ***Chica / chiquee / chickee / chiqitita*** — (*Spanish*) Girl or lady

"Celina," I said consolingly. Then to the table: "Man, we can't stress her out with work on the side."

"It wouldn't be any extra work, Atlas," Celina said, "I like doing it. And I get paid most of the time, which is fine by me."

Celina had to go again; she had been checking her watch throughout the conversation. We let her get on, she had fresh batches of pistachio chocolate that were about to be ready. We told her we would be back again.

We finished the fondue and Henryk leaned back with a stretch.

"I just had an idea. Crazy inspiration. I think I'm high from this chocolate. But anyway. Did you notice how Celina liked what she did? Like a lot? I just realized that that's what I want."

"You just realized this now?" Simon asked.

"Yeah, bro. Yeah, it's exactly what I'm going to do."

"You make it sound so easy," I murmured.

"I like what I do," Lukasz attested. "I don't always like it, but I mostly like it."

"But would you be doing it even if you didn't like it?" I asked.

As I expected, no one responded. They continued around me.

"I'm going to school," Henryk said. "I've tried the work thing, and I can't do it. Not this way. Fuck ladders. I'm going to climb grade point averages."

"What are you going to pursue?" Martin asked,

"I don't know. Something scientific, I think that's just natural. I don't know what yet. I'll figure it out by tomorrow. No, nevermind, by, uh, whenever. I'll figure it out."

"I'm so fucking sick of work that I literally think about ways to get hurt on the job so I can't go," Simon said. "I'd be down for school, guy. Let's fucking do it. You and me."

"You know what?" Henryk said. "I'm going into biology. That's it. Or something like it."

"I've got to find something that comes so easy to me. Is there a major in absurdism?"

"Maybe you can make it one."

"Here is the plan," Henryk leaned into the table. "I can't tell you how lucid I am right now. It suddenly makes sense. Ok, here it goes. Me and Simon are going to rock the school thing, right from scratch, year one with the teens. Martin, you're going to rock that magazine, by next year we'll be at this table celebrating your editorship. Lukasz, you're going to keep it real in university, kill that shit, then take your pre-law exams. Atlas, you uh, you keep sous-chefing."

"Thanks," I tried sarcasm.

"And we're all going to get our own place. We're going to rent someplace, a townhouse or apartment or something. It'll help the focus, I think. Think about it—away from the rigor of home, or the fucked-up'dness at home," Henryk motioned a hand in my direction, "And just onto our own vibes. We can smoke when we want, trip whenever, sleep on our own schedule, whatever."

"I'm behind you, bro."

"You know what? That sounds like an awesome idea," Martin nodded. "Brilliant, my man. We can move to the east end of Mississauga to be closer to the TTC[6], and school, and work. Or even downtown proper."

"Downtown's too expensive. I got my car, but I'm feeling the transit. Driving downtown sucks," I said.

"Definitely. We'll look. All of us. I'm not kidding about this, this will happen."

"You can get all feng shui and make something real nice for yourselves. Something to channel your energy," Lukasz said, laughing because he had mentioned earlier that he couldn't get into that oriental history elective he wanted.

---

[6] ***TTC*** — (*English*) Toronto Transit Corporation

"We just need to get feng shui—or whatever, *atoned*—with *ourselves,*" Simon said. "We'll get the kind of energy that made us all walk in here bummed out from our hard knocks and now suddenly laughing and enjoying life. Feng shui or not, let's do it."

Red door; clean drains; grow
fruits—or find a way to live
within our bodies.

GORILLA TERRORIST
[Simon Arcan]

I had spent the last two years of my life in labour. It was awful. I am too much of a man of action to be wasted on work.

So I quit my job. Henryk quit his job too. It might have been the happiest thing either of us has ever done in our short adult lives. Henryk is a gentleman, so when he was ready to quit he wrote an apologetic two-week notice. Considering neither of his parents had ever quit a job, he did it fairly well. He shook his boss' hand as he left.

Me? Fuck it, I've never been a polite man. Well, once, but that was because I needed to get the job I was quitting. A two-week notice would've been an excessive waste of my generosity. The company was a corporate vampire who treated us like nothing more than its set of fangs. On my last day, I popped confetti crackers all over the place and played the *Last Post* on a tape-deck attached to my hip. It would've been more shocking had I done it when people were there, but I was a commercial cleaner. I worked after-hours across Mississauga, keeping the suburban corpocrats from seeing their greasy fingerprints. Hopefully the next cleaners had a good sense of humour.

This coming September brought a change for us. University for me and college for Henryk. Both of us were tired with the grind, the meaningless cash grab that kept the city lit up twenty-four hours a day. Instead we riled each other into a frantic academic buzz, now passed the age where highschool transcripts were really assessed— *mature* students, they said—so we could finally cut a hole in the fence they erected for us at the end of highschool.

My dad was pretty pissed off about the whole deal, because I asked for money, and Mami just wanted to make sure I kept busy. Atlas was jealous; he became disillusioned with university and quit after his first year. Martin congratulated us. He believed in the Holy Academic Sepulchre—the library cemeteries, the funeral procession lecture halls, the liturgy of knowledge.

But tonight—tonight we had something to shake off two years of slavery to the capitalist machine.

Henryk and I: jumpy with adrenalin, indignant with righteousness, humble with masks in a backpack. We also had two ratchets and a pack of cigarettes in there.

"This place is the burial chamber," I said.

"That's what happens when you spend your life running away from death," Henryk said.

"Yes! Putting up traffic lights and security systems!"

We talked nonsense on the curb across from our old highschool. Its colours looked saturated with amber under the street lights.

"Mother Earth's guerrilla army," Henryk uttered.

That was who we were tonight. For Henryk, this meant doing a good deed for the planet; for me, it meant doing good for ourselves.

Henryk considered our old highschool's architecture with cigarette smoke in the way. It was our fossil; all the denials and short-comings, all the D's and pink slips packed in that building, trapped in amber. The orange street lights were our only guides tonight—and orange rightly so. Just like the lights, Henryk and I were suspended somewhere between a red passion and a yellow cowardice. *Rage Against the Machine* blasted in the Sunfire (borrowed from Atlas) on our way over. We were pumped. After parking the car discreetly we stalked the streets like secret soldiers on a crucial operation. We ended up at the school. Our destination point.

"We gotta go, dude," I said.

"Is it time?"

"It's time enough."

We cut off the school's main street into the adjacent residential neighbourhood.

Our plan was simple.

"How's this one?"

"Looks like a pig. I bet it sucks half-a-tank a day."

Henryk stooped at the SUV's bumper. I slipped the ratchets out of the bag and handed him one. He removed the license plate. I moved up the block, eyeing the cars parked in the street. Henryk stuck the lifted license plate into my opened backpack.

"Whoa, Rambo," I pointed to a Hummer parked across the street, "Really? Where's the war, soldier?"

I snatched the license plate off the enormous bumper of the pimped-out war machine. Henny and

I continued up and down the block, methodically choosing license plates to remove. Within two hours we had twenty plates from Suburban Urgency Vehicles, and ten from pick-ups. They rattled like crushed pop cans in my backpack as we headed for the highschool's football field.

"We have thirty, right? We can set up six rows with five headstones each," Henryk calculated.

"We should've gotten some flowers. Like those fake fabric flowers."

"We can add them tomorrow. Totally take ourselves out of the heat by mocking our own protest! We'll deliver flowers to the cemetery site, like we're disregarding the intended message."

"Or enhancing it."

"Masks. We need masks."

"Oh yea, I've got a glow-in-the-dark skull and a gorilla, which one would you prefer?"

"Let me have the skull," Henryk said.

"I guess we're both guerrillas anyway."

We were across the street from the school property again, waiting for traffic to clear so that we could cross without witnesses. Henryk watched the parking lot camera intently.

"I think we should put our masks on now," Henryk urged, thumbing to the camera's pole.

"No way, that's bait! Two guys standing on the side of the road in masks? Someone's going to call the cops. Let's just wait 'til we're halfway across the street."

I lit up a smoke as we casually drifted to the nearby bus stop (though it was after hours for the transit). Henryk's head darted up and down the street. There was a mall and a few of Mississauga's main intersections near our school. It was busy, even at eleven o'clock on a Sunday night.

Finally a gap appeared in the traffic. We both seized the opportunity and jetted to the other side, donning the masks as soon as we stepped on the curb of the school property. Keeping a determined gait we crossed the parking lot and stepped onto the football field. The schoolgrounds occupied a whole block; it was built like an island. The football field was slightly raised from the rest of the block. I looked around. I couldn't see cars passing so they couldn't see us—I noted this to Henryk to assure him that we were safe. At centrefield Henryk kneeled, unzipped his backpack and let the license plates crash onto the trimmed lawn. We began our sham cemetery: six rows with five plates each.

More than half way through Henryk crawled beside the pile of plates and sat with his knees in his arms.

"Man this is wrong," he said, with a slight tremor in the word *wrong*.

His expression was impossible to read behind the skull mask.

"What?! Ah, guy, don't give me this shit now. It's too late to think about wrong," I exclaimed, throwing my hands into the air.

"They're not going to get it. They're just going to be pissed. They're going to spend more time thinking about whodunit than what caused someone to do it."

"You know blame is easier than thought."

"Fuck. I know."

Henryk crawled back to the rows with the last few plates. His skull mask just hinted at its glow-in-the-dark properties. He cocked his head and nodded.

"You know what? Fuck 'em."

"Don't trick yourself. You know that's even easier than blame."

In under fifteen minutes we had the simple display erected. It looked shitty in the dark. We couldn't wait until morning to see the reaction it would garner. We made a solemn procession off the property, making sure to escape a different way and cut through residential neighbourhoods without our masks to confuse whoever was bound to watch the video tape tomorrow.

> Feel me sweat, hear me
> grunt, watch me pimp the system
> before I'm the ho.

OH CLAIRE
[Henryk Zdicz]

It was a long, cool spring, and I, for one, needed to get out. I needed to see the sun, I wanted to breathe fresh outside air. Of course, really fresh air would mean a long drive out of the city. The air just felt better beyond my suburban walls.

Atlas, Claire and I went down to the Oakville lakeshore for a coffee. The storefront windows were wide, and elms hung over the sidewalks, still leafless, pencilled in against a grey sky.

I wished the sun could have come out. But you can't wait forever for a tease.

Warmed from the coffee and the conversation we decided to hit the real lakeshore—the actual banks of Lake Ontario. At least, as real as you could get for such a developed bank. Most of it was concrete, or covered with gravel and sand trucked in when the suburbs began their creep westward.

There were small docks that interrupted the shore, where rich lakeside mansioniers dipped their over-compensation into the water to claim a piece.

Then there were the man-made bays that the rich inlanders used. At the mouth of one there was a concrete pier, about a hundred metres into the lake, ended by a peppermint-striped lighthouse. In summer it was a beacon for youth who just got their driver's license and wanted to go out, to smoke a joint or just hang out and watch the lights around the lake.

We pre-empted summer. We sat at the end of the lighthouse, bundled in our layers, our legs hanging off the end of the pier. Claire watched the horizon deeply while her hair whipped around her face.

Atlas had met Claire Chandran in his first year of university. He had late classes, and the cafeteria had an old discordant grand piano that had strings missing. Atlas played this piano late at night, after classes, when no one was in the café but it was still open in good campus trust. The way he tells it, she was in there one night, studying poetry while he was half-heartedly playing piano. He said she just came up to him, sat beside him and asked if he had a lighter. He did, and he went out for a smoke. Atlas didn't smoke cigarettes, but he would if it was a good idea at the time. He thought it was. Atlas never had luck with girls—the man was a virgin, but I'll get to that later. Claire also didn't smoke; she fully intended to smoke a joint, which pleased Atlas because he had one tucked in his ear under his hair.

I thought the story was exaggerated. I was sure the actual situation was a lot more awkward given Atlas' *spaciness* (for lack of better term). Either way, they became fast friends. It was strange, because even though it had only been a couple years, you could almost be fooled into thinking that they had ESP. If you asked Atlas if he had ESP when he was on acid, he would say yes; any other time you asked he would vaguely say that everybody does. Personally, I thought behavioural patterns between humans were easy to pick up on if you really wanted to, and the two of them wanted to, so they made some kind of subconscious connection.

Even now Atlas and Claire kicked their legs over the pier in a slow synchronicity, and neither was looking at each other, they were peering at opposite ends of the lake.

One time, I asked Atlas to try ESP with me. I valued experimentation. If I found out that I didn't have ESP abilities, that would be normal—if I found out that I did, that would only be a plus. Atlas and I pressed palms together and he slowed his breathing. Then he told me to clear my mind, and asked me to picture a shape. As soon as I visualized a triangle, Atlas said triangle. This, at the time, blew my mind more than I could explain. It could've been the acid, but really, it was an ethereal experience.

If I really had ESP, you would know the one word on my mind right now:

-

That's right.

Atlas said something about the water, and Claire *mm-hmm*'d. I started talking about the weather; something everybody can always talk about. In highschool Atlas and I tried to keep weather journals, where we recorded the weather and our general mood. I lost mine after a year of carrying it around. Atlas still had his, I think.

Atlas pointed out the smokestacks of the coal-fired powerplant to the east. They looked like four burning cigarettes stood upright in an ashtray.

"They remind me of the hospital smokestack," Atlas said. "You remember, Henny? It was the smokestack for their incinerators. Like, where they burned all the garbage that they couldn't otherwise dispose of—"

"Like bodies," I added.

"Yeah, bodies, I guess. I watched that smokestack almost everyday in highschool. You could see it from any third floor classroom that faced the hospital. I don't know why I watched it. It was just so..."

Atlas trailed off. Claire and I nodded.

Claire talked about the final essays she was working on. She was older than us, in her fourth year of university, pursuing a double major in sociology and philosophy. She was brilliant; she had a photographic memory and could recite quotes from books she had read when she was four.

But the reason why I liked Claire—and the reason why I liked Atlas, too—was that they were both adept listeners who would take anything you said to *mean* something. I could say anything I wanted to Atlas, especially if Claire was around.

"I have to tell you guys something..." I said. "I'm taking a vow of, uh, abstinence."

"Abstinence?" Atlas asked.

"Yeah. I'm off sex. I want to sublimate my energy somewhere else."

"What do you mean, man? You going to practice some black magick shit on us now?"

"No, I'm saying that a body only has so much energy in it, and it can only do certain things with that energy, and I want to put that energy into something else."

"I think if you say *energy* one more time, you'll get back to Kansas," Claire laughed.

"Simon's got everybody illuminated with his energy logic," Atlas informed Claire, then asked me, "So, what's your energy going into?"

"I don't know. I'm just saying that I feel like I can do it now. That I can move on, I guess."

"Man, those ladies really swept you."

"Glass houses," Claire said to Atlas.

The water looked like thousands of glass houses shattered in a pit, tussled by wind and its own turbulent forces. I examined the water for a moment or two. I didn't hear what Atlas and Claire discussed.

"Henryk, my friend, I see your abstinence and raise you a celibacy vow."

"For some reason, I don't think you have a *vow*, per se."

"Maybe it's a pheromone deficiency," Claiure offered. "I have to say, and I know this is weird to say, but it's true—I've never felt like, you know, making it with you. You know, fucking. So it could be a hormonal thing."

"Yeah. Maybe."

Atlas didn't look as disconsolate as I was sure he felt. Claire didn't know how he had talked about her when they first met. First, his ecstasy at their meeting; then the bewitchment of her calls and text messages. They made him believe that he had found a soulmate. Again. There had been Jeanne, and before that Catalina. Probably countless others before that. As long as I had known Atlas—and this would verge on fourteen years of friendship—he had his heart repeatedly broken. But the real story to tell was that no matter the circumstance his heart regenerated. At least I had gotten a handjob or some head before my heart was broken, and even then my cum couldn't heal my heart. Poor sad Atlas, all he wanted was to be loved. And it was hard for the man to come by.

The wind blew, and Claire leaned onto Atlas' shoulder. He tamed a smile she wouldn't be able to see anyways.

"If it's any consolation, I've always wanted to fuck you, Atlas," I joked.

"That's sweet. Maybe I shouldn't get in between you two," Claire laughed. "But I think we should get out of here."

"Why?" I asked.

"Yeah, she's right. It's cold anyway. Let's roll."

Claire and Atlas walked arm in arm back to the car. When we passed the small park uphill from the lakeshore, I scrambled up the metal structure and slid down the slide on my feet. As I came down I noticed a cop car cruising along the street. I skipped to keep up with Atlas and Claire.

"*Dzein dobry*[7], pig. Five-oh!" I announced. "But you guys already knew that, right?"

Claire shrugged and Atlas watched the cop's faceless inquiry as he passed. I laughed and shook my head at the two of them. I asked what was going to happen next, but neither answered me right away. They walked with their heads bowed, arm in arm. Claire looked up the street, then looked at me with her cute smile.

"Would it freak you out if we told you the future?" she asked.

"Yeah, it would."

"It'd freak me out, too," Atlas said.

"We all know the future's for the future. Isn't that why you really believe there's still hope for the earth?" Claire asked.

Claire was cryptically referring to a conversation we'd had our last time at the lighthouse, which had been at the end of the past summer. Tedious to

---

[7] ***Dzein dobry*** — (*Polish*) Good evening

repeat, but the main gist was that Simon had ranted about how the world was doomed to go to shit, and Atlas claimed we were already in shit, and I was saying that if we knew that we were getting into shit, in true and actual perdition, we could stop it. Since we were aware of it, I argued, we could stop it, or maybe just delay its arrival. Claire shared my hope, but she shared a lot more of Atlas' nihilism.

"Besides, man, you could only know what you're in at the moment. And even then..." Atlas then and repeated now.

We got into the Atlas' red Sunfire. He took the longer yet more scenic route through the suburban sprawl. I noticed all the vegetation between the concrete and bricks. It was a restless struggle. Almost hopeless, yet beautiful, to see the elms cowering over the streets, punching through a square of soil, so shameless and poised.

Claire hummed along to the instrumental tune I popped into the tape deck. In a few weeks it would be warm enough to have the windows open. Then the music could really blast.

Hear us coming up
the street, with our windows down
singing at the world.

...IT COULD HAPPEN LIKE ANYTHING
[Simon Arcan]

It was getting past the hour of indecision. The line would be drawn soon. Either I took up school after a labourious purgatory, or I took to my servitude and fell in love with purgatory.

After three years I still wasn't sure what I wanted to do with my life, nevermind what I wanted to take at university. It was an intimidating reducer.

I poured through the magazines of all my choice universities when I was bored, but especially when I was feeling riled up, like after I watched the news or got harassed by cops. After the magazines I re-read the information online, like something was going to reach out and grab me, take me in.

Every single course looked decent. I felt like I could conquer most of them if I really wanted.

Chemistry. Forgot it from highschool but I knew that shit. I wanted to be a chemist at some point. I could double as a prime producer of psychotropics and work through Dr. Alexander Shulgin's formulas.

Engineering. Too much math. Demanded some kind of logical-thinking that I only saw on television, but someday I wanted to come up with something cool and revolutionary.

Revolution. Was that a major?

Anthropology. Sociology. Observations about ourselves. I observed things all the time. I could write a book and re-mould how people thought of themselves. I wanted to change what we knew about ourselves at some point.

Astronomy. Space sciences. I wanted to ride a wormhole at some point.

Business. Not hard, c'mon, that's a fucking joke course. Did they teach you how to convince a monkey to pick stocks for you? Or did you need a zoologist for that? The business school grads were the same as the 'phenomenal athletes' of poker championships. All bullshit. The DOW stood for Don't-Overwork-Whitey. I could die my hair grey early on and become a CEO; do nothing and bullshit my way out of anything. I wanted to bullshit at some point.

Theology. Atlas & Henryk & I experimented with all the major religions. I didn't know to what end, but it brought me hours and hours of first-hand experience, something those old bald-heads couldn't teach in secular classrooms. I could become a great teacher of theology, because that's what theology bred, teachers, those who wanted to do nothing else than know something you do not, and be able to feed it to you at their generosity's whimsy. I wanted to be generous at some point.

The pamphlets didn't help at all. They only muddled matters worse. When I was younger my dad had told me that I could do *anything*, and you know he worked his ass off to make it true, but by the time everything was supposed to come together in a happy Huxtable moment after graduation, I fucked it up and broke the spell.

Anything seemed like a lot then. I could handle it now. Not before, not when I was still filling the shell of myself. Not then. But now I was finally ready to meet *anything*.

The deadline was coming close. It was time to make a date with anything, but it was proving difficult. Because that wasn't what was offered. *Anything* didn't exist cohesively. I couldn't choose a single major, though I forced myself back to the magazines at my desk with the empty forms beside them.

Perfect time for a distraction. I went downstairs and made myself a cup of tea from a small tin of leaves Atlas gifted me randomnly last Sunday.

Upstairs in my room I emptied my desk and sat over my mug. I inhaled the tea deeply.

It smelled like walking the African savannah on a damp, rainy day. It smelled like foreign sex. Like getting right into the muff and smelling sweet cunt. It smelled like the sweating over-worked masses catching a bus along a dirt road…a poncho burning over a lemongrass-fed fire…that man drying out his poncho…an Arab woman's dethroned pheromones…Atlas always wondered how I could be so scatter-brained but still convince everyone I was still sane.

Then, over the visions in the smells and the power of random sinuosity, I came to a sudden decision that I wanted to be atoned with people. I wanted all those smells to be my own; I felt they were. Political science, for whatever reason (and with very little contemplation), would be the best way for me to tackle the post-secondary circus. It was time for me to join in the act.

Sparrow hit my window!

Right now. Just clunked as I started filling in the forms. I rushed to the window and searched for the songbird. It had fallen to the first floor awning. It rolled around a little, shaken. I guess it could happen like anything. I sighed deeply and went back to my desk. Polly sigh—poli. sci.—the choice for me. If I mailed the package right away it would get there just in time. Time to sign my life away with my vocation's chime.

Goodbye, indecision; the next time you see me I will have a name.

Realized my dad
had said, "you can be anything,
but not everything."

PROMETHEUS SHOULD HAVE NEVER CAME
[Simon Arcan]

"...then the suburbs will catch fire."

Atlas pulled a sigh from the spring air. He rubbed his eyes and shifted on the log he was sitting on. Henryk tugged at his chin thoughtfully. He looked at the ground in front of Atlas. Lukasz looked embarrassed at having listened to Atlas long violent rant. He cleared his throat and nodded to ease the silence.

"Serious *Salvia* vision," Lukasz ruminated.

"Sorry."

"Naw, no apologies," I assured Atlas, slapping his shoulder. "Whatever it is, it is. You can't change what you see."

Henryk glared at me; without words he pleaded me not to encourage Atlas. I shrugged. Henryk was inclined to believe Atlas' so-called visions were psychobabble, the kind of stream-of-consciousness that revealed nothing more than what the seer perceived of himself. Henryk checked his phone to busy himself.

"Anything from Conrad or Martin?"

"Nope," Henryk said. "But they know where we are."

The next ten minutes passed in relative silence as the four of us waited. We were in the Valley (or rural escape in the escarpment) on this day of reckoning—the day of Conrad Ernestway's convocation. Martin had gone to the ceremony and he was bringing the man himself here for a massive session in celebration.

[Henryk Zdicz]

A log was fallen over a dry creek bed about a kilometre into the forest, lending a nice bench for all of us. We waited half an hour before we heard rustling through the underbrush and saw Martin leading Conrad.

We gave Conrad props and showed him the blunt Lukasz had rolled. He told us it was the best thing all day. He looked out of place in his semi-formal clothes. At least he had put on boots, because it was a warm afternoon and we expected to get some hiking done. We were kept cool by the lofty canopy, but there was a heavy humidity.

After an enlightening session we followed the creek further upstream. Simon and I knew it stretched another two or three kilometres but became harder after the first kilometre because there were ledges where waterfalls would have run had the creek not dried out. Atlas egged us to go on. Conrad tightened the backpack he brought around everywhere and joked that he was ready to go climbing in the Alps.

En route, Martin commented on how genuinely happy people looked when they were handed their diplomas. Martin was looking forward to his own convocation. Conrad walked with a bowed head. He didn't have a reply, only a wry smile; until he finally spoke up.

"Yeah, they can get tattoos of their bachelor degrees but it wouldn't do any good out here. You can't eat off that shit."

Solemnly we considered his perspective. Simon told us he'd chosen Political Science as his major. Martin congratulated the man. When I was asked, I said my decision was pending, but that I was still psyched. Conrad shrugged.

I felt guilty thinking that post-secondary was a waste of time because it was my parents' utmost desire to have me graduate with a degree and make them proud with a degree. They would tell all our family back in Poland. They had always told me, 'There were no good jobs anymore without a degree.' So for them, being a cog in the machine was the easiest choice. But why would I want to take the easy way?

To take command of the controls and push the buttons that made the cogs move—that was the place to be.

Too bad that wasn't a choice.

Down the riverbed we came to a clearing, where Simon commissioned Conrad to stop and roll the next joint. In the meantime Atlas and I grabbed armfuls of firewood. Lukasz and I negotiated our lighters through the sticks to the newspaper in the middle. The paper caught and burned out quick.

"I think this wood's too wet," Lukasz deduced.

"It did rain yesterday," Conrad said.

"Fuck. Sorry, I don't think we'll get a fire today, bro," I told Conrad.

"No worries. I'd just end up burning my diploma anyways."

[Atlas Sangman]

Shapes filled my head. The *Salvia divinorum* hit me harder than usual. I couldn't find words, I couldn't pull coherent thoughts together. But I knew some things now, things that I hadn't known before the *Salvia*.

Simon was pissed off about the fire, but he was usually pissed off about a lot of things. Henryk thought it would be easier to hike back along the main river. I had no intention to move, but I trudged along behind the group.

I wondered what my mother would've thought about my vision—though I never intended to tell her—I just wondered. I bet she would say something like, "You've been with those Algonquins for too long, you think you're actually one of them."

Story of my life. It suddenly occurred to me that I enjoyed nature so much because it was as homeless as I was. My mother went backpacking in the Andes after university, bumming around with two girlfriends. She met an Incan boy in one of the mountain villages. Nine months later I was born in Toronto.

All would've been cool from there, except that my mother developed a habit that turned into a full-on addiction. Mom was so drunk most days that I walked myself to and from kindergarten. That got her in trouble. So I was sent to live with my only living relative, my Algonquin Uncle John—my mom's step-brother from her dad's second marriage—for a long time the entanglement of inter-relations made me believe that we were all blood relatives. I lived on the reserve with him, north of the city, until eighth grade.

"Let's just chill here, man, I need a cigarette," Martin said.

We sat on the banks of the river. I stared into the water and watched my face bounce on the choppy current.

On the reserve all the kids targeted me because I wasn't actually native. At first it was just name-calling, the usual bullshit that occupies childrens' social play time. One Halloween I was chased into the bush by some older guys. They caught me at the edge of town and beat me until I fell down. They let me run on a little more, then caught up with me again and forced off my shoes. They left some bruises and a broken rib. They also left me almost three kilometres from my uncle's house. I started limping back home and got picked up by the RCMP. They drove me home, then told me that I had to tell them who did it. I didn't. I pretended I had too much of a headache to remember.

The next day I started homeschool.

—In this Salvia reverie my memories were so crisp, so resal, so light compared to the mud that weighted down my boots—

I dunked my head into the river. When I came up, I heard everyone laughing. I shook and wrung water out of my hair.

"You alright, Atlas?" Martin asked.

I nodded.

"Maybe we should keep going," he said.

I shook my head again and reached over to him. I asked for a cigarette; he obliged.

The smell of tobacco—the smell of Uncle John's hands as he flipped the pages of the textbook in front of me. We went through the standard textbooks, but we also went over other educational books from the library. We also learned from the elders; especially the tribe shaman, who was infertile, so his legacy would disappear without an apprentice. My Uncle learned from him, and he taught me. Uncle John made learning a way of life, not a chore or a fault of nature.

But when Mom came crying back to me, and asked me to move in with her again, I felt like I had learned nothing at all.

"Too bad we couldn't've started a fire," Lukasz lamented.

We all nodded quietly.

"Summer," Henryk vaguely preluded.

We all nodded again. Conrad, who sat behind all of us with his thick sunglasses squaring his face, moved slowly through his backpack.

When my mother came to the reserve to get me she said she had been sober for forty-four days. I didn't know if that was a long time or not, because at the time I never drank (shit, I was finishing eighth grade). So I went back. Because mostly, I didn't have a choice. I started highschool back in the city. That was where I met my Homeboys.

[Martin O'Neill]

Conrad took the thin folder that was holding his diploma out of his backpack. He opened it, and slipped the diploma out of it.

I had enjoyed Conrad's convocation. I never even expected to be at a convocation, even though my own was imminent. I met his parents, who were so proud that they could not hold back cheeky smiles and emotionally charged tears.

Conrad began to fold his diploma. I did not say anything, though my instinct told me to—I just watched him carefully fold the paper, rubbing the crease in with his palm. After a few folds he held up his origami: a paper boat. He smiled a bit, then walked to the river's edge. He stooped, and carefully set the boat on the riffles.

"Whoa!" I shouted, and got up to grab the diploma.

Simon laughed. Atlas watched the boat calmly float by him on the current.

"What are you doing?" I asked Conrad.

"Sailing," he answered.

"Sailing!" Simon shrieked with laughter.

I tried to badger Conrad, but he did not explain himself. Henryk said we should keep walking. We passed the boat on the river, but nobody stopped to grab it. It bubbled along, the ink already streaming from the parchment.

Lukasz and Henryk talked at the back of the group. They stopped us and pointed to a massive bramble of shrubs. They said there was probably dry wood in there. Conrad, Atlas and I had given up on the idea of a fire, so Lukasz and Henryk went to look. When they came back with armfuls of dry wood, the rest of us went in to grab dead branches.

Lukasz and Henryk arranged the deadwood into a tipi. They filled the inside with the graduation programme and lit it. Soon we all circled around a rudimentary fire.

I had to piss, so I walked to the reeds by the river and relieved myself. While I did I watched the clouds, then watched them reflected on the jerky river. Something opaque caught my attention. The distinct shape was hard to mistake—it was Conrad's diploma sailboat, marooned on a smooth stone. I zipped up and picked the boat off the water.

When I was back at the fire I dropped the boat into Conrad's lap. He looked at me, then at the wet paper. Conrad picked it up delicately, dangling it at eye level. He scoffed and took off his sunglasses.

Then he tossed his diploma into the fire.

We stared at it: captivated, bewitched. It was hypnotic. First the paper steamed and became wrinkled. Then, as quickly as it had become wet, it caught the flame and shrivelled into ashes.

Simon's eyes grew wide as saucers. His mouth curved into a mad smile. Conrad watched the paper burn, stolid.

False accomplishment,
kindling, origami—what
diplomas are for.

BRING IT BACK
[Simon Arcan]

You slap the strings until your fingers hurt. At that point, you're ready to play. Marshall Bridges told me that, and he played bass in four local bands before getting signed and dying the week later of a meth overdose. In the Mississauga underground the man was an icon—the true dichotomy of hero and idiot.

I wouldn't take any advice on word only, so I upheld his wisdom because it worked for me. That was why when nine-thirty rolled around I was totally stoned with aching fingers, standing on a darkened stage with my friends shifting their weight on anxious feet.

A kid with a beenie and puberty beard announced our name with no banter.

Malik Ceiss hit the guitar strings before the guy was done, so no one heard who we were, and to be honest I didn't care if they knew. Most of the crowd was way too fucked to care. And the straight-edgers were too elite to want to remember us. Izzy Duomo kicked in the drums and we harmonized immediately out of the preliminary noise. The cheap incandescents of the Lodge weren't dimmed for the mood, they were only dull from low wattage. Henryk Zdicz sang the melody and we swung to the groove. Who knows what the fuck the crowd was doing. I had my eyes closed. This was not for them.

I would hardly call our music hip hop, or hip rock, or rock & roll for that matter, but that was because I didn't call our music anything but music. We just jacked up the volume and played. I guess, though, in the grand scheme of the industry scam called genrefication we had some jams that were hip hop influenced. Which people expected, I guess, because Malik and I were mulatto. To the audience, it fit better than what we played from the heart, from that no-nonsense chant of chicanery, the harangue of the no-mind soul. Hip hop was from the head. It was constructed. Measured. It was the only time we counted anything, actually. But for what it was worth, I didn't think it counted. Henryk only played it because he could take a break from singing.

Fuck yeah, homie, my time to shizz-ine.

It was hardly Nas or A Tribe Called Quest but I tried my best. Considering I didn't really try. The rap wasn't mine. It wasn't even a rap. It was one of Atlas' old poems, the kind he used to write during class and show me, before he got tired of doing that. He stopped showing me his poems during the tail end of his first year of university, when he pretty much gave up on everything else. I think he thought I didn't care. Hence my unproclaimed shout-out. He never claimed it as his own, he even dismissed any ownership when I asked if he wanted credits on our EP. Whatever.

> Atlas told me
> breech the mind, find what you find,
> bring it back for us all.

A BOTTLE ON THE NIGHT TABLE
[Martin O'Neill]

I don't why, but every time I looked Conrad in the eye, I saw the glint of a billion bats emerging from a cave, like Hunter S. Thompson freaking out in the Mojave; except not so manic, it was more subdued and sinister. Conrad could never be batty enough to desert himself. Maybe his sleep schedule brought the image, but I thought the bats were after something else.

"Hey, Martin," Conrad greeted me hastily at the side door.

He led me to the set of couches he had in his basement apartment. Posters of gloomy bands presided over the crowd of angled walls. Conrad did not sit, but I did. I felt awkward in Conrad's room, mostly because his bed was just on the other side of the couches and I could smell the musk of his nest. Lining the walls Conrad had bookshelves overstacked with classics—all the Iliad's and Mahabharata's your mind could indulge in one lifetime, all in one basement, in the hands of this great writer who seemed very small and measly in his thin yellowed shirt and three-day-old beard.

"How's school treating you?" he asked, trying to sound casual, avoiding eye contact with me.

"Pretty good, I guess."

I did not have the heart to tell Conrad that I also was getting paid to do what he longed to do--write. That I toiled my days away pining for that scholarly validation at a magazine that heavily edited all my work. I was Athena's Echo, and don'tcha know that bats can't hear an echo. Conrad could not keep tabs on many peoples' lives at a time.

"How is everyone?" he looked at me, finally, with one eye.

He stood hunched over the coffee table, looking like he was waiting for me to invite him to sit down.

"Everyone's alive and they're not planning on quitting anytime soon, so..."

"Heh."

"It's good. Haven't seen you 'round lately, and I thought—"

"I've been busy. My life is just...a tremendous hurtle, and I'm on one leg."

The crux of literature's academia: the student at the feet of masters. I wondered if he understood the hidden metaphor in his metaphor.

"Yeah, tell me about it," I said

"I read some of your shorts," he said.

"Jeanne left them right?"

At the pronunciation of her name I caught myself, but it was too late. Conrad cringed subtlety with his eyes. It had been six months since Jeanne ter Baark left Conrad, but it might as well have been yesterday for him.

"I only read a few."

He made himself look busy. I sat back on the sofa, feeling stupid for having insulted my host, and wishing I could crack a beer. Fuck, I could be at home right now.

"I have someone you should read," he continued, heading to his bed area.

He stopped by the night table, stared at it hollowedly for a minute, then crawled over the bed and reached for a book. He made sure to pick up his weed on the way back.

Conrad handed the book to me, then proceeded to break up ganja on the coffee table for a joint.

"Melville wrote poetry?"

"You should take a look."

"Yeah, for sure, man, for sure. Never read any besides *Moby Dick*."

I flipped through the book, not really reading anything, just looking at the shapes of text flittering across the pages. Rectangles slid down the pages like a vertebrate.

I was more interested in wishing Conrad had said more about my writing. Melville was not really my style, I did not have time for tedious recounts of forgotten wars. What about my writing?

We casually talked about nothing while the pinner was rolled—Conrad's classic pinch of weed between thin paper—then smoked it outside, under the heavy shadows of the back porch light.

Bats. Fucking bat country out here, man[8]. Conrad made eye contact with me a total of five times, and each time a flood of bats made looking back at him difficult. I wondered if Jeanne saw the bats. There was no room in a healthy relationship for two people and a cave full of bats.

---

[8] Props & acknowledgements to Hunter S. Thompson.

"I've been writing lots," Conrad told me once we were inside again.

He showed me his work station: a cleared desk with his laptop sitting square in the centre. So neat, so precise, so acute in its form. Conrad patted the back of the chair like it was his prized mustang.

"A lot of work. I'm also figuring out a master's thesis. It's draining. Not enough hours in the day."

"What have you been writing?"

"A novel. Some poetry, some random stuff."

"A novel?"

"Yeah."

"What about?"

"I'd, uh, rather not say. Not until it's done. Bad luck."

"Yeah, for sure. That's really cool, you'll have to let me read it when it's done."

As we sat back on the couches I realized the reason why I rarely hung out with Conrad one-on-one much: he had nothing to say. Especially for someone who apparently wrote like mad all night.

"I have some stuff printed. A short story or two," he said.

"I'd love to read them."

"Let me get them for you."

He handed me the papers he already had in his hands. I buried them under the Melville collection.

"You can pass those around to whoever wants to read them. I want to know what people think. It's important to write for an audience. It'd be good to know what they're saying as much as it's good to know what you're saying."

"I'll let Atlas look it over, too. He's wanted to read your shit forever."

Conrad cringed again at Atlas' name. This one piqued my curiosity.

"He's asked for you. We all have. You should come out, man, come smoke a joint and do whatever, just enjoy the warmth of the outer world before hibernation season."

"Maybe. Jeanne and Izzy might want to read those."

"Izzy definitely would."

Conrad had mentioned Jeanne to confirm my thoughts. I had to prod with Atlas again.

"Izzy's been jamming with Atlas a bit."

"Izzy can kick out the jams."

"Atlas loves playing with him."

Conrad let the conversation drop. Not today, not these six months past, not in the next century would the bats leave his cave.

I said I had to go, like I was busy at 11:30 on a Thursday evening. I promised to text him the next time we were passing by his neighbourhood—but I would have to think of the politest way to ask him to leave his bats at home first.

On the way out I noticed he had a bottle of liquor by his bed. The amber liquid caught lines of the lamplight. It was uncracked.

"Been doing some late night drinking, eh?" I asked casually, adjusting the jacket I had not taken off, "Atta boy."

"No. No, actually," Conrad coughed out a laugh. "I haven't even cracked her. I won't. It's kind of an empowerment thing I'm trying out. I don't want to drink it, though sometimes I do want to. I have to stop myself. It's been there for a long time."

Six months time, Conrad?

"Well, bring it out with us and we'll have a good round with it. Fuck the paperweight mode."

Conrad turned a sigh into a laugh, then sat down on his desk. He leaned on his elbows and watched me leave.

By the time I got home and crashed, Conrad still sat in pyjama pants at his empty desk, gazing between the empty page on the computer screen and the virgin bottle of liquor.

Everyone lives with
their misery until it
kisses them goodnight.

OM BY ACCIDENT
[Atlas Sangman]

Beauty in urban decay. Faded plastic store-front signs. Buses trawl flat-faced, devastated in their infinite circling. The jobless, homeless, and destitute looking for no other place than where they are. Beauty parlour sluts fix their exaggerated eyelashes to magazines, they don't care who I am, I am not glossy in their magazines. Faded-hair grandmothers revive their wigs to new devastatingly juvenile colours. They will have something to talk about tonight at the canasta tournament.

I already felt drained by the time I pushed the back door and stepped into the white kitchen. I fixed my apron in the bathroom mirror, fantasizing about how easily my crooked nose would be fixed by standing in front of a bus.

"Yo, Blanquito[9], you done shaving your legs?"

But not today.

I stepped back into the kitchen, where Loco was moving between shiny bowls and the oven.

"About time, man. Yo, grab me some more olive oil."

"Sorry, man, I slept in."

---

[9] **Blanquito** — (*Spanish*) "Whitey"

I covered for my slow trolling to work. I decided to skip the bus today and walk to work instead.

"Ye, ye, whatever man."

We worked at our respective opening duties, prepping the kitchen for the rest of the staff that would soon arrive to dress the dishes for the hungry customers. Loco—'Alejandro' to the government— was the chef, and because the restaurant couldn't afford to hire him a properly trained sous-chef I had to do. Nepotism, almost, because Loco was the former coke-toting thug who used to be the group-appointed leader of the Latino group in highschool; the Latino crew who had a love-hate relationship with me because I was from their bloodlines but not from their cultures. Nepotism, almost, because it was a very Latino thing to do.

"Done, man, everything's ready," I said.

"Right on, bro. *Vamos a fumar*[10]."

In the back alley we smoked a joint. Down the alley the traffic rumbled passed, all high on their routes, their appointments, their briefcases, their cellphones.

"Damn. That's good shit."

---

[10] ***Vamos a fumar*** — (*Spanish*) Let's go smoke

"Yeah, man. Hey, where'd you get that necklace?"

I pointed to the wooden OM emblem that hung off wooden beads around Loco's neck. It stuck out above his shirt. He fingered it for a while until he finished inhaling.

"Observant, Blanquito, hey? OM. It's a Hindu symbol."

"Naw, I'm familiar with the symbol. Where'd you get it?"

"In Thailand, dude. In a small village, this little girl was making them."

"Cool."

"Ye, and I had no idea what the symbol was until later. It was a complete accident. I lost it for the past few months. I'd worn it for eight years straight man, never took it off, it brought me mad good luck."

"Good luck?" I laughed, because I thought the word *luck* was the punchline.

"Listen, man, I was looking for this bitches' earrings that she claims she left at my house, and I was looking and looking and I found this, then I found her earrings. I give her her earrings, ready to tell her to fuck off, and she wraps her arms 'round my neck and just goes to town, man. It was crazy shit. I loved that girl at one time, then she just fucked me over. Now...shit...the tables have turned."

Loco spoke animatedly with his hands, reliving the previous night's escapades. He stared at a dumpster as if he saw something else, then continued toking on the joint.

"Man, sounds like it just brought you trouble."

"Naw, s'all good man," Loco said. "Straight up, afterwards, she just said she wanted to keep it casual. Y'know, like—what?? When does that happen?"

"The universe conspires."

"In Thailand I bought it, then the next week I was in Singapore and this random lady and me sat in a park on the grass and she told me what the symbol meant to her. And then after that—"

"What'd she say?"

"She explained what it meant. Then what it meant to her. How it changed her life, man. And I was like, it's just a fucking symbol, y'know'm'saying?"

"Money's just a symbol."

"You can't trade this necklace for food, man."

"Maybe not."

"After that I met so many other people who told me such deep stories 'cause of this thing, man. But y'know'm'saying, it all comes back to the root of travel. That kind of knowledge only comes from travel. It's essential. For any chef, especially"—Loco was able to evoke his rebellious intellect when he wanted—"Like a magician, man, they don't just do the same old tricks that every person in town knows. Naw, they go far and wide to look for new tricks. Same with religions, they get more relevant because they travel, they adapt. Even Jesus travelled up and down the Silk Road and learned everything about life that he tells about in the Bible. He wasn't no son of God—he was just a man who travelled and picked up new tricks and new recipes along the way. When the fuck you going to travel, Blanquito?"

"I don't know man. I'd like to."

"Then why don't you?"

"I don't know man."

"Well you gotta get the fuck outta here some time."

"Yeah. I will."

"Here comes Mr. Bossman."

The restaurant's manager pulled up in his used sports car. He ignored us while getting out of his car, and spoke to us only when he reached the door.

"Hope you guys didn't get too fried."

"Naw, Boss, just enough for the flavours to come alive," Loco answered.

Our manager looked both ways down the alley nervously, then opened the door.

"You guys should take off your uniforms at least."

"Sure thing, Boss."

The manager could have cared less about our pre-shift ritual, he knew we were apt even when high. He even included two dishes that Loco and I invented, stoned, one lazy afternoon.

For now we laughed at our boss' bogus rim caps that imitated expensive chrome rims. We speculated on how busy the day would be, and assumed the Thursday rush would come strong, but then dip after sundown. Friday was a day to loath, but that was tomorrow.

"So, man, you never told me. What do you know about OM?"

"I know a little bit," I said.

"Good or bad?"

"I can't even imagine how it could be bad."

"Some people are closed-minded," Loco pointed with his chin to our boss' BMW. "Some people just don't understand."

"True," I considered how much I should tell Loco; like Epictetus said, no good came from philosophizing with non-philosophers. "So...yeah. What does OM mean to me, man? It means someone buying a necklace by complete accident then never wanting to lose it again."

Loco paused, studying my face. Then he cracked his smile capped by a black moustache which exaggerated it.

"Ye, bro. You sure you've never travelled? Shit...Let's get to work, *hombre*[11], before we convince ourselves to get the fuck outta here."

> Steady humming chant
> percolating through souls to
> brighten faded eyes.

JOHNNY WALKS
[Martin O'Neill]

Malik Ceiss always did this. He would call me over, then I would reach his house only to find out that he was still at work for another half-hour. I should have come to expect it.

Today, at least, his mom was home. She hugged me and welcomed me in. Their neighbourhood was affluent, to say the least. Mrs. Ceiss exemplified the upscale suburban housewife, either wine-buzzed or

---

[11] ***Hombre*** — (*Spanish*) Man

ignorantly joyful, a little smiling chocolate chip in this over-floured neighbourhood.

"Have you eaten?" she asked.

"Not really. But I'm good."

"Oh please," she pulled me with friendly waves into the kitchen, "You have to eat. I bet you boys won't eat well enough in your new place. All microwave meals, I bet."

"Well, Atlas is a cook, so I'm sure he'll keep the house well fed."

"How is Atlas?"

"He's good. Busy with work. But good."

"That's g*ooo*od," she sang.

I took a seat at a stool along the large island that cordoned off the kitchen from the breakfast nook. Charlotte Ceiss loved me like a son. She was that kind of mom, with a heart too large for her own chest. I had known Malik for twelve of my twenty-one years, and Charlotte had been there to have seen me awkwardly shed skin over that time.

"How is the magazine?"

"It's going well. Tough, though. I just hope I can stay on for my whole co-op term."

"Oh, I'm sure you're doing fine. I read your first article there. It was well written. I don't think it's exactly your style, or what you wanted to write, but it turned out nicely."

Charlotte piled a plate with food and set it in front of me.

"Eat up."

It was always odd to be served food in a house that was not yours. But her cooking was hard to pass up. While I contemplated my food Charlotte whisked around the kitchen.

"Malik should be home in about twenty minutes. My Dad's wandering around, but don't mind him. I'm doing laundry and doing some cleaning, but you just make yourself at home, okay? Take anything else you need."

"Thanks, Charlotte."

I lowered my head and ate, wanting to bury my face in the potatoes out of shame for not being able to feed myself, for relying on the kindness of others, for bending so easily under the thumb of kindness.

The food was fantastic, of course. I scanned the newspaper on the counter while I ate.

World Economy on Brink of Failure Again, page two.

1 in 90 Children Born With Autism: Study, page three.

On page five there was a colour photo of a field of scraggly poppies growing against a horribly indifferent mountain range. Apparently the Afghani opium fields were being attacked by a new disease to the hurrahs of the various foreign armies stomping through the mountains. I chuckled aloud at the inset photo of an armoured soldier amongst a group of dirty children.

I noticed movement outside the sliding glass door to the backyard. An old man unsteadily bent to a flower pot and plucked a decorative plastic flower from the soil. He put it to his face, then carried it with him. I had not met him before, but I figured he was Malik's grandfather. He came to the glass door and fumbled with the handle. Malik's grandfather had Alzheimer's, and it had progressed too far for treatment. The withered man spent his days in a speechless stupor. Malik told me how he did not even know who he was, or which room was the bathroom.

When he finally made it inside I bent my face to my food again. He wandered around the kitchen. He put the plastic flower in the sink, and moved a dish rag into the fridge. He stood still for a few minutes. I watched the man carefully. He looked concerned about something. Finally his head jerked up and around. He caught my eyes. His crystalline blue eyes sparkled vacuously. We stared at each other for about a minute. I did not know how to react. Finally, he winked at me and smiled.

I immediately broke eye contact. I shovelled food into my mouth. I watched out of my peripherals as the man wandered out of the kitchen then right back in. With effort he pulled back the stool beside me and sat down.

"Hello," I said.

The man stared at the countertop without reaction.

"How're you doing"—I had forgotten his name; but really, it did not matter, "Johnny?"

Johnny held his hands together in his lap and stared distantly out the kitchen window. Slowly he looked at my dish, then at me. I smiled as warmly as I could. The corners of my lips parted to show teeth, the way they did when my smile was forced. I continued to eat while Johnny stared at me. I looked back up, meeting those handsome blue eyes again. He smiled.

"I bet your flower there smelled great, eh?"

Johnny stood and left the room. Glass shattered, followed by Charlotte's hurried footsteps from upstairs.

"Oh, d*aaaa*d," she cooed.

Johnny came back into the kitchen and stood across the island from me. Charlotte came in the room with a dustpan full of glass.

"I'm sorry, Martin," Charlotte sighed, "I hope he didn't bother you."

"Oh no. Not at all. This food is delicious, by the way. A pleasure."

"Thanks. Dad, come on, let's go into the living room and watch some TV," Charlotte took Johnny's hand and guided him away.

Johnny stopped her. He smiled at me and winked again. I winked back. Charlotte caught a sob in her throat. I looked over to her and fumbled my fork awkwardly. A tear crawled over her high cheekbone. Her lips scrunched into a frown. I understood that Johnny had not displayed those emotions in a long time. It had been so long since Charlotte had seen him be anything as close to human as he had just been.

I bent my head again, dragging my fork through the sauce on my dish.

Empty plate, heavy fork,
fake flower, headline woes,
forgotten hunger pangs.

THE GULP
[Simon Arcan]

So many fallacies.

When Uncle Frances built The Gulp, he told the architect to build two back doors. The architect argued for weeks, trying to tell my Uncle that it was impossible. I guess my Uncle was right, because the architect got himself fired.

Uncle Frances hadn't been right often throughout his life. Or at least he was made to feel like he made a lot of wrong decisions. I remember when we went to eat supper with him on the odd weekend, my father would be so uncomfortable that he would give himself indigestion. Uncle Frances riled me up, and I liked the man; we planned games and imaginary plays in the summers. Dad called Uncle Frances 'Uncle Pansy'. He told me never to sleep in the same bed as him. Mami didn't care as much as Dad did, but I think that was because Dad lost a lot of fights over Uncle Frances. Uncle Frances was gay, and he didn't give a fuck about it. In the eighties he might as well have been a neo-Nazi, he probably would have caught as much flack. Which was unfortunate because he was my favourite family member. His downtown apartment smelled nice, and he always had the most interesting guys over that weren't uptight like Dad, they talked liberally about anything. I guess when you *are* the politically incorrect you can be as politically incorrect as you like.

It was also a shame—but a big point on Dad's offensive—that Uncle Frances caught syphilis. He wasn't even ashamed of that. It took Dad six years to finally admit to me that Uncle Frances had contracted an STD, but I knew six weeks after the diagnosis.

In the late stages of his illness Uncle Frances changed. He was still eccentric, but now with a definite underlining of madness. He was a stock broker by trade, and he pooled all his money together to open up a gay bar: The Gulp. Uncle Frances named it after the first sound Dad made when he told him about it.

The Gulp was a popular establishment. Lesbians and gays drank, danced, hooked up, and did whatever they wanted under the madcap smile my Uncle put on from his VIP balcony. It was a sanctuary, without the leering gaze of the straight masses. The gay movement had already gained ground legally and politically; the social perception was a slow monster to breed.

Or not to breed, I guess, was the point. Which I thought was brilliant. If I didn't like pussy so much I would have liked to be gay. There was something practical and efficient about it. There was nothing practical and efficient about me. I quit my job months before school started, which was short-sighted, but I had had enough. Fortunately Uncle Frances was a nice enough man that he offered me a job at the club. Against Dad's better judgement I took the job.

So that was why I had tight pants on, and my nipples showed out the side of a velour vest. I carried drinks between soused men who openly thought about my asshole, about what it would be like to grab my afro and slap my ass. Not like those retentive drunks in heterosexual bars, who wondered the same thing, but drowned their thoughts with more liquor and obscenely skanky women.

I set martinis for four guys who were on their second bottle of vodka. They practically made out while I emptied the tray. The one nearest the end of the table slapped my ass and stuffed a five dollar bill into my pants pocket. The end of the rolled bill poked my dick, which felt weird. I smiled anyways and pinched the man's cheek.

Although I never knew this, gays do not necessarily like lesbians, and vice versa. It wasn't premeditated on my Uncle's part, it just turned out that the men gathered on the lower part of the split floor, and the women on the higher level.

"Hey sexy," a man spoke into my ear at the bar while I waited for more drinks.

"What's up brother?"

"Hmm-haha, brother. When's your shift finish?"

"Late."

I learned quick that it was best to be brief and vague.

"I'll be around late."

"Cool. See you then."

My friend Ayn worked as a waitress for three years and told me how sick she got of men trying to fulfill their sex maiden fantasies with her. I was glad, at least, that I couldn't be convinced to consider some of the proposed escapades.

"Have you ever had your asshole electroshocked?" another man sloppily asked into my ear.

Fortunately my next drinks were going to the upper level. Serving the lesbians was so exciting I actually got nervous. Everytime I expected a curious couple to ask me if I would be interested in a threesome. But these lesbians were hardcore; they had zero interest in my broad shoulders or the exaggerated bulge in my crotch. They were all about the cunt.

The hot nights were fun—made interesting by costumes, the constant crowd, and the thumping electronic music that kept the dancefloor rumbling. I enjoyed those nights, even when I came home at three in the morning with glitter on my face, and the gangsters riding the bus with me laughed and weighed how much they wanted to kick my ass over how much I would enjoy it.

The other nights, like Tuesdays, on those boring days when nobody had the libido or gusto to give themselves up to their pleasure centres, those nights were sad. These were the nights of the desperate. The social alcoholics. The ultra-lonely that reached out so hard for company. On these nights the spinning lights seemed vain, and the music played lower because these people preferred to talk and drink, not go nuts.

It was on one of these nights that I broke the waiter law and drank on my shift.

While I waited to notice people looking around for a next drink I downed my own. The bar wrapped around two sides of the room, so I could watch the bar, which was usually packed solid on a busy night. Tonight only two girls sat at it.

The whole bar was built of mirror. It was a job in itself to clean it. It was super reflective, so there was a particular placement of the lights that hit the surfaces just enough to trip you out but not burn your eyes. The girls at the bar talked expressively; then one of them started fingering her phone, so the other took out her own phone and pressed buttons.

They were so goddamn sad I cringed for another drink. I went behind the bar and fixed three drinks. I brought two of them to the girls and offered them on the house. Something had to get them unplugged from their wireless lives.

That started the trend that got me fired. All the isolated parties were so fucking sad, they provoked something that made me just want to help them. At the end of the night everybody had cleared out, and I finished the last bit of liquor from one of the bottles of rum. Uncle Frances came in to cash out at one in the morning.

He smiled at me. He noticed all the empty bottles under the counter, and the curious shortage of cash and receipts to match up. I didn't have a single receipt, and I was too hammered to make up a better story.

"Simon," Uncle Frances grabbed my shoulder and sat me on one of the stools. The music was off but the lights still swung slowly, "This isn't the place for you. What you did wasn't entirely wrong, it just can't happen here. This business is my life."

I gulped. Tried to hold back the vomit. It was too late.

"I'll call you a taxi."

"Naw, *Tio*[12], naw, I'll take the bus."

---

[12] *Tio* — (*Spanish*) Uncle (Aunt: *Tia*)

Fallacies: bitter
sweet vomit, blurry-eyed, trying
to find two back doors.

TO THE CEMETERY
[Atlas Sangman]

Sometimes when we had to leave a place but we weren't ready to go home we shot out of the city and rode the fringe roads back in. It was relaxing. The four of us let the music do all the conversing. Some spacey drawn-out jazz wailed over the tape deck, just the kind of soundtrack you needed when you had to cope with the end of an ecstatic purge.

The roads out of town were darker; all the more reason for headlights, the total of which we saw was four, plus our own, which made for an overall blackness that nobody minded because nobody saw it, our eyes were still painted from over-stimulated phosphenes and retinas and imaginations. Jeanne knew how to throw a party.

Henryk cracked his window. Even at 80 km/h, a cacophony of birdsong and insect buzzes spiked the music. To our backs, downtown hedonists were also sleepless—but they needed reasons, they needed party invites, they needed cocaine, lights, coffee and alcohol—here, where it truly fell dark, earth's creatures never slept. The wild was never quiet. Maybe that was how you lived when you only lived for a few days, weeks, or months.

Jeanne ter Baark had just returned from Cannes. She spent the last winter living in the south of France, painting under the apprenticeship of a French instructor, Madame Baudelaire (no relation to Charles, much to Martin's disappointment). Six months under the sun, invoking the sensualities of colour, crashing like the Mediterranean waves as the sun fell to discover the fleshly appetites on a strict diet of canvas, oil paint, and red wine.

Madame Baudelaire still housed the majority of Jeanne's work, because the cost to transport the one hundred and thirty-eight pieces was outrageous. Plus orgies couldn't transport well without being spoiled. Jeanne showed me some photos of her new work, tittering close to me because she couldn't explain anything she had painted, it just came forth like the shells that washed onto the shore.

"Madame Baudelaire and I, we'd walk barefoot on the rocky shore outside of town and pluck the most beautiful shells. Then we'd pay our models with these shells. Madame Baudelaire said nothing but beauty could acknowledge beauty, and that beauty is everywhere, so the beautiful are everywhere too."

Jeanne's subtle Dutch accent had kept its rigour but became softened by the French she learned.

"To pay the landscape we gave ourselves to it, Atlas, isn't that so *charnelle[13]*? Isn't that the way you imagine life came upon earth? By giving itself to itself? *Lui pour lui. Et toute pour lui-meme[14]*. Haha!"

Jeanne had been a prodigal painter before her sabbatical, she had shown her work in Mississauga's galleries when she was only sixteen. But that had only been a debut: the virgin showing what she had to offer. France had married Jeanne to her craft. This was the artist in fruit. The artist with her loins spread vastly across the earth; a maw unto which modern times would peer into and see itself reflected back.

I loved Jeanne. But she could never love me back now, not with such a demanding lover.

So from the brightly coloured decorations and mismatched lamp-light of Jeanne's new apartment we dove into the darkness.

The simple, impersonal darkness.

---

[13] ***Charnelle*** — (*French*) Carnal

[14] ***Lui pour lui. Et toute pour lui-meme!*** — (*French*) Him for him! And all for themselves! (although Jeanne was intending, "One for all, and all for each other.")

"Cut through here," Henryk directed.

"The cemetery?"

"It's a nicer drive."

There was no complaint from the backseat. The road through the cemetery was winding, and I slowed down. The back window opened; Martin clicked his lighter. I opened my window to feel the cool wind blow back my hair.

Old oaks hung over the road, accented every now and then by elms or short shrubs, but generally there was an open view of the cemetery's rolling hills. There was an eerie new fashion, to stick solar-powered lights over the graves. The flowers brightened the gloom during the day; the lights did the same for the night. Sprightly LED lights dotted the hills, some blinking like ghastly lighthouses, some shifting colours, some stolid and sombre like the tombstones behind them. Even out here in the city fringes a dark night was rare; here in the cemetery the sedated lights flickered on every night like a reawakened heartbeat for the dead.

"The lights are on, but nobody's home," Henryk commented.

The cemetery ended abruptly onto a major thoroughfare that was empty at such a late hour.

The streetlights blinded out the night above and I felt awake again.

How life came to earth:
giving itself to itself—
dead cemetery.

THINGS WE LOST IN THE MOVE:
[Simon Arcan]

Atlas had this comb he never used and I say had
because now its redundancy is fulfilled in the lost
netherlands of lostness—along with that old
gumball machine Martin had filled with ibuprofen
—Henryk's black reading lamp—a wholesale
package of tinfoil—a few scraps of paper where I
had peoples' phone numbers written down but I
never phoned them yet so I guess they were
unimportant—a ziploc of nuts and bolts for that
extra table—our newly bought set of spoons—a
book Henryk thought he had—the Guinness Book
of World Records Martin casually noticed was
missing—a glass hash pipe—a box of paper clips—
the extra Zeppelin tape I never told Henryk I traded
for the CD—pie plates Atlas thinks he might have
used as drip trays for his mom's spider plants that
will keep her occupied while she is trying to dry out
—we all know it's bullshit but who cares pie plates
are cheap at the dollar store—some lame nature
posters Henryk collected from our highschool's

National Geographic collection—Martin's S key on one of his old typewriters—guess all his stories will be about an ex—fuck sex—he said he could repair it but we lost our tools—or at least I ignored my dad and did not take the mini tool box he had clandestinely snuck onto my pile of stuff—nail clippers—my Che Guevara flag—Henryk's highschool science notes—on a positive note we found a glass door knob in Martin's boxes that he cannot account for—on another positive vibration we do not really give a fuck about the shit we lost because it is only a fraction of all the things we have lost throughout the years—the four of us have already become too cynical or too wise to believe we can move without losing—all movement is loss.

So while we are on the topic the four of us have also lost structured homes with a mom and dad and sibling(s) whose dynamics will shape the outcome of our futures more than we like to admit—secure budgeted resources to replace what goes wrong— hope Atlas does not get fired—a place to escape from each other—parental workplace-backed insurance policies—quiet suburban streets where between eight o'clock and five-thirty you can hear your footsteps echo if you run and if you run and somebody happens to see you they will think it suspicious and safely and appropriately call the police—long walks to public transit—secret porn viewings—arbitrary punishments for when shit hits the fan—old family recipes—a clean house—air conditioning—a stocked fridge—thanks mom—a responsible adult—curfews—masked highs—guilt —a reason not to walk around naked—visits from relatives—traditional holiday nuances—the embarrassment of having our whacky friends come visit—a need to muffle orgasmic moans in pillows —laundry hampers—a sink void of dirty dishes—a good excuse to leave the house.

BENIGN TUMORS
[Henryk Zdicz]

We planned a larger house-warming, but on the day after we hauled in boxes to the new townhouse, Unit 3E, Jeanne and Lukasz showed up at our door with a small homemade cake. We had seen them recently enough that the small talk was minimal, and as we ate cake we continued our previous conversation.

"Atlas, you been to the mountains. Right?" Simon pointed out.

"Yeah, man. Once," he said.

"Alright. So what's it like? Did you meditate on a glacial mountaintop or something?"

"Maybe. But there was something else about it. Something just, uhm, *sensory*. Y'know? I think it must be the tiny drop in oxygen, because of the altitude. You could walk through Jasper and be amused by the architecture and the weird cliché catering they got going on, and even *then* there's something ethereal about it. It just felt different. I think it'd be cool if we all went."

"This summer," I said.

"This summer," Simon repeated.

"Do we drive it?"

"Drive it? O-kay Kerouac. I think it'd be a brutal drive," Simon said. "We could get drunk on a plane."

"Flying wine is something like heaven," Jeanne noted.

"Steaks on a plane!"

"Fuck first class. But I say we do it. Matter of fact, I might even go alone, y'know, if everybody else changes their mind."

"Oh, I'll come with you, Sy," I nodded.

"Ah I'm so down," Lukasz said.

"Atlas? What are you saying?"

"I dunno, man, we'll see. I'm not really in a fortune, plus the house and all, so—"

"We'll find a way," I said, "We'll find a way to the mountains! I think we should even go mapless.

What's the use of a map? All the roads tell you if you're going east or west. It's all square out there. My dad flew it before, he said it looked like the most boring game of chess ever."

"Maybe some farmer's daughter can hook us up with some shelter on the way." Simon added.

[Simon Arcan]

We all considered the adventure quietly, listening to the raspy vinyl record. The sofas were cushy and there was a pot of tea in the middle of the table that incensed the room. Atlas dimmed the lights, and we all just hung out to the music. I, for one, was too tired to even think of doing anything.

"But for now," Henryk said slowly, "I'm just going to stay focused on school. If I'm not working, I might as well be tearing down that institution."

"Me too, guy, I'm telling you, this is our militant training. I bet we can find a way to work together," I said.

"Man, the only thing you guys could do together would be to sabotage industrial corporations," Lukasz joked.

"Yeah, could be. It'd be an alright idea," Simon said.

"One day at a time, guys. C'mon, give me a break, I'm just trying to get through these academic hoops."

"Henryk, you're brighter than any piece of shit professor I've seen bred out of those tight universities," Jeanne said. "Darling, you've got more than they know to offer."

"Man, what would it take to establish a university?" Atlas asked. "Is it just a business thing? Or, like, just a want-to-do-it kind of thing?"

"I think it's a lot of things," Henryk said. "I don't think it's easy either way. Anyone honest probably couldn't do it. You'd have to be slick in some way."

"*Everybody's got something to hide—*" I sang.

"*Except for me and my monkey[15],*" Jeanne added.

[Atlas Sangman]

After a pause to groove to a bass line Jeanne said *The Satellites* were getting back together. None of us knew they broke up, but nobody said anything.

I drank most of the tea. Simon said the tea tasted like summer sex, which I didn't understand.

"Do you mind if I sketch?" Jeanne asked.

---

[15] Much love to the Beatles (here quoting "Everybody's Got Something to Hide Except Me and My Monkey" off the White Album)

No one answered, because it was implicit that she could. She took out her sketchpad and a couple of pencils and slowly made stripes on the paper.

"Ji-Ji's going to go wild with her canvases, I bet you're going to have to burn some of them to keep you warm one day. You should get a monkey."

"I've already got you, Simonkey."

"Will you bear my resemblances for me?"

Simon sometimes just talked nonsense while we all nodded along. It was easier that way. Simon could knot himself into paradoxes and make those his point. If Claire had been here, she would've been able to stop him short, but—

"The point being that I am a fruit as much as you —I mean, you know, not in the slang gay way, but in, like, the way of bearing fruit. We are the apple tree, if you will. But more like a beaver. Did I tell you about energy yet, Jeanne? Were you here for that revelation?"

"Don't think I was," she answered.

"No. And we don't need to go into it again, man," I answered Simon's real question.

"What? Why not?"

"Because, man. It'll just trip everyone out, and we'll all focus on it way too much. It'll redefine the whole evening."

"Maybe that's just the way she needs to go."

"Suffice to say, Jeanne, it's that we are energy," Henryk said. "I think Sy's just saying that we're all doing stuff, like being productive in the world. Like beavers, I guess."

"Sounds interesting."

"I'm sure you'll hear it another time."

"Fine, I won't spill my thoughts. But I will say that Captain Obvious missed the part that we're not just productive, we're essential to the product *and* what it was produced from. If I'm not making an impact on this world—if I'm *not*—then what am I? A benign tumour? Growth for growth's sake? The earth does not waste."

"There are a lot of junk satellites in orbit, Simon. We waste, so it must be natural."

"Growth for growth's sake?" Simon repeated.

I noticed the enthusiasm of the room sizzle out as the cake's sugar buzz wore down. The small jade plant Henryk had moved into the den bent under its own weight, it needed watering. I also had violets and a Christmas cactus in the room—neglected plants Henryk and I were trying to nurse back from my mother. I left the room, fetched and filled the watering can, and brought it back to the den. Nobody moved; they remained collapsed in their cushions. I watered the plants slowly, studying them up close. Jeanne motioned me over after I finished the last pot and showed me her sketchbook. She had sketched the three plants in succession. Then quickly sketched in with wide strokes: a rudimentary man feeding the plants water. She smiled at me and told me I could have it, but I declined. I couldn't take it. The picture was hers; she could use it. Jeanne smiled and told me that I was easy to draw, whatever that meant. While I was up I refilled the pot of tea, and when I sat back on the sofa the conversation had completely shifted gears, and Henryk was playing his guitar while Jeanne and Simon tried to figure out a song they both knew. I sat back, without a voice.

> Grow like benign
> tumours under the sun—vagrant
> zombie flowers.

AN AUGUST TO-DO
[Lukasz Skarbek]

- move $ from savings
- ~~ask boys for help to move~~
- ~~give two weeks' notice~~
- ~~pack books~~
- borrow wok
- print class schedule
- ~~buy oz~~

- ~~new papes~~
- ~~steal milkcrates~~
- buy new socks
- get batt for watch
- change cellphone plan
- ~~start big grocery list~~
- ~~KEEP IT REAL~~ (and keep it up)
- get $ from Henny
- convince mom we don't need a landline
- ~~get Manny to get his shit together~~
- ~~get new clothes you greasy mofo~~
- tell Sy to fuck off
- ~~find ritalin hook-up~~
- ~~take it easy~~
- ~~get new 'Loo gym membership~~
- buy antacids
- vitamins
- *do something*

LISTENING TO THE LOGOS
[Simon Arcan]

Hopelessness.

That is what made the mall such a frustrating place for me. The food court smell of grease-laden belly filler—the shiny halogens key-lighting smooth plastic models in haphazard outfits for any number of social occasions—bass-thumping plain drum kit music to muffle the good sense of outrage —the maps coded for your convenience with the scrawl of a consumerist prophet roll-call—all too much for me; I needed something real, something tangible, I needed something I couldn't buy. But Lukasz was going back to Waterloo and needed things.

"I got a list," he said.

"For what?"

"Of things I need to buy."

"That's unfortunate."

It was a Thursday afternoon but the mall was already packed with what I assumed was the weekend crowd. Teenagers outnumbered the old people, so it was clearly past four o'clock. A short, shaved-head pseudo-thug ran into my shoulder as we rounded a corner. A group of girls with matching booty shorts talked while texting other people. The confusion!—the escalators' slow rise that I beat by running up—Lukasz jogging to keep up—the glass elevators we passed with a stagnant young family leading a baby carriage, staring out of the glass like the faceless models, dressed up with nowhere better to go than here.

"Here, man, I can get some jeans here," Lukasz led the way because I hadn't been in a mall in years.

After ten minutes of leaning in various racks of clothes Lukasz lifted a pair and asked me what I thought. I told him I thought they were jeans. He tried them on but they looked like any other pair of jeans would.

"Eighty. Not bad."

"You mean eighty dollars?" I asked, trying to keep my voice low. "That's fucking ridiculous. Man, check out my jeans. They're the same shit. Nine bucks at the thrift store."

"Yeah guy, but they're grimey. I don't want welfare jeans, I want fresh shit."

"Did you know they were nine bucks before I told you?"

On to the next store. Lukasz filled his hands with practical items too: socks, watch battery, antacids. We passed the toy aisle of the big box store, and I couldn't resist. I pulled Lukasz down the aisle and turned on every single musical, motion-activated, noisy and/or lit-up toy I could reach. The aisle exploded in a ramshackle rattle of senseless nursery rhymes—*Mary had a little gagagaga yayaya ha heeee ahuahuahua zeep zeep zop Mary had a little*—we moved on but the music stayed, like a parade that no one was watching.

Lukasz went back to the pharmacy to look for some vitamins, and hidden between Vitamin D and

Echinacea I found a stack of numbers, the plastic numbers the store used to post the latest discount prices on their low-quality/high-quantity goods. So we wandered the store for the next few minutes changing random prices, lowering them even more —9.99 to .88, 47.96 to 12.93, 103.99 to .13. We had just changed our last price when security blocked the check-out counter and asked us to leave the store.

"I have stuff to buy," Lukasz answered bluntly.

"You're not going to be buying it here," the security guard said.

"What? This man wants to spend money at your establishment and you're refusing him service?"

"That's bullshit," Lukasz scoffed.

"If you'd like to stick around and debate about it you're more than welcome, and we can call up the police and hear what they think, too."

"What an amateur," Lukasz sneered.

"Fuck you," I tossed the items in Lukasz's hands to the floor. "We don't want your shit anyways. I should've shit in your potty-training toilets, too. Yo," I added, throwing up my middle finger as we were leaving, "Invite the police to this, motherfucker."

We passed the store's white-light threshold to the brown tiles and sky-lights of the mall, to continue our market mayhem. I considered that maybe it was a good idea to go to the mall and get kicked out so I could have a good excuse to never come back here.

"I need some tees," Lukasz checked a list from his pocket.

So we found a store that tried to be punk in every facet, except that it was a corporate retailer that exploited the culture they wanted to sustain for their own profit. So many logos—the logos were too many to count, some impossible to name, just symbols upon symbols, some upon words that meant nothing—they were stickers, posters, hats, t-shirts, sweaters, bikinis and socks, shoes and wallets. The teens who came into the store were already covered in logos. Lukasz held up shirts and hid himself behind these logos.

"Why in the hell would you want to support these companies for?"

"What do you mean?"

"I mean you're gonna be a fucking billboard for these guys. And you gotta pay insane prices—who pays fifty dollars for a t-shirt?"

"I like it. The design, man—"

"There is no design, it's just the company's name. I don't understand. Man, can you imagine if with all this exposure these logos become symbols in our collective unconscious? And guide our decisions? For what? For a hefty fucking profit margin? I just don't *get* it."

"Look, Sy, I brought you 'cause you seem to have an eye for fashion that I don't necessarily have."

"It's all accidental then, bro, 'cause I'd never pay a goddamn cent for any of these threads."

"Fuck off. I knew I should've waited 'til Henryk was free," Lukasz muttered.

"He'd at least know better than to be a fucking paperboy for consumerist bastards."

I talked loud enough that people near-by could hear. I was afraid it would be the only way they would ever allow themselves to consider the pure irrationality of their purchases. For some it was hopeless, their parents led them, picked up clothes for them, stood in line with their pubescent children hiding behind them, asking for one more sweater—hearing me—then hearing their parents' much more authoritative teeth sucking and finding comfort in the silent swipe of the credit card in the tight maw of the debit machine.

But it was a sweet tight pussy that twisted tighter —at the racks I was bound to find something I thought was funky, something I had seen other people wear. And I wasn't above aspiring to be someone else sometimes. One sweater I considered, for modernity's sake. Fortunately Lukasz was already at the counter making his purchase.

Finally the hopelessness was beat—the sudden breath of fresh air beyond the mall's double doors, the exhilaration Lukasz felt with armfuls of new things; me, relieved to be outside and knowing that I could get as dirty as I wanted and not feel guilty because I didn't spend a sarcophagus of money to cover myself.

The afternoon sun built up an awful humidity that finally let itself go into a warm rain that smelled funny. Lukasz raced to the car but I lagged behind.

"C'mon, man, let's get the hell outta here."

"Are you out of that mall spell? Finally. That's the most sane thing I've heard you say all afternoon."

Fresh out of words—lost—
found something perfect to say—
there, on my t-shirt.

TATTOO
[Atlas Sangman]

It had been a long time since I was last afraid.

I think the last time I was truly afraid was when I was twelve. Once the older boys on the Reserve got the taste for beating me senseless. They threatened me constantly, telling me that I would end up dead before my next birthday. But I made it through that miserable birthday.

So almost ten years of frightlessness. If anybody asked I wouldn't tell them I was afraid right now, but they could probably tell by my shaky appendages. I couldn't stop shaking at least one of my limbs since the six of us—Martin, Simon, Lukasz, Malik, myself, and birthday boy Henryk— had walked into the tattoo parlour.

When Henryk got his first tattoo we were eighteen. I fully supported the man. But it was never something I considered.

So when Henryk brought it up again two weeks ago the idea remained in a similar foreign precipice of experience, far from me. Then he convinced everybody else to get a joint tattoo, an ink bond to show our camaraderie.

My skin was baby-ish. I could barely sprout facial hair. I had never decorated myself in any way. I hated my body, but I was used to it the way it was. I didn't want to ruin it anymore.

"C'mon, man, just get something little. We can all think of something to get inked. You don't have to get it across your forehead. It can be discreet," Henryk pleaded.

I did a lot for Henryk.

Apparently I did this for him on my right bicep.

Martin, Lukasz, Malik and Henryk were experienced, all inked in the years past—Simon hadn't but he was more excited than I was. He flipped through our artists' portfolio on the waiting room sofa, laughing at the stupid ideas people came up with to have permanently inscribed on their skin.

Henryk was the first on the chair. The metallic buzz of the needle made me cringe. It sounded like a small saw cutting through metal.

I wasn't metal. I was a delicate bag of skin.

"Don't worry, Atlas," Martin soothed me. "It doesn't hurt. It's just a strange feeling. Like a ringing in the flesh. You get used to it. You'll like it."

Which was nice to hear, except it was hard to hear over the *ZZZZZZZZZZZ* of the needle coming from the other room, sounding like a swarm of killer bees.

Under the bumble I heard Henryk talking with the artist, occasionally laughing softly. I ignored Simon, pointing out all the places he thought would be the most painful to get a tattoo.

"The crown of the skull. The inside thigh. Your eyelids. Your cock," Simon listed. "The inside of your lip. Atlas, your pussy lips. The inside of your lip. The soft side of your forearm."

The superfluidity of stupidity was that people chose these places to have a needle jabbed into their skin. Henryk's second tattoo complicated that notion, though, in that it was a choice to represent something unchosen. On his left forearm, on the soft skin where you could so easily see your veins, he had five numbers in blue ink. They were originally a gift his grandfather received from the mangled teeth of the Auschwitz concentration camp, where he had been sent after being captured for participating in Poland's Nazi resistance movement. His grandmother remembered that number vividly, it was impressed on her memory as it was impressed on his frail arm; when he returned home from the concentration camp he took off his shirt she traced it with her fingers, and was forever horrified by it.

Thirty minutes passed quickly. Henryk came bounding into the waiting room, shirt off and all smiles, showing off the new ink we would soon all share: *S.A.U.G.A.* For (obviously) the *Society of Artists, Unknowns, Geniuses and Adventurers*, the name we synthesized one high night for our rag-tag group of friends.

I jumped up from the sofa and headed for the chair. I couldn't bear waiting. The tattoo artist was burly, his ass flapped over the ends of the rolling chair. He asked me where I wanted it and I pointed to my right bicep and tried to explain that I wanted it going downwards, like Chinese script, except I could barely form a sentence.

The needle clicked on, the man dipped the pointy end in a small pack of black ink and drew the droning apparatus to my arm. Without warning he poked my skin and I jumped.

"Don't do that. Just relax," he instructed.

"Oh yeah, yeah. I'm cool."

I squirmed in the seat. He started at the top of the arm, so the needle's vibrations carried through my collarbone and rattled my spine.

Why am I doing this to myself?

There was no easy answer to an easy question.

After about twenty minutes the pain had melted into an ooze of euphoria. Each time the needle pricked my skin I felt calmer, stronger, happier. When the tattoo artist wiped my arm down I leaped off the seat.

"Whoa, buddy, take it easy. I gotta bandage you up."

He sat me down, wrapped up my arm. He explained all the care to put into the tattoo. I could care less.

"You got all that? Alright dude. Come back when you get the itch again."

I came around the wall with the same Seussian smile Henryk had worn. I skipped carelessly into the waiting room and peeled back the bandage so everyone could see. Simon cocked his head over my arm, stepped back, and slapped the fresh tattoo. The slap stung, it made me reel back—but I didn't give him hell. I just smiled.

All things come to pass.

> The illusion of permanence
> is the permanence
> of illusion.

NO ROADS BACK TO ABERDEEN
[Simon Arcan]

Coming late into class is like a slow tai chi. You float to, then into, your seat. You don't want anybody to notice you; this isn't highschool anymore, the spectacle of tardiness has lost its entertainment.

I hate being late. Late & hungry. Late & hungry & hungover & buzzing on that desperate black coffee.

On my first day of school. Howdy-do-dee teacher, I'm the fuck-up you wish never signed up. The professor watches me climb to the back row while he continues introducing the course.

Fuck off, old man. Just say what you got to say and if I pick it up, good, if I argue against it better, and if I do nothing than we both wasted our time. I loathed university on my first day.

What might make it better was ganja. I should've smoked this morning.

Instead I convinced myself that I was going to try to be the sober soldier running on passion alone.

I would have to rethink that proposal.

I think Atlas spent his first day in university like me: trying to get stoned. He said it was how he met Kaya, rolling a joint in the quad after orientation. But Atlas was looking for different shit than me. He probably just sat in the trees and left his mark nowhere. He left no one a reason to expect him around.

That snooty motherfucker, shitting all over the credibility Henryk and I were finally chasing. An extra semester in highschool, and internet courses, and we *still* had to wait until we were over the age of 21 and highschool marks didn't matter so much to get accepted.

Henryk had pragmatics in mind—so he went to college for forest management and I pursued political science at university.

The instructor used the word *sustainability* and I checked out the girls in class. There were more seats than seated. I wondered why the fuck it was so hard to get in to this place. Then when you were in you complained the whole way through. People already complained. They asked about the succession of tests, how many papers and how long —like that was going to make a difference.

Hello, annoying dude at the front of the class. You have made yourself known on day one. Good job.

These kids were damned stupid,. I couldn't believe these were the minds who outcompeted me three years ago.

Look at me, such an old man. Twenty-one year-old man too old to have patience for dem dere kidren playin' therr on the lawn.

The class would pick up Unit One on Thursday. We had to be caught up on our reading by then. I didn't know what book he was even talking about.

Everyone solemnly moved to their next class. They all must have felt like me: they already hated this ride.

I had enough time to sneak in a cigarette, but why ruin a good moment? I fished down the hallways, up and down until I found the classroom, then joined in the party again: meeting the old head who would talk to us about shit we'd have to know to write papers he liked, and how to write tests he approved; the subtle feeling that this was the end of the world, and you had to know things to rebuild the human race; staring at the girls in class and trying to read them according to their clothes; bringing two fingers to my face and inhaling, but blowing no smoke out; then rushing out at the end class like it was on fire—then we were channelled down naturally lit hallways to smile and laugh amongst ourselves, planning how much we'd have to eat at supper in order to get a nice smash on in the evening.

There was the nagging feeling that I would be disappointed with this institution. I inspected the halls, wandering the corridors without names. I watched people who were busy watching other things. I sat for a second and felt horrible about my decision. I had woken up to Nirvana on my alarm clock. The song replayed in my head.

I sat down at a bench by the window in a quiet stairwell. I thought about Kurt Cobain, because his voice sang in my mind. I wondered if he ever went back to his birthtown, Aberdeen, and considered what his life had become. It would've made a good song, if anything. I guess I could write a song, too, about my disorientation at a location, about a disassociation by a paranoid consideration.

But I had more important things to do. I needed to keep myself busy.

I figured I could buy my books. Might as well —I already had a fucking epic of intellect that I had to absorb for this first week. The bookstore was in the basement I never knew existed. I found it after I scoured all the hallways, building my own map of the school. I noted where all the bathrooms were.

The bookstore was small, it was crammed with books, like all our heads would be by finals. The blocks of books excited me. There was a lot of power in this basement, it was a fucking landmine. It could fall giants. That was good. I would find the library next.

There was deliberation with the numbering system, some retarded child of the Dewey decimal system. My books from today's classes towered by my eyes. And there was still tomorrow. Man, this landmine is heavy. It wouldn't ever be mined out.

At the counter I told the clerk that I couldn't find a book, it wasn't on the shelves.

"Did you look?" she asked.

"Uh. Yeah."

I wanted to add: Why the fuck wouldn't have I looked?

"What's it called?"

"I can't remember, but it's for Delgado's Contemporary Political Science class."

"You don't know the name?"

"Uh. No, sorry."

"If you don't know the name, I can't look it up."

"Can't you look up the class and see what texts are required?"

"No."

"No? Why not? That seems a little ridiculous. Aren't you the *school* bookstore? Why would you work as a separate entity?"

"I'm sorry, do you want me to check out the books you have?" she asked, ever impervious to jumpy first years.

"No. Listen to me. I asked questions. Do I have to speak to the manager?"

"I am the manager, sir."

"Fan-fucking-tastic," I blurted. "Great. That explains everything. You see this?" I asked the girl behind me—but it was too late to stop—"You see how they treat us? Like we're stupid, heh. Not even the dignity of ownership."

The girl just raised her eyebrows and nodded for my sake.

"You can't separate the hands from the head," I said back to the clerk, even though I didn't know what that meant.

She started scanning my books. I walked away. I didn't even look back, I knew that the line would be staring at me.

Outside, I paused by the doors and lit another cigarette. I inhaled, looked around. People crisscrossed the quad. I walked and puffed my cigarette, not going anywhere in particular. The campus map stopped me, because I'd never noticed it before. I studied it. I tried to find the way out from where I was.

The map stares at me and laughs—
do you know the way
back to Aberdeen?

CASH RULES EVERYTHING AROUND ME
[Martin O'Neill]

"Have you thought about what we're doing?" Simon asked.

Atlas, Henryk, Simon, and I walked down the street, spilling off the sidewalk. Atlas swung around trees near the curb. I smoked a cigarette and tried to slow Simon's pace. He was almost skipping, darting; this was how Sy got when he left the house in the early evening. His power seemed to surge in the dying sun. Henryk dressed the nicest, he boosted the overall visual integrity of our group, who otherwise would have been simple stoners on their way to get munchies—who otherwise would have been stoned if Ozzy had called us back earlier. Munchies would be nice, but it wasn't the focus. This was an appointment we couldn't miss.

"We are giving in to social paranoia. They say everything's wrong when it isn't. Money is the way out. I don't know if I want to do this."

"We have to, man," Atlas said solemnly.

"But isn't it our choice to value our own life in our own way?"

"Sy, it's only insurance, man."

"It's a necessary rip-off. Just do it, get the cheapest rate we can, and make our peace," Henryk explained.

"How many rip-offs does it take the feel comforted?" Sy snuffed. "Whatever. I'm washing my hands clean of this. I'm Pontius Pilate, y'all, I'm not responsible for what goes down."

"We're almost there," Henryk reminded us as we crossed a street.

Henryk would have to stay sharp for our meeting with the insurance broker. He usually was on the ball, so the onus was on him to figure out what to do. My dad had given me the card for this insurance broker he knew from college. The guy operated a one-man show out of his house, which was conveniently close to where we lived. That's about as much as I understood about the insurance industry. I knew they made us afraid of fire and water and the world in general to make us pay for imaginary safety nets that might or might not break your fall.

Yeah, sometimes Simon was right too.

"I say we don't buy insurance but copyright *ourselves* so that if people want to use our names or identities they'll have to pay us. The phonebook, the police, telemarketers. Everytime someone reads our tombstones they'd have to sign a cheque."

Simon could get to a point of ridiculous clarity. We laughed when he ranted, sometimes only because it was insane that what he was saying wasn't true.

"I'm going to do that. Next time a telemarketer calls I'll ask for their manager and demand my royalties. *Yo, you can't say my name like that. You owe me*," Henryk laughed.

"Then you give them my number, and as your copyright lawyer I'll tell them we'd have to sue unless they pay up."

"Why would you run a con on a poor telemarketer like that?" Atlas asked.

"I can't believe you'd even ask that question."

"Check it out," Henryk pointed up to the war-era porch of a narrow house.

"That's him," I confirmed, checking the business card against the name etched onto the glass.

"Perfect," Henryk said.

He stamped his foot when he said it, reminding me of a Viking laying claim to land.

"I've never been in this part of town," Atlas said.

"It's higher middle-class, these old homes," Henryk explained. "Lawyers and optometrists and dentist and the like. They keep business close to home, I guess."

It must've been implied that I would have to introduce people to this guy, even though I'd never met him and only talked to his secretary.

The door felt so thin it was useless. The glass shook when I knocked.

It was a while until a plump white-haired man answered the door. He was smiling all the way down the hall. He opened the door and waved us in.

"Hello guys, hello. Come on in, please, take off your shoes."

"That doesn't sound safe. What if the house catches fire? Oh my god, we'll all die. We need some insurance, doc, we need it real bad," Simon mocked, over-dramatizing.

Luckily the door frame was small and I filled it, so Mr. Roshburg, our beaming insurance agent, did not kick us out right then.

"You know, I don't mind house calls," Roshburg beamed. "They usually turn out the best."

"Oh yeah, thanks."

"So what do you got for us?" Atlas asked.

Atlas was the only one with any substantial inflow of money, so he offered to pay the bill. We were all counting on Atlas agreeing to the deal so that we could get our house.

Mr. Roshburg led us to his office. It would've been the living room in any ordinary house. The staircase was shut-off by a door and the kitchen entry sat at the back of his office with a curtain partition.

His full suit, minus the shoes, made the whole office feel like he was a senile man playing doctor.

"Please, sit."

He sat in his big leather chair. We faced him in the wooden chairs moved in from the kitchen.

"Would you guys like coffee or something?" Roshburg asked.

Simon said yes while the rest of us shook our heads.

"Maybe I'll have one too, if you're making it," Henryk said quietly.

"It's already made."

Mr. Roshburg pressed a small button on his desk and the curtains exploded behind him. A woman carried out a tray with three coffees and sat them in front of Simon, Henryk, and Roshburg. Atlas' leg pumped offbeat to Simon's knee. I hoped they would make it through this grown-up situation. I was relieved when Simon took a quick sip of the steaming coffee then thanked the lady.

Mr. Roshburg started right into his pitch.

"Now look, boys, insurance isn't cheap, but I can help you out with it. Martin, your father is a fine man who has my business for sure."

"Thank you…" I said, but I didn't know why.

"So I printed out some rates you can take a look at. There are a couple different options. The choice is totally up to you, but I can definitely go over each one."

Atlas laughed politely as our response.

"I don't know if this is against the rules of your salesmanship, but could you just tell us which is the...the one with the lowest price," Henryk finally said.

"That'd be the basic coverage. But it has a high premium."

I think we all wanted to ask what a premium was but we didn't want to show any weakness. The sale would be a taekwondo match that would demand unprejudiced focus. Just like Atlas paraphrased from the *Art of War* last night during our preparation session: when you're strong, look weak; when you're weak, look strong. Atlas said it posed like a ninja, and it impressed us. I started to doubt the concept now, as we sat awkwardly, cooped up in uncomfortable chairs in this man's living room. I felt underdressed.

"How high of a premium?" Henryk tried to keep up.

"Twenty percent."

"Twenty," Henryk repeated.

That sounded high. A fifth. Enough to get you drunk.

"If you keep up with your payments it's easy to not get in over your heads."

"What does it cover?"

Atlas was just as meticulous as Henryk when he shopped, something he picked up from living with his impoverished drunk mother. He could stare at two packets of gum for ten minutes before deciding he could do without gum.

"Fire, flood, roof collapse—"

"Roof collapse?" Simon repeated.

"Yes."

"Does that ever happen? What are the chances? That's the *basic* coverage?"

"Yes."

"Do we get big-bad-wolf-blowing-down-our-house coverage?"

"If…you mean wind damage, then yes. Fire, water, wind and—"

"And roof collapse."

"Yes."

"Sy, man, don't start," Henryk tried to whisper to him, but we all heard it.

"What is the next package up from that?"

Roshburg had this answer practised, polished in the mirror, and repeated to dozens of poor ignorant folks such as ourselves.

Roshburg was a good salesman; he had already picked up that Atlas and Henryk were the ones that he needed to convince, so his eyes darted between them while seldomly me or Simon. Henryk leaned forward, listening intently. Simon stared passed Roshburg's chair to the line of framed photos behind him. Something was brewing in that boiling pot of his mind.

Roshburg blinked and it captured my attention. I stared at his eyes until he met my line of sight. It was only a glimpse, but the glimpse said it all.

In his eyes big piles of money grew around him, until it covered him.

But then he was back to spitting his gib about insurance packages in his light green room. Everything was tidy and kind of homely, and his square-cut suit was profane against the domestic background. Simon finished his coffee. He looked bored. Henryk still strived to pay attention.

"Could we have a few minutes to talk about it?" Atlas asked, and I realized I hadn't been paying attention either.

"Yes, take all the time you want."

Then, like a knife through an old lady's blouse, Roshburg disappeared into the kitchen. I don't think he expected us to buy much, but he must have felt pride about his delivery.

"What do you think?" Henryk asked Atlas.

"I don't know."

"It was hard to keep up with," I admitted so that they wouldn't ask me.

"True, man, there was a lot to take in," Henryk conceded friendlily.

"Fuck this guy," Simon concluded. "Roof collapse? Like, is he serious? That's bullshit, he's trying to tack on some obscure insurance we'll never cash in on."

"It was in the basic coverage. It must happen enough that they think it's basic to insure against it," Henryk said.

"I'd like to see the numbers."

"The high premium of the basic coverage sucks," Atlas said. "But the next coverage up is too much a month for us, I think. I want to live humbly, man, I don't want to be buying into paranoia."

"If we're so against it why are we buying it?"

"Because we need to, man. You heard the landlord."

"The house is close to all the places we need to be, and we're adults, and I'm not moving back with my parents," Henryk reasoned. "Let me have my brother's away-from-home college experience. Even if it's only half-way across town."

"Fuck this cream."

There was a moment's repose to take in Simon's out-burst. Then Atlas continued on. He looked stressed out. He rubbed his chin while his knee shook ferociously.

"I say we stick to the plan—the cheapest shit we can get."

"Go basic."

"Go basic and go home."

"To our home."

Everyone looked over at me. I fiended for a cigarette and wished I'd taken a coffee.

"Sounds good," I answered.

"Back to the basics," Henryk confirmed.

We waited another five minutes, convincing ourselves and commenting on the creepy family photos staring at us from behind the desk. Simon wondered if some had hidden cameras. I looked into the portraits and thought he might not be far off. Sometimes cameras, sometimes windows.

When Roshburg returned we told him our decision. He presented a small pile of papers to go through. We awkwardly watched him flip the pages, then offer the page to each of us for a signature at the X. We all shared one pen. If it had been a fountain pen, it would have felt like we were signing the Declaration of Independence.

Roshburg smiled cheerfully all the way to the door, where he let us out with a mighty wave.

Simon waved back once Roshburg closed the door and invited him to play poker with us so we could steal back our money.

Wood and nails traded
for claustrophobic nightmares
to insurance men.

EL JUEGO LINDA
[Simon Arcan]

Las gritas de mi memoria[16]. How loud they come. They swoop in unexpected, as if they're after something, lynching a hold to some loose strand of attention easily tugged away but not pulled off.

I am easily distracted when I'm trying to study.

The books have information but the mind has knowledge. I flipped through the fat Poli.Sci textbook, twirled my pen, and expected something to happen.

"¿Simon, *digames, por que estas tu mirando la cielo cuando la juego es al herba*[17]?" Mami would ask, nudging me and smiling with her unstraightened teeth.

---

[16] *Las gritas de mi memoria* — (*Spanish*) My shouting memory

[17] *¿Simon, digames, por que estas tu mirando la cielo cuando la juego es al herba?* — (*Spanish*) Simon, tell me, why're you watching the sky when the game's on the grass?

I had been studying for two hours already. Attention was bound to wane.

My mami was happy on two occasions: when it was hot and sunny, and when she watched soccer games. Both would be ideal, but this was Canada. Back home mami would spend long tropical evenings watching the neighbourhood boys face off against regional teams. When she was younger yet she watched my *abuelo*[18] play for the national team —a true legend in our family, and somewhat in our country, in a minor sports kind of way.

"Your *abuelo* would start at the goal box and he could run to the other one passing the ball between the players until he was at the net, then—*ai*[19]!" she shot a hand out in front of her. "*Todo vezas*[20], straight to a *gol*[21].*"

In the stands we always sat by the men who brought drums and cheap trumpets to play songs during plays and to celebrate loudly when their

---

[18]   **Abuelo** — (*Spanish*) Grandfather (Grandmother: **Abuela**)

[19] **Ai** — (*Spanish*) Hispanic way to yelp (also replaces "oh" in English semantics)

[20] **Todo vezas** — (*Spanish*) All the time

[21] **Gol** — (*Spanish*) Goal!

chosen team scored. I think many of the non-Latino players were confused by the unruly excitement; especially the teenaged provincial teams. Only the Latino players understood.

The drummers passed a bottle of dark rum between themselves. They would've smoked cigars if the guards were not so stringent on adhering to the rules. In an outdoor field! All the men complained loudly at the uptight Canadian rules.

Because during half-time there was always a whole fifteen minutes to complain about Canada in some way—in Spanish, of course, this was a matter of national security—like: it was too cold; the English people couldn't understand their accents; their landlords were raising rent again, trying to kick their *pobre culitos*[22] out onto the street. They said that that was where this country kept all of their coloured: on the street.

"In Santo Domingo they don't beg. Even the poorest of the poorest without a single mango[23] don't sit on the streets and do nothing. They get a job. They work around the house. What, those

---

[22] ***Pobre culitos*** — (*Spanish*) Poor asses

[23] ***Mango*** — (*Spanish*) Slang for a dollar

people don't have family? *¿Estan locos²⁴*? Who wants to lay in the street when it is minus forty and *mi pelotas²⁵* are falling off?"

"Luchos, you don't know nathing about losing your balls, your wife has kept dem in a jar in de kitchen *por diez años²⁶*."

"Don't give me shit, *negrito²⁷*, you haven't even used your balls since you moved to Canada. You think these white girls here can dance? Ha!"

"In Santo Domingo they dance in the street, you remember? They played soccer in the street," Mami recalled.

"You could smoke and have a little bit of rum!"

"But Trujillo *era un ijo de puta²⁸*."

---

²⁴ *¿Estan loco?* — (*Spanish*) Are they crazy?

²⁵ *Mi pelotas* — (*Spanish*) My balls (testicles)

²⁶ *Por diez anos* — (*Spanish*) For ten years

²⁷ *Negrito* — (*Spanish*) Little black one; used as the character's nickname

²⁸ *Trujillo era un ijo de puta* — (*Spanish*) Rafael Trujillo, tyrant and dictator in the Dominican Republic between 1930 and 1952; some might have said he was a son of a bitch (but not to his face when he was living)

"These people don't care, they don't care, they let their family die in the cold and let the children become lazy."

"I think de game ees starting again, heh?"

"¡*Otra vez*[29]!"

"¡*Andas, andas*[30]!"

And little Simon sipped his cola from the cheap concession stand, watching these embers from a distant fire, these vanguards to the world of boredom from the world of spice, dance and soul. Where people fought for what they cared about. Mami spoke little of Tio Hernando, but from what I pieced together, he was a mercenary revolutionary soldier. He left for Bolivia in 1969, only eighteen, to help Che Guevara unify South America from the inside out. He was too late, Che had died the year before, and the movement was shut down by the CIA.

I highlighted the CIA heading as it came up in my reading. Beside it I penciled in *Control of Intelligent Amity*.

A crisp photograph was all that was left of Tio Hernando. In black & white monochrome he stands with one leg up on a box of ammunition, greasy

---

[29] ***Otra vez*** — (*Spanish*) Again

[30] ***Andas*** — (*Spanish*) Go

beard and tilted hat obscuring most of his face. He smiles wide and holds his gun like he knows how to use it.

I wish I could have met him. It would have made the Cuban revolution chapter easier. Now I had to do it the hard way, at arm's length from the people who experienced it.

I flipped another page, highlighting more words. More terms to be memorized. Definitions. The incantations of hardening fruit, the rattle of acorns in a windstorm. There is a certain dialectical finesse that politicians used when tight-rope-walking above the heads of the fist-shaking public. It was perfectly exemplified by those stupid holiday songs remade with barking dogs—all pointless, all to make the suicidal winter-weariness feel like there is still a manipulation they can feel proud of.

Buzzword bullshit. That's what it was. That should've been the only definition we needed to know for the political sciences.

I flipped to the next page.

A tinny trumpet squealed in my ear. Another *gol*. Mami jumped off the bleachers, nearly knocking me over.

"*¡Muéstrelos cómo jugar[31]!*" she shouted while the players returned to centre-field.

The referee blew his whistle and the play started again. Mami watched intently, her audacity renewed from the *gol*. She instructed plays under her breath.

"Simon, *mira. La gol era hermosa. Si, chico. ¿Pero, digame, es la gol possible sin el juegito[32]?*"

"No, mami. You need a game to score."

"*Claro*," Mami sang, "*El juegito es qué acomodadores el sudor. El juegito es lo que aviva el fuego de pasión. Los demás son lo que es quemado. Entonces permítale quemar. El juegito es todo[33].*"

I slammed my textbook shut. I paced my room, contemplating why I didn't have a soccer ball any

---

[31] ***Muéstrelos cómo jugar*** — (*Spanish*) Show them how to play

[32] ***Simon, mira. La gol era hermosa. Si, chico. ¿Pero, digame, es la gol possible sin el juegito*** — (*Spanish*) Simon, look, that goal was beautiful. Yes, child. But, tell me, was the goal possible without the game?

[33] ***Claro. El juegito es qué acomodadores el sudor. El juegito es lo que aviva el fuego de pasión. Los demás son lo que es quemado. Entonces permítale quemar. El juegito es todo*** — (*Spanish*) Right. The game ushers sweat. The game fuels the fires of passion. The rest are the things that burn. So let them burn. The game is everything.

more. What did it mean if I learned everything I needed to know from a soccer game?

Another page flipped—
the football field's grass
entangled by the players.

THE SECOND MOVEMENT

THE ESSENCE OF SENESCENCE

STRAWBERRY FIELDS FOREVER
[Atlas Sangman]

(Sorry, Present; this is not For you, but it is Of you)

Catholic highschool taught that alchemy was for greedy magicians, so it was difficult to really appreciate the genuine alchemy practiced back in the day. It took us a while to figure it out.

Alchemy of the moment: to change prosaic occurrences into bona fide, pure, golden moments. To blend elements otherwise naturally monotonous and ordinary, and turn them into something outlandish, daring, joyous. Rememberable.

So this is how I remember it.

Summer, four years ago. We had just started grade twelve. School was a daily drag. Nights wouldn't come quick enough, and when we were in their midst they were impatient to leave again.

I remember Henryk pointing out the North Star. We were just amazed that we were able to see stars among the airplanes in the sky. That serene country darkness enveloped us. The first strange thing was that we weren't alone. Lucy Sparrow was with us, along with her friend Tracy Qing and Jean-Grey Lechelle. Simon sprang the initiates on Henryk and I, and we weren't happy about it. I was especially paranoid because that made six people squeezing into my five-seated sedan.

Henryk was more concerned with what came later. He called it the Loot. To the rest of us it was fruit. The Fruit Loot—that was why we were in the countryside in the middle of the night. Like law-abiding adult citizens in every way, except that we preferred to do our picking under the stars, and we didn't like to pay for what we picked.

Strawberries, raspberries, blackberries, Macintosh apples, pears, blueberries; none of us knew Ontario as an agricultural province, but it had its fair share of the Fruit Loot. Fortunately for us Mississauga was not far from the farming fringe, so we were able to make the trip in just over thirty minutes.

Not bad, except that Jean-Grey lay over Lucy, Tracy and Sy in the back. Sy insisted that nobody would be satisfied with the trip unless he made every effort to make it sexually-charged. He did a decent job while Henryk and I watched for five-oh and rocked out to the Led Zeppelin side of the tape. I watched Lucy's expression to Sy's cock remarks in the rearview. I diverted my eyes when I saw her embarrassed laughing eyes catch mine. Lucy's first words to me upon entering the car were the only ones she had meant for me all night:

"Cool. Tapes."

She searched my centre console's tape collection until Sy directed Jean-Grey to dive into the backseat.

As we neared our target farm Henryk turned down the music and gave prompt instructions.

"Okay this is almost it. Yeah, it's up here. There's a small fence, nothing we can't jump. Me and Atlas came through here a few days ago during the day. Everything looks ripe. There are baskets in the trunk. Don't take more than you can carry. We gotta stay together. *Together*. For sure. Don't fuck around, we will leave you out there."

"No we won't, man," I said, anxious that Jean-Grey, Tracy, and Lucy would take it the wrong way and think we would actually abandon them in a field.

"We stay in for twenty minutes. Any longer and we're fucked."

"And we gotta stay quiet," I added.

"Yeah, like little bo no peep. And, um..."

"They might as well know, man."

"Know what?" Simon asked.

"There might be dogs."

"What?! Aw man...this is supposed to be fun not —"

"There just *might be*. We don't know for sure."

"I saw those dogs, man."

"We'll see. So long as we stay quiet and don't stay long we should be okay."

Henryk and I smiled at each other. There was an absurdity to the things we did at that time. Like getting ourselves into trouble, testing our bodies and minds, experimenting with obscurities.

"We got a couple masks, too, man, if you're super paranoid."

"I want a mask," Tracy said.

She didn't sound like she wanted to be here. Jean-Grey dragged her two friends out with us at Simon's invite. Lucy nodded along with Tracy and asked for a mask too.

"Skeletor or Snoop Doggy Dogg?"

I parked the car on a gravel side road. Everyone grabbed baskets out of the trunk and the masks were distributed. Her skeletor mask was the last thing to come out of the trunk before I slammed it, so Lucy and I were at the back of the group. Henryk reassured the group of our safety record. But I didn't hear a word he said. Lucy held the glow-in-the-dark mask in a swinging arm and that held my full attention. It was the only object illuminated on that dark country road. Between us the sound of gravel crunched like half-uttered words.

We reached the spot along the fenceline Henryk and I had scouted out as our jumping point. He and I held down the barbed wire so that everyone could cross. Once inside we crouched and pointed out the different rows of berries. We would work from strawberries to blueberries, then finish on cranberries. Henryk checked his watch, then motioned for us to move. Clandestinely we plucked the fruit, using our fingertips as our eyes until nightvision adjusted, which didn't happen until blueberries, when it became harder to see because of the dark berries.

Tracy giggled, muffled by the Snoop Dogg mask, and Lucy shared her nervous laughter behind the glow-in-the-dark mask, which was eerie to see bobbing between the rows.

But then we heard the barks.

"Oh shit," Henryk gasped.

"Naw, those weren't fucking dogs, were they?" Simon asked.

"Yeah, those are definitely dogs," I needlessly stated the obvious.

"Okay, hold on, stay calm. Just start moving towards the fence. Move, move!"

Henryk stressed his whisper. The barks got closer and closer, and then something came crashing through a nearby row. Everybody immediately scattered.

"For fuckssakes," was the last thing I heard Henryk say.

Into the inky night: six suburban kids weighed down by baskets full of precious Fruit Loot and pockets full of cellphones and keys. My clothes were unprepared for this adventure. I heard something rip loudly as I dove over a row. The barking dog sounded distant, so I stopped to catch my breath. I wished I could have appreciated the stars then. Instead I searched madly for the fenceline.

Then something ripped over the bush and I jumped excitedly, both at the movement and the sudden light in my face. I froze when I noticed the shape of the light—the facial proportions of the feared nemesis, Skeletor. I laughed, and Lucy ripped off the mask.

"I can't see anything behind this thing."

"They're not made for looking, man."

"I'm so glad I found you. I was out of my mind. Thank God, you have the car keys, right?"

"Yeah, I guess I do," I said gaining a new preparedness. "We gotta get to the car, man. Then we can phone everyone and pick 'em up wherever."

"Do you know the way?"

"Yeah."

But I didn't. I lead Lucy down the row, until we went far enough that we should have hit the fenceline, so I turned around and found the fence at the other end. Once we were on the road we were already laughing about the whole thing. We checked each other's baskets and named different dishes we could make with the assortment of berries.

We reached the car safely. Lucy took shotgun, which was exciting because she was now my wingwoman—her life ran parallel to mine for that short drive. She phoned Tracy, who didn't answer, so I phoned Henryk.

"Yo, Rickshaw," I said.

"Wuddup, Atlantis?"

We had secret names for our escapades. This is important for anything that involves night and the possibility of police.

"Man, where are you?"

"In the fucking field of dreams, dude. Where are you?"

"In the car."

"You bastard."

"I'm with Lucy, man, we're safe and clear. If you get out to a road we'll be able to find you."

"A road. That'd be nice. We'll try to find one. Well, Jean-Grey and I at least. Simon is looking for Tracy, she fucking flipped. she took off after the old hound dogs found us and saw we had no beef jerky for them."

"Damn. Hopefully she's okay. Lucy tried phoning her to no avail."

"Simon's on it. He'll find her."

"Tracy? Is Tracy alright?" Lucy asked.

"Yeah, no worries. K, round up the troops and we'll be cruising the roads for you."

"Okay."

"Peace."

"What happened to Tracy?" Lucy asked again.

"I don't know, she just flipped out and ran off. Simon's looking for her."

"Oh no."

"She's fine. Just scared. Probably thinks Sy's a dog. Which he is, I guess."

I started the car, assuring Lucy that everything was okay. We would peruse the local roads until we came across four suburban teenagers. It wouldn't be hard. Nevertheless Lucy was visibly nervous.

The tape player clicked on as soon as we got rolling, turning from the Led Zep side to the Beatles' side.

"I love the Beatles!" Lucy gasped.

"I know—"

I wished I hadn't said that. I didn't want her to know that I knew all the buttons on her backpack.

"Hey check it out. A whole unfenced field," Lucy looked out the passenger's window.

"It looks like strawberries."

"Should we stop?"

"I guess. Henny would stop for strawberry fields."

"We should've just come during the day," Lucy said.

"I guess..."

"No. No, you're right. This is a lot more fun."

We snuck into the field with our baskets and filled them passed the brim. During the adventure I started humming the tune to *Strawberry Fields Forever*[34]. Lucy sung along with her sweet high voice and I joined in. Once we were in the car, alive and giggly from the cooling night air I fast-forwarded the tape in short fits to find the Beatles' own rendition of the song.

"*Always know sometimes think it's me...*"

"*But you I know that it's a dream.*"

---

[34] Again, a shoutout to the Beatles. Here quoting "Strawberry Fields Forever" off the Magical Mystery Tour.

Let me take you down to that generational hobby farm. Baskets full of strawberries. Our eyes scanned the road like retro-clocks shaped like cats, eyes to the left, eyes to the right, tic toc, tic toc, until we found perpendicular figures on the road that couldn't have been encroaching trees—yup, dig that crooked haircut—suburban children lost on rural roads.

"Fancy we find you guys here," I said as they loaded the backseat.

Henryk didn't appreciate sitting in the backseat, awkward with Jean-Grey in his lap. Nadia, one of his many girlfriends, waited for his text message tonight, and his phone was stuck in his back pocket under the weight of one and a half bodies. Lucy and I laughed wildly in the front seat, recounting our liberation from the fields and our sweet strawberry discovery. Tracy had a massive gash in her leg that she complained about. It bogged Lucy down. I was just happy that Lucy was sitting shotgun.

Atlas Sangman: This road's so quiet.

Lucy Sparrow: I love it. You can hear yourself think. Even with the engine. I want to live on a farm someday, have a llama.

AS: It's so dark.

LS: Is that Venus?

AS: Could be. Although I think she's sitting right beside me.

    LS: Oh, Atlas.

AS: What?

    LS: You're such a sweetie.

AS: I love you.

    LS: Atlas, (*blush*). You know I love you. Madly.

AS: Strawberry fields.

    LS: Forever.

Except that conversation never voiced itself, it only echoed in my head.

"Flip the tape."

Henryk was used to being in shotgun, he was the *de facto* DJ and MC of the Sunfire.

In my time of dying. Want nobody to moan[35].

"Yeaahhh."

"*All I want...*"

"*For you to do...*"

"*Take my body. Home.*"

"*Well, well...*"

Well back to the suburbs. The regular intervals of orange streetlight, the ashamed blue night high

---

[35] Led Zeppelin! Here quoting "In My Time of Dying" off Physical Graffiti (also shout out to Bob Dylan's stunning version, and Blind Willie Johnson for the original composition).

overhead. The city was tucked into bed so we could sleep easy. I dropped the girls at Tracy's car. Us testosteroned boys knew we wouldn't see those girls any time soon after tonight's fiasco. I bid Lucy goodnight briefly, but only briefly, and Simon parted with a suggestion on fresh morning milkshakes next week at school. (We would actually keep the Fruit Loot in my trunk for munchies until they rotted, then we fed the leftovers to the birds in the Valley).

"You and Lucy, hey?" Henryk lead me on.

"Yup," was my slim answer.

"You fag. Did you guys exchange recipes? And trade apron patterns?" Simon teased.

"Yup."

"Fuck...Nadia," Henryk moaned. "She texted me twice. No reception in farm country."

"Whatever. Not like she's expecting you. Fuck her. Oh wait—have you fucked her?"

"Fuck off."

"Yeah...that's what I thought."

"Man, who cares? Dig these lights, don't they look so foreign after being in the countryside? They look like jewels," I said.

"I say we get hella high on that bombastic bud you got and munch on as many berries as our guts can take before we instant-diarrhea."

"Deal."

My past concedes
on objects that survived it—
wild strawberry fields.

THE FOREST BENEATH THE TREES
[Henryk Zdicz]

My choice was sudden and it went unannounced
until we had moved into our place. I told Atlas first,
and he was genuinely interested, more than he was
about Simon's political science major. I told him I
was going to study ecology. Martin was happy at
any pursuit of knowledge, and I was ahppy for that.
We had a good ecosystem to offer forth new
growth...or something like that. I would revamp
that once I learned a little more.

I could have gone to university and learned
ecology from a book. But I needed education, not
second-hand notions. That's why I finally chose to
go to college.

Simon gave me a hard time for going to college.
In Canada, college meant low-budget low-brow
hands-on learning. What the intellectuals forgot was
that after four years they were going to finish with a
degree in post-modern avant-garde German

literature and would need to create a need for what they knew—look at shrinks, they popped up everywhere because they knew how to pimp themselves out. They figured out how to create a needed niche for themselves.

What colleges offered was a practical guide to pre-established needs. Canadians had thought themselves too modern and too complex for practicality, that was why immigrants drove the buses for drugged-up, under-slept, stressed-out university graduates. The bricklayers made the houses for the academics to become shut-ins in.

My urban bones needed nature, not theories. Every fucking corner had a theory—theories about what shoes were best, what fashion meant, what it meant to be human, theories on who I could become. What I needed was something that needed me. Something solid like the Canadian Shield.

My mind meandered so fiercely in the backseat of moving vehicles. Natural reaction to driving in straight lines, I suppose. Spruce poked the late morning skylight. We—the eighteen of us that made up the Forest Management course—plus Cayce Kooten: instructor, professional biologist, photographer, ornithologist, ichthyologist, botanist, lichenologist, lepidopterist, and fourth-generation Canadian—were piled into three vans that convoyed northbound on Highway 400 to the boreal forest for a day-long field lab.

The boreal forest: the world's largest unbroken forest. The earth's circumpolar olive branch crown; its five-o'clock-post-glacial shadow.

Out of some kind of otherwise inexperienced shyness I scrambled for the first van in the parking lot. Cayce (he refused the stuffy 'Dr. Kooten') calmly commanded the wheel and led the caravan. It was the second week of classes. I didn't know anyone. I held back a fart since Barrie and didn't know how much longer I could keep it back.

The old coot lectured softly, pointing over the steering wheel at the forest.

"You see the rocks are peeking through the soil here. Evidence of glaciation. Farther west, in our prairies, much of the bedrock was overlain by churned up soil, mixed rock, and glaciofluvial[36] deposits. Here massive glacial sheets, as they retreated, exposed the bedrock. So, northern Ontario, Quebec, in fact the whole Canadian Shield, is exposed bedrock from glacial retreat. Plants made the best of it. Succession—just like we covered last Monday. Mosses and lichens first colonized, breaking down the rock and adding organic matter,

---

[36] *Glaciofluvial* — (*English*) Land-forming process related to glacial rivers and streams

all very slowly of course, and then other non-vasculars and vasculars colonized, and soon the trees came. Which in their own due course have seen many changes, succession being further set-back, or reset, if you will, by fire, disease, weather. Animals moved in as they could, of course. And just like everything else humans have made the best of it too. Sudbury's nickel deposits are so easily accessible because of the exposed bedrock. Then you have oil, forestry, anything else we can possibly take."

I shifted in the seat for the fourth time that minute and peeked around the van. The two people in the backseat were asleep. The girl in shotgun responded to Cayce's notes with peremptory *uh-huhs* and *ohs* and *interesting* remarks. Her politeness made her seem older than she was, or stupider, so I stayed quiet but listened attentively to Cayce.

Because unlike most of the people in the class, I knew shit all about forests. I knew they grew and I knew I liked them. But I wasn't from Timmins or near Algonquin Park (or ever visited them for that matter). My parents weren't even born in Canada, and even in Poland they were urbanites. I was so disconnected with my own land. That was probably why I was listening as hard as I was trying to hold my flatulence.

"Do you think global warming will break down the Canadian Shield quicker?" Lady Shotgun asked out of what I could only guess was pressure to maintain her integrity in the conversation. "Because, like, that might mean that they are sensitive areas that could be protected and not exploited."

I looked over to my companion in the middle row. She raised her eyebrows, rolled her eyes.

"*Well*..." Cayce began.

He stretched the word like a safety net—soft enough to not make you feel stupid, but firm enough to make sure you knew you went wrong.

"Oh—Great Bear Creek," my middle row friend read a passing sign. "I love that place. Great tasting fish."

It felt wrong to speak over Cayce. I leaned back in my seat to separate the front from the middle.

"Do you fish much?"

"Whenever and wherever I can. It's calming. And delicious. You can't find that combination much elsewhere."

"True," I chewed on the word.

Not that I am a sexist—surely a good prelude to my impression—but fishing was typically a male sport, with tall outdoorsmen casting phallic reels into a pond. The woman to my side didn't flaunt any tomboyish tells. Her fingers were painted red. She wore mascara, even though we were going into the bush.

"I don't know your name," I asked to conform to my curious expression.

"Philomena."

"I'm Henryk."

"Henryk."

The *ik* stuck to the roof of her mouth. We shook hands cordially. Her palm was soft and warm, it made mine feel beefy and fumbly.

"Do you fish much, Henryk?"

"No. Well, I try. I'd like to do it more. I'm not very good."

"You're not very good."

"I'm just not so successful."

"Do you enjoy doing it?"

"Yeah. Like you said, it's calming. I wouldn't eat a damn thing out of Lake Ontario or the Credit River or anything, so I don't know about delicious —"

"Well, if you enjoy it..."

The silence felt heavy. I was about to continue with some useless small talk, but Cayce pulled off the highway onto a gravel road that bit into the quiet.

Ten minutes off the highway any sign of development (besides the road) was historical enough to blend into the natural scenery. Rusting signs warned of bears and crossing deer. A dusty glass Coca Cola bottle lay in the ditch. Cayce pulled the van off the road and got out. Soon we all stood around the vans in the dry ditch, a semi-circle of semi-urbanites trying their best to be dressed for the weather without usurping a faith in fashion.

The morning chill had shifted smoothly into an overcast afternoon. Autumn was slowly drawing that grey arctic sky over Canada. Philomena nudged me. Someone was already shivering. He was ready for Yonge street, ready to be seen. The trees with their eyes forever turned the other way made him seem so vain I snarked a bit. A single bird tweeted while Cayce explained our purpose here.

"...then let's call that a day," he said.

The class was split into teams of three. People aggregated with those nearest them, so I found myself in a group with Philomena and the girl who sat shotgun. She introduced herself cheerily as Jodie. With a satchel of equipment, the class split to their assigned co-ordinates. Jodie spoke the whole way, even as her breath was pulled from her tiny frame trying to support the large rucksack perched on her back. Philomena looked as unenthused as I did. I was glad I had that camaraderie, although I felt bad for Jodie. She must have been just as lonely as us.

"So," Philomena hummed a little, "Where are you from, Henryk?"

I held both my backpack straps. They dug into my shoulders. I tried to control my huffing, looking between the trees while I responded.

"Do you mean like, where I came from this morning? Or where I'm *from* from?"

"First, where did you drive from this morning?"

"I actually took public transit. I live in Mississauga."

"Me too!" Jodie cheerfully added.

"Cool."

"What highschool did you go to?"

"And where are you *from* from?" Philomena asked over Jodie.

"Poland."

"Have you guys ever watched *Eighty*?" Jodie interjected.

"Like, the television show? No, I've never watched it," I said politely.

"Oh because its this race around the world, and when they passed through Europe they went to Poland."

I nodded, because the last time I watched TV I caught a documentary on the Siberian taiga forest. I would have brought that up, except that I wasn't eighteen and I didn't care much about the world of television, which used to mean a lot to me. I guess I grew out of it.

"And where are you from? *From* from," I asked Philomena.

"Right here. This is the beginning of our transect."

"Great. I'm warm. Are you guys warm? Isn't that sun wonderful?" Jodie jabbered.

Philomena took the gear out of her bag while Jodie read our instructions. We started north through rocky mosses. Philomena and I finished our tasks at the first plot before Jodie, who was having issues with the mirrors and measurements. I bored a tree to count its age. I took a picture of the bark's texture. One of the birch snags had shed its bark. It showed the smooth xylem, and it was etched with the wiggles of some kind of insect larvae. The carving made an image of a face. I ran my fingers along the lines.

I reminded myself to pay attention to how we got here so I could come back with Atlas.

Philomena caught me taking pictures.

"Nice camera."

"Oh, thanks. One of the few things I've splurged on."

"You know what's weird? I have the same camera as you."

She turned around, back to Jodie, because I started in her direction. It was an eerie coincidence, but I didn't know how to respond to her.

"I've always wanted to get more into photography," Jodie said, "Maybe I could use these field trips to start."

But Jodie had forgotten her camera. We walked to our next plot. I eyed the vegetation carefully, noting the parameters we had to observe. This time I measured trees. It would trip Atlas out if I told him that I had used Pythagorean Theory today to calculate the height of trees, but he might just ask me what was the point of measuring the trees at all?

So I told Philomena instead.

"I never thought I would ever use mathematics in any serious way in my life."

"No? I believe mathematics has something important for us to understand."

"What's that?"

"Always carry a calculator?"

Philomena tried a joke, but it was clear that it was because she was keeping aloof. It was too easy for the forest to make you feel open.

I kicked pinecones to clear a spot to dig a small hole at the next site. I felt the soil. Felt it for specific things, not just for feeling—for its texture —which I had trouble with because I had never really felt soil before. Philomena came over after she finished boring a tree and grabbed a handful of soil from the hole while I worked.

I watched her play with the soil.

"Doesn't it feel like we're in kindergarten, but just a lot bigger and more serious?"

"I hope I can always feel like I'm in kindergarten," she said.

"Have you guys ever watched *Solitary*?" Jodie asked over the bushes.

"Not a chance," I told Jodie. "I don't even own a TV."

"Are you serious?"

"Who needs that hassle?" Philomena nodded in agreement with me. "You can get enough drama in real life."

"Could you imagine if Vikings had TV? They would've never crossed the Atlantic. They would've gotten slaughtered by the people who were actually living life, not passively watching re-runs and news and shit."

I didn't want to feel so comfortable with Philomena, but I did. I had a two month abstinence going that I intended to keep. I had had too many exasperating relationships after highschool—some that hurt, some that were awesome then hurt, and others that never intended to hurt but did.

"Nice.," Philomena said. "Historic."

The *ik* stuck in her mouth again.

"Sorry, I'm a nerd. Should've warned you."

"Not at all. I'm actually a history nerd too. Actually, I'm a bachelor of history."

"You're not seeing anyone right now? Shit, I'm a bachelor too."

"No, I did my final dissertation on the history of science. Which kind of reminded me how much I adore science. That's why I'm here." Philomena laughed abruptly. "Sorry, I don't know why I'm telling you this."

"Tell me something about the history of science that I didn't know."

"Other than it's an actual subject?"

I laughed along with her. Jodie tried to laugh a bit as we met her by our packs.

"All done?"

"Yup. Ready for the next one?"

"This one's the last one," Philomena said.

"Oh. Okay great. Reverse declination back to the vans?"

We started back along our transect. I inspected the forest again. I stopped half way back, stooping to the ground to get a better look at the mosses. Philomena stopped too, pulling her camera from her bag.

"George Washington Carver claimed he could talk to plants."

"What?" I asked.

"That's something you didn't know about the history of science."

She snapped photos of the mosses and lichens spread like a lumpy shag carpet.

"Is that true?"

"That he spoke with plants? Probably not. But it's true that he claimed it."

I took my identical camera out of my pack and took photos of the densely complex moss arrangements. I used macro to turn the miniscule moss into a forest. Then I felt the feather moss with my palm. Philomena laughed at me, but she had been touching plants the whole time we were in the forest. I picked up my lens cap and looked at the small area it was covering. I counted twelve different forms of mosses and lichens in that small area.

"Are you coming?" she asked.

Philomena already stood a few metres away. I noticed that I had been staring at the ground for a long while. She smiled at me, then looked up at the trees. I turned the camera her way and snapped a photograph.

"Yeah. Let's get back to the suburbs before I decide to stay here."

Under the cap lens
lives the whole
of what we call a day.

THE IRRATIONAL FAMILIAR
[Simon Arcan]

My father stood akimbo in the middle of the den, eyeing every edge of the room with suspicion.

"Where's Mami?" I asked.

"Working," he responded, not looking at me but around me.

"Why aren't you with her?"

"I wanted to check out your place. How much did you say it was?"

"Rent is cheap. Especially 'cause it's split."

"*Cheap*. If you were working, it'd be cheap."

"I'm working," Atlas piped in, leaning on the support beam dividing the kitchen from the den.

My dad eyed Atlas and nodded his head. Grumpy—as per usual—he pointed to a heating register like he had found a hole in the wall.

"Your heat gas or electric?"

"I don't know."

"Heating is all covered in the rent," Atlas tried to justify our ignorance.

I appreciated that Atlas had left his lunch sitting in the microwave so he could join me in touring my dad around. Dad had a knack for being a pain in the ass, especially when he wasn't in control, which was exactly what this house was: not in his control. It was something I had that he didn't (besides patience, an open-mind and humility—but don't ask Atlas, he'd say I was lying).

"Not if it's electric. Then you're paying."

"Electricity is covered too."

"How much did you say rent was?"

"Not much."

"How much?" he asked, his tone inferring that he wanted a solid number.

"A million and a half dollars," I said cheekily.

"Works out to about two-fifty a month, split between the four of us."

My father grunted.

"Is your water-heater gas or electric?"

"I don't know. Who cares?"

"Give me your tools and I'll see."

"We don't have any tools," Atlas said, ever patient with parents.

"No tools? Jesus Christ, you monkeys think your music is going to build houses?"

"Dad, who cares if it's gas or electric? What will it change if you know?"

"It's in the basement, so you can see it if you'd like," Atlas talked over me.

"How old is the place?" my dad asked.

"A century, probably. Maybe a millennia."

"When was the last time the roof shingles were done?"

"I don't know."

"The landlord takes care of that kind of stuff," Atlas said.

"Do you let the landlord wipe your ass for you too?"

My father was notoriously nitpicky for what I thought were useless things. The stupid shit that I would have to give up my mind to learn. You know —plumbing, heating, cars, I dunno, carpentry. Those were the kind of nuances I would worry about when they came, those weren't things to build a life on.

But worrying about those things made my father his living, which gave him the ego to think they were important, so whatever. I let him know early on in my childhood that I had no interest. I worked at his commercial cleaning enterprise, the piddly company he'd put together to lift us out of poverty. But he had issues with profits, mostly because he couldn't ever find them, but I guess you can't teach a new dog old tricks.

A vastly proud man, my father was once a contractor, hired by construction companies to design various components of their buildings. He loved it. The schematic was his native habitat. In his office he hung old blueprints of now-defunct buildings. They were his Picassos. In his younger days, just years before I was born, he was hired by a hotel chain to help design the waterworks of a number of new hotels in the Caribbean. He got working vacations in St. Lucia, the Bahamas, Trinidad, and the Dominican Republic. It was on the last island where he was at his most ego-inflated, most rum-intoxicated, most power-drunk —where he managed to wrangle the woman who would become my mother from a shanty-town, dress her up and limo her into fancy clubs, dizzy her with the exotic dreams of a winter wonderland in the north called Canada, where everyone was free and money flowed like the tropical flowers bloomed, and where she would be happy fucking him *ad naseum*, or until a baby was born.

Too bad that he knew little about waterworks and how they function, because apparently, before long, the hotel in St. Lucia crapped out, followed by the Bahamas. The Trinis, on the verge of floating in their own shit, pre-emptively shut down their hotel and warned the Dominicans to fire that *piruja*[37]. Dad got fired. But before he left he managed to get Mami a Visa and fly her to Toronto. It wasn't long until I was stewing in her belly. He panicked and married her. I thought my Dad was an ugly motherfucker so it was no wonder he rushed into marriage, it was no wonder he scooped up my Dominican bombshell mother before she figured out that he was just another white-collar bozo trying to get away with doing an expensive form of nothing.

"Where's your bedroom?" he asked.

"Upstairs."

"It got air-conditioning?"

"No."

---

[37] ***Piruja*** — (*Spanish*) Whore

"We could install a little unit in the window."

"Why?" I asked.

"We'd have to pass that by the landlord first," Atlas said, obviously annoyed that he had to keep repeating the landlord's almighty auspices over our home.

"He'd never know," my dad shrugged.

"I think he'd know if a box was jutting out my window."

"You're such a smart ass," he pointed out.

"He sure is," Atlas tried to joke.

"And you're the one kissing it," he said to Atlas.

"My lunch is cooking so I'm going to go eat now."

Even Atlas could only take small doses of my father.

"Don't you want to show him the studio?" I asked Atlas.

"Naw, it smells like cigarettes and liquor," Atlas said, grinning at me, now out of view of my dad.

I could've throttled him. I don't think my dad would have minded.

"Smoking again? Jesus Christ, Simon, what is wrong with you? Are you wasting my money, going to school? Are you just planning on getting wasted and pissing away my hard-earned money?" he spoke reservedly, but clearly pissed off. "Do you know the kind of hours I put in to save for your education? Do you want all your mother's hard work to go to waste?"

"Dad..." I sighed, noticing like I always did when we were fighting how much darker my complexion was than his, "I'm doing good in school."

"*Well*," he jabbed at my grammar.

"Whatever. I'm working hard. Atlas was just joking. That's how obvious your temperament is."

"If you think rock-and-roll and your buddy there working a kitchen is going to get you through this world, you are far from having to worry about *my* temper. You guys better clean up."

He picked up the jacket he'd thrown onto a sofa and made his way for the door.

"I won't tell your mother. I won't embarrass you. But when she comes..."

He left the statement ominously hanging.

Blood filled his face as he slipped on his shoes, half upside-down.

"You better not embarrass yourself."

Then he left.

"Thanks for coming by," I said graciously to a closed door. "Fuck!"

I found Atlas eating in the kitchen.

"Sorry about that, man, I couldn't help it. He's intense."

"Naw, naw, don't worry about it. Not your fault. It's his own fault. So caught up in blueprints that he doesn't see the things going on between the lines. It's okay. Fuck him, guy. He's going to give me some weird dad-hating complex. If I don't have one already."

"He's a nice guy."

"That just proves that either *you're* the nice guy, or just a moron."

Slammed doors, hugs, slaps, good
night kisses—the family
is irrational.

PROPRIOCEPTION
[Atlas Sangman]

"You know what's weird?" Simon asked. "They sell paper at twenty-two cents per page. But after five hundred pages, they discount you. What the fuck is up with that? I don't understand how something can cost less when you get more," Simon vehemented.

He flipped mechanically, page by page, through a massive political science textbook.

"But then if you buy a book, with just some glue attaching the same paper, it costs so much again! It's like, unless we touch it, it ain't worth shit. Can you imagine that? And here we are today."

Simon was making a copy of one of his nine textbooks he had piled in two backpacks.

"Are you even allowed to scan a book?" I asked.

"Do you think Modest Mindy over there, who's getting paid less than the company makes on paper, is going to stop us? I don't know man…"

His arms busily threw open the copier top, flipped one page, whipped the top shut and pressed the fat green button. It was as simple as that. In typical glorious-manic-rebel mood he pissed off the bookstore, or they pissed him off, or something. Either way he had to get his books on the black market. He said there was a guy in his class who wore a pin on his backpack that said "Sell me Weed". Sy couldn't help saying that he could hook him up with some serious shit. The guy said he'd pay. Simon considered. He traded nine books— convenient that this guy was in his class—but I guess birds of a feather weather the same weather— nine books for a half-ounce of weed. It was almost Harvest Day, and all of us were looking forward to it. Soon it would be time to reap.

If no one's told you about Harvest Day yet, it's because they don't want you to find out. We found ourselves a date for salvation. Henryk and I had found a massive stand of about three hundred plants in the Valley. Eighteen ganja plants. The holy herb. All for us. When we first found it in spring we tried not to get too excited, we just monitored the spot to make sure this wasn't a gang's secret crop. But no one ever came to the Valley. Then the plants started flowering. We visited a few times a week, hanging out, watering and fertilizing the plants. We tried samples and felt nothing, and figured it wasn't ready yet. But since then they had grown over a metre high, full of buds. Salvation was close and, who knows, maybe I could be reborn twice in the same lifetime.

Simon got the books in advance and told buddy he could get him a good deal on white widow tomorrow. Luckily PaperTape Supplies was open late on Mondays and our drug dealer never slept.

"If you get arrested I wonder if they'd charge you with copyright infringement or trafficking."

"I'd say I killed a man. Let them get me good. I'll have to kill a man first."

"Chill Cypress Hill."

It was weird now that Simon and Henryk were in school and I was the one working. It suddenly made the school lifestyle seem fun—I could see why they were in such a malaise when they worked. Now I wanted to ride the wave again—second-hand knowledge kills but at least it keeps you busy. Plus Simon was already getting himself into trouble. That's when you knew it was going to be fun.

But alas, I was the one exhausted from work.

"Harvest Day is going to be insane. We are literally going to making a killing. Imagine. Just imagine how much," Simon said.

"Hopefully nothing goes wrong."

"What could?"

"That's exactly what a character would say to foreshadow bloodshed man, I don't want to hear that. Anything could go wrong."

"We'll be fine," he overacted, being cartoonish.

"No one's around by the credits, I guarantee it now. You just jinxed us. Straight up jinxed."

I felt tired and Simon exhausted me. He was a lot of energy to take in all at once, especially since I saw him everyday. Simon was an activity sometimes, not a person.

I leaned against the wall and stared out over the store. It was a forest. Reshaped, yeah, reformed and unrecognizable, but still a forest. Henryk would give Sy shit when he found out how much paper he printed. Simon wouldn't care.

"Scan-a-lan-lan. Scan this bitch. PaperTape supplies, yeah, buy our shit," Sy rapped out.

"Are any of these books by Disney?"

"Disney?"—he missed my joke, but whatever —"What do you think I'm studying? Fairy tales? I don't know who makes these books. Whoever they are doesn't care. They charge surplus on the books. The intellivision-gen—uh, I mean, the intelligent borrow the books and scan them and the stupid people buy them. That's their marketing strategy. It'd be mine, at least."

The lights were so white. So fluorescent they radiated. There were no shadows in this store. No shadows! And too many colours. They were offending. They actually bothered me. There was nowhere they could go either. I leaned against the wall heavier.

"I should get Henryk to do the same. We'd save money, if anything," Simon continued.

My legs were below and my head was above, but in what context I didn't know. The outside world was floating by, literally detached, floating around like glitter in water, fluttering, alive but so far away, and I—where was I? I had no real sense of my body. My legs, yes, hips, chest, arms, head, all there, everything present, but where was it present? If I could find Simon I would ask him.

I slid down the wall. I tried to blink my eyes. I heard new sounds now: something like a trumpet being played by a drum kit.

"Yeah when I get home I think I'm going to nap. Or have some beer. You're just going to nap here? Should I come back in the morning?" Simon asked.

"Simon…" I called out. "Simon…"

"What's up man, you okay?"

"Simon…"

"Is someone coming? The copyright police?"

Then suddenly everything snapped back again. Everything came back to normal. My tongue loosened, my neck unlocked, and I looked up at Simon. He still worked away with his copies.

"I'm okay," I said, exhausted, "No, I'm fine."

"I'm tired too."

I climbed back up and sighed deeply.

"Yeah, I guess we're all tired."

"How 'bout you do some copying for now and I'll run to get some coffee."

"Sure."

"I'm going to grab a coffee for Ms. Mindy too."

"Couldn't be so innocent, could it?"

"If you get busted, don't mention my name. Just say you didn't know. You're just learning to read."

I took over for Simon. He slipped on the coat he'd tossed on the floor and laughed.

"It'd suck if I didn't come back, eh?"

"Yeah. It would."

Sometimes where you are
goes on a break somewhere else,
leaving you the bill.

CARRYING CAPACITY
[Martin O'Neill]

Atlas perched on the kitchen chair, thoughtful over his plate. He seemed subdued. He slowly sipped from a mug between bites.

"Hey, man, do you, uhm, do you think I can take down that grad picture?" Atlas asked. "The one on the fridge."

"Sure. Doesn't matter to me. It's your picture," I said, skimming through the newspaper.

Henryk had put the photograph up. In it Atlas was squeezed between his mother and his moustachioed uncle with an exaggerated smile that made him looked like a happy muppet.

"But we should definitely leave that one of the four us camping. I think it's a dope picture," I clarified, hoping he would understand that I was trying to keep him from tearing his memories into pieces.

"Oh, for sure, man, I wouldn't think of taking that one down. It's just, uhm, it's just that everytime I see that other one, like when I pass the fridge and get a brief side-glance—just sometimes I see my biological father instead of my mother, and he's cupping my eyes"—Atlas showed me on an invisible model—"like that, but he's behind me and I can't see his face. It's weird. I just don't know why I see it, 'cause it's so obvious that it's my mother, overdressed and smashed."

"That's cool, brother, don't worry about it. Take it down. I know what you mean," I said, although I was not sure if Atlas actually knew that I really *did* know what it was like to look at a person and see their inner-thoughts revealed through their eyes.

"I'll take it later," Atlas stood and took his plate to the sink. "I gotta rush to work, man."

"Have a good night."

"Peace."

I folded the paper I was no longer reading and headed upstairs. On the way up I stopped by Simon's room. His door was open, and he was sprawled on his bed with books stacked around him.

"Building a fort?" I asked.

"More like a tower..." Simon said without lifting his eyes from the page. "What's up with you?"

"Nothing."

Simon closed the book and wiped his eyes.

"Did Atlas leave any food?"

"Don't think so."

"Damnit."

"I'm going to cook up a pizza later. You can have some if you want. Hey, tell me something: what was the coolest thing you learned today?"

"That letters don't say a damn thing. Why do you ask?"

"Just a game Henryk used to play."

"Sounds like a shitty game."

"I'll let you know when I start that pizza."

Down the hall, I stopped at Henryk's door. It was closed, but you could hear heavy music behind it. I knocked and waited. The music lowered, and Henryk opened the door.

"What's up, Martin?"

"Oh nothing, man. Just wanted to let you know I'm starting a pizza soon," I said.

"Sweet. I've had so much coffee today I need some starch to soak it up," Henryk said, waving me into the room.

He plopped into his desk chair and swivelled around to face me on the bed. There was an imposing feeling in Henryk's room. He walls were all occuiped by shelves upon shelves. None of his surfaces were left empty, except for his bed.

"What was the coolest thing you learned today?" I asked with a smirk.

"Oh, you bastard. Yes! I was going to ask you. But I'm glad you asked."

"Tell me."

"I'll try. It's new shit to me. I haven't been in school since I didn't-give-a-damn, and now that I do give a damn it's totally different. But anyways—it's a simple letter: K. The eleventh letter. But why K? Actually *why* doesn't matter. What does matter is what it symbolizes: *carrying capacity*," he said carefully, "How much the earth naturally, in any given ecosystem, can support life. Like a budget almost, but more complicated and not so arbitrary. Throwing off the carrying capacity is like overloading the system, or leaving it in some kind of deficit. It can cause the whole ecosystem to go awonk."

Henryk used his hands to draw me a graph that I imagined floating before him. His hand rose, crested, then oscillated across his face.

"And that much is what the earth can hold. Imagine that. All based on an energy budget. Shit, Simon could be thinking something sharp. Remember? His energy thing or whatever? I don't know."

Henryk spun in his chair and asked me my original question. I shrugged and told him that I learned that it was a slow celebrity news day. It didn't surprise me, because the newspapers I sporadically bought were wasted on news about the lives of people I did not know, almost like my walking literary heroes, but real life, and -vincible. Henryk nodded.

"I haven't read about current affairs in a long while," he said.

He motioned to the science textbooks on his desk.

"The old news is all I got."

"Don't worry," I told him, standing up to leave, "You're not missing much. I'll save you the time— a lot of shit has stayed the same."

"I don't know if that's good news or bad news."

It all passes, comes
and goes, -vincible, like old
pages in a book.

VAGABONDS UNITE!
[Atlas Sangman]

Wednesday afternoon, 3 P.M.

Pedestrian traffic seems set on a breathing rhythm: out, it swells; in, it shrinks. The morning rush sighs, rises from bed, then lulls in traffic until it reassumes a waking sleep over keyboards. At lunch there is a shameless burp: the streets rattle with gas compressed by morning meetings. The afternoon falls quiet. The collective breath is held until the end of the work day. But while the faceless concrete giants held their breath, some traffic managed to scrape by, so that you found the occasional individual who meandered, lost without a heel to follow.

So somewhere between with-held breath and the cheer of five o'clock I hummed quietly in the corner of a downtown café, itself on a quiet corner of Queen street, west of Ossington. The Addiction & Mental Health Hospital across the street gave the block a topical open-aired feeling. The hospital's lawn was vast for this part of town, dotted with tangled beech trees drooping like the scattered patients accompanied by their nurses. This was a nice place to come think.

Claire was touring the Museum of Contemporary Canadian Art, just down the block opposite the front door of the Hospital. Afterwards she was going to meet me here. Although I felt that she wouldn't meet me, I came anyway. Sometimes our house was a depressing place to go back to after work. Henryk and Simon always had something on the go, something propelling their days forward, and Martin was always trying to meet his deadlines, and anyone else who visited came on their spare time from varied pursuits and projects. So for a boy trying to live on his daily bread it was difficult to finish a day of exhausting work only to realize I had accomplished nothing.

From a window table, I watched a chubby man across the street blessing passers-by, gesticulating the sign of the cross with his whole upper body. Couples ignored him and old ladies stared at him, either forgetting or failing to admit that this man did not see the same world that they did.

Then the man caught my eye through the window, and he also shot me a stressed sign of the cross—and bells jingled.

The café door slammed closed. It was a broken door I had ignored for the past twenty minutes.

A thin lady walked in. I recognized her immediately.

I would hate to relive highschool here, or anywhere, but to explain Lucy Sparrow's significance would take a novel. The short version is unflattering: Lucy was the girl I always wished I could've asked out. Instead of getting to know her, I took the easy way out. The easy hard way, I guess. I admired her from afar and made an ass of myself whenever I did have the chance to interact. I'm sure Simon would have a fun time explaining the details. And maybe he would be more honest than me.

Either way, I didn't want to see Lucy Sparrow. So I made myself believe that I hadn't seen her. Except that I had, so my peripherals coyly tried to pull her into view. She ordered a coffee. Double latté with a shot of strawberry flavour.

Strawberry Fields Forever. That was the last time I had spent any significant time with her.

I hoped she wouldn't see me. Moreover I hoped that if she did see me she treated me the way I treated her. The Golden Rule. Leave without saying anything.

"Atlas?"

I turned around with an excessively surprised expression that I pulled back too quickly. Even the schizophrenics wouldn't have believed me.

"Lucy. Hey. How're you doing?"

She stood at the counter, still waiting for her coffee.

"Not bad. What are you doing here?" Lucy asked, eyeing the building beyond the window.

"Just having some tea. I was waiting for someone, but I don't think they're coming anymore."

"Oh—oh thanks," Lucy accepted the proffered coffee then stepped closer to my table, "It's strange that I should see you here."

"Why's that?"

"I don't think you come around this part of town much."

"No?"

"I probably would've run into you already."

"Do you live around here?"

"Yes, in those lofts just around the corner."

"Sweet. Very bohemian of you."

Lucy swung on the ball of her outstretched foot. She wrinkled her brow briefly, asking herself something, then stopped swinging.

"I know there are lots of tables, but would you mind if I sat with you?"

"Sharing is caring," I said stupidly.

I moved my pot of tea and Martin's magazine to make room for Lucy at the table. She spun the magazine around.

"*Glossolalia*," she read. "Are you a fan?"

"Do you remember Martin O'Neill? From highschool."

"Yes."

"He's a writer for the magazine. I gotta support my man."

"Oh yeah, I've designed some spreads for the mag."

"Really?"

I was surprised that Martin hadn't mentioned running into Lucy.

"They're not overly impressive and I get fine print credit. But I do it because I love it. What've you been up to? Are you still—still studying philosophy?"

"Naw, man, if I was I'd be across the street there preaching with ZZ Top," I motioned to the sidewalk holy man to make sure Lucy understood I was not associated.

Lucy laughed. She hid her smile behind her hand. Cute.

"Naw, I'm working myself stupid. Figure if life's taught me anything it's that I won't be a millionaire or a genius or anything other than another set of hands. Which I still have both of. So..."

"Hmm," Lucy said instead of saying what she wanted to.

"How about you? I guess this is your fourth year."

"Don't remind me. Four years and I feel like I've lost both my hands."

"At least you'll have your degree."

"Yeah. At least."

My phone buzzed in my pocket. I checked the text message:

Claire: *atlas im sorry. prof wants this report today. insane! ill see you tomorrow.*

Lucy and I started our sentences at the same time. I conceded, gesturing for her to go first.

"I was just going to ask who you were waiting for."

"My friend Claire. We usually get together on my days off."

"Cool," Lucy diverted her eyes.

"She's not my girlfriend," I corrected, "Just to clarify. Just to update you on my misery," I laughed. "My progress on that front has been as pathetic as every other avenue."

"Join the club."

"I founded it."

Lucy laughed, staring out of the window. "In a city like this you'd think finding someone wouldn't be so hard."

"It isn't. I, for one, make it hard on myself."

I wanted to reach out and take the words back. That wasn't something I would tell just anybody. I hoped Lucy understood that.

"It should be hard. Whatever. I have other priorities."

We sat in silence for a few minutes. I finished the last of my tea. Lucy continued to stare out of the window, so I watched her. Her cheeks had become sunken, her eyes bulged further out. The skin, once dappled with juvenile acne (a fraction as bad as my own) was now smooth. Her lips were still full, formed now into a more pronounced pout—she had hardened since highschool.

I felt an unusual merriment as the afternoon sun brightened on Lucy's face. It heaved a golden mask on her that made her squint and turn her chair to the side.

"Nice weather we've been having," she said.

I sat up from my usual slump and leaned on the table.

"I have a weird question—and don't take it the wrong way—actually, you should take it in a good way—or just take it in your own way—but, uhm—

would you want to get out of here? I know a real cool pub in Kensington that's got cheap pints and might be fitting for a bohemian such as yourself."

"A drink?" Lucy considered. "I would totally be up for a drink. To tell you the truth I have nothing to do tonight. And I loathe going back to my loft right now. It's in quite the disarray."

"I'm feeling you, man. Except that I don't got a loft. Which sucks. But you know—"

"Let's go."

I consciously tried to slow my pace. Excitement made my legs over-reach their normal gait. A man stopped us half a block into our walk.

"Can I take a picture of the lovely couple?" he over-caressed his words with wetted lips.

Lucy and I looked at each other. Neither of us had the heart to tell him we weren't a couple. He raised a tin can to his eye and directed us to stand together. We obliged.

"Lovely. Lovely, lovely couple. This is a lovely photo," the man walked away quickly flapping a delusive polaroid.

"That's probably the nicest thing anyone's said to me in months," Lucy said.

"That's sad, man."

"I know."

The walk to the Kaleidoscope Lounge felt shorter than it was. The end of our trip was made quieter by the foot traffic that began to crowd us.

"Funny, I've never heard of this place," Lucy said.

"Seems like something you'd've heard of. I come here every now and then for poetry readings. And jazz. I'm telling you, man, very bohemian. They could rename this the *Sparrow's Cage*."

"Clever."

"Is tonight an open mic?" I pointed to the placard out front.

"Oh no."

"Well it's not 'til later."

"I think that'd totally ruin it."

"Or might make it perfect."

"It's gotta be hard, right?"

But I didn't hear her because I led the way through the thick wooden doors. It was early so there were plenty of tables. We went to the top floor and found a window seat. I ordered a beer. Lucy started with a strawberry daiquiri.

"*Strawberry fields forever*," I sung.

"You remember."

"I'm lame like that. Perfectly sentimental. Memorific[38] to a fault."

"Memorific?"

"And sometimes I make up my own words."

"How's this one for you? Vamption[39]."

"Does that have to do with virgin tramps?"

"Vampire fiction."

"I was close. You don't read that shit do you?"

"Unfortunately. But only because vampires are the perfect heroes for this age."

Outside, the east-leaning shadows collapsed onto the street. I tried to understand what Lucy meant. But if highschool had taught me anything, it was that I didn't understand many things. I asked for an explanation.

"Look at all the villains throughout history. There've been animal monsters, like griffins, and demons, and otherworldly figures. Then you have the wolf-man. Half animal, half man. Scary stuff in itself. Nevermind that he hunts innocent people. Then Shelley introduces us to Frankenstein's monster—a monster created from the strongest pieces of ourselves, yet lacking humanity."

---

[38] ***Memorific*** — (*Atlasian*) Awesome memory, to the point of defect

[39] ***Vamption*** — (*Sparrow*) Vampire Fiction

"Frankenstein was boring."

"I know. Plus Miss Balders made it so much worse."

"So much worse."

"That was our first class together, wasn't it?"

"Yeah."

Lucy hid an ephemeral blush. She was embarrassed that she remembered that.

"Anyways," Lucy continued, "Then comes along the vampire. Who is human. But more. More than human. It's a cannibal, first off, that needs humans to live. They need life to live. The elixir of life: blood. The vampire's super strong. Emotionless. They can be men or women, not like those other monsters. They're a sexy master of seduction. They twist the minds of innocent humans. Afraid of Christianity. They live by night, the time that humans historically have feared. And still do, look at all the lightposts in this city. I really hate that it's always light here. But I'm rambling."

"Naw, you're not done, go on."

"But vampires were historically scary. Now, I don't know. I just don't see how we're all that different from vampires. Except that we don't have fangs that draw blood."

Lucy shrugged. The beer's bubbles disappeared on my palette. We ordered a second round and I changed subjects.

"I bet you have a huge portfolio by now. Have you showed anywhere?"

"No," Lucy aimlessly played with her drink's umbrella, "I can't say I've done anything amazing. School's already fed the egos of all the flashy kids. They've already made websites and branded themselves and whatever. It takes a real solidarity of character to go through with that. I wish I could. I haven't. It's been tough. There are so many artists and designers in this city trying to make it, you just need luck to find your way."

"Someone once told me that luck is when knowledge meets opportunity."

"That sounds nice."

"Yeah I thought it sounded stupid as well."

"It was really strange that I ran into you today."

"Unexpected things—" I started, but Lucy kept talking.

"I always thought I would. I'm surprised it wasn't through Malik or Simon, though. Did you know I designed their album cover?"

"Yeah. The mirror hallway."

"It's embarrassing—"

"I thought it was awesome."

"I just mean the man in the picture. At the time —well, the figure was based on you."

"Naw," I said, trying to erase what I just heard.

"It's true and totally embarassing to admit."

"Why me?"

"It was just that at the time—"

"Fuck it. I guess there's a time for all things," I interrupted so I wouldn't have to hear the explanation. "Even a time for me to be a muse. Even though usually it's me chasing muses. Me making a mockery of myself in front of my muses to somehow evaluate myself. I'm getting way too personal."

"And I'm not?" Lucy gazed into her second strawberry daiquiri.

There was a new sadness that encompassed Lucy. Over the past four years I imagined her the same way I did in highschool: creative, innocent, shy, removed, sober, all the things I wanted to be— me, *deshabillé*[40]. Yet not me—the opposite—pasty white, blond, kind, figured out.

Figured out—so unlike me. She always knew she was an artist. Her parents supported her. She was happy to have been accepted to OCAD. It was a highlight in her life. OCAD wasn't the accept-all

---

[40] **Deshabillé** — (*French*) Undressed

school like the one I went to. But she deserved it. I thought so, at least.

Lucy twirled her straw and ordered another drink.

"And the Louvre was fascinating," Lucy continued her story about globe-trotting. "It truly is the epitome as far as collections go. But to be real, I mean, to be absolutely honest, the more fascinating art were all the people looking at the canvases. There were these two lesbians holding hands, walking down the hall towards the Mona Lisa, flanked by these religious renaissance paintings. But they were the real renaissance. They were in love. It made me jealous, but it also made me really appreciate their love. It made me understand love from a different perspective. That's what I think art does."

But despite her alcohol-inspired openness Lucy was sad. Or maybe I only knew her sadness through my own. We wanted to be so much more, we saw so much more in the world than we could share. That made anything else we did seem so menial.

I polished off my third beer and ordered a fourth round. The fall sun tumbled to its bed, and we defied it, the perfect heroes for our age.

"I love this place. It is truly bohemian. Like, look at that girl. She's not even wearing shoes!

She's barefoot. That's relaxed. I wished I didn't have to wear shoes. But then I'd get hepatitis, with my luck."

I kicked off my shoes and raised my eyebrows to Lucy. She cocked her head and laughed.

"But I'm not wearing socks."

I peeled off my socks, tucking them into my shoes. Lucy sipped her daiquiri then slipped off her flats.

"You're a bad influence, Atlas."

The way she said Atlas made me giggle.

"If I get Hepatitis I'm blaming you," she said.

"I bet we can make it home without shoes."

"And if we do?"

"Then I owe you supper."

"And if we don't?"

"I owe you supper," I said, recklessly bold from the alcohol.

"So—haha! So—"

"Everyone's a winner."

"And how do *you* win?"

"I get to feel the city trembling under my soles. I get to feel your heartbeat through them. I get to soak in the pure vibes that the shoemaker is afraid we'll find out about. I'll save fifty bucks a year not buying shoes. And I'd get to see you again."

"There's a band starting—is that the open mic band?"

"Naw, that's the *Chilly Cats*."

"That's the lamest name ever."

"I know. Them *Chilly Cats* hoowwwlin' in the alley. What's your number?"

"Abrupt."

"Yuh."

"Do you know I've given out my number to, like, thirteen or so guys and none of them have ever called me."

"Well how do you expect me to not call you if I don't have your number?"

"I think it'd make a good random chance bad."

I realized then, as Lucy looked down into her drink that I couldn't fool myself. I was over Lucy Sparrow. Whatever weird fantastical image I adored was gone. But I was glad I revisited the idea tonight to concrete it. Tomorrow I would wake up with a headache and a hard-on, and Lucy's ghost would ask me where to go. We would lay in the figment of my imagination, naked and expended, and I would realize that I had nothing to say to Lucy.

Hopefully I wouldn't have to go that far tonight. I wouldn't have to break Lucy's heart to find out that she would break mine.

"It's getting late and I'm pretty buzzed," I said.

"Me too."

"I oughta get home."

"Hey—you wouldn't happen to have any weed would you?"

I paused. Lucy lay her hand on my forearm. I was ready to leave so I played aloof.

"Since when do you burn?"

"Since every now and then."

"Naw, Lucy, naw. I got no weed."

"You're lying. You don't have a little dime to roll? We can smoke back at the loft if you're paranoid or whatever."

"I—"

"I have money."

"It's not about money."

"Then what's it about?"

"What do you want, Lucy?"

"Let's have a good time. Let's have the good times we never allowed ourselves to have in highschool."

I drained my glass. Lucy jiggled her bare foot. It tugged at my pants.

I looked at the tables that had filled since we reached the Lounge. The *Chilly Cats* played a blues song I didn't recognize.

"Do you still hang out with Simon?" Lucy asked.

"Yeah. I live with the man. Him, Martin O'Neill, Henryk Zdicz and I all live together."

"That's the bunch—Simon told me, once, but I thought he was high—"

"Probably."

"I met him at some random party. He told me that you only get what you give back."

"Weird. Sy usually makes up his own clichés."

"It made me really self-conscious. I think he was trying to help me be less shy but it just made me more shy. I've thought about it since."

"And what's the conclusion?"

"I haven't figured that out yet. All I know is—wait, did that guy just dedicate this song to no-one?"

"I wasn't listening."

"He just dedicated the song to no-one. Hold on."

Lucy searched her purse for her camera. It was an expensive digital-SLR, one of those heavy cameras that needed two hands and a single sharp eye to operate. She left the table for a better angle. At the edge of the stage she snapped photos, moving slowly from vantage point to vantage point.

I considered Lucy's offer. I had more than enough herb—it wasn't a question about my adequacy. Lucy was playing happy, and that concerned me. The daiquiris made her smile compulsive—but I felt there was an underlying frown that made the smile a reaction against something more sinister, more representative, more *real*. No, I wouldn't be a conquest. Was that why I always liked Lucy? Was that what attracted me? My shores were well-guarded, I could be better than that. Maybe Simon had said what he did to Lucy back in the day to help me in the future. He said he could see the future, although I knew he just said that to mack on ladies. But imagine. Imagine I really did know what Claire was going to text me before she did, imagine that I knew that I did have an intention besides general vagabondry when I left the house this afternoon.

I could imagine.

The open mic started. Neither of us wanted to stay.

I went to the bathroom. When I returned Lucy was collecting her things.

"I'm buying," I said.

"No, no. I got my own."

"Don't worry about it, Lucy. I got it. I work, I'm not the broke artist. Let it be my treat."

I paid at the bar. I felt stupid being barefoot, but no one said anything.

"So are you ready to owe me a dinner?" she asked.

I led the way, shoes in hand. Lucy swayed behind me, her flats between her fingers.

"Where do you live?" I asked.

"Queen West. A place called Liberty Village."

"Holy fuck. No way. That's just—nevermind—I mean, whatever, I've smoked at that place. Ended up there after a party once, had to wait forever for a cab, but real nice place. Real chill."

"No way!"

"What?"

"I've seen you there. I didn't think it was you. But it must've been."

"I was just looking for some liberty."

"Me too."

The shadows had completely overtaken the streets now. There was only the hint of orange in the western sky. I could eat that western sky if it would give me some illumination. Instead I burped and tasted beer in my mouth again.

Blue and orange light,
cool pavement underfoot, eyes
glassy—lonely city.

} LET'S GET TOGETHER SO WE CAN FALL APART {
[Atlas Sangman]

Thursday Morning, 3 A.M.

"...and Romeo has that corner over there with the rosy sheets, and Lily's got the painter's drop-cloth, and Drew has the black bedsheets—he's some eccentric writer type who you hear ticking away at night. Like, Lily can barely keep her eyes open so she doesn't care, but I have trouble sleeping so I hear every letter he types out."

"Is it any good?"

Lucy hid her laugh behind her hand and recrossed her legs. She tapped a spot on her bed.

"It's too far to pass joints from where you are."

"True."

But it was also true that I was afraid that the bed would swallow me into its maw, and there I would light a match and find Lucy curled up in the acidic bowels, hungry for companionship. And me with all my fresh visions of the outside.

Life sometimes must get lonely..[41].

---

[41] Infinite respects to Bob Dylan! Here Lucy and Atlas listen to Bringing It All Back Home. The two songs quoted are "It's Alright Ma (I'm Only Bleeding)" and "It's All Over Now, Baby Blue"

Tinny music scratched from the second-hand record player. It was quiet, as to not disturb the roommates, and fell to a distant rasp when I crawled to the mattress. Lucy shuffled over and handed me a book of matches. She stuck the joint in her mouth and pointed it to me.

Say okay, I've had enough, what else can you show me?

I burned out two matches before I lit the tip of the joint. When Lucy toked her cheeks collapsed into her mouth and her eyes closed. She looked pained. It looked like she tried to inhale herself—blackhole therapy, maybe. Delicately she balanced the joint between two fingers and passed it to my face. I watched Lucy exhale a breath of relief. The candles she lit beside her bed baked her face, the shadows skittish veils through which Lucy watched the cherry blush between my lips. The burn's crisp sizzle ebbed with the record's popping. Bob Dylan squeezed out a harmonica melody, exchanging words as I offered the paper twig back to Lucy.

Look out the saints are coming through...

"I'm vibing on your canvasses. They're awesome."

I referred to the various projects safety-pinned to the cloth walls.

"That takes an eye that I don't have to capture it, man."

"My parents...they always told me 'we're not your entertainers' so I had to find a way to entertain myself. It never helped me understand who they were. But it helped me find something useful, I suppose."

Supposition. Those supple lips of Lucy's rolled around the joint. She passed it back. I kept my eyes on her lips.

There was a draft that ruffled the sheets—a slight tremor. Faint keys tapped spasmodically from beyond the curtains. Lucy wavered in the candlelight. Shadows jumped behind her, each leaning forward to watch the space between us. Lucy took the joint back on her delicate wrist. It was thin—just a sketch—I leaned my elbows on my knees, lead-headed—Lucy's knees buckled so easily, and her skin held the same tremor as the sheets. There were only bedsheets separating these four people. The sheets that kept Lucy an individual also provided her with an anonymous space to undress, and create, and touch herself. The floor creaked from an unseen footstep. Lucy leaned a light head on my shoulder. The roof hummed—the sheets trembled—Lucy's head grew heavier—I staid my posture despite all the flowy things about me that needed to collapse, that, like the sheets, were held up by strings taut on nails stuck in bricks, themselves laid over each other, over wood that rotted slowly, hidden, which was drilled into the earth, which heaved and shook over centuries trying to get out of its slumber under the restless ocean—so I had no choice.

Is drawing crazy patterns on your sheets...

The roach was too small to deal with. Lucy plucked it from my fingers and gently lay it on her night table beside her broken watch, her empty glass, her retainer, and her mascara.

Lucy swayed for a moment, and I felt that I swayed too. She waited to hear what she wanted to; I waited to see what she needed to hear.

Strike another match, go start anew...

Her movement was fluid. She crested towards me—our eyes locked in a gaze that said nothing, only hinting at a question—she ebbed, she lifted, she swirled. She, like any good wave, fell back.

I leaned over her. Lucy snored softly.

I will blow out the
flames, tip toe to the door
and close it behind me.

THE PASSWORD
[Martin O'Neill]

"Can you believe how they make us so suspicious over passwords? Like they're some secret cult magic spell. What the fuck! Caps lock? Oh, fuck you."

Simon told me he wanted to use the journals I had access to at my school. So I brought him. I needed to finish a report anyways. But I forgot how Sy gets when he's out.

"Do you think that's how speech started? Like, with a password. And like, it spread by who needed to know it, and different languages appeared from the different secrets? Wouldn't that be weird?"

Simon clicked through pages of an online search page as he talked to me. He was too distracted to notice the room fill up. Several exhausted individuals sneered at Simon's monologue, but a few shook their heads quietly.

"I am the Googler! *Goo-goo-g'job*! *Did you mean: go get a job*? Haha!"

I knew I wouldn't be able to work with Simon sitting beside me, so I put on headphones. But even over the music I could hear Simon mumble something or laugh. After forty minutes Simon ripped my headphones off and moved my head towards his screen. On the twenty-inch hi-def screen Simon had a close-up of a wet pussy.

"You bastard," I said. "Now security's coming to bust us. They catch people looking at porn all the time and they even fine them."

"That's fucked. Good thing I'm clean."

Simon had found a student ID card in the quad on the way to the computer lab. It worked out perfect, because access was the only issue.

"I could get out of here. I'm done," he said.

"You're done?"

"Yeah, check it out."

Sy scrolled through ten pages he had of references listed neatly under sub-headings with short-hand notes typed underneath. In my twenty minutes I had read three articles and idly checked my email inbox twice.

"Want to go? Are you done?"

"I'm nowhere close to done. But yeah, I can come back, it's all good."

"What's our time?" Sy asked.

"Let me check."

"Didn't you just check your phone?"

"Yeah," I opened the phone again. "Twelve minutes 'til the next bus."

"We can totally make it."

At the front of the building there were a few loiterers taking advantage of the last warmth before winter to inhale their cigarettes with calm steadiness. The shaky cold would come soon enough, the entrance would look as bare as the mangled trees that loomed from little squares of dirt between long stretches of pavement. Right outside the doors three teenage cadets stood, pushing calendars on passers-by.

"Calendar to support the Cadets?"

"No thanks."

They hadn't remembered we passed twenty-minutes ago and denied them. I turned to Simon to offer a cigarette, and he stopped to grab one from my pack. He turned with a discontented look to the cadets behind him.

"What the fuck is wrong with you?" he asked them.

Their smiles flattened out, except for one who stared him down with a grin hanging off his right ear.

"Smiley, smiley, smiley," Simon turned to the uniformed line-up and walked to the grinner. "Here's a date to circle. The date your casket comes back from Afghanistan."

"Hey, screw off," one of the others stepped up in defence.

"Oh alright, cap-ee-tan.. I'll step off. What the fuck were you laughing at anyways, you clowns? Why don't you go to Iraq and get amputated?"

Sy lit his smoke and stepped closer to the trio. They looked between me and each other. The grinner's eyes were lit up with excitement. He glared at me, then stared down Simon—I saw little coloured pegs moving in strategic lines across a map—a line of pegs knocked over by the roll of dice. The one who defended the group took another step in Simon's direction, then stepped back—in his eyes I saw fighter planes plough through war smoke clouds in attack formation. The third broke the tension by offering a calendar to a suited man.

Simon stopped within centimetres of the grinner's face. He looked ready to upper-cut the dumb smiler, but Simon only contemplated something. Then, quicker than the soldier could think, Simon licked him. Right over his lips. The kid reeled, and the two beside him yelped and jumped back. Simon collapsed in laughter then faked a punch to the diaphragm. The trio leaped back from Simon. Simon laughed again, then walked away. I let him pass me, to make sure he didn't have any after-thoughts. I watched the soldiers. Right before I turned around they were already laughing. They had already convinced themselves that they had won that battle. Too bad they couldn't see the whole war.

Simon was not too far ahead, but I was still out of breath by the time I caught up with him.

"Sy, what happened?"

"Those fucking guys. Fucking soldiers without a cause. They were fucking laughing at me! Both times we passed. They just cracked up when they saw me. Shit, give some people a uniform and they get all boisterous."

"Boisterous," I repeated.

Sometimes Simon impressed me in ways I never thought I could be impressed.

When we reached the bus stop Simon got me to check the time. We were four minutes early. He pumped the air and jumped on his toes like a boxer.

"Hey. I know that chick."

He pointed down the line of people to a short girl with long hair. She wore big sunglasses, with a lip ring neatly punctuating an otherwise featureless face. She stared across the street, the trademark white ear-bud wires dangling from her hair.

"No way," I said.

Simon knew a myriad of people I never imagined he could possibly know.

"She's a model," he nodded with a smile. "A model. C'mon."

He strode over to her and ducked in her view. She shook her head and plucked a bud out of one ear.

"Hey Bunny," Sy said coolly.

"Simon?! How's it going, baby?"

"It's all good. You wouldn't happen to be heading to Mississauga were you?"

"Oh no, heading the other way. I'm waiting for the next bus."

"You're early."

"I'm always super early for the bus."

Simon smiled devilishly at me.

"This is my homeboy Martin, by the way."

"Hello, Martin," she extended her delicate arm, and answered my unasked question, "I'm Bunny. My license says Brianna, but I barely use it so who cares? So? What are you up to tonight, Simon? Something wild?"

"The only wild thing going down tonight is the wild rice I'll be cooking up."

"Ooo, wild rice?"

"Yes, and jerk chicken. You want to come by? Have you eaten?"

"I was going to hit up some sushi before going home to shower."

"I can leave your chicken raw, if you want. C'mon, we've got our own place, we got some liquor, some good food, some good people. Martin will be there."

Bunny smiled cleanly, hardly creasing her face. She looked Simon in the face, but it was hard to tell where she was looking through the sunglasses.

"Okay. But I have to go by nine. No later. No funny business."

Simon held up innocent hands.

When we got home I went up to my room to put away my backpack. I checked my emails before I went back down. The smell of jerk spice already wafted through the kitchen.

Bunny sat in a stool, leaning on the bar with a gin & tonic in a mason jar. Simon zipped from drawer to drawer in the kitchen.

"Do you know where the flipper-ma-jigee is?" he asked me.

I joined Bunny at the bar and watched Simon give his impromptu cooking lesson. Bunny giggled and cheered him on. He credited Atlas with the dish, called it *Atlas' Jerking Special*. Bunny asked about the house and who lived there. Simon glorified the four of us like we were some revolutionary think-tank. Without anything to add to Simon's play I only shrugged when the attention shifted on to me.

"But now I must be primal again!" Simon said. "I must go out to the woods and stake out my claim, must build the highest fire and cook the biggest chicken."

Simon left for the backyard BBQ juggling the plate of seasoned chicken and the flipper-ma-jigee. Silence would have settled between us if Bunny had not stopped smiling. It made it easy to start small talk.

"So how do you know Simon?" I asked.

"How does anybody know Simon?" she asked in a tone that made me want to know more.

"Yeah, tell me about it. Are you in school now?"

"Yes, for—wait. Guess."

"I'm not good at that."

"Just guess, I bet you'll get it right."

"Uh…I dunno. Photography? Graphic design? Fashion?"

"*Ding-ding-ding*! Fashion girl. Make my own clothes," she ran a hand up and down her side for demonstration.

"Nice. I like the stitching."

Who likes stitching?

"What do you do, then?"

"I model. Not for Playboy or anything chachi[42] like that. Victoria Secret is as naughty as I'll get."

"Is that where *Bunny* comes from?"

"*Hee-hee*. I guess. How about you? What do you do?"

"Journalism. I write for *Glossolalia*."

"Oh? What kind of reporting?"

"Mostly current events. Political events, too."

Because I knew that was what every girl wanted to hear.

"Oh that's fantastic. There's so much cool things that go on and so many of us know so little about it all. Sweet."

"I bet modelling is a lot more fun."

Bunny shrugged and sipped her drink. She looked out the back door for Simon, but the BBQ was out of view. Her profile was sleek, her skin pale. It looked like someone had sculpted her face. Her eyes were unhidden now, the sunglasses folded on the counter. She had clear chestnut eyes, a true marble texture. When she caught my eyes over her emptying glass she blinked for a moment and the light slid across her eye—I saw Bunny lean forward

---

[42] **Chachi** — (*English*) Slang; reference to something trying to be cool (or cooler than it is); reference to Chachi Arcola, the loveable tough-kid from "Happy Days" who loved Joanie

into a mirror, frowning, staring with those chestnut eyes forlorn, the colours drawn from her face, droopy eyebrows foreboding some great sadness— then she blinked and raised her cheekbones from the glass. A fresh smile brought me back to reality.

"Simon's not going to give me food poisoning, is he?"

"No…" I looked away so I could answer normally. "He's learned a thing or two from Atlas. Worst he can do is burn the food."

Simon did end up burning the wild rice on the stove. But the chicken was fantastic. I was really impressed, I would have to pay closer attention next time Atlas cooked.

Photograph on my
retina—punched out like a
ribbon of passwords.

INVASIVE
[Martin O'Neill]

"Claire Chandran, tell me something. When was the last time you bought fish on the street?"

"Never, actually. Plus, we're not on the street. So I think my current chances are low," Claire said.

"True that, true that," Simon said. "But see I have bought fish on the street—fish tacos, in fact, and they were legit. But I mean, when do you ever see someone selling fish in the Valley?"

"I don't think he's selling. He's collecting. Just like us, right?"

Simon and Claire spoke theatrically as we walked through the tall grass. We passed the old fisherman without acknowledgement.

Henryk led the way with Lukasz. Atlas looked back to the car and asked me if he locked the door. The Valley was not a place you would worry about someone breaking into your car, Atlas was just paranoid. And thorough, as per Henryk's instructions. Henryk's backpack had two other backpacks stuffed in it, plus clippers and his plant identification book. Simon carried the other backpack with tupperware containers and a bottle of sparkling wine for after.

There was a spot—a *haven on high*, as Henryk called it—up a dry streambed in the Valley that harboured a living stash of our favourite intoxicant. Henryk and Atlas counted 18 plants, taller than either of them. Lukasz calculated off generic figures and estimated 54 ounces. 1728 grams. 4.5 pounds. When he told us these numbers we knew we had come by some fortune.

I was a little concerned with what we had done to deserve it. Or what we would have to do.

Henryk and Atlas tended to the plants throughout the summer. They had tried smoking the flowers as they developed, but it never got them high. Despite the trials, Atlas was optimistic that it would grow potent as it ripened.

So as summer cooled to autumn we waited impatiently. We were like children with excitement. Finally leaves crunched under our ill-chosen footwear, though the canopy still looked full. Henryk periodically stopped at different plants and tried to name them. Simon told him to shut up, so Henryk just stopped telling us. Along the way we smoked a joint—it felt appropriate. It was warm out, so we all enjoyed the hike. Then Henryk started to get excited. We were close.

There was a short shelf where a waterfall would run in the spring, but it probably had not flowed in years. After a short climb, Henryk ran ahead to stand in the middle of the clump of plants. We each studied the plants as we came to them. I took one in my hand and looked at the leaves and the flowers, then smelled it. It did not smell like what we thought it was. But what did I know about cultivation of any kind?

"So?" Simon asked, arms akimbo.

"Let's do it."

Henryk opened his backpack and handed out supplies. Atlas and Claire clipped plants into one bag, and Simon and Lukasz did another. I partnered with Henryk and started cutting the flowers and leaves off the plant.

"Is this how you do it?" I asked.

"Um, I guess," Henryk shrugged, "Just make it, like, look like it would look if we bought it."

But Henryk stood idly by while I started clipping. I asked him what was up, and he shrugged concernedly.

"Shit. This just doesn't look enough like it. No, not like I thought it did."

"What do you think it is?" I asked.

"I don't know. Actually, I actually it's a weed. Nothing psychoactive at all."

"So, like, just hemp?"

"No. Just a natural weed. You know? Like dandelions or Canada thistles."

"I didn't know dandelions were a weed. They're everywhere."

"Yeah, exactly."

Henryk grabbed his plant identification book from his backpack and flipped through it.

"And Canada thistle? Why are they weeds?" I asked, still concerned over the vilification of my favourite plant.

"They're not native."

"Haha! Dude, we're not native. I guess Atlas is kind of native."

"We're all native somewhere."

"So these plants basically immigrate to this country and that makes them weeds?"

"It's more complicated then that," Henryk said without looking up from the book.

The other four laughed while they collected, running a competition as to who could fill their sack the quickest—Simon shouted out that the game should be called reverse-sex. Or wedding sex, as Lukasz added. I asked Henryk if I should tell them to stop and he shook his head. He contemplated a page of his book.

"Check this out."

The page had pictures of the plant and detailed description of identification features. The name acrossed the top said *Potentilla gracilis*[43].

"*Potent*-tilla? Gracious and potent, right? That sounds good," I said.

---

[43] ***Potentilla gracilis*** — (*Latin*) Scientific name for graceful cinquefoil, a perennial, rhizomatic forb native to Canada

"Yeah, but it's not the herb we're after. It's useless. Well, actually, it says here that the Cree smoked it to cure headaches.

"The name's really misleading."

"Yo," Henryk shouted to the others, "Stop. Stop clipping."

"Fucking clip-blocker," Simon called back.

"Stop. It's not ganja."

The others stopped and looked at the plants again.

"I knew it didn't smell right," Simon said.

Atlas emptied the bags and folded them back into one another. Nobody spoke. Simon led the way back down the stream, with Claire and Henryk in lag. Claire talked with Henryk, she tried to cheer him up. She told him that it was good exercise, and that the lead up to the Harvest was the best part, and it lasted months. Henryk shrugged and Simon spoke up from the front, saying how the best part was the months of getting high afterwards. I pointed out that at least we got half the pleasure—and Henryk told us how stupid he felt. Nobody comforted him, but no one bugged him about it.

We crossed the river upstream from where we had originally, and walked back on the flat floodplain on the other side. The old fisherman was still perched on the riverbank, leaning his fishing rod into the river. He tugged at the line and eyed the ripples carefully. When we were close he called out good-day to us as we passed. Atlas and Claire smiled and waved at the man. The man nodded slowly to Henryk and asked us how our hike was.

"Fine. Just fine. How's fishing?" Henryk redirected the question.

He stopped beside the fisherman. The rest of us lingered nearby.

"The fishing's good, but that's not a good thing in this case," the fisherman said roughly.

"What do you mean? I didn't even know there were fish in this stream."

"Not too many, especially not these days. What I'm looking for will succeed anywhere. And it is. I'm with the Fish & Wildlife department."

"Cool. I'm actually studying ecology right now."

The fisherman nodded. He took off his large hat and we could see how wrinkled his face was. His skin hung over crystal clear blue eyes. White hair fringed the back of his head.

"*Channa argus*[44]. You know that one?" he asked.

---

[44] ***Channa argus*** — (*Latin*) Scientific name for the Northern snakehead, an exotic invasive species to North America that is detrimental to native fish populations

"No."

"Northern snakehead. It's an invasive fish moving up to Canada. From Asia."

"Invasive," Henryk repeated.

I cringed a bit when he said it. I noticed Henryk wanted to get away. But the old fisherman insisted.

"These fish can technically walk over land. They're impossible to stop. And they're vicious. Huge biomass. They're are the peak of trophic levels. But they're throwing the whole ecosystem out of whack."

"Why?" Henryk asked, biting his lip. I figured he must have caught himself asking the question he had not wanted to.

"I'd love to know. That's why I'm out here. Want to see one?" the fisherman asked, pointing to his case.

"No. No thanks. We have to go."

As Henryk walked away the fisherman eyed the rest of us. He met my eyes and locked for a moment. In a flicker I saw violent streams pouring down his face, boiling with foreign fish that looked no different than us.

I patted Henryk's shoulder. I could see the disparity in my friend's face.

"No worries, right?"

Henryk nodded without conviction. I knew he disagreed. But right now wasn't the time to worry. Worry implied hopelessness. For now, we still had hope. So for now, I was right.

"No worries," Henryk said.

That fine borderline
fusing invaders into
lost, wayward natives.

SNAG
[Henryk Zdicz]

Since Harvest Day was such a waste, I wanted to find something just as good to replace it. The discovery had been mine. The operation was my responsibility. And I fucked up. Simon was pissed. He looked forward to the Harvest more than any of us. I tried to reason with him that we never had any of the crop in our possession in the first place, and more inconvincingly that a loss now meant a gain later. Atlas had told me that comforting perspective on the silent empty-bagged ride home from the Valley.

That gain would come because I would bring it. I called up Oz and asked if he still needed a runner. Conveniently, a package of MDMA needed a ride up north that week. Oz seemed intrigued by my random phone call. His car had broken down that very day and he was wondering how he was going to make his run this week. He hired me right away.

I brought Atlas along on the three-hundred kilometre trek north on the 400 highway. It was his day off and, more importantly, he was the only one of us with a car.

The Sunfire zipped through fragments of enormous rock. It was Thursday, which meant I would only miss two classes. I considered it a field tour of northern Ontario's boreal forest. Everything was round.

"Everything is round," Atlas nodded, staring down the road.

"Yeah?"

"The lakes feed the clouds that feed the lakes. And all the sponges take what they can, happy in the middle."

"True."

Atlas had an intuitive grasp on the information I was just beginning to realize. I learned about the hydrologic cycle in grade five but never fully comprehended it, never fully put myself in it.

"Do you know the guy we're trading with?"

"Not exactly," I admitted. "I have a phone number that the guy doesn't want me to call unless I need to. We just have a time to meet. Sketchy, I know. The guy must be mad paranoid, he's trafficking MDMA and cannabis in the middle of the forest."

"On federal land."

"That's right."

"On stolen land."

"Not everyone's a winner."

Which was another reason why Atlas was with me. The forest where we were meeting up with our man was on the Wildwood Algonquin Reserve where Atlas' uncle lived. It wasn't a place where Atlas was popular (that place probably didn't exist) but at least he knew the forest and some faces and would be able to get us out of a jam.

"Tell me something about the forest," Atlas asked.

"Like what? I've only been in school for three weeks, man, I don't know very much about anything yet."

"Why does the forest look dead?"

"No, it's just old. A lot of old growth up here. In the places where the loggers haven't gotten to at least. A lot of old stuff."

"So many broken trees."

"Yeah, but they make the landscape the mosaic it should be. You know, they form the tapestry: new growth, old growth, lakeshores, hilltops, valleys, etcetera. All the different habitats. Like all that biodiversity. That's what it's about. Woodpeckers and owls use the snags—"

Atlas knew I could ramble once I started. It was too long of a ride to just drone out to music. So I told Atlas about forest ecology, or at least what I knew about it. He was intrigued by the natural role of fire. I was too. All the things that can go wrong in the city were natural and correct in the wild.

Atlas asked me to re-explain parasitism.

"Mistletoe is a parasite?"

"Yeah. All the plants in the family are, to some extent. Mistletoe takes away the tree's nutrients and slowly kill it. Huge stands can go rusty."

"Damn. Mistletoe is a parasite, lovers!" Atlas called out to an old couple that passed us in the left lane.

"You're going to take this next exit," I said.

"Naw, it's the next one, man."

"No, wait, two more. You're right. Just get ready to exit."

"Aie, aie, *kapitan*[45]."

The Sunfire peeled off the highway, now on the secondary highway that led us right to the

---

[45] ***Kapitan*** — (*Polish*) Captain

Wildwood Forest on the Algonquin Reserve. This was native land. Our highschool textbooks told us that this was as close as we were ever going to get to seeing the land as it was before we (Europeans) arrived. But I had enough common sense to know that was a rotten bag of horseshit.

Atlas turned the music up and became sullen as the paved road abruptly turned to a gravel one. He squinted—when Atlas squinted I didn't bother to joke, I knew he was in no mood for it. We passed a wrinkled old man walking in the ditch. I watched him as we passed, but Atlas kept his eyes square on the road. If I had been with anybody else or in any other place I would have suggested that we picked the man up. Sorry, grandfather, not today.

Atlas knew his way. He broke off of the main road, cutting around to the far north side of the forest. Strategically he parked behind a large clump of willows and reminded me to lock the doors. We got our backpacks out of the trunk and checked that we had everything we needed.

Water. Compass. Snack bars. Two ounces of pure MDMA. Hash pipe. My plant I.D. book. One five-inch hunting knife. Car keys. Cellphones. We wouldn't need more than half the shit we brought, but I liked to be prepared. In the event that we were fucked over, it was better to have more than we needed.

We had about a two kilometre hike to the exchange point, the rocky north shore of small Lake Miskwanibi[46]. I stopped frequently and tried to identify interesting plants. At each one Atlas crouched beside me, scanning the pages as I flipped through, trying to match form to name. Atlas called out the names of birds as they tweeted in the canopy overhead. I never realized how many birdcalls Atlas knew. Then again, he could've been making them up. I didn't have my ornithology book with me.

"What's this plant?" Atlas asked.

"I don't know. It's already dead."

"Dead?"

"It's already gone to seed."

"Zombie flower."

We reached the lake in good time despite all the stops. By the time we sat on a massive boulder over-looking the lake I had named fifteen different plant species. Satisfied and now acquainted with my surroundings, having known them by name, I kept an eye out for our man and enjoyed the autumn sun. Atlas sat cross-legged with his back to me, staring out at the lake. I scanned all the crevices in the

---

[46] ***Lake Miskwanibi*** — (*Algonquin*) Red Lake (Red: Miskwà; Lake: Níbí)

forest that I could see, watching for movement. Atlas pulled a piece of paper from his backpack and wrote on his knee. A raven crossed overhead. It landed on a snag in front of Atlas.

"Hey, Raven," Atlas called out, "Where is our man?"

The raven cawed in response then stupidly flew away. Atlas watched it fly back to where I saw it come from. It perched on another snag with its back to us.

"Is he coming from that way?" I asked.

"No. I don't think so."

We waited another hour for our man to show up. We were pissed off that he kept us waiting. He approached empty-handed.

"Hey," he waved to us when he was close, "Are you Rickshaw?"

I smiled upon hearing my pseudonym, and nodded.

"Yeah. This is Atlantis."

"You got the stuff?"

"You got ours?"

"Yeah. You gotta follow me, eh, I parked down an old seismic line there with my pick-up. I thought that's where you guys were going."

"How far is it?"

"Oh, maybe fifteen minutes."

We followed the man through bush to the seismic line. Along the way we stumbled through some conversations that were stunted by paranoia. This was a serious drug-deal, one on a scale we had never conducted. We didn't want to leave ourselves open for anything. We were vague with every question the man threw at us. He kept asking us if we wanted a ride back to our car so the exchange would be easier. Atlas turned him down everytime.

We finally reached the man's white pick-up truck after twenty minutes. I had gotten turned around a bit, but thought I still knew where the car was. I hoped Atlas knew, just to be sure. The man walked us to the back of his ratty old pick-up truck. The bed was full of small, bunched conifers. The tail-gate had little block-letters, the individual-letter stickers you buy from a hardware store. It read *TREES 4 SALE.* I smirked as the man pulled down the gate and unbunched a few spruce boughs. He reached inside and started unloading kilo-bags of pot. I grabbed the neatly-wrapped MDMA from my bag. Atlas stuffed his back-pack with the bags of herb.

Oz never told me how much pot we would be trading, but we assumed off the price of the MDMA that it would be a lot less than what we got. By the time we packed away all the bags both our backpacks were filled to expanded zippers, and a third back-pack Atlas had brought, just in case, was also filled. The bags looked like chubby faces filled with too many marshmallows. It seemed very campy, very appropriate. I handed the man the bags of MDMA.

"How is it?" he asked.

"Pretty good," I said, even though I hadn't tried it myself.

"Pretty good, eh? Yeah, Oz usually out-does himself with every new batch. You guys sure you don't want a ride back to your car?"

"Yeah, man, thanks. We'll take it from here."

The man nodded, then drove away. The trees in the back jumped around as he rumbled over the rough seismic line. Atlas shouldered the two bags and looked up a tree. I followed his gaze to see a raven perched on the crown.

"Hey, Raven," I called out this time, "Where's our car?"

The raven did nothing. It continued to watch us from the tree top.

"What're you doing talking to the birds, Henny? The car's that way."

I followed Atlas back to the car. We didn't stop this time, we were excited by the weight of the bags. I was sweating by the time I recognized where we were, in the flat of willows near the road. But the car wasn't where we parked it.

"What the fuck? Didn't we park here? Or maybe it's down the road, there."

I walked to the next clump of suspicious willows but the car was not there either.

"Fuck," Atlas said dejectedly.

"What? Is this the wrong road?"

"No, man, this is it. That is definitely where we parked our car. Look, there are our fresh tire marks. But check it out, man, there's other footprints. More than just us, man. Fuck. I can't believe it. These fucking guys."

A heavy fist grabbed a hold of my stomach and twisted. I dropped the back-pack and stomped the ground a bit. I cursed. Atlas rambled about how stupid he was to have trusted them. He asked me why they kept tormenting him like this. He looked like he was about to cry.

I guided him back into the woods to keep out of sight of the road, just in case.

"Don't worry," I said, "Don't worry. We'll find it. We'll get it back. Besides, if we don't, I'm not too upset about being out here."

"Yeah. Yeah, easy to say when the whole fucking place doesn't mock you."

"We just need to think. Just peace out and think. Turn the mocking into clues. Something will come. We'll get it back."

But I was not so sure.

Stolid I perch on
tree snags, looking at nothing,
like zombie flowers.

AUTOSTOPOWICZ
[Henryk Zdicz]

Hitch-hiking is a long-lost art in the New World. My *babcia*[47] would hitch a ride from outside of Gdansk all the way to Gdynia in the rain to see family and friends. Not only was hitch-hiking legal in Poland, it was a recommended form of travel until the 1990's, when I was a toddler, so that if I ever wanted to experience how it had been I would have had to be on that road beside my mom, tugging at her dress.

Atlas' mom hitch-hiked across South America, it was how she met his dad. But us, the spawn of foreign free-wheelers? No, the art was lost on us.

---

[47] ***Babcia*** — (*Polish*) Grandmother

I still tried. I walked backwards on that gravel road, staring down at the faint point where road vanished into horizon and distance became minimized. Atlas didn't bother, he walked ahead of me, still carrying the two backpacks full of herb. Between us the only silence was our shoes scraping the gravel.

"You should stop wasting your arm's strength, man, we're not going to get a ride. Not from these fucking people. They'll probably drive by in my own car and piss on me when they pass. Way to fulfill the stereotype you dumbfucks."

Atlas was sore about losing the car. He wanted to walk back to the nearest town to call the police and report the car stolen. I reminded him of our back-packs full of copious amounts of marijuana. I decided it would be better to head onto the reserve and find out through word-of-mouth if anybody had seen the car. Atlas knew the elders would be kind enough to help us out, it was just the periphery of the young that he thought would fuck us over given the chance.

"Just chill, Atlas, chill. Innocent until proven guilty, right?"

"You don't know, Henny," Atlas stopped me. "You weren't there. You don't know what these guys did to me. Like, why would you strip a comrade and make him walk back home with his bare ass showing? Why? Just because I was whiter than them? I wish I didn't have to be pissed off with them. They're the only true North Americans yet we've cut them off from our new North America. And I take their revenge. Plain stupid, man. I have nothing to do with them being the way they are, I'm just as dispossessed as them, but they can't get passed their own predicament. It's just like the Nazis for you. Would you trust them?"

That was how it was when you hit a nerve with a friend—they knew all your nerves too. That is how you can tell who your friends are: by how close they hit your nerves.

My *dziadek*[48] was a warrior. A true Polish hero. When Hitler stormed the country in six days many people laid down, but not all did. *Dziadek* was one of those who stood up against the tyrant until the end. I never knew him, because he got hit by a car eight years after the war was over, but the old cracked photographs and my *babcia* told me everything I needed to know.

"No, I wouldn't trust a Nazi, but the Algonquin people are far from Nazis."

"They're my personal terrorists."

---

[48] **Dziadek** — (*Polish*) Grandfather

"Yeah, like dude over there is a real threat."

I pointed down the road, where a wrinkled old man walked slowly in the ditch. He had his hands in his pockets, contemplating the grass.

"Actually, man, we should go ask him if he saw anything."

Atlas' face brightened. We marched across the road to the man. Atlas waved his arms and I got excited. I had never met a real Native person before. I only encountered them in history books, which sucked because they cannot talk back to you when they were locked in those pages.

"Enkoodabaoo[49], how are you?" Atlas inquired politely.

"Eh?" answered Enkoodabaoo, "What do you want?"

He looked us over with a careful eye, trying to continue walking though we were in his way. His eyes were deeply wrinkled. His scraggly moustache was the only thing that looked young on his face.

"I am John Sangman's nephew. My Uncle John hunts moose with you."

---

[49] ***Enkoodabaoo*** — (*Algonquin*) One who lives alone

"John? You mean Hassun[50]? Yes. I remember. You lived with him for a few years, eh? Achak[51]. I remember now. You have aged, *mukki*[52]."

"This is my friend Henryk."

I nodded.

"What are you guys doing up here? Come to visit Hassun?"

"Well, kind of. I wanted to show Henryk the forest. He's an ecologist."

"Oh, a scientist, eh? You come to tell me what I already know?"

Enkoodabaoo laughed heartily, displaying two missing teeth, and telling me with his laugh that he was only giving me a hard time. The man probably knew all the plants by friendly nicknames.

"How long have you been walking this road, Enkoodabaoo?"

"Today?"

"Yeah."

"Maybe two, three hours. Don't have no car. Don't need one. I was born with two cars right here," he pointed to his legs.

---

[50] **Hassun** — (*Algonquin*) Stone

[51] **Achak** — (*Algonquin*) Soul/Spirit

[52] **Mukki** — (*Algonquin*) Child

"Well we've run into some trouble."

"Achak, trouble always finds you well."

"I know. We par—"

"I think that *pauwau*[53] cursed you when you moved here."

"What's a *pauwau*?" I asked.

"A witch."

Atlas ignored the point and continued with his own.

"We parked down the road there and when we came back from our hike the car was missing. Did you see anybody drive by in a red Sunfire?"

"Red Sunfire?"

"Maybe it was the *pauwau* again?" I joked.

Atlas looked coldly at me. I bowed my head and watched my shoes. Atlas could be so fucking sensitive sometimes.

"Yeah I seen it. Cop car came cruising down here. Of course he pushed me around, he thought I was drinking. Stupid. He sees me every other day on this road and everytime he thinks I'm drunk, eh. Yeah, he came down this road, then when he came back he was followed by a tow-truck that had a red Sunfire hooked up to it."

"Fuck."

---

[53] ***Pauwau*** — (*Algonquin*) Witch

"Eh, watch your mouth, Achak. I'll tell Hassun and he'll whip your hide."

"Is there a pound in town?"

"No but there's Bearclaw's lot. Right beside the dump."

"Great. Alright, man. Well, thanks, Enkoodabaoo, you helped a whole lot," Atlas said.

"Yeah, thanks, man."

"Eh, you tell Hassun to bring you out for the next moose hunt. We'll get a big one."

"I can't shoot, you know that."

"You can learn. You just tell Hassun. And stay out of trouble, Achak. And take care of Nootau[54], here," he said, stretching out a hand for me to shake it. "Or should I ask Nootau to look out for our *mukki* here?"

"Nootau?" I asked.

Enkoodabaoo laughed again and waved us off. We went off in the opposite direction, our backs pulling further and further apart until I looked back and he was gone.

"What does Nootau mean?"

"I dunno, man, my Algonquin's not all that good. I only know a few words here and there."

---

[54]   ***Nootau*** — (*Algonquin*) Fire; Enkoodabaoo unknowingly translates Henryk's last name Zdicz, itself a play on the Polish word znicz (torch; flame; fire)

"Do you think it's something bad?"

"Naw, I don't think so. If it was bad, you'd have known it."

"Who's the witch?"

"Man, 'nuff with the questions. Let's just get the fucking car so we can roll a big spliff and get home."

The road parts the way
Back home, in the fire of a
shaman's lost *pauwau*.

LA PULL-IT OR LA OOF
[Martin O'Neill]

"The question is a simple one, *messieurs*[55]," Jaquelyn proposed. "*La poule, ou l'oeuf*[56]?"

"What?" Simon asked.

"The chicken or the egg. *Il parle pas français*[57]?"

---

[55] **Messieurs** — (*French*) Sirs

[56] **La poule ou l'oeuf?** — (*French*) The chicken or the egg?

[57] **Il parle pas francais?** — (*French*) He doesn't speak French?

"No," Henryk answered.

"*Quelle malheure. Qui d'autre[58]?*"

"*Seulement Atlas et moi pouvons parler[59].*"

"Well I need to work out my English anyways."

Henryk and Jacquelyn laughed together. I wished I spoke French, or even Celtic for that matter. For me, it was English through and through. At least Simon spoke Spanish. Henryk and Lukasz both spoke Polish. Simon's new classmate Kenny spoke cowboy. Atlas knew broken bits of a dozen languages, half of them learned from Claire. It was Henryk's intention to help Atlas learn fluent French from his new college friend, Jacquelyn, originally from Trois-Rivières. Her English was not as bad as her disclaimer alluded to.

"The metaphysics besides...these scientists say that it must have been, truly, the chicken that came first," she said

"How do they know?" Simon asked distrustfully.

"Logic. The proteins in the shell are created solely from the synthesis of the parent's cells."

---

[58] ***Quelle malheure. Qui d'autre?*** — (*French*) That's too bad. Who else?

[59] ***Seulement Atlas et moi pouvons parler*** — (*French*) Only Atlas and I can speak

"Yeah, that's right," Henryk spoke distantly, "Plus, it would make sense that there was an asexual chicken whose genes mutated or changed to sexually reproduce. Like, uh..."

"Daphnia[60]."

"Who's Daphnia?" I asked.

"Water fleas. They reproduce—"

"P a r t h e n o g e n e t i c a l l y," J a c q u e l y n overpronounced.

"—Yeah."

"Which is?"

"Where the female only produces females, asexually, without males, until harsh environmental conditions, like drought, or salinity, or whatever, then they produce males. The males sexually reproduce to provide more genetic variation. They create offspring able to withstand the harsh conditions."

"I don't see how that's anything like chickens making it with big bad cocks," Simon laughed.

"It makes sense," I rubbed my chin.

"Well I understand it, but it still doesn't make any sense to me," Simon shrugged.

"Then it all comes down to semantics, man," Atlas leaned forward thoughtfully as he spoke,

---

[60] ***Daphnia*** — (*Latin*) Genus of small crustaceans

"Because if the chicken is the cause for the egg, doesn't the chicken then become the shell for the egg?"

"*Ooo*...the chicken is the egg!"

"The chicken is the egg. And the egg is the chicken."

Jacquelyn's cheekbones bunched up her eyes when she smiled. She clearly understood why Henryk told her she would like Atlas. Atlas smiled shyly, though he missed the critical point of eye contact that could have sealed his sexual fate.

"And both are delicious," I added to level the tension.

"And that's what counts, there, sir," Kenny said.

The conversation paused while everyone took a moment to drink. The autumn evening was warm enough that we were able to hang out in the fenceless backyard on the plastic patio set Henryk and Atlas found on garbage day. The set was incomplete, so Simon and Kenny sat on stools from inside. They were perched higher than the rest of us. When Simon got his bouncy knee it shook the table, testing the balance of our beer bottles. Two citronella candles burned slowly in the centre of the table to keep the lingering fall mosquitoes at bay, but they did little to protect our ankles. Mine felt like a bag of itchy marbles. I scratched mechanically with one hand, the other busy putting a cigarette to my mouth.

"I read in the news—Atlas, you may find this interesting—that they rediscovered this old library in Tibet or some shit," Henryk said. "But this library is in a cave. It was hidden for nine hundred years behind a fresco that finally crumbled."

"Why was it hidden? Why were Buddhist texts hidden in a Buddhist country?" I asked.

"I don't know. Maybe they were worried about Islamic invaders."

"Or maybe they had the meaning of life."

"I love the clouds, when they catch the light of the sun in the evening," Jacquelyn cooed.

The sky was striated by the colours of the rainbow. Each of us craned our heads for as long as we needed.

"Baudelaire said that nature is perfect because it displays all the colours of the rainbow in any single scene," I paraphrased.

"All the colours of the rainbow?" Atlas repeated. "How about the other ones?"

"What other ones?" Kenny laughed.

"Oh, y'know, love, and justice, and unicorn," Simon mocked Atlas.

"Atlas believes that there are not only colours other than the ones we know, but that he's seen them as well," I explained to Jacquelyn.

"Considering that we only see a small slice of the electromagnetic spectrum, I am not surprised."

"What, you got X-ray vision, Atlas?"

"Naw, man. Maybe if you just—"

"Whatever," Simon interrupted. "Don't encourage him, chickee, he's got 'nuff just trying to convince himself of reality sometimes."

It had become clear that Jacquelyn had taken a liking to Atlas just by the gentle way she spoke to him and agreed with his odd notions. Simon and Kenny, devastatingly alpha males, immediately picked up on the pheromones and put poor little Atlas in his place.

"The man's half insane!" Simon cried.

"Or half saint," Henryk defended.

"Same shit."

"Man, I'm right here."

"Don't worry, someone will change the subject. Someone always does."

Cue: me.

Unlike Simon, who had a different outlook on what it meant to help a brother out, I followed Henryk's route of soft encouragement.

"I bet those scripts they found would make an awesome book. I just love the way Tibetan letters look, even if I can't understand them. Think: shapes make sounds that make meaning."

"Oh yeah," Jacquelyn agreed with my idolatry of the written word.

"You know what's better than reading? Writing," Simon said.

"I just can't believe those people'd waste their time on digging up some dusty old papers when they have some real issues like food and water," Kenny said.

"No doubt. Liberation! How about resistance against a repressive government?" Simon said.

"I think there is value in discovering culture," Jacquelyn countered. "That is how you can join people together to form a resistance."

"Yeah, but Simon's not into books," I said.

"You and your goddamned book fetish," Simon said to me.

"*Ooo*, kinky."

"It's about more than just the object. It's about the experience," Atlas argued with Simon.

"Yes, I love turning pages," Jacquelyn added.

"Fuck that—why turn pages when you can turn your life around?"

"Simon's also only ever read one full novel by choice," I explained to Jacquelyn.

"Oh? Which one?"

"*Fahrenheit 451*[61]."

"I've never read it."

"Well you should. Wait, maybe they made it into a movie. Fuck, someone should make it into a movie."

"So how can you judge when you've only read one book?"

"One or one-hundred-and-seven like Martin—it doesn't matter."

"At least your one book wasn't the Bible."

I groaned in appreciation of Jacquelyn's unappreciation.

"I read that novel," Kenny said, "But it ain't very good."

"Naw...but if you *lived* it—then what? You'd probably want to write all about it."

"Then tear it up, man. Would've been just as good," Atlas muttered.

"What I think is wrong with modern society is this exact thing," Simon began, "That we're more concerned with unearthing secret chambers than

---

[61] *Fahrenheit 451* — (*Name*) Ray Bradbury science-fiction novel about a dystopian society that burns the written word

making them, y'know? All that's so Hollywood, so fake, so historic. D'you think those old Buddhists wanted to find old caves with secret writings? Naw, guy, they were *making* them. They were *in it*, y'know?"

"That's right," Kenny said.

Simon was jumpy on his stool while he spoke. He looked at all of us in succession, then settled on Jacquelyn.

"And that, *mademoiselle*[62], is why I've only read one book in my life."

Everyone fell silent. Even Jacquelyn, new as she was, could read Simon's willingness to jump on any conclusion. Finally Atlas broke the silence.

"There are thousands of reasons, and thousands of people to keep them."

"*Perception*[63]," Jacquelyn said.

"*Perspicacité*[64]."

Jacquelyn and Atlas finally shared eyes. Meanwhile Simon and Kenny convened a trip upstairs to the studio. Kenny would practice his harmonica while Simon practiced his country blues.

---

[62] *Mademoiselle* — (*French*) Misses

[63] *Perception* — (*French*) Perception (surprise!)

[64] *Perspicacité* — (*French*) Perspicacity; acute mental vision or discernment

After they left Jacquelyn checked her watch and cursed the bus schedule.

"We'll have a good time. A party," I said, trying to encourage Jacquelyn to come back.

"We should hit up the 'Loo," Henryk suggested.

"Isn't that the bathroom?"

"In Britain, yeah. What kind of English do you think we are?"

"I don't know. The English kind. Can we at least have some *poutine*[65]?"

"You have to taste Atlas' poutine. International poutine—it's got curry and cumin."

"Oh, I love cumin."

Atlas shyed away from the attention. After Jacquelyn left Henryk and I tried to pry open that hardened shell of his. It was no use. Atlas was stolid—and not even stoned yet.

Somehow I felt bad for my friend. I also recognized that his life's path might be beyond the dating scene, even if I did not understand what that meant.

"If you're not interested, I'd definitely be," I said, uncharacteristically chauvinistic.

"Go for it, brother," Atlas smiled.

---

[65] ***Poutine*** — (*French*) Quebeçois pronounciation of poutine: puh-tin

"C'mon, she's digging you. Just give it a chance. It'll be a good time."

"I had a good time."

"I think Henryk meant—"

"I know what he meant. And I love the love, Henny but, like, maybe there won't be any scoring. You just keep setting up good times, because I certainly won't. And don't worry about what happens because it'll happen as it needs to."

Henryk bowed his head. They both had such a profound understanding of one another. Plus Atlas had a way to make Time feel like enough of a victory. Still, Henryk felt he owed Atlas a Jacquelyn, a momento of their time.

"I know. I'm just looking out for you," he said.

Atlas snuffed the citronella candles. They waited until I finished my cigarette. In the meantime we contemplated the colours fading to dark shades in the sky. Henryk pointed out Venus in the eastern sky. I punched my cigarette into our tincan ashtray.

"It's getting chilly," I said. "Let's go have a chicken omelette."

If the present is
fed the future will always
have a bellyful.

I, P.O.D (PHENYLETHYLAMINE, OXYTOCIN, DOPAMINE)
[The Fourth Wall]

This was, unofficially, the third party in Unit 3E since the homeboys moved in. Its life before them could not be told, and since they moved in no one had really kept count. If the count was based on preparation, this would have been the second party, but in scale, this was the third. The first was their house warming party in August, where they were welcomed to the neighbourhood by the police who informed them of the eleven o'clock noise curfew. The second was in September, just after school had started, once the neighbours got used to the ruckus.

It was Thanksgiving. In other parts of the country young adults were sitting at family dinners with basted turkeys, a number of fixings, and a cornucopia centrepiece, recounting their adventures in university, or introducing their new-found significant others. In certain neighbourhoods within the GTA there were a number of families doing just that—which was evident by the number of people buying turkeys, as noted by Henryk and Simon when they went shopping for party food . But in this house, and certainly in many immigrant homes, Thanksgiving was as foreign as they were. It was a holiday. A day off work, and for most immigrants, it was not even that. It was a time-and-a-half workday. Besides that, it was some abstract celebration for the rape and pillaging of the currently disparaged Native peoples. It was a day for pirates, for unfair bargains, for taking advantage, for greed, for pride, for puritans, for parliaments, for patriotism, for a framed freedom— in short, for all the false pretenses the country was formed upon.

So it was befitting that four bastards of the land held what they hoped would be a raunchy party that Thanksgiving weekend. It would, actually, last all weekend, except that the length was not well advertised. These days no one really wanted to party on and on, everyone looked forward to the end of the party, to those end credits where they could reminisce about who was there and what they did.

So Friday night was spent smoking copious amounts of herbature and hanging out in the studio. Jeanne came with Jésus and Tori, and the whole group jammed on the collected musical instruments. Despite the haze, despite the dimmed lights and in spite of the quickly over-taking night the room vibrated with the sweet sounds of harmonious rapture. The kind that inmates would have hummed while doing forced labour in the southern States. A sound that was beyond the bubbling teen emotions, yet born from its steams. A sound that was not necessarily depressed, or euphoric, or upset—but certainly emotional and unleashed from cherished lockets of passion. Even Atlas and Martin, who were not musicians, found the occasion nurturing enough to throw in some vocals or bang the djembe Jésus lended to the studio for the weekend.

The Satellites were hardcore like that. They lived their music. Jeanne, Tori, and Jésus— otherwise known in the local music scene as The Satellites—were going to occupy the studio for the weekend (drummer Wude had taken up a high-end retail job to pay for their recording requirements and would be sleeping peacefully in his own apartment). Their stay was evidenced by the stack of sleeping bags in one corner. That night, after the homeboys rolled into their respective beds with their fingers torn and their ears still ringing, the Satellites recorded a short acoustic set of four songs that would be released later on. For now it was their lullaby.

In the morning the crew had a hearty breakfast at noon. The Saturday party was the one they told everyone about, so people started arriving early enough that there was beer in the backyard, wine in the kitchen, and pot in the studio before supper.

Henryk fired up the BBQ despite the cool weather and cooked Atlas' homemade hamburgers and roasted vegetables. The party-goers, at this point mostly the usual suspects who were familiar to the house and the homeboys, revelled at Atlas' cooking and Henryk's pyromastery.

When the rest of the guests arrived, either by invite or by word-of-mouth, the house had a gentle smell of home-cooking that could have fooled anybody who wanted to be fooled into thinking that this was a halfway house's Thanksgiving celebration. Which it was, in a way.

Except that the usual prohibitions of halfway houses were not only missing, their opposites were endorsed. Simon insisted that everyone put the intoxicants they brought onto a central table so everyone could share. So that you did not bring something you could not share, and no one could experience something someone else could not. It was an interesting concept to a few people who still hid partial stashes of their goods on their persons, because it was hard to break with convention, even under the auspices of someone as conventionless and radical as Simon.

Because even Simon had a gram and a half of cocaine tucked into his jean's pocket that no one would know he had.

Nevertheless there were a myriad of psychoactives available, and a myriad of people to take them.

At some point in the night Kenny left the party.

There was the Table. The Trip Ticket Table. Henryk had a name for everything. The drunker Kenny was, the funnier Henryk was. Henryk did not even need to make sense. What was a Gulag? Or Auschwitz? Was that a Polish sandwich? It was difficult to tell. Henryk stuck around the Table for a short portion of the night, getting his fill.

Atlas moved stealthily around the table, making quiet conversations with the person nearest him, who was never Kenny. It was someone who made Atlas consider something heavy, then laugh in response.

Maybe it was their accents. Kenny noticed that the drunker Simon was, the more Simon's words slurred and took on Latino inflexions. He noticed it first with the word *Revolución*[66], a word Simon announced as a girl, after much consideration and head-shaking reluctance, dropped an ecstasy pill from a jewellery box.

"Someone get Jeanie a trumpet. Put it to her lips. *¡Revolución!* Let the pure youth revolt be

---

[66] ***Revolución*** — (*Spanish*) Revolution

heard, man, be felt *con las manas* over *semanas*[67] after the quake of the first shake"—Simon was absolutely fucked, Kenny thought.

Kenny first eyed the Table the way a poor man looked at jewellery. He had never known drugs, at least no illicit ones other than massive amounts of beer and whiskey, which he was very familiar with. His half empty whiskey bottle acknowledged the fact. But Kenny was interested.

He scanned the room, trying to understand what he thought a drug trip would look like and how it actually looked. It looked like there was nothing special happening. Nobody was naked, there were no freaky body painting exercises, there was nobody trying to fly out of the Studio windows. People talked. And laughed. And touched shoulders, which Kenny found weird, and they half-hugged, and loved each other in a way Kenny thought he couldn't because he had an inexplicable fantasy to pull out his gold-plated Smith-&-Weston and pluck off the idiots who wore their pants too tight or the girls with ridiculous facial piercings.

In the first conversation Kenny had with someone new, he got into a heated argument about guns. Which was unfortunate, because Kenny never

---

[67] ***Con las manas over semanas*** — (*Spanish*) With the hands, over weeks

realized how strongly he felt about his position until this pansy Asian asshole Tori confronted him about it.

So the second thing Kenny did was join in on a marijuana session occurring in the bathroom between Henryk, Lukasz, Atlas and Jacquelyn, who had the strongest accent of the four. That stupid Quebeçois accent. Kenny harboured a deep resent for the provinces (other than Alberta, of course) that he couldn't explain or even fight against. But Kenny held his tongue. He realized, after a few hits, that it was impossible to yell at anyone in candle light. It made everything so chill—*chill*—just like Atlas told him to do when Kenny tried to stand after the first toke and nearly ripped the shower curtain off the rods.

His heart raced. Kenny's first time getting high, not much happened. He felt tired, then went to sleep. But this time was different. When he returned to the party below he realized how difficult socializing was, and how thirsty he was, and how loud that one chick in stripes talked, and how the lamp in the den gave off an octopus' shadow, and that Bunny was sexy, and that Atlas said something meaningful that Kenny promised himself he would remember but he did not. Kenny did not drink any more whiskey, but had another beer, which helped him relax again.

Jeanne ter Baark slept that Saturday afternoon, and after Atlas' delicious supper she felt refreshed. Not like a short bicycle ride through the rolling hills of Èze, but it satisfied her, which was not something she was familiar with. (Being satisfied, that is). Over a gin and tonic Jeanne held small talk with people she had not seen in a while. But there were many faces she did not recognize. She preferred to be a host, there was a certain magical centralness that she found comforting.

She watched Atlas, the former love of her life. But both had diverged silently, consenting to chase bigger dreams that neither could explain. So neither could find a middle ground, somewhere between a paintbrush and a spatula. Jeanne was hurt (more than she wanted to be) when she saw Jacquelyn and Atlas laugh over something they both talked about freely, happily (removed from the party), innocently sitting close (to share a place, maybe something like a middle ground). (This broke Jeanne's heart, so she had another drink). She found the people she wanted to paint most, and gravitated to them.

This worked well, until (three a.m., when only Atlas and Jeanne were left awake) and Atlas and Jeanne smoked a joint together while cooling off on a walk around the block. (This was nothing like finding fresh bread in Cannes, but it satisfied her). Atlas was in a good mood, which put Jeanne in a good mood. At the neighbourhood park the two swung like they had years ago (when they first met). This made Jeanne want to see Atlas closer, which made her want to kiss him. Atlas did not resist. In fact, he fell into a trance as Jeanne's head grew in his vision and their lips were so close together that they tingled. The kiss lasted because neither wanted to end it. (Then they giggled at each other).

Punchline:

Jeanne stumbles back to the Studio, where a very unabridged Jésus was fucking Jacquelyn.

Atlas collapses into bed with a hard-on. He is too drunk to deal with it, and he falls asleep after stripping and climbing between his sheets.

Jeanne stumbles through the hall (trying to remember whose room is whose). The first door she tries is the right one. Atlas is half-asleep and confused, and sees a shadowy figure approach him. It's a haloed Jeanne. The door closes behind Jeanne, and Atlas sits up in bed. (Atlas asks what's up). Jeanne needs a place to sleep. What's wrong with the studio? Nothing, Jésus and Tori just spread all their stuff around and left no room. Jeanne was welcome to sleep in Atlas' bed (he would sleep on the floor). (Jeanne did not know Atlas was naked until) she coaxed him to stay in bed. (He does not understand). Jeanne stripped in the dark. Atlas shyed away until Jeanne told him he could look. If he did not, he would not know what he was feeling. So when Jeanne slipped under the covers, Atlas had a new hard-on (that felt warm on Jeanne's cold thighs). He cooed. But he thought about Jacquelyn. Where was she? What if she came in and saw? But there was nothing that tied Jacquelyn to Atlas besides this night (and Henryk's good intentions). So Atlas felt Jeanne's breasts. Plump. The nipples enticed him, (he unobtrusively fingered them) and he could feel the heat grow between their loins. Atlas' tongue tasted like chocolate. Jeanne's tasted like nothing. (In Nice Jeanne's kisses tasted like red wine, but this was more satisfying). Jeanne knew Atlas was a virgin. Atlas knew Jeanne was not. This made him feel privileged but afraid, so he opted for using his chocolate tongue to do something to Jeanne that he had once only fantasized he would. Now he sincerely doubted he could. (That was, give her a massive star blast orgasm). Jeanne always wanted to feel Atlas' cock (which was larger than she thought it would be; such a humble man for what he was endowed with). Jeanne's pussy tasted like a fleshy honey that became wetter and easier to slip his tongue into. (His tongue cramped, and he wondered if he was ever going to make it). Jeanne made it. Then she invited Atlas in. (He slowly came over her body, the tarp she had always wanted to know him as). Atlas felt like he should say something (but he did not). Jeanne pulled him into her and Atlas felt a shock pulse from his pelvis up his spine. He thought about Jacquelyn, but only for a passing moment (as Jacquelyn's footsteps were covered by the scent of Jeanne's perfume, which was, Atlas remembered, the same one she wore the first night he met her). He moved within Jeanne *as* Jeanne, their breathing not laboured as much as desired, each exhalation a new exhilaration voiced. A moan, a yelp, a grunt. (Atlas was quieter than the sculptor in Monaco, but this was much more satisfying). Jeanne liked feeling so vulnerable under Atlas' wiry frame.

Atlas and Jeanne fucked passionately for what seemed like an eternity, without regard to the party (or to the other social bubbles of their lives). Just two conjoined bodies moving as one, inside and around one another. Atlas tried to recite a mantra that would stave off his climax (but he fumbled the words). Jeanne's moans became unfettered. She came. (Atlas exploded into her).

As they lay in each others' arms Jeanne hummed a quiet tune to herself. Atlas composed an ecstatic poem in his mind. If either had any unsatisfied urge left, they would have pursued their creative bursts. However, both lay motionless. For once, happy. (For once, satisfied).

It was Bunny's second time naked since she got up that Saturday morning. At noon she had a shoot with a gay photographer named Blaise who taped X's over her nipples and asked her to frown.

Late Saturday afternoon, Simon poured bubble soap into the bathtub and made Bunny feel giggly. Simon loved to see Bunny naked, and Bunny enjoyed baths, so it worked out that after they ate Atlas' home cooking they ventured upstairs for a warm soak. Simon was on his early ascent on E. Bunny was only buzzed off a little champagne and the smell of cumin, which made her think of sex. She had smelled cumin on Atlas' hands as he passed out food, so as the bubbles crowded out her nipples in the tub she found herself thinking about Atlas. She wondered if he would last longer than one minute in bed with her. She thought this about many men she encountered. She had thought Simon would last when she first fucked him, but he did not. At least he had the decency to made sure Bunny came.

In the tub Simon applied a guarana and ginseng body-wash to her skin gently, with a sculptor's seriousness, and though his cock grew hard while he did it, when he was finished he simply climbed into the tub and became brother Sy shaping the bubbles into simple figures. Bunny sipped her champagne and laughed.

Bunny did not know Simon purposefully left the door unlocked, until Martin stepped in and stopped with the doorknob still in his hand. He shaded his eyes and asked Simon where the Looking Glass was. Simon avoided a response and invited Martin in. Bunny invited Martin in. Martin met Bunny's eyes and tried to avoid looking down her neck, though Bunny noticed he did sneak a look, which made her smile and sip her champagne again. It was empty, so she asked Martin for a refill. He uhmed and ahhed and finally left on task. Simon cocked an eyebrow at Bunny, and Bunny asked Simon if he could leave. Simon obliged, slowly drying himself with a towel then heading to his room to get dressed.

When Martin returned to the bathroom he found Bunny alone, with her shoulders above the bubbles at one end and her legs above on the other. Bunny motioned Martin in, but he declined. He did not want to get wet, it was cold outside and he would inevitably need a smoke sooner than later. Martin would not even sit. Bunny was not aware that Evelyn Chidor had shown up while Martin was downstairs filling the glass and he wanted to get back to her. It was a difficult decision for Martin, but Bunny was cool with it. She needed a smoke as well, anyways. She stepped out of the tub and looked around for a towel that Martin could not find. His eyes were distracted. Bunny finally found a towel in the cabinet under the sink. She told Martin she would find him outside for a smoke. Martin nodded, though he would be taking an unannounced detour first. He would need to stop in his room to let his erection work itself out before he went back downstairs.

Evelyn watched the party intently from the doorway. She had just started university, so she was no virgin to parties. That said, this one was different. There were countless bottles of liquor, everyone talked with their vocal levels controlled, there were no sloppy compilations of people in odd rooms, and there were weird substances she did not recognize on the table with liquor.

Martin returned with a determined gait down the stairs. Evelyn told him that she had been sent by their mothers to deliver a large casserole. Their families had been close friends before emigrating from Ireland, and Martin had watched Evelyn grow up. So Martin thanked her for the casserole.

He gave props to a man passing them, who thanked Martin for 'that line', which Evelyn assumed was a phrase in *Glossolalia* that Martin helped him produce. Martin seemed embarrassed about the ordeal and asked Evelyn if she wanted anything, conceding, at the same time, that she was still young and probably better off leaving. A short brunette put her hand on Martin's chest and asked him if he was ready for a smoke. Martin apologized to Evelyn and admitted that he smoked, and that he needed to go.

Evelyn shrugged and admitted that she smoked too. Martin held the pack out to her, but Evelyn shook her head. She needed to make a phone call first.

Sensitive. That would best describe Lukasz. On the ride from Waterloo with Jean-Grey and their old friend Ayn, he got caught in an argument about monogamy and found himself arguing for it. Ayn was a strong academic feminist and Jean-Grey, Lukasz thought, was just from a broken home.

Bubbly. Lukasz tasted the beer in imaginary gulps before he cracked a real one over a fat hamburger handed over by Henryk.

Cavil. What Ayn raised when Lukasz asked if he could get her a burger. Ayn did not eat meat or accept chauvinistic butlering from a man anymore —especially not Lukasz, but that was because they fucked two years ago and Ayn became openly disgusted, lamenting that she allowed herself to succumb to her body's animal instincts, though she was well aware that they were perfectly normal, natural and evolutionarily necessary. So Lukasz got high as hell on a blunt with Atlas, Henryk and Jeanne in the studio until they were all irregularly banging instruments and making some sort of tribal sound off.

Caducité[68]. The first word Lukasz heard out of Jacquelyn's mouth. She spoke French to Atlas when she entered the studio, and they teetered out of the room. Henryk left too, for more beer, and Lukasz was left alone with Jeanne, whom he had spent very little time alone with. They talked about recent news: how Lukasz was in his last year of university, and how Jeanne was painting and trying to find design jobs downtown. Henryk did not come back for a long while, but Lukasz enjoyed the conversation with Jeanne so much that he never noticed. Then Jeanne's glass of wine became dry,

---

[68]   ***Caducité*** — (*French*) Caducity; transitory, or perishable

and Lukasz remembered that he had wanted another beer, so they left the studio.

Jeopardy. What Lukasz thought he was playing when he went to fetch a beer and a couple stopped him and presented statements that Lukasz did not understand, so he answered with questions.

Savour. What Lukasz's palette did for his last Polish import beer, the six pack he and Henny splurged on for the party. Polish beer had a certain robustness that lacked in Canadian beer. He and Henryk reminisced in the backyard over cigarillos and their Polish beer, remembering their homeland. Though both had a different fragment of the country imprinted on their young memories, they had a national camaraderie.

Over-rated. That is what someone told Lukasz imported beer was. What a fucking joker. The man had a big belt buckle that ukasz wanted to punch under.

Highbrow. Lukasz was an honour roll student, and smoked an ounce of chronic a month, but he could not bring himself to debate school subjects at parties. Lukasz appreciated the way the Homeboys were able to stay hardcore as fuck, pumping Wu-Tang while debating high level politics, but Lukasz was never one to participate. Parties were for the enjoyment of the small blink moment, not the contemplation of big picture frescoes. So while a debate raged in the living room Lukasz went outside and engaged Ayn and Conrad in simple conversation, the kind he needed to clear his mind from too much thinking.

Jewel. That is what Lukasz thought Ayn was. Normally, there was a tonne of emotional rock that separated the two. But when Lukasz was as drunk as he was, he thought he could fork those rocks right out of the way. So he started with a joke to continue his excavation. Eventually Ayn was distracted by Celina, who took her away. Then Lukasz was left alone in the empty cave he cleared for himself.

Heart-warming. That was how the cherry-coloured ladle above the stove made Lukasz feel.

Unidirectional. The way Simon moved through the house, the Pied Piper of the party in appropriate attention deficit, leading a load one way, then another in the opposite direction. Lukasz was impressed and followed Simon in his escapades to the Trip Ticket Table, where he paused. Simon urged him to take an E pill. Lukasz declined. He stayed away from synthetics. Instead, he downed a couple grams of mushrooms, then felt guilty because he did not know who he had taken them away from. Simon insisted on the legitimacy of the

Table's rules, then led Lukasz upstairs to his room where they listened to a hip hop record while Simon snorted a line. Lukasz casually smoked Simon's hash pipe near the window, ensuring to send the smoke outwards.

Honk. Simon's snorting made him sound like an angry animal.

Tangy. The taste of the mushroom juice that seeped from the quid in Lukasz's cheeks. By the time Lukasz swallowed the mash Simon was hacking at the pipe in turn. Simon called Lukasz his nigga, which made Lukasz feel included, like he really *knew* Simon, though he could not feel the lips Simon could not feel either.

Hmm. Cocaine was an anaesthetic that Lukasz could have used to ease his sensitivities. But Lukasz was too sensible to need erasing.

Votary. The perfect word for Atlas. (A staunch worshipper). (Of something). For the time that Lukasz spent with Atlas he wanted to believe everything the man said. He would have carried Atlas' cross, if it was small or tangible enough.

Uneaten. The last crumbs of shrooms. Lukasz could hardly feel the effects of the few he had munched, so he took the rest. The effects would come, eventually, just like everything. Lukasz went to find Ayn.

Evelyn returned to the party with a certain grimey attitude. She had phoned her mother, who was at the O'Neill's house, but also made a quick trip to the nearest strip mall. She took off her conservative zip-up hoodie, baring her shoulders, which was scandalous as far as she was concerned. She stopped at a drug store to buy lipstick. She considered a dark crimson, then a blazing scarlet, but settled on a natural tone. If she had time she would have painted her nails. Alas.

Atlas answered the door, which was surprising, because no one answered the door the first time she came. He let her in and asked her if she wanted to eat. She told him that she had come for Martin. Atlas nodded and fetched the man. Before leaving, Atlas told her something she forgot immediately because some fat dude bumped into her and asked her if she wanted a shot. Evelyn was new to the party scene, and did not understand the severity of intensity, so she accepted, and was soon downing sweetened liquor with a man who could physically dilute the liquor content in his fatty tissues; the fatty tissues Evelyn abstained from pork and fast food to avoid. When Martin found Evelyn she was giggly. Seeing Evelyn laugh so liberally made Martin feel happy that she came back to the party. He held out his hand and guided her to the backyard for a smoke.

Roxa had not been invited to the party. Not directly. Martin invited David from the magazine, who invited James against Martin's keen avoidance, who then invited his girlfriend Roxa. James decided against going, but Roxa didn't find that out until David had picked her up.

Roxa knew nobody at the party. If Roxa pretended that she was looking for someone no one would suspect anything. This occupied Roxa's time for the first little while.

If Roxa had known any of the Homeboys, she would have known that Simon was going to be the first to find her.

"Wuddup? I'm Simon. Sy. *Sigh*. I don't know if I know your name."

"Roxa."

"*Bienvienedos*[69]. How's your drink? You need a touch up?"

"Sure."

"What's your poison?"

"What d'you think?"

Simon considered Roxa's playful guile for a second.

---

[69] ***Bienvienedos*** — (*Spanish*) Welcome

"I see, I see. Yeah, whatever I like, hey? Sure."

"A business woman," Atlas intercepted Simon at the Trip Ticket Table. "Check the quota…secure your stocks…buy, sell, sell."

"A business woman? What the fuck are you talking about, guy?"

"How do you know?" Roxa asked.

Atlas had already left.

"Business woman? Martin must've invited you. Sure wasn't any of the other three of us."

"Why not?"

"*Chiquita*, you must not know any of us. How about a tour of our wonderful *casa*[70]?"

Simon showed her the different rooms with a circus-esque embellishment. Roxa thought that if Simon did not try to sound like he was joking, he would make a decent salesman.

Simon hugged several ladies and a few men throughout their journey. He was clearly a man with faith in community. He quickly sold Roxa on that idea. He also sold her on his capacity to care. Whenever he ran into a lady he hugged her and asked something that seemed special. Roxa adored that he actually cared.

---

[70] *Casa* — (*Spanish*) House

Simon also sold Roxa on showing her the rooms.

"Each has its own aura. Its own air, even though the windows all catch the same old Mississauga air. That Mississauga air, *chiquee*, it comes from all corners at once and carries everything everywhere. But you know that. It blew you in."

"It's blowing me away—no—not away from here. I mean—"

"I know what you mean."

Simon showed his room last. He did not explain anything when he entered, he just stood at the threshold and let Roxa explore it on her own.

"I like this desk."

"Thanks, I hardly use it."

"This duvet is beautiful. It looks Mexican."

"It is. But it's hard to tell its beauty without feeling it."

Simon did not need cheesy lines, but he had an abundance of them. Roxa rubbed her cheek and lips on it, then Simon suggested she do the same with her other cheek and lips.

As Simon covered Roxa, she pictured him as the ringleader of this crazy circus, and every good business woman knows that you needed to convince the CEO before you sold anything. In this case the CEO had sold her, but every good business woman knows you never admitted to being sold until you handed over the transacted goods or services.

So Roxa passed over her goods.

Kenny returned to the table while the party was winding down. At least he thought it was. He was new to this idea of an extended party, his parties back home usually passed out by now.

He eyed the drugs left on the table. He recognized the E pills from all the people who were talking about them. The jewellery box was empty, though, and the bags of weed were useless since Kenny did not know how to roll a joint. A small bag of mushrooms had been ravaged. There was a small bar of liquor bottles, but none would've beat his whiskey, which he wasn't in the mood for anymore. There were orange pill bottles: codeine and oxycodone. There was an empty bottle of cough medicine, which he thought was odd. He hoped nobody had been sick enough to have offered cough medicine as defence against their inevitable contagion. Fuck. It made Kenny want a cigarette. And some guidance.

So he found Martin, who, of course, was smoking in the backyard with a group of quiet talkers. Kenny asked for a cigarette from Martin, who obliged. Kenny smoked nervously, apart from the table, on the concrete step to the kitchen. Martin eventually included Kenny in the conversation, and everyone turned their chairs to accommodate Kenny's presence. One young redhead, who hung onto Martin's every word, announced she needed to use the bathroom and abruptly left, which braked the conversation awkwardly. Nearing the end of his cigarette, Martin decided to go in for a line. Kenny wasn't sure if that meant a line of cocaine or of poetry, which they'd just finished talking about. Martin invited Kenny along, and three of them walked purposefully passed the regular party-goers for Martin's room.

His room was lined with shelves of books, which Kenny had not noticed until the other dude noticed. Conrad fingered the spine of a copy of *Lolita* and bitched about Jeanne's presence at the party. Martin apologized but did not sound genuine in his apology. Kenny connected the dots and started on a brave macho rant about women and their infinite infidelity. Conrad did not look at him the whole time he spoke, which Kenny thought was rude—but in his chemically-induced jovial mood, Kenny considered that maybe it was because of his exaggerated cowboy slur, or maybe it was because Conrad didn't need consoling, or that he had heard the spiel before.

Martin interrupted Kenny to present Conrad with his line. Kenny asked if the white powder on the mirror was cocaine, and Martin answered in the affirmative while Conrad drowned him out with a snortle. Kenny watched Conrad tip his head back and continue to snort. He recalled all the pamphlets the RCMP had presented over the years about drugs: the failures, the disappointments, the addictions, the malfeasance, the miscarriages, the rapes, abuse, suicide, murder, theft, and insanity. Kenny shook his head. He would not snort crack cocaine. Martin corrected him on the term, but Kenny didn't care.

Martin let a little bit of another crystal powder onto the mirror and asked Kenny what he knew about ketamine. Kenny's family owned horses through much of his youth, so he knew that ketamine was horse tranquilizer. How did Martin have ketamine? Did he have a horse? And he never told Kenny?

No. Ketamine, Martin explained, was a dissociative in humans. A mild hallucinogen. Kenny laughed because he thought it was absurd that horse tranquilizer was actually used as a recreational drug. So he accepted, more to denounce the idiocy than to get high. Martin shrugged and started cutting up the crystals, which, upon closer inspection, looked like small shards of translucent glass.

Martin taught Kenny how to snort a line, and Kenny did. One in each nostril. The act of snorting was exhilarating in itself, except that the powder immediately plugged his nose to the point of discomfort. He continued to inhale until he was able to breathe. At that point Kenny collapsed on the bed.

Conrad would not have come to the party if Martin hadn't invited him. Thrice. Conrad appreciated Martin's coaxing. Plus he knew that the Homeboys loved him.

Conrad spent a considerable time with Ayn when he first arrived. Ayn got chatty for her first few drinks, and Conrad was unusually chatty that evening, so it worked out well for both. Lukasz floated in and out of their conversation. Conrad was hardwired as a writer so he was exceptionally observant, and he noticed that Lukasz returned for Ayn the way Conrad once returned for Jeanne: to seek her out as the stable mast in his Moby Dick quest.

Conrad became sympathetic towards Lukasz's cause. He tried to subtly convince Ayn that Lukasz was: 1. A cool guy; 2. A valid & commendable choice as a partner; and 3. A smart man. These were things Conrad thought Ayn would need in a partner. Conrad had to work with extra sensitivity; he knew Ayn studied psychology and could find his holes easier than he wanted to expose them. Then Celina sat on Ayn's lap and ruined his work with the mindless chatter of the drunk.

Conrad stayed for a while with Lukasz. His pupils were dilated, and Conrad wondered whether he had gotten into the shrooms.

Conrad thought he could see all that he needed to, then. He left Lukasz staring at the stars.

Martin asked Conrad if he was having a good time and apologized for Jeanne's presence. Conrad shrugged. He noticed Martin's nostrils were red and that Martin had beads of sweat on his upper lip and his forehead. Conrad followed Martin outside for a cigarette with a redhead. A cowboy joined them. The cowboy was so obviously out of place Conrad felt bad for him too.

Not that Conrad liked cowboys. He had never been a fan of westerns. They were *über-cliché* and unoriginal. But he had no way of knowing that this surly man was a cowboy, besides estimations from his speech and his tragically unfashionable tucked-in plaid shirt. He could have just been home-schooled.

After the redhead left for the bathroom Martin itched his neck and rubbed his nose. Conrad lifted an eyebrow at him and mock snorted. Martin nodded. Conrad nodded. Martin invited Conrad and the cowboy to his room for a line.

Conrad was no cokehead by any measure. In fact, this was only his second time trying it. He was impressed that after the first time, years ago, he never felt any immediate fiending. He had never thought about cocaine until tonight. It could have been sparked by: 1. Jeanne's impairing presence; 2. The tragedy of Ayn denying Lukasz, an out-of-body mirror experience that made Conrad feel common; or 3. The look he noticed Jeanne shot to Atlas, blatantly ignoring Atlas' flirting with another girl. These things made Conrad inhale the silty powder extra hard and demand another one after the cowboy, Kenny, took his line of ketamine.

The K made Kenny fall onto the bed and stare at the ceiling. Martin shrugged it off and told Conrad it was normal procedure. Just let the man lay. Conrad could not have that, so while Martin took his own line and cut a couple more, Conrad read aloud a poem from the shelves above his head. That kept him occupied until Martin passed the mirror and Conrad was able to go under again. Or go up. He was not sure. His skin tingled from the warmth.

His leg shook. He leaned over Kenny and assured him he was going to be okay. Kenny formed an incomprehensible sentence.

Martin and Conrad fiended for another smoke, so they left Kenny in Martin's room. Conrad stayed behind for a second, and repeated where they would be and that everything was going to be okay until he got an affirmation he could understand.

Conrad pushed the lightswitch down and left Kenny in the darkness.

Kenny was wrapped in a blanket of incomprehension which was neither warming nor comforting.

Where was Kenny, anyway?

Kenny needed his mother. He needed to throw up. He needed to lay down. He was lying down. Okay. He needed to stand up. He tried. The lights were out, so he had no idea if he made it or not. His arm curved over his head, grasping for something, and his legs moved. He watched himself from behind his body. Kenny never saw Kenny this way before. Because that Kenny, with the arms and chest and legs and hair was a different Kenny then the one who watched that Kenny. The Kenny who watched Kenny could have been in Alberta. Which, in Kenny's mind, he was—on his quiet rural route, watching this absurd live video stream of himself in

Ontario. Kenny watched Kenny laugh. The laugh was distorted, it came out all wrong. But that made Kenny laugh more. He completely forgot that he had taken a strong dose of ketamine, which would've been dangerous if he freaked out. Most people think they are going to die the first time they trip hard on ketamine because it dissociates your mind from your body. For Kenny, this was actually welcomed. It was better than his whiskey. Better than that lame marijuana he smoked earlier. This was Kenny. This was K.

K found the door from the light along the floor. He directed his body to it. Then he fitfully guided his body down the stairs. His body found it difficult to move swiftly. Instead it stomped like a retarded horse. He'd get shot, K thought, if he was a horse on the ranch. But this was Mississauga. This kind of thing was acceptable.

Simon slapped K on the back and K spun around, nearly falling on Simon.

Are you drunk? *No.* Are you okay? *Yeah, great.* You look fucked. *I might be; what are you, then?* What am I? *Yeah.* I'm Simon. *That's unfortunate.* You're out of your fucking *cabeza*[71], man.

---

[71] *Cabeza* — (*Spanish*) Head

It was funny because it was so ludicrous. K watched the same urbane hipsters who before made him feel inferior. They were so impractible it was imprudent, these jocular children who could not farm, fish or hunt. They couldn't sustain themselves if the very conspiracies they discussed fervently came true. They would be screwed. Who had ever heard of the last man on earth needing a drive-thru to get fed? These people needed their hipness in order to stay relevant. Otherwise they were nothing.

K? He was something beyond hip. He could survive, with or without television and shaving cream. Yes, maybe K would stop shaving now. He could grow a beard like his grandfather in the dirty thirties, when the dust collected in the curly hairs on his face and made Grandpa look like a prairie sage, and despite the lack of water, food, shelter, clothes, and essentially everything else, he survived. That was something K could be proud of. But these kids couldn't survive. Not these cowards, whose parents ran from their countries because of wars, famines, or whatever else.

Loony. K told Simon he was Loony. Simon had probably never even seen a loon, except on the tail of a dollar coin.

K was unsure how long he sat in the living room staring at the party-goers, contrasting their lives to his own, but at some point he glimpsed Martin and remembered the crystals he had snorted. He wanted more.

What's up, Kenny? *K.* You doing alright, man? *K, Marty, I want some more of that K.* No, you don't need more of that shit. It's a one hit kind of thing. *Fuck that, how many lines have you had?* Blow is different. *C'mon, don't give me that bullshit.* Alright, Kenny, but I'm not responsible for you anymore. *You left me in the dark.* Look if you don't want to have an amateur blackout, you better just stick with your one line and chill the fuck out. *You left me in the dark; you already gave me my blackout.*

Martin slapped the baggie of ketamine into K's chest and walked away. K marvelled at the little crystals then went to find Simon and the Looking Glass.

Roxa lay naked on top of the sheets, dazed by euphoria and the candles Simon had perfunctorily lit. She heard occasional voices from below but they were so far from her. Now Roxa was no longer a stranger. She was alone now, but not a stranger. Roxa shifted her legs and felt her thigh's stickiness.

She watched the candles and recalled what Simon and her had just discussed moments before.

"The electrical grid..." Simon said, running a hand over her skin. "We're plugged in now. Not to the power grid, but to the real grid, the one between humans."

"What do you mean?" Roxa laughed, still light-headed from her orgasm.

"Check it, *chiquee*, the electrical grid works on a touchy balance. Supply and demand. Supply cannot overwhelm demand, and demand cannot overwhelm supply."

"Supply and demand," Roxa repeated the concept she knew so well.

"Yeah, but naw, that's not what's important. What's important is that all of us are hooked up to this grid at all hours. Everytime we flick a switch or turn something on or anything. Click! And boom, that supply and demand metes out, y'know?"

"So that's why you lit the candles? To save energy?"

"Naw. But yeah, I guess. I'm just metaphorizing what I'm trying to say: that we're hooked into the human grid, that endless energy-force-life-flow, y'know?"

Roxa stroked Sy's curly hair and watched the candle shadows flicker on his chest.

Simon left for water, leaving his warmth on the sheets. He dressed and told her to come down whenever she was ready. Roxa nodded and considered a nap.

But Roxa could not sleep. She was not a stranger, and she wasn't a whore either. She did not feel comfortable sleeping in this foreign house.

Roxa was not a stranger and not a whore and not stupid. Her eyes found Simon's trash bin, conveniently set near the bed. On it's edge their condom hung, still glistening in the light. Unseen before, Roxa noticed another condom on the floor, also still wet. Simon was so impatient when they fucked that he'd almost forgotten to use a condom then. Their sex was fierce and urgent. He definitely had not used two condoms.

Roxa was not a stranger and not a whore and not stupid or weak. But Roxa understood, as Simon's body heat dissipated from the bedsheets and Roxa's nipples stiffened, that virgins stay smart by staying strong: that her opposite wouldn't have bought into Simon's charisma.

So Roxa was not sure what she was.

The house was exponentially quieter when Martin decided that Evelyn needed sleep. He helped her upstairs to his bed. She insisted on taking off her jeans and her bra for comfort. He left the room to let her change. He took the opportunity to brush his teeth.

When he returned Evelyn was under the covers. She turned towards the door when she heard Martin lumber in. She asked him for a teddy bear, and Martin apologized because he did not have any. He prepared a makeshift bed on the floor and prepared for an uncomfortable sleep.

Martin would not fall asleep easily. Cocaine is not exactly a lullabying siren. He left the room and grabbed some codeine from the pillboxes. He popped the codeine and saved some oxycodone in case the codeine did not work. He crawled back to his floor bed.

Evelyn broke the silence.

"Martin, thanks for letting me party with you guys."

"No problem. Anytime."

"Your friends are cool."

"We're not always like this."

"I know. That's why I think you guys are cool."

"G'night, Evelyn."

There was a pause, then rustling in the sheets.

"Martin?"

"Yeah?"

"Could you come up here? I want to talk to you."

"I can hear you from here."

"Please?"

Martin climbed onto the bed and lay on top of the sheets, facing Evelyn. His eyes had adjusted, and in the darkness he could make out the oval shape of her face. Evelyn continued in a whisper.

"I want to kiss you."

"I...I don't think you should. I'd love it, but—"

"But what?"

"You shouldn't."

"I know."

"I'm going to go back to the floor now."

Martin yawned. It was a welcomed yawn. The codeine was already calming his racing mind.

"Wait," Evelyn said.

"What is it?"

"That girl Jacquelyn told me something interesting. She's pretty. I wanted to kiss her too. Then she told me this."

Jacquelyn had discussed with precocious little Evelyn the chemical nature of love. She used her current experiment, Atlas, as an example. How at first they become aroused by each others' company, and hormones flooded the brain—phenylethylamine, oxytocin and dopamine (Evelyn had forgotten their names, but later Googled them)—so that when the flirt occurred the hormones peaked. They made the persons feel jubilant, exhilarated, completely magnetized. They alerted the desirous sections of the brain. Touches were amplified. If you didn't check yourself, Jacquelyn said, it was easy to get lost in the hormonal high's upward screwdriver—eventually control was lost and culminated in *chaud lapins*[72], as Jacquelyn said. Fucking, she clarified.

"That's how she controls herself. Interesting, right?"

Martin began to nod off during Evelyn's explanation. He pictured a scenario play out that involved two Erlenmeyer flasks and fizzy chemical reactions.

"But if you get too turned on, you're fucked."

Evelyn laughed at her vulgar use of the word *fuck*, which sounded extra harsh in her mouth. Martin grunted and asked her if she was still turned on. She wasn't. She did not ask him.

Evelyn said goodnight and turned around in bed. Martin had his eyes closed, but explored her with his nose that, though clogged, could pick up her fruity shampoo. He could also feel her warmth on the other side of the bed. If he reached out his hand slightly, he could have felt her skin.

A slight dizziness made Martin uncomfortable, so he turned over in bed. In the darkness and through half-shut eyes he considered his computer.

---

[72] ***Chaud lapins*** — (*French*) Literally, hot rabbits; slang for sex

His pornographic shrine. But Martin was too blitzed to entertain himself. He was not even sure he could get a hard-on, though he was sure if Evelyn was involved he could. But Evelyn already snored softly behind him. Then Martin understood why he had given himself an incredible tolerance for intoxicants: for other times, to fool himself into thinking that he could party hard; and for this time, to lay next to Evelyn Chidor in bed and not ruin her integrity.

So Martin basked in his skin flask, a decomposing cocktail of blood, flesh, alcohol, THC, tobacco, cocaine, codeine, phenylethylamine, oxytocin and dopamine.

Failing to fetch me at first keep encouraged,
Missing me one place search another,
I stop somewhere waiting for you.

Walt Whitman

THE THIRD MOVEMENT

SYMBIOSIS DOLDRUMS

FORMULAE LADY LAY
[Henryk Zdicz]

There was something nostalgic about winter. It was four o'clock in the afternoon but a storm had darkened the skies for the past two hours so the night's coming darkness would be nothing new. The bared elm that crowded the front of the house tapped the window in the wind. Atlas clanked dishes and utensils while he cleared the kitchen for cooking. He looked removed when he told me that you needed an empty kitchen to cook. It made sense at the time, because in fifteen minutes the counter space was packed again.

Atlas poured the wine he had mulling with coca leaves on the stovetop. I sipped the brew and decided music would be in order for our project, so I ran upstairs for the CD player. Atlas liked listening to reggae when he cooked. I drowned out the muffled music coming from Simon's room upstairs and watched Atlas prepare the flour, eggs, and butter.

Atlas' serene focus reminded me of when I was younger and my mother made cabbage rolls and perogies by hand. She would spend a whole weekend preparing a massive batch of food that she had lovingly folded together. My mother nurtured my appreciation for fresh food.

She had not made much by hand in the past few years. Anything could be bought at the grocery store for a fraction of the cost and time.

"Do you know how to knead dough?" Atlas asked.

"Of course," I answered. "Want me to?"

"Could you? I'm going to set-up the pasta roller."

"What did you use in the dough?"

"Whole wheat flour, eggs, some hemp powder, a dash of salt and a few spices."

I never knew how to use spices. For me, cooking was a repetitive formula: specific compounds that created a specific set of circumstances. The tangents Atlas took confused me. But those tangents were also why he was good at his job.

Simon came downstairs while Atlas and I were rolling and cutting the pasta.

"What the hell are you doing?" he asked.

"Making pasta," I said proudly.

"I know. What's wrong with the shit in the cupboards?"

"That's different."

"Right. You didn't get to waste as much time with the store-bought stuff. Hey, you guys got any rubbers laying around?"

Simon politely addressed the question to both Atlas and I, though he really only asked me.

"Not one. Six months, my friend," I reminded him of my abstinence.

"Six months. Wow, what a fucking waste. You know," Simon propped himself on a stool and grabbed Atlas' glass of wine, "I'm seeing Jean-Grey tonight, and she said she could grab Tatum if I could grab Martin. You know where that mofo is?"

"I think he's doing some interviews downtown."

"I thought so. Not going to tell her that, though. She can still bring Tatum."

"You might be more of an idealist than Atlas," I joked.

"Except at the end of the day, man, I'm going to be able to eat my pasta too," Atlas mumbled.

"You guys think there's some kind of magic. Some impossibility to overcome with sex. I don't get it, guy. It's simple science. You put a cock with a cunt and you're going to end up with a fuck, y'know'm'saying? Your friend Jacquelyn told me that too, and let me say that she knew a thing or two about that formula."

The pasta roller's handle crashed to the floor. Atlas grabbed his glass of wine back from Simon and went to the pantry to rummage through cans. I tried to communicate silently with Simon, which was impossible. He kept asking *what?* So I stopped trying.

Atlas came back to the counter with cans of tomato paste. He paid no attention to us and got the tools he needed for the sauce.

"Whatever guy, if Martin does come home let him know he's missed out," Simon shrugged.

"Peace."

Simon left me alone with Atlas. I rubbed my hands together to erase that whole conversation.

"Time to sauce it up."

I was unable to lighten Atlas' mood. He forced a smile when he knew I was trying, but that was because he was polite. Finally, when the sauce was simmering and we were ready to get the pasta boiling, I leaned against the counter with my arms crossed and stared at Atlas.

"Dude, I'm sorry about Jacquelyn. I thought she was tight."

"Nothing for you to apologize about, man."

"You know it's not as easy as he says. There's no formula," I half-tried to convince myself.

Atlas kept his hand on the stove knob for a second, cocking his head as if he was going to say something. Instead he shook his head, and clicked on the stovetop burner. With a soft exhalation a little blue flame zipped around the burner ring.

Puzzling equation:
solving for X when X is
the correct answer.

THE CURATOR
[Simon Arcan]

I flipped through my cellphone's contact list, like I usually did when I was bored. It was a good distraction from my homework, which I had hacked away at so hard this whole week. I thought I deserved time to lay my hammer down and leave the rock unchiselled for one night. But Atlas was working, Martin was at his magazine's anniversary party, and Henryk was studying like a madman for his plant identification test on Monday.

"C'mon, Henny, the plants aren't going to change. You'll remember them all the same without one night's study," I tried to convince Henryk.

"I'm not going to fail. I refuse. I want to do good. Don't you?"

"Yeah."

"Next weekend, man, next Friday we'll all do something together."

"Alright."

The only problem was that next weekend was next weekend, and I was yearning to burn *now*. I wanted out. I wanted to taste the city. Fuck these books for one night. How could it hurt?

I highlighted the middle contact on my phonebook list: Kenneth.

I sent the call, listening intently for my new friend's drawl.

"Huh-lo."

"Yo, *caballero*[73]."

"Hey."

"It's Simon."

"How're you doing, Simon?"

"Alright, guy. Pretty cool, I guess, except that it's Friday and I got shit all to do. What're you saying?"

"What am I saying? About what?"

"What are you doing?" I reiterated.

It was easy to forget that a person spoke in a slang developed to suit the people they interacted with most often. Our miscommunication got me excited about hanging out with Kenny. Our language could clash and he would be starry-eyed at my new words. I could teach him how to find his way through the streets. He would be the receiver of all my useless knowledge.

---

[73] *Caballero* — (*Spanish*) Gentleman

"Well, I just had some supper," Kenny said. "My parents are watching T.V, I think. I'm studying."

"Studying for what?"

"Polly Sci."

"Do we have a test next week?"

"Nope. Just keeping up is all."

"I'm thinking about doing something, big city style, y'know?"

"Big city style?"

"We can grab a mickey and just walk around, and I can show you some cool things off the tourist pamphlets, and maybe we'll hit up some bars and do it up right. Rock a little ganja."

"I don't smoke weed."

"Whatever. S'all good. Just, c'mon, what're you saying, Kenny?"

There was a moment's silence broken by Kenneth's good-natured cowboy crackle.

"Aaalright. But no craziness. No fights. No jail."

"That's up to you, my man."

I arranged to go to his house to pick him up.

There was only a short bus ride separating our houses, but it might as well have been an entirely different city. His neighbourhood had houses that rivalled our whole townhouse row, with wide sprawling lawns that gave the front doors a sense of distance. From the custom-carved door frames the owners watched the world in their housecoats and said whatever they wanted, scratching their balls and snifting their brandy. That was a happiness money could buy.

I knew some kids that grew up in this 'hood, some cool peeps that were down-to-earth too, or at least they thought they were—I had no problem with the folks—I had nothing but my friendship to give to them, and they were just as generous. Atlas said we had good karma in that way—but on the inside those rich fuckers knew they were better than us. Their social strata was too engrained in the functions of society. Money is success. The rich are the winners and the poor are the losers. I know they thought that shit because the rest of us poor motherfuckers had no choice but to live by the strangle hold of those rat bastards.

But whenever I went to one of their backyard pools in the summer I told my dad. I loved to watch him flip. He would trade swimtrunks with me any day. This was the neighbourhood I would have grown up in if my dad wasn't allergic to money.

Instead I hopped off the bus, grabbed a transfer for the hell of it and started my walk, belly full of pasta.

I expected a Texas gate at the end of Kenny's lawn, but it looked suspiciously normal.

Kenny spared most of the details of his family's story. All I knew was that his parents were successful cattle ranchers. Big Oil bought out their land. They had been well-compensated.

Kenny answered the door shortly after I knocked. I expected to wait longer…and that a butler would answer the door.

"Hey, Simon," Kenny greeted me.

"Wuddup K."

"Come on in."

I hesitantly walked inside. Kenny closed the door behind me. He waited for me to take off my shoes before saying another word.

"Hey, Mom? Simon's here."

"Okay, honey."

I followed Kenny's back with my hands in my pockets. The decor was more basic than I thought it would be: no saddles or bullhorns on the walls anywhere.

Kenny's mom was in the kitchen, busily moving over the counter with a knife in her hand.

"This is Simon."

"Oh, hello, Simon," she said without looking up at me.

"Hi."

"I told Kenneth that I could've come to pick you up. It's getting cold out there."

"It's a little cold. I like the walk though."

"Well next time I can pick you up. You're in Political Science with Kenneth, is that right?"

"Yeah."

"How are you enjoying it? Kenneth here says he's got a paw full of trouble for the first semester."

"Oh it's all good. I don't mind it."

"Well that's good. Are you guys staying for dessert?"

"Not sure" Kenny said. "What were you...er, what were you *saying*, Simon?"

"I was thinking we'd hit it up ASAP. I mean, we're on foot for the most part, and public transit leaves so many time gaps in your schedule," I tried explaining my thought-process in the most logical, mom-friendly way. "You ride on their schedule."

"Kenneth's never rode public transit."

"I've taken a taxi," Kenny said.

"That's not public transit," I clarified.

"Your big first ride, honey," his mom ribbed him for my benefit.

I didn't want to seem unappreciative, but I didn't care. I just wanted to go on and get out.

"The next bus downtown is at quarter to seven. After that it won't come 'til eight. Then we'll really be running late. We can eat somewhere downtown if we need to. I'll feed you full of city, then take you through its bowels."

"That sounds disgusting," his mom said. "Kenneth, please be careful."

The subway ran every five minutes. It took Kenneth forever to actually leave, so when we did I picked up the pace to the subway station.

"I hope we're not late for this bus."

"We won't be," I said.

"It's 7:10."

"Yeah, we'll be alright."

By 7:30 Kenny had paid for his first subway ticket, and five minutes later we were riding the bullet. Kenny kept it cool, not saying much. The way his eyes flickered, and the way he constantly smiled signalled something devilish.

"We should hit up the LCBO[74] before it closes. Get some liquor," I said.

"You guys and you're crazy government liquor shops."

We got off on Bay and each bought a mickey that we stashed in our coat pockets. Kenny mused about how he felt like a Native with his paperbag follies.

---

[74] **LCBO** — (*English*) The Liquor Control Board of Ontario

"Haha! You're crazy man. You gotta keep that shit down though. You can't say that kind of stuff around here."

"Why not? Are there Injuns in the Big Smoke?"

"They're the only real citizens of this continent, my friend."

Atlas would tear this guy a new asshole (proverbially…Atlas was no fighter). I would have to clean this cowboy up. For now we'd get drunk. The lessons would come later.

In a paved alley I cracked open my rum and Kenny cracked his whiskey and we took the harsh first gulps. We clinked mickeys as an early streetlight flickered on.

"So where're you going to take me?"

"We're here. This is it. We are where we need to be. Wherever we are is where we need to be. Did you think I was going to tour you around on a fucking bus with polite indications of where some historic locations were? You think this shit is some walk-around tour of Toronto? Man, this is *it*, this is living it. This is putting the pieces of the puzzle together as you find them."

"S'long as I don't get raped, I'm good to go wherever."

"Good. Lessgo."

"Where to?" Kenny jogged to keep up with my sudden pace.

"I don't know."

This, an alley—
this, the endless sidewalk: living
is the museum.

THIS AIN'T THE BACK FORTY
[Simon Arcan]

Me still. Where did you think I'd go?

Out of the corner of my eye I watched Kenny. His cowboy boots clunked on the staircase. If they didn't catch attention then his laugh did. I would've regretted hanging out with the man if I wasn't so drunk.

Over the course of the night Kenny lectured me on what it meant to be a cowboy. He pointed out some alleged fakes leaning against tables near the bathroom. I hadn't noticed them. I eyed the ladies who passed and nudged Kenny's burly ribs only to get that obnoxiously grunted laugh. *Hurh-hurh-hurh.* I imagined Canada's highlands sounded like a chorus of belching joy.

More beer! More beer! Pitcher upon pitcher. Lecture upon lecture. If you asked Kenny he pretty much knew everything you wanted to know.

We got kicked out of the second bar because he tapped a passing waitress' ass. He blamed it on me so we both got hustled out by the bearded bartender.

"You can't do that kinda shit."

"Aw, them smelly buggers don't know how to show a woman what she's worth."

"It's a bit of a walk to our next stop."

"Walk? Goddamnit, don't you city people ever drive? No quads or big honkin' trucks, but at least an old clunking Model A or something. Goddamnit, I'm gonna get junkie thin hangin' out with you slickers."

At the fourth bar the hip hop music made Kenny feel uncomfortable, so he tried to convince me to leave. I enjoyed watching him out of his confort zone—he lowered his head and surveyed out of the top of his eyes, fiddling with his glass and tapping one boot nervously.

I knew what was going through his head over and over. I could see it held back on his eyebrows that would fold in the middle everytime a black guy passed us for the bathroom. I twirled a bit of curly hair at the back of my head and taunted him.

"I dig this song. Listen to that bass line."

Kenny just shook his head.

"Wuddup? You don't like hip hop?"

"No," he scoffed like I was supposed to know it.

"Really?"

"I bet you don't like country."

"Yeah, actually, I do."

"Name one country singer."

"Garth Brooks."

"Everybody can name him."

"Country and hip hop are essentially the same music. All music's the same when it's making money. It's just some bullshit lullaby about money and euphoria and ego."

"Country ain't bullshit."

"Okie dokie."

"Not like this nigger music."

What. The. Fuck.

Behind Kenny, a man slowly turned around to look at him. He arched an eyebrow that raised a parallel curve in his baby blue doo-rag. He looked me in the eyes, then he evil-eyed Kenny.

"You can't say that shit, guy. You're gonna get your ass beat."

"Whatever."

The man considered Kenny for a moment, but he must've thought Kenny was early for Halloween in his cliché gear, so he turned back to his table.

"Just shut. The fuck. Up. It offends me when you use that word. I'll fucking choke you with your own saddle, redneck."

"What?" Kenny cocked his head challengingly.

"Let's take this outside, motherfucker."

Outside I punched Kenny in the arm lightly and threw my hands up.

"What are you doing? You're trying to get yourself killed, or what?"

"I'm just sayin' what I'm sayin'."

"Say it, say it all, whatever. But not here. Not now. Time and place, man, time and place."

"That place was queer anyway."

"It's almost closing time. So whatever. Let's just fuck it. You can come crash at my place if you want."

"I don't know my way home."

"Then I guess you better not piss me off anymore."

We walked slowly. I was pretty drunk. I made a couple of wrong turns. We ended up passing the bar we left before I figured out which way we should've been going. To save time I cut down an alley, hoping K would keep up. Cowboy boots made terrible walking shoes. He clunked along behind me.

Two blocks later we hit a residential road. It was the quickest route back to the subway station. The street felt abandoned. When voices broke the silence, we both spun on our heels.

Maybe the old church was right, maybe the physical earth is not round. Or maybe their only blasphemy was denying that the world was round.

"Yo, son."

The tall figure turned from silhouette to form to silhouette as it passed under the streetlights. There were four of them. I knew before recognizing him that it was the guy from the bar. The man in the blue doo-rag.

Of course. The world is round.

"Yo, b. Now, look who it is. Niggas. Y'all know who this is, *niggas*? And that nigga who was with him," the man pointed to me. "This cracker paying you to hang out with him or something?"

"Naw, man, naw. Just chill," I pre-empted the situation.

"I'm chill, guy. Just wanted to make sure Billy Bob wasn't harassing you. 'Cause I heard he's got some nice names for us. Eh, Bobby?"

"It's Kenny."

Kenny had a smug look in his face. He turned both feet to face the approaching party.

"Ohhhh. Kenny. Oh, aight, *Kenny*, whatever the fuck you say. It's just that, y'know'm'sayin, I just don't go 'round calling people niggas and crackers for no reason, like I'm some ghetto motherfucker who has no intelligence or who doesn't know how to be respectable in society. But do you do that, Kenny? My name's Lex, by the way, unless you wanna just stick with nigga."

Kenny puffed up his chest, putting his hands coolly in his pocket. Lex pressed right into Kenny's chest.

At any moment the air could snap—that quiet block would explode to smacking fists, heaving knees, huffs of testosterone. Lex's crew circled Kenny, and I backed away. When I hit the curb I sat down on it. I found a cigarette butt and lit it.

If it had been anybody else I would be right in there with them. But—

Kenny pushed Lex first, so Lex snapped right back with a fierce punch to the face. Kenny jumped on Lex, and the crowd of three dove onto Kenny, mobbing him. Under the drunken haze (made worse by the streetlights) the mass of men became difficult to distinguish. It looked like everybody was fighting each other. It was hard to tell who was who, if that was Lex dropping his fist or Kenny lifting a stiff leg to the face.

"That's a nigga for you. There! Now run tell your friends that some niggas did that to you. Eh? That was what you wanted from us, right? Right, motherfucker?"

The commotion stopped. One body lay on the floor, in the middle of the street, while four hung over it. Lex looked over to me. He had forgotten about me. I watched him watch me. He took a step towards me but stopped. There was a car coming down the street.

"Lessgo. Don't let this man pull that kind of shit next time, brother," Lex shouted to me.

The car's headlights lit up Kenny's folded body on the pavement. I ran out to make sure it stopped. There were dark spots growing underneath him. He spat. The car stopped a few metres from us and I could see that there was blood in blotches beneath Kenny. I grabbed him by the shoulder, helping him to his feet and taking him to the curb.

The car continued and we were in the orange darkness again.

"You alright?" I asked.

"I think I broke a rib."

"Wanna go to the hospital or something?"

"Why didn't you jump in?"

"I don't fight."

"Why didn't you help me?"

"You started your own shit, K. You deal with the problems you cause."

"That's not how we do it back home. We fight for our men."

"And I do. But this ain't back home. This ain't the local bar where you see the same faces everyday for decades and people get to know your humour and shit. This ain't *Cheers*."

"Those fucking niggers."

"Holy shit! Did you not just learn your lesson? Or am I, like, an outdated Mother Goose?"

"I should've brought my nigger-stick with me."

"You need sleep."

"That just ain't decent. I'm going to get my shotgun. This is my land that those idiots are makin' a mockery of."

"Naw, naw, naw. That's not how it goes down. Let me tell you what's going on. You're gonna go to sleep. You're gonna wake up with a headache. You'll forget about most of tonight. But you'll remember what's important. You're crashing at my place. We'll clean you up before you go home to mommy looking like a fucking rag doll. Hey, don't forget your boot out there in the middle of the street."

This ain't your land.
This ain't the back forty,
whatever the fuck that is.

IF SUFFERING DOES NOT COUNT THEN WHAT'S THE POINT?
[Martin O'Neill]

"So help me through this shit," Atlas tapped a pen against the stack of papers which comprised the Canadian Census document.

It was not rare that all four of us hung out, but it was rare that while hanging out we had a goal to accomplish.

"Fuck this census. I don't want the government tracking me like they know me. Like they have any right to interrogate me? Fuck that," Simon said, to nobody's surprise.

"Well I'm filling it out, so do whatever you want, man, I'm still counting you in."

"Whatever."

"Let's do this," Henryk sat attentively on the edge of the sofa.

"I already filled out the address, all the preliminary shit already. List the people who live here. Alright, alright..."

Atlas scribbled away. He read the questions aloud in a mocking monotone.

"Did you leave anyone out of the list of who lives here because you did not think they should be listed?"

"You shouldn't've included Sy 'cause he's an anarchist terrorist, and Martin 'cause he's funding the Irish militia," Henryk said. "We're cool though."

"Hey, if they didn't want to support a free Ireland they should've come with their guns blazing," I interjected jokingly. "Instead they let us migrate and borrow their money."

"Oh shit, are they going to ask about the size of our arsenal?" Simon joked.

"Is anyone who lives here a farm operator who produces at least one agricultural product intended for sale?"

"See? What the fuck do they gotta know that for? Shouldn't they know that by how they tax? Or what? The redundancy of bureaucracy!" Simon said.

"Well, we do consume at least one illicit agricultural product intended for sale, but I don't think they'll approve," Henryk admitted.

"Does the farm operator make daily management decisions related to the farm?"

"How much weed do we have left?" Simon asked.

"Okay now for the personal stuff. Sy you're up f —"

"Fuck that."

"Alright, fine. Henryk."

"Go."

"Birthday..." Atlas knew all the easy things. "Sex...Marital status?"

"Ho'ing around."

"Not an option. I'll put single."

"You cunts are basically like my harem," Simon laughed.

"Ah man, imagine we put common law for all four of us?" Henryk asked. "Common law covers same sex right? Fuck it, none of their business. Put common law."

"No way," I protested, only half-jokingly. "I don't want to be a contestant for a top secret spy job with CSIS and have my gay census results be the deciding factor against me."

"Put common law on mine, I don't care," Simon said.

"Sorry, Martin, the harem has spoken. Henryk, you're relationship to me, as *Person One*."

"We should put that each of us are each others' fathers," Simon laughed again, having way too much fun.

"I'll just put roommate for all of you. Okay, daily activities. Do you, Henryk Zdicz, have problems hearing, seeing, communicating, climbing stairs, bending, learning or doing similar activities?"

"Only on the weekends."

"Does a physical or mental problem reduce the amount or kind of activity you can do at home?"

"Sometimes."

"At work or school?"

"No."

"In other activities?"

"No."

"Okay. Where were you born? Poland. Are you now or have you ever been a landed immigrant?"

"Yes."

"In what year did you become a landed immigrant? If exact year is not known, enter best estimate."

"Probably 1923."

"Can you speak English or French well enough to conduct a conversation?"

"*Oui, bonjour* [75]."

"What other languages are you conversable in?"

"Polish, Swahili, Zulu, and the language of love."

"What language do you most often speak at home?"

---

[75] ***Oui, bonjour*** — (*French*) Yes, hello

"Nonsense."

"What were the ethnical or cultural origins of your ancestors?"

"Really?" I asked. "They ask that? That's kind of cool. They can probably string together a crazy web of origins on this continental vestige of the forsaken," I voiced, thinking about my crazy web.

"Or they're trying to organize a systematic holocaust," Simon protested.

"Say mostly Caucasian, for my ethnic origins," Henryk answered. "Then one part Ruskie. Some German. A little French. But Caucasian, I guess, covers most of it. Maybe throw in some gypsy and Mongolian in there, just for good measure."

"Can never be too sure. Where were your parents born?"

"Both in Poland."

"Have you completed your highschool diploma?"

"I don't see how one relates to the other," Henryk took a defensive tone.

"They don't, man, this is the next section. This shit's boring, I'm going quickly and filling in what I know about you already. Next: last week, how many hours did you spend doing unpaid housework? Huh, that's a question for all you motherfuckers. When was the last time any of you did dishes? Or swept?"

"We leave that to the bitch," Simon murmured.

"Hey, I do dishes," Henryk said.

"I vacuum," I claimed my share.

"True enough. So Sy's the lazy motherfucker. Do you even make your bed?"

"Why? I'm just going to mess it up again."

"Last week, how many hours did you spend working for pay, or self-employment?"

"Does keeping myself entertained count as self-employment?" Simon asked in response.

"Do you have arrangements to work in the next four weeks? Did you look for paid work in the past four weeks?"

"No."

A sudden guilt fell on Henryk. It made him sit back with his head down, his eager smile gone. He knew when Atlas was getting disappointed. I recognized it too. With Atlas, you had to know him for a long enough time before you could figure out what he was chiselling away from himself to slowly reveal.

Atlas had a good reason to get us all together to do this. We could have easily filled it out individually.

"Could you have started a job last week, had one been available?"

"Yeah. I could've. If—" Henryk started.

"When did you last work for pay or self-employment, even for a few days?"

"Summertime."

Atlas had stopped writing the answers down.

"Atlas, I detect something more than a census," I interjected, breaking the fourth wall so he knew I was being serious.

"Naw, man, it's nothing like that."

"You're not even writing down the answers. Plus, you know these details about us. What's up, man?"

Atlas sighed. He sat back in the armchair. He chewed on the end of the pen before answering.

"I'm just so fucking strung out from work, man. I put in so much of my good energy in, y'know? And I'm getting so little back. I wake up every morning revived, ready to take on the world, and I come home smelling like fried shit and my feet hurt, my back aches, all of you are roaring for the night and I'm purring asleep."

"Why don't you find a different job?" Henryk asked bluntly.

Atlas did not answer. The four of us sat in silence; the three of us in contemplation, and Atlas resting his head on the back of the armchair with his eyes closed. If anyone spoke before Atlas did it would break him. I watched Sy, expecting a retort. When he looked at me I shook my head to make the moot point.

"I'm just tired, man. I'm sorry," Atlas said slowly.

"Don't apologize, Atlas. You have nothing to be sorry about," I explained, speaking for the dejected Henryk and the objectionable Simon. "You work the hardest out of all of us and you know we all appreciate it. You are the man around here. If you're tired, sleep. We'll all keep the place together. If we're not, give us hell. We're adults. We'll handle it."

"Plus summer's only a semester away, we'll get some money back to you," Henryk added.

"I'm not worried about the money."

"I know."

Anybody could have made the point that Atlas had bitched about going to university and quit. Now that he was doing what he thought he preferred to do, he was bitching about it too. But we had all been there before. Bad faith had bound all of us to something we did not understand. Atlas had a purpose of a magnitude higher than the census could survey. But there was just no way to tell him without leaving the hopelessness of no final answer, no stars you could point to to draw the constellation. It was a gestalt of stars that formed Atlas' constellation.

There was just no way to tell him.

"I'll finish the census," Henryk offered.

"I know what you need, homeboy," Simon perked up. "You just need something to stay awake for."

"No, Sy. That won't solve anything."

"Oh? No?"

"Oh shit."

"Don't."

There was just no way to tell him no.

Count the muscles, the
bones, the teeth in the gums—that
does not make a smile.

PERISHABLES

[Simon Arcan]

"Holy hell. Dig this, Henny. Eff-bee-eye shot a two-headed sasquatch on Parliament Hill. There you have it. Straight up."

"Stupid rag," Henryk agreed.

I picked up the tabloid, whose headline professed the second-coming of Jesus in a Memphis garage.

"How many of these do you sell?" I asked the cashier who was busy scanning a bachelor's processed dinners.

She glared at the magazine, then met me with eyes as glossy as the paper I held in my hands.

"I mean, seriously, who's buying this shit? Some stupid motherfucker must be, 'cause the shelf's half empty—"

"Maybe it's half full to convince people that someone thinks it's worth buying," Henryk said.

"No doubt. You know what'd be funny?" I flipped to the centrefold, "If they had a full page rolling paper right here, and were like, roll a bat with this and write our next issue."

"I bet we could fiction up some better shit than what's in there."

"Yeah, and it's called the rest of these stupid magazines. Poison! A store full of poisons."

Henryk and I dialogued half out of boredom, but mostly in show for the other people in the grocery line who were numbed from the halogen lights. The two of us had volunteered to be responsible for procuring food now. Atlas was busy, plus he cooked. And Martin couldn't be trusted, he would come back with bag loads of frozen pizza and chips and pop.

Henryk knew how to shop for soul food. For him grocery shopping was a rehearsed porno: the organic act of gathering materials for nutrition, stamina, cleansing—repeated, precariously, once a week with only slight differences to add some emotion to the ceremony.

Me, I was just frugal as fuck and wouldn't let some corporation poison my body and render me lazy for their own benefit. I wouldn't be enslaved by my own needs.

I ploughed the shopping cart against its wobbly wheel while Henryk walked ahead, thoughtfully offering suggestions for food.

"Cabbage. Gotta have cabbage. Dark greens—I love kale. Munch this. Iron rich. Iron, man. Fish, got to have fish."

"Check out how fresh this salmon is."

"Sure. As fresh as it can be flying in from Newfie-land or Bud Columbia. So long as it's not coming out of Lake On-dump-io."

"We're out of cereal."

"Here, rolled oats. Some of this horse grain too."

"Naw, man, there's gotta be a cheaper brand."

"We're going to need a look-up counter then. How many cereal choices do we really need?"

"You need enough to stand in this aisle and forget about your choices and revert to the commercial you've seen most. It's just shocked soccer moms blacking out and ringing out jingles like a locker combination they've gotta remember."

When we got to the check-out counter we had a cart scantily full with fresh meat and whole grains covered in vegetables and fruits. It was easy to be defiantly healthy in the store. Later, when the munchies got the best of us, we'd crumble and crave cookies, trans-saturated fats, and monosodium glutamate.

We checked out our own goods at the self-checkout. The robot had no idea that our vine tomatoes weren't the bulk roma tomatoes, or that our green peppers were red and orange, or that we had the pricier organic bananas and apples. It was the store's own fault—if they didn't like it they could fire me. I hadn't read the operating manual. I'm just an innocent shepherded customer.

We bought a box of chicken, whose price tag we covered with the cheaper package of chicken gizzards.

Henryk stuffed twenties into the thin mouth. Oz paid Henryk and Atlas well enough to cover our groceries and then some. It was a clean deal with the robot. Henryk's dirty money was now anonymous with the rest of the filthy bills. The supervising cashier dutifully twirled her pen and stared blankly, bored, her lip ring the only indication that she wasn't always a comatose pawn. There was life beyond cabbage and fresh salmon and microwave dinners.

I wheeled the wriggly cart to the Sunfire, on loan to Henryk. We would have to pick up Atlas after his afternoon shift. As we loaded the trunk I stared up at the billboard dauntingly overlooking the parking lot. We had never come to this budget grocery store, there was a closer one to the house. But I convinced Henryk to come out this way so that we could see the billboard with Bunny sprawled across it, wearing only jeans. Not that that was anything special, there was a dirty magazine full of provocative billboard ads across the city at any one time. Our pilgrimage was to support Bunny, or at least sneak a peek at her supple skin.

Henryk continued to load our fabric bags while I stared up at the planar body. Her eyes were marked with long streaks of glittery blue make-up, her hair was flying back, her lips parted in a pout— breasts down, ass up, feet wrinkled in geometric point—she slithered forward although everything about her pulled back. Then her eyes—usually bright, flickering between thoughtless innocence and composed sardonism—were stark, surrounded by suggestively coital eyebrows.

Henryk shut the trunk and stared up at the billboard. He wrung his face in contemplation, then grinned. Bunny would be plastered on the wall for a month, preserving the jean company's shiny new hook over the older neighbourhood's bricks and plaster which crumbled away beneath it. The dilapidated old buildings looked like creepy old men oogling the modern femme fatale. Bunny stared beyond all of them, out to nowhere, like a zooed animal pacified by its caged protection.

Henryk started the car while I searched through the tapes Atlas haphazardly stacked in the middle console. I couldn't find anything to suit my mood. I asked Henryk for a suggestion and he shrugged. He idly stared over the steering wheel.

"Wuddup?" I asked.

"I didn't want to stare. But I can't not," he pointed with his head.

"Why not?" I asked before I looked.

An old man, with a yellowed beard tickling his belly, stooped over a rusted shopping cart. An empty can rattled in the bottom like an organ grinder's dancing monkey. He crossed slowly in front of us.

"He's probably just going shopping."

"Hey, man," Henryk giggled. "That's not funny. He's probably hungry. And he's come to scrap for food. Too bad we didn't buy any non-perishables."

"How could we have known?"

"Normal people buy non-perishables," he said.

"Normal people are fucked over by their easy food."

"It would be nice to be able to give the guy a hand. Good karma, you know? I didn't exactly make this money doing productive things. It would be nice to see it do some good."

"Chill out Robin Hood. Let the man be."

"I guess he needs a lot more than non-perishables."

"He's just as perishable as the rest of us."

The old hobo was out of our view but we continued to stare over the dashboard. My cheeks filled with a buzzing. They wanted to giggle, to sob, to lash out and harangue someone in a suit, to be slapped, hard.

Squeaky wheel whistles
mindless jingles unheard by
the men in their car.

A HARD DAY'S WOK
[Atlas Sangman]

"Hey there, m'boy, they got you cooking for 'em?" Waydie asked.

Kenny's dad had looked me over carefully before approaching me. I smiled to reinforce my benignness, and he roughly smiled back.

"I enjoy it," I said. "I don't mind."

"Jesus, you should come over more often then. We could use a coosie[76] in this household. But it's good on ya. It's a good way to feed it forward. There's nothing worse than having all the talent in the world but having nowhere to put it."

I offered an inquisitive *humph* to fulfill the Waydie's thoughtfulness. He sauntered over to a cabinet and pulled a stumpy bottle from it.

"How're you liking city life?" I asked, more out of discomfort than curiosity.

"Doesn't take as much hazing—in fact, feels like yer being herded here and there. The streets always have cars on them. People don't seem to sleep. Well, it might not be for me, but I can get used to it."

---

[76] ***Coosie*** — (*English*) Old school mid-western slang for a cook

I wanted to ask if he was too old to bother getting used to anything.

"It's a good thing we're here though. You can take and take from the world, but eventually you have to give back. That's what some folks don't realize."

Waydie poured some scotch into a mug and leaned his ass against the kitchen counter. He crossed his arms in thought and kept his eyes trained on nowhere in particular. I continued to cut vegetables, trying to give myself a thoughtful air by nodding my head.

"It's an easy thing to forget, that. That you're life is here on earth," Waydie continued in his slow drawl. "Some people expect that they can take their chequebooks with them when they die. But yer born naked and alone, and die that way too. And I've seen a few funerals in my time, and boy I can tell ya, I've never once seen an armoured bank truck following a hearse. You leave all that stuff behind. Some folks don't realize that. Not even my wife, sometimes, and certainly not Kenny. I forget too. That's why I try to remember. If you believe in reincarnation, like the Hindus with their caste system, then even when you're done with this body, you leave, and maybe you show up here or there, but either way, you don't get back what you left behind. Not even yer memories. Now I believe reincarnation in the Indian way, because I've got some Cree blood in me. I know that my life happens here on this earth, in this body. Whatever happens after or happened before don't matter 'cause it's gone or non-existent."

By this time I had the wok heated. The onions and garlic sizzled as I dropped them in, so it became difficult to hear Waydie's voice over the popping oil.

"You know, that canola oil could've been grown by my neighbour."

"Oh. Cool."

"He was an asshole."

"Oh."

"Just like that, all the quarrels and conflupmtions we make, we just keep that miserable old war going. No different than Vietnam, or Iraq, or anything. You just hate to be born in the crossfire, so why in the hell would you put up any fire to begin with?"

Waydie refilled his mug with scotch. The man was iron tongued. He kept a stolid face while he gulped his liquor.

"I'd hate to be reborn as this chicken," I joked for lack of anything imposing to say (and for fear of revealing my core beliefs).

Although my suffocated childhood had left me with too much to say, my conflagrant teen years had taught me that what I had to say probably shouldn't be shared—with the wrong people, I guess, was the proper addendum to that. While I liked Waydie from the little time I had known him, I didn't want to be the ambassador for urban culture. I didn't want to be the one who left bitter counter-culture spit in his conservative blue mouth.

I wondered if Simon had spoken with Waydie at all.

"That chicken serves us both well," he said. "But you should've used beef."

"Sorry. I didn't want to raid your freezer."

"It's okay, boy. When yer in this house, act as if it's yer own."

"Thanks, Waydie."

"All in a day's work. I open my house so you can open yer offerings to others. That is how it works."

I smiled as Waydie left the room with a fresh mug of scotch. I would've let Waydie's words swelter in my thoughts, but I had food to cook. The smell of cumin, cayenne and curry opened my nose, and I stirred the wok with a religious fervour.

Onions sizzle, meats
corrupt, spices martyr and
the hungry get fed.

A GOLDEN THREAD AND A FAITH IN FABRIC
[Henryk Zdicz]

"Oh, oh, yes! The alignment of the planets. Nibiru will descend. I'm telling you, twenty-twelve is very real. Why wouldn't it be? Do you believe anything different? The energy of the earth tells you, doesn't it? It's creaking like an old man, like it's tired of this parasite it has caught whipping around this crazy universe."

Goldie spoke wildly, closing her eyes when she accented points and tipping her red cup of fruity mixed drink while she gestured. I'd forgotten how I started conversation with Goldie. That could be attributed to the five beers I'd had, or to Goldie's stunning beauty.

"Atlas!" I called after him as he passed. "You gotta meet my friend Atlas."

Atlas needed female companionship. I would help him with that. And I needed a reason to stop talking about something I didn't care about. Atlas would help me with that.

"His name is Atlas?"

"It's weird, I know, but you'll like him. Atlas!"

I wrapped my arm around his thin shoulders. I leaned into Atlas' face and pointed to Goldie.

"Goldie. Her name's Goldie. You'll like her. Tell him what you were telling me, Goldie."

I leaned away after I slapped Atlas on the back. I watched as if I was behind a two-way mirror. The voyeuristic angle was amplified by my bottle's prodigal attachment to my lips. Atlas was empty-handed, but wore a long beaded glow-in-the-dark necklace some couple handed out earlier. It was dull and vain in the dim light, struggling to glow. Still, its light trailed in my vision.

"Uh. Hey."

Atlas knew how to catch a lady's attention.

"Your name's really Atlas?"

"Yeah," Atlas laughed politely.

"Really? Wow, that's cr-*aaa*zy."

Atlas wiped his mouth and eyed me. Without words I knew he badgered me, asking if I really thought he would like her. I slowly nodded in animated response.

"What were you saying that got Henryk all flustered?"

"A threesome—no!" Goldie tried to joke, but couldn't follow through. "Twenty-twelve. Have you heard about it?"

"No."

"Really?"

"No, yeah, I have. I was just joking."

"Ohmigawd, I'm telling you, twenty-twelve is the *end*. Do you know it? Have you heard that the centre of the Universe is going to be aligned with the earth? And it's going to send all it's weird energy and whatever right to us, and we're going to receive it, and it's going to *change* things."

"Time wave zero," Atlas mumbled.

"But how are we not aligned with the centre of the Universe all of the time, if it's the centre?" I asked the question previously posed to Goldie, for Atlas' benefit.

"Good point. But, man, I'm no math pro," Atlas shrugged.

"Neither am I. There's regularly stuff in the way, Henryk. All that stuff will be out, just enough, for the centre to be directly aligned with us."

"That's a lot of stuff to move just for us," Atlas said.

"It is. And a whole bunch of religions and ancient sciences and stuff come to the same year: twenty-twelve. But obviously the Mayans are the ones *everyone* knows about,"—she said this like she was personally offended—"Do you know that the previous shift in the Mayan eras was when the Spanish visited them for the first time? And it totally changed them, didn't it? They thought it was the god their prophecy predicted would appear, and they just let it happen. But we don't have to be like that. We can listen to the prophecy so we know what'll happen. Then we won't be blind when it comes."

"But what if it has to happen and we can't change anything?" Atlas asked.

"Then we'll have a good time. At least we'll know it's coming."

"Interesting," Atlas considered.

Atlas knew how to hold his cards when he needed to. I first thought this wouldn't be one of those times. Usually guys like Atlas fumbled their whole stratagem when a lady as dazzling as Goldie showed interest.

I stepped back into focus from my watchful repose to try to urge him along.

"Atlas what're you saying about twenty-twelve?" I asked, then added to Goldie, "The man here's a shaman. His ancestors probably wrote the prophecies. If anyone knows what'll happen, it's this guy here."

Atlas smiled with his head bowed. He stared off beyond us, out of the living room window into the dark night outside. Goldie said something neither of us heard.

"Naw, nothing'll happen, man," Atlas said. "It's all bullshit. If any change'll come it's because people brought it about by their own will. The new age movement, man, all that shit, it won't go nowhere because all those people are waiting for some magical esoteric sign to appear in the sky. They're waiting for the stars and planets to align. If we wait for that, fuck, we'll be waiting longer than any of us ever can. Because it won't happen. People bring about change. World War Two, the French revolution, the spread of Christendom, the Beatles, man, they all happened because people did something. Not because the cosmos aligned. But, the cosmos won't align, man. The universe is just not linear enough for that. It's round. Everything is round. We'll all find that out. Maybe in death. Maybe in the here and now."

I stared at Atlas' smiling lecture face. His eyes shifted everywhere, not trained on anything in particular. I nodded and added 'yes' throughout the conversation because he said what I believed but didn't have the clarity to tell Goldie myself. She wasn't so impressed. She tilted her head from side to side while he talked, taking sips of her drink and watching people milling around behind us. I grabbed Atlas' shoulder and shook him amiably. Goldie laughed.

"You guys. You went through all this trouble, Henryk, just to fuck with me? You guys are rid*iii*culous."

"At least she left in a good mood," I said once she was beyond earshot, which wasn't far in the loud house. "Man, why'd you say all that? I bet you could've theorized her right to a quiet place somewhere, you know what I mean?"

"Thanks for trying, Henny. I appreciate it, man. Maybe I'm not so cut out for hook-ups, y'know?"

"Still. I'm still going to try. Believe you me. You will get fucked. Yes. But," I lead Atlas to the kitchen to get us another beer. "But why'd you tell her all that? You usually tell people what they don't want to hear, which is usually the opposite of all that."

"Because, man. You know. Belief in yourself before belief in another."

Tell the girl before
she forgets that she brings the
cup to her own lips.

CONFETTI FACE
[Martin O'Neill]

"I brought some cookies for the less fortunate."

Tatum was less than able with her words, her accent was still hurdling over an angular Siberian dialect.

"Thanks. We could've used some sleeping bags and drinking money," Simon soused.

"What?"

"Nevermind."

"Where are we hitting up?" I asked to break Simon's endless flirtation.

"I'm thinking we cruise dee-tee, find a hopping bar or something. I dunno, just find a—"

"Like, somewhere to dance?" Atlas asked.

"Whatever the *chiquitas* want. Of course dude."

"Atlas doesn't dance," I explained to the ladies sitting on our couch, parenthesizing the way people did when they wanted to show themselves to be close and comfortable enough to divulge interior information in front of others.

I could tell the trio was somewhat uncomfortable. Tatum sat with Bunny and Jean-Grey Lechelle. Jean-Grey sat at the edge of the sofa with her hands in her jacket pockets, legs straight out, as if she was cold and ready to leave.

"Let's not go dancing," she suggested.

"Dancing is bored. We should dance with the words," Tatum offered.

"Sexy."

"Fantastic."

"Fox trot," Atlas said.

"How about the Vulture Perch?" Simon suggested.

"Sounds like a sketchy bar," Bunny said.

"No. We should hit up The Imperial," I suggested. "If not, then there's lots of other stuff around there, too. But—"

"How about we just hit the fucking road and see what we see?"

"See-saw."

Atlas ever the awkward man, always with the stupid last words no one needed to hear. I felt bad for him, but the ratio was right for the night. Simon was thoughtful, even if over-hopeful for a foursome, so credit was due on his part.

We left the house into winter's overcast evening. That afternoon it snowed. The wind thrashed some brown leaves from their branches. I always thought the city looked better after snow. The colours became saturated, the greys justified by the similar hues in the sky. The sadness leaked from the asphalt and sewer grates and bricks and powerlines, and was appropriately mirrored without bucolic sunshine. Bubbles were left in our footsteps. I avoided popping them. Simon walked ahead with Bunny. Jean-Grey was cross-armed between them, and I fell in step with Tatum. Atlas sulked behind.

"How long have you been in Canada?" I asked Tatum.

"Two years."

"Nice. Your English is very good."

"No, you don't have to say. I love the language but I spend too much time speaking Russian with my family."

"Passion is the first step, I suppose."

I looked over my shoulder to check on Atlas. His hair swooped back and forth in front of his face.

"I think you'll find a good resource in all of us here. If there's a word you need to know, I'm sure one of us can help you out. I'm a writer, too. So if you need help with—"

"Yes, you write for magazine."

"Oh yeah. Did Simon tell you?"

"No, you told me."

"Me?"

I did not remember telling her. I had not met Tatum before, and I was sure I would remember anything I had ever told her. I admired Tatum from the corner of my eye. She looked ahead, discerning our route. She looked a lot like Audrey Hepburn. Like a lot a lot. Almost identical. It was unbelievable. Was Hepburn Russian? Where was a search engine when you needed one. Too bad Henryk was having a quiet family dinner tonight.

Simon entertained us on the subway with his gaunt ad-bashing. He would not stop until someone got offended. It didn't matter who. The advertisements offended him—so it was fair that he shared this offense with others. A man in chequered pants laughed at Simon, shaking his head. You could see the words *crazy kids these days* escape his lips. An old couple tried to ignore him, but it was difficult. Fortunately our ride was short.

We got off on Queen (which Sy had a good time explaining to Tatum) to pass the shops that made cultural life in Toronto worth waiting in traffic and dealing with assholes for. Simon eyed the vinyls displayed in the record store, and Atlas spied the bongs in the hemp shop. I eyed Tatum further. She dressed in the same fashions as the mannequins non-chalantly posing across the street, but her face looked pasted on her shoulders, especially against the dulled streets. The way her skin glowed against the rocks made her seem so much more foreign.

Tatum caught my sliced eyes. I wanted to dart away but I couldn't. For a second our eyes snapped together, magnetized, and I noticed how hazel they were. Tatum's eyes took on a glassy complexion, a wholly empty sombre glare that seemed mismatched with her toothy grin. The eyes became mirrors where I saw Tatum looking concentrically at her own face—then the mirror shattered into a trillion indiscernible pieces.

So much more foreign.

The Imperial Pub was empty when we showed up. Turned out, though, that the folks never crowded this bar, which was probably why we liked it so much. The walls were lined with heavy oak bookshelves. The titles ranged from Fitzgerald to Homer, from modern to someone else`s modern. This was the kind of place where bearded professors came to discuss their stuffy ideas. The professors whose wives had long ago divorced to maintain sanity.

The perfect stable for fables. Two pitchers to start, tall glasses all around. Even Bunny, whose delicate hand was made for Cosmopolitans and Sex-on-The-Beach doubles, clutched a heavy stein.

Three hours passed in a flurry of fizzy beer and conversational belching.

Simon embarrassed Bunny by telling everyone the origin of her name. Tatum told her grandmother's life as a Soviet spy. Atlas avoided being himself and sounded like an idiot too many times, so he eventually fell into an alcoholic stupor and kept his responses to laughter. We all made the waiter feel uncomfortable with ample friendliness. Every trip to the bathroom became a more euphoric journey, until we finally hit the cool air outside and I lit up a cigarette. Smoke curled around my head, and I lit Tatum a smoke using the lit cherry of my own. I studied her face in close proximity. The blue monotones of night blushed with the reddish glow of the butt. They touched, and intensified.

As the beers thinned Tatum's blood her accent grew thicker.

"Thunk ew[77]."

"No problem, darling," I said.

"Durlen. Haha! So conginitul. Luvlee is yoor ize."

"Munchies back at the house!" Simon shouted. "Yo, Atlas, you down for some cooking? Yo, Atlas is the dopest cook. Straight up. He can fuckin' sautée your panties right off."

"I gotta work cross-town tomorrow," Jean-Grey said.

---

[77] ***Thunk ew…durlen…conginital…luvlee is yoor ize… pull-chreh-teh-deen-us…*** — (*The International Language of Broken English*) Thank you…Darling… Congenial…Your eyes are lovely…Pulchrutidinous; beautiful

"We got rides," Simon assured her. "You come with us. You eat, you rest, and feel brand new in the morn."

"Hey, what's going on?!"

I pointed down the block to where Dundas Square shone under an artificial daylight. There was music, excitement, and the roar of people shouting.

So to the light we flocked.

At the east end of the square a small stage offered a band with enough members to leave little elbow room. People squeezed around the stage. At the peripheries people watched, danced, talked, and presumably sold illicit materials. Never-ending advertisements flashed in neon colours overhead—too bright in the day and retina-piercing at night. It was overwhelming. We moved, together, apart, unanimously without consent into the crowd, joining the moving bodies and soundwaves. I became entirely lost in it all, too dizzy—but the crowd was the perfect excuse not to end the night, the lights the damning reason why we would not nod off, the music the reason to be anything other than sleeping beasts. In the midst of the bodies, and the many scarves and indie silk-screens, I thought I lost my friends' familiar faces, although everyone had become one entity by now. I bumped into Tatum, who leaned close into my ear, ungracefully passing her lips over my ear lobe, then exclaiming too loudly:

"*Pull-chreh-teh-deen-us*!"

I nodded, though I did not understand what she said. She smiled, all teeth. She danced ahead of me. So European in the way she unleashed her passion. I moved closer and connected my groin to her ass. She responded, pushing into me. Conscious of our backwards embrace I felt all the other people who touched me. There was no escape from the mass, the web, and no reason to want escape. As the song concluded my voice was torn up from my chest, I shouted clamorously with hundreds of others. A pop broke above. Multi-coloured confetti sprinkled down.

The band thanked us. There was no way for us to thank them but scream. Tatum followed me to the edge of Dundas Square, where we met up with the rest of our group. Everybody was too short of breath to comment much beyond brief exhilarations. Atlas shook the confetti out of his hair. He helped Jean-Grey get the cofetti off her head. Tatum's sweaty face had confetti stuck to it. We cleaned each other on the walk back to the subway.

Underground, the lingering ring of amplifiers was strung taut between us. In the fuzz Bunny,

Jean-Grey and Tatum decided to go their own way. Jean-Grey seemed overwhelemed and upset. Too much apart time. She hadn't wanted to be part of something bigger. She had just wanted to be with us. Anyway, the night was over.

As Simon, Atlas and I stood at the subway door, we waved to the girls. The windows started to slide by like a slow film strip. Tatum and I held eyes. She had her feet kicked up on top of empty seats. On the sole of her furry boots rogue confetti caught my eye. How long would she carry that impromptu mosaic with her?

"Tatum is beautiful!" I raved to Simon.

"Yeah, bro."

"I mean, fucking stunning. And she looks like Audrey Hepburn, doesn't she? Just like her. Wow."

"Yeah dude. She chose Audrey Hepburn."

"What?"

Simon shrugged.

"And why the hell did she think we'd met before? I've met Bunny, and remember Jean-Grey from highschool, but not her. Maybe we met in a previous life. Eh, Atlas? What do you say? You pick up on any vibes?"

"Naw, man, we *mos def*[78] have met her," Atlas tittered, still unable to speak without laughing.

"What? No way. I'd remember a face like that."

"Yeah you would, man."

"That's because she didn't always have that face, genius," Simon said—but seeing my blank expression he sucked his teeth and said, "Shit, guy, she had plastic surgery."

"What? Really? That's shitty."

"Naw, naw, not like that, man, not, like, recreationally," Simon took his time with his words as we climbed the stairs up from the underground. His voice echoed in the stairwell. "Her boyfriend. He beat her. Like, regularly. But then, one time, he beat her so fuckin' bad he nearly killed her. Brutal. It fucked up her face beyond recognition. She needed to reconstruct the whole thing. So she chose Audrey Hepburn as a, uh, a model, I guess. Good choice, right?"

The cold night air hit us as we exited onto the street. The night looked darker. I opened my pack of cigarettes, imagining Tatum's face falling to pieces then being puzzled together again. There was something at the bottom of my empty pack. I held it

---

[78] ***Mos def*** — (*English*) Slang; most definitely—and shout outs to the emcee

upside down. Confetti fell out, back-flipping as it sailed for the ground.

Litmus confetti
test: whether it makes you smile
or loathe the mess left.

A BITING COLD
[Henryk Zdicz]

Atlas didn't care to know about it, but twice a month I went to visit his mom.

She lived in a rented bungalow on the east side of Toronto. She had about fifteen metres of sidewalk, walkway, and porch, but it was more than she could handle. Between my visits, when the snow fell knee high, she wouldn't leave the house. When it was waist high she went mad with delirium tremens, and I found her shaking on the sofa, staring at an empty TV screen.

Atlas' mom, Caroline, was a hardcore alcoholic. It was no secret, which made it sadder. She knew she was addicted, Atlas knew she was hooked, even her family knew she was a lush. She told me everytime I visited that she had a new ulcer from the drink. Then she would offer me a beer.

She caught the habit when Atlas was young. It started out of sheer desperation—or at least I thought so, after hearing the drunken story from the lady herself—as an escape from what she realized was her eternal poverty. She was terrified about becoming poor. Her parents had always been steady. Her grandmother told her she would waste the family's riches getting drunk, although the family never actually had riches. Like all epic sad stories, her descent began years before it started. Caroline's mom died in a car crash while on vacation in Kashmir. She lived with her grandparents, but that was short-lived, because they were. She moved back in with her dad, who had re-married. Her step-mom was a cheery Algonquin woman who loved her more than her real mom ever had. But then her dad died from pneumonia. So she lived with her step-mom on the reserve.

That's where she learned the fine art of drinking your face off. It was unfortunate, but true—so much more hurtful in its truth—I was ashamed to know this dark side of Canada's indigenous people, who who had been so exploited that they were rewarded a martyred honour in all our history textbooks.

When Atlas' mom was old enough to have a baby, she did. But between her drinking and the fights over an out-of-wedlock baby, the baby was born premature and died. That gave Atlas' mom the perfect excuse to drink everyday.

The alcohol filled her with grandiose ideas, like starting a business, which she tried, and travelling the world, which she did. That's how she ended up under an itchy alpaca blanket in the Andes with Atlas' estranged sperm donor.

After Atlas was born, she managed to stop drinking. But then she started again, and it got so bad Atlas moved in with his uncle on the reserve. Since then he tried moving back, but she was unendurable.

I hated that she was so unambitious that she didn't even bother to leave the house for days at a time. I hated that she offered me a beer everytime I saw her; those were always her first words to me. I hated that she let her plants die, even after I bought new ones and helped her develop a watering calendar. I hated that she had tons of pictures up all over the place, but not a single one with Atlas.

But she was my psuedo-brother's quasi-mother, and I would love her.

Like Simon says, the nuclear family is the most irrational institution our society has created.

So after a half-hour bent over a shovel, I finally sat down with Caroline for that promised beer.

Sometimes I felt so weirded out being in her house without Atlas that I wanted a reason to go as soon as I got there. Today Caroline lazily smoked while the TV played highlights of the hockey game. It had been months since I watched TV, and it was hard to get back in the habit. Instead I watched Caroline. She casually talked to me without looking away from the TV, even when commercials were on.

"How's Atlas?" she asked.

"He's great."

"That's a lie. That boy is a disaster. He's going to die one too."

Caroline was blunt at her best. She tended to put Atlas down. It was no wonder that the man had some serious self-esteem issues. She doubted him, constantly. And at every off-colour remark about Atlas' character I wanted to jump right into her face and yell that my bro was a saint, the man paid our rent and worked his ass off for everything but his own advancement.

"How's school?"

"Pretty good."

"Learning anything good?"

"Yeah, I guess."

"Good enough. It's almost a shame now that everyone has to go to school to be something. Back in the day it only took hard work and persistence. Now it just takes four years."

I bit my lip so I didn't tell her my diploma was only two years.

"But, that's the way of the world. That's why Atlas is never going to make it, that poor bastard."

My eyes wandered up a cabinet, where she had photos. I settled on a frame on the top shelf. It was a spacious photo of the Andean landscape. I remembered the photo. Atlas had a copy. He said it was the only photo of his father.

"At least you got some smarts, Henryk. You've got something to work with, but believe me, even that's worth nothing. You could fail even worse than Atlas."

I stared at Caroline, expecting a laugh. When none came I sighed and finished the last swig of beer. I remembered that crazy old man Atlas and I ran into on the reserve when the Sunfire was towed. He had a word—*pauwau*?—for a witch who had cursed Atlas. Of course, that old goof knew better than to actually believe in a mythical figure, but the word did fit someone like Caroline. No wonder Atlas hated himself! No wonder he couldn't speak fluently with women! No wonder he cared more about death than feeding himself! No wonder he lamented his life's failure—how could he turn out any other way when he was made to believe that failure was the best he could hope for?

I clunked the beer bottle on the table loud enough to get Caroline's attention. She watched me for a minute, then asked if I wanted more beer. I declined her offer and told her I had to catch the bus.

As soon as I opened the door I cringed in the cold gusts. I admired my work on the driveway. The snow piled a metre-and-a-half on either side. White Christmas this year, if they could find us.

But wait. My masterpiece! All down the sidewalk tire tracks pressed into the small drifts of snow left from the shovelling.

I heard an electric elk bugle at the end of the block (at least what I thought an electric elk sounded like, or just an elk for that matter). I stared down the block. There was a man on an ATV, doing donuts in the street with his kid hanging off the back. Real safe, buddy. And thanks, asshole, for leaving that packed snow.

"Fucking asshole."

Caroline stood on the front porch. She stared at the man on the ATV than waved me closer.

"That dick loves to make a racket with his toys."

"Aren't you cold? You're barefoot."

"I'm fine."

"I can shovel up the mess. It won't take—"

"No, don't worry about it. The snow'll just fall again. You go home, Henryk. And thank you, thank you so much."

Caroline embraced me. The hug lasted longer than I wanted it to, but there was nothing I could do, the ATV made another pass and drowned out any possibility of tender words.

What hands take away
machines put back in neat rows,
so we never finish.

POPS GOES *
[Malik Ceiss]

"Malik."

It had been a long time since I had heard my mother's voice quiver. At first, I thought the heater was broken at her office. It happened once, two years ago. The temperature dropped so much the fax machines whirred but didn't print anything.

"Malik...it's Pops."

Mom's voice dropped. I looked over the various people milling around the store, trying to find my mom's face in theirs.

"What about Pops?" I asked.

"They phoned. They said he's in critical care."

"What happened?"

"I don't know!" Mom snapped. Then she reproachfully sighed, "I wasn't there. The hospital phoned."

"But they didn't say—"

"Malik it'll take me an hour in this weather to get down to the hospital from work. The highways are slick. I need you to go down to the hospital. I need you to check on Pops."

I wouldn't tell her that my boss was already pissed off at me because I couldn't make it to work on time, or that I was a prime suspect in a recent CD-stealing conspiracy.

"Okay. I'll be there in, like, twenty minutes."

I told my boss there was no choice. If he fired me I would tell him my grandfather died. Luckily the man was in his mid-thirties and depressed that he was a lowly record store manger in the same mall he perused as a hopeless teen. So he shooed me away without much argument.

One winter the heater stopped in the entire mall and it got so cold the escalators whirred but wouldn't go up or down.

I could have waited for a bus, but it would have taken me longer. Plus I needed a cigarette. My fingers went numb within five minutes. A lackadaisical guitar riff chugged in my ears, in between gusts of frosty wind. My shoes became wet trudging through the browned slush. Twenty minutes later, when I stepped into the hospital doors, a prickly slap rejuvenated my skin. The ends of my hair had collected frost and my lazy facial hair was frozen in tiny curls.

If I had stood at the nurse station wordless any longer they might have pointed me to the fifth floor, where the stabbing victims were guiltily recuperating.

Except my nervous words flickered out like the fluorescent light in the file room behind the cock-eyed nurse.

"I'm here for Mark Ceiss."

It felt so foreign to call Pops by his real name. Not that he would recognize either name anyway. He could be Johnny or Steve or Pajamas or anything. At the door the nurse repeated the name.

Pops lay limply with his eyes closed like a final pale monument to his life.

Alzheimer's is not a disease, it is a slow rebirth within this lifetime. Or at least that's what Atlas once observed. At the time that logic made the first years of Pops' descent manageable. Now Atlas' words seemed too easy to understand to be true.

The soft clinical smell of the hospital made me feel old. It made Atlas' words seem like toddler's babble.

The nurse waited at the door for a few moments, maybe to ensure that I wouldn't steal the old man's wallet. She didn't know that the only thing in the wallet was my mom's business card with the message: *If found, please call Charlotte Ceiss immediately.*

Or maybe she did read it, and was afraid he would lose that.

Then he would forever be lost to the oblivion.

The snow pelted the window, the storm was kicking up in time for the evening rush hour. I wasn't exactly sure what Mom wanted me here for, so I stood over Pops' still body until I had to pee. I used the bathroom, then sat in the seat beside the bed.

I had watched enough movies to know that this was a time for tender words. They would be the last words I would ever be able to share with the man.

Except that I had already had my last words with Pops when I was nine.

"I was too young when I went to France. And too dumb! I should've studied up. But there was no time for that, no time," Pops retold his war story for the thousandth time, "I never understood a damned thing those people said. But when we were leaving, at the end of the war, everyone kept coming up and telling us: *Mercy buckets*! *Mercy buckets*!"

"I've heard that story before," I told Pops.

For a nine year-old it's difficult to hear an old man re-tell stories. It's something that still embarrassed me: the faint hint that there is nothing new.

I wanted to tell Pops that it would be nice if he told me about his time in France. But the only sound he made wasn't even his. The cardiograph beside his bed beeped regularly. I checked my cell phone to see if Mom had phoned.

New text message: Mom was on her way.

The question was whether Pops was on his.

Mercy buckets!

I had cried over Pops' death when I was twelve and his Alzheimer's progressed beyond repair. He was a dead man walking. He spent everyday safely locked inside, but he had definitely left the building.

The room's heater, which provided white noise, stopped. The cardiograph's beeping became louder. I wondered if the heater had stopped working. I wondered if it would become so cold that the cardiograph would whir but not keep a beat.

But the heater started up again, and I leaned back in my seat, and the plain lights dulled, and the beeping became melodic, and when I woke up my mother cradled my head, and the cardiograph whirred but did not keep a beat.

BE BENT, BE VACANT, BE WORN
[Atlas Sangman]

Tradition was tradition. Who could break a date?

If I could, I hid it from myself. That's why when Henryk asked me if I was going to join him and his mother at midnight mass on Christmas Eve again, I said I would.

It would be wrong to tell someone that what they believed was wrong, and it was especially rude if you didn't know what was *right*. I had picked up a recent habit of going to the Buddhist temple a couple times a week before work. But I was still baptized—the water could hardly run off me—that sticky holy water that oozed from my mother to my self. Maybe my father wasn't a Christian. Maybe the mountains of missionaries that swept South America missed him, maybe he was held up in a tree wrestling a jaguar for supper, maybe he was an Incan hermit, maybe he was just a drunk fucking pagan.

I guess that's what's cool about everybody's dad. They can be whoever you wanted them to be, as long as you never really knew them. That was part of the paternal stitching that supported society —the idea itself a supportive father.

I guess that's why Jesus called God his Father even though God never called him his son.

I would never judge who was right, only what was right for me. I tried reasoning that point with Henryk, who knew I experimented with religions like they were new drugs, but he was unswayed. He just didn't want to talk about it anymore—besides, these days, religious holidays were just imaginative excuses for fake happiness.

Mass was pretty lamentable. Christmas Mass was like beating a dead pope. The ritual's real meaning was the furthest thing from people's minds. There was no sentiment here. The parishoners just wanted someone to cook them dinner, then get drunk so they could forget about the rest of the shitty year. Maybe for some this was the season to get back on the wagon, sing those hymns, and feel redemption. Whatever.

Fuck this.

I looked over to Henryk. He sat still, eyes ahead, not scanning or watching—just a cloudy-eyed stare to the front of the church. Mrs. Zdicz sat on the farside of him. The pew hurt my ass and the service hadn't even started.

There was a calm in this building, though. It soothed me, reminding me of the dimmed enchantedness of churches in my youth, when holy ghosts and Jesus and God sat on the rafters, moving around to avoid people trying to catch a glimpse— the priest like some kind of schizophrenic who wanted to be your friend and introduce you to his old friend, that mighty nice invisible hippie Jesus Christ—*Yeshua*[79], you found out, once you took Catholic religious history in highschool—the mild-mannered mason or carpenter who just happened to be the Son of God, by the way.

That was what I wanted to tell Henryk, but he was just staring.

He remembered all the incantations. He knew what to say and when to say it. Maybe that was why he was so good with women.

I wanted to tell him that, too. Henryk would only remind me to shut up: this was only one hour of my life. And if I liked it, apparently I would get it back later.

---

[79] **Yeshua** — (*Aramaic*) Original iteration of the name Jesus

Maybe that was the problem with Jesus. He made it too easy not to trust him. He made it easy to be cynical.

An old lady finished posting the hymns for the night.

"Yo Henny, check the hymns. Hymn 666?"

"Did they know we were coming?" Henryk whispered back.

"Don't you think they would've skipped that number in the book, like how they skip thirteen in buildings?"

"I guess it's just a number."

"How many Jews and witches did we burn?"

"I didn't burn shit, man."

"Henryk!" Mrs. Zdicz whispered sharply.

"Sorry, Ma."

"Why do you embarrass me everytime we come?"

Henryk smiled and faked knocking me on the head with the bible tucked into the pew ahead of us.

"Henryk, please. Stop being stupid," his mother pleaded.

"Fucking Able."

"You are not exempt, Atlas, from this. Just because your mother will not take you does not mean you can go to hell happily."

"Sorry."

But I had to be honest.

"I just don't want to be here."

"You are free to go," Mrs. Zdicz flipped up a palm towards the door, but I couldn't budge.

I knew I had no right to go.

The priest entered and we all stood. We all obeyed. He walked solemnly to the altar, led by those all too bored altar-servers in their white robes, all of them thinking about who in the congregation they would jerk off to tonight.

The priest didn't notice me or Henryk, he didn't even acknowledge any of the regulars. This was serious shit. I guess there was no room for people. Maybe if Jesus came back no one would notice because he would walk right past us in a pious gait.

I tried to enjoy the music. The organ was electric, hardly authentic, but its vibrato was still eerie. It felt like the ominous background in a horror movie, right before you stepped into the world of the strange, the dark, the unknown— Martin would love it—the soundtrack as you stepped into the Twilight Zone:

--*Skip, Skip, where did you take us?*

--*I just don't know, Midge. This used to be my old house.*

--*But, Skip, this is a church. You weren't raised in a church, now were you?*

--My room was right there...where the altar is...and my mother chased me through the garden, over there, near the choir.

--You must be mistaken. This church has been the only thing here since the town was built.

--No. It can't be. I lived here, I tell ya.

Cut to the narrator.

"Peace be with you."

"*And also with you.*"

"We lift up our hearts."

"*We lift them up to the Lord.*"

Offering our hearts! A living sacrifice. We had softened up since our ancient times. Maybe that's why the gods were so pissed off with us.

I half-listened to the introduction, the pomp ceremony, the engrained chants. The service was familiar, I remembered it from when I was young. My mom would go every other Sunday, just to see her old auntie. Then we would go to a bakery. That was the best part.

My Uncle John never went to church. He did go into the bush, though, which he called his church, but it was nothing like this.

When my mom tried the twelve-step program she tried taking me to church again. I went once. She went twice. Finding god wasn't so easy in our family, I guess.

On the ride home Mrs. Zdicz complimented the priest and his sermon. She seemed cheered by the hour. Henryk nodded along complacently while she spoke in happy quips.

"What did you learn, Henryk?" she asked.

"I don't know, Mama."

"And you, Atlas?"

"I'm not sure," I cleared my throat, and noticed we were close to the townhouse. "Maybe I learned that people pretend Christmas is about things that it's really not about."

"Maybe," she said.

Henryk hugged his mom when she dropped us off, and then she hugged me. She watched us walk to the door. Inside, Henryk sighed and asked if I wanted to blaze.

On the walk upstairs to the studio Henryk thanked me again for joining him.

"No problem, brother. This time of year is for union. Whether it's something I enjoy doing or not," I said.

"Yeah, church just trips me out. It feels haunted, even though it's only a decade old."

"Naw, man, I've never felt farther from God than when I'm at church."

"Lucky you," Henryk laughed.

He paused before opening the Studio door, like he was going to say something. He only chuckled, then opened the door.

Your young men will see
visions, and they will proclaim
the Spirit's message.

THE FOURTH MOVEMENT

LET'S MOVE ONWARDS & OUTWARDS

LET'S BURN OURSELVES A FUCKING PASTOR
[Simon Arcan]

"I don't like 'em fancy talkers."

I gave Kenny a sidelong glance, wondering how he could say that with *Global Political Theory: Realism to Post-Constructionalism and Beyond* faithfully tucked under his arm.

"I mean you gotta know how to use the words, but when you're with your fellow man you don't gotta flower it up."

"Then you're shit out of luck, my man," I said.

"D'you think those girls'll be at this shin-dig?"

"I fathom they will be."

"Huh. Fathom."

I rushed Kenny through the halls, across the quad, and to the stuffy room on the first floor of the Thomspon Building, that was the philosophy teacher assistants' office during the day and home to the *'Pataphysicians' Office*[80] after hours. Inside there were four people: a pair of tall twins, one

---

[80] *'Pataphysics* — (*English*) Philosophy of that which trancends metaphysics (Alfred Jarry: "['Pataphysics is] the science of imaginary solutions, which symbolically attributes the properties of objects, described by their virtuality, to their lineaments")

dressed in punk façade and the other in indie flannel; an Asiatic who suited up as a Rastafarian; and a stocky tomboy whose features flattered her refusal to wear make-up.

"Wuddup," I presented myself, looking around the room. "Simon. Kenny. I saw the posters."

"Did you *read* the posters?" questioned the Rasiatic.

"Naw, I just saw the shapes and matched them to the pictures on the door and thought I'd win a prize. So where the fuck's my prize?"

Kenny looked at me disapprovingly. His eyes showed disappointment with the female turnout. The Tomboy wasn't one of the girls he thought would show up. I guess he should've looked up what 'pataphysics was.

"Smart ass!" the Indie Twin declared. "Give him a membership card."

The Rasiatic threw a button at me which I half-dodged. Kenny caught his and admired it with confusion.

"Your membership card is your knowledge that this is who you are. Everyone has buttons— everyone's a 'pataphysician."

"But if we had to explain..." trailed the Rasiatic.

"I'd probably have to explain to you that your homeland is definitely not Africa?" I retorted.

The Rasiatic looked too comfortable in the armchair, his legs swung up on one arm, his dreadlocks lazily tucked under a tea cosy—his Babylon was long gone.

These people thought they were so smart, with their office and buttons and off-beat thought patterns. I turned to leave, patting Kenny's chest to signal our departure.

As I reached for the doorknob the door opened. The man coming in nearly ran right into me.

"Holy shit," he exclaimed, right in my face.

We stared at each other for a little while.

"Are we going to kiss?" he asked.

"I don't know. I didn't read the script."

The man cracked a smile.

"First on the list. We need to reconsider lists. Aren't they just a physical embodiment of a supra-rational paranoia? What's your name?" the man asked me.

"Simon."

"Simeon the Holy Fool[81]! And you? You look like you tagged along. Wrong room, cowboy?"

"My name's Kenneth."

---

[81] ***Simeon the Holy Fool*** — (*Name*) Syrian Christian monk, patron saint of holy fools and puppeteers

"The Holy Fool and Cowboy have joined our ranks, which are rankless, and in fact, they have joined nothing, because that's what all this is."

"I still don't know what the hell a 'pataphysician is," Kenny said.

"Perfect. Then you know exactly what it is. I'd do a round about introduction, but then this would feel like a cheesy movie, now wouldn't it? I'm Hugh Min, by the way."

"I had an idea," the Punk Twin spoke up, ignoring our exchange. "I got a hook-up with the person working the coffee dispenser in the cafeteria. I was thinking we highjack it and exchange the coffee with sewage. Start your day with your own shit!"

"That's good," the Tomboy said, "But fucking gross. Why are you always pushing the shit-centric ideas?"

"Anal expulsive," noted the Indie Twin.

"We could do the human muffins again," Punk Twin offered.

"We do not do *again*. We don't do *again*. Negatory. We do anything but again," Hugh said.

"Shit, you guys just looking for a prank?" I asked.

"Not just a prank, Holy Fool."

"Prank is what the cops call it, man. That's them keeping you under semantic arrest," The Rasiatic said.

"Pranks are easy. Do you like it easy? Because if you do, you should leave."

"Huh," Kenny snorted.

"We crack social graces," Hugh explained. "We shatter shiny toothpasted grins. Make anti-perspirants perform their so-called necessities. To make people lean off the edge of their own being, to stretch their neck over the edge of their furthermost reality and peer into the Void which comprises the entirety of our true being. That's not a prank. That's called real life."

"Sounds like an acid trip."

"Say that again."

"I don't say things again."

"Yes. *Yasss*. Did you motherfuckers hear that? Did you *hear* that?" Hugh hopped onto the sofa beside the Tomboy, then giggled like a madman. "Here is a man who lives by *experience*. Lives by the daily *tick tock tick* and not by calendars, advertisements, feces, Jesus Christ, fuck all. Are we all seeing this? Like an acid trip! *Yasss*."

Hugh would have disturbed a different room. But here he jumped between everyone, barely sprouting sentences, and everyone nodded thoughtfully. Kenny laughed, leaning on the wall. He tried to get me to laugh at the irrationality of the situation. He cocked his head and played with his eyebrows to express his disbelief. I shook my head. I would've said something, but it would have embarrass Kenny. He didn't need alienation in this foreign land.

"Dig it, man, you know what we can fucking do?" I said, excited by Hugh's excitement at my random observation. "Bring the trip to people. Like, y'know, everybody drinks at a party and even those who don't still drink something. So we dose drinks we provide at an open concert we throw in the fourth quad down in the gully. I know bands. I got a link for mad amounts of mind-blowing LSD. It can be done. And we can do it."

"*Yasss*. The Void, man, the *Void*. We can *see* it. *They* can see it. We can bring it to them. Without dying. But like dying. Listen to the Holy Fool. Haha! Cowboy, round up the calvary, Jimmy get your bass and Jake your fucking incoherent punkers, and *gah*, bitch get your lesbians and witches and let's burn ourselves a fucking pastor."

Either you get it
or pretend nothing happened—
the page turns idly.

STUCCO
[Martin O'Neill]

The early evening makes me feel self-conscious.

I tucked one arm under the one stretched out with a cigarette. I posed thoughtfully in the glass. I watched my reflection in a dark store front, half-listening to Simon and Henryk argue about the validity of museums.

"The library and the museum. Both cemeteries," Simon argued.

"Nay," countered Henryk. "Where else does human society come more profoundly alive than in the past? That's what distinguishes us from that pigeon or that tower. A knowledge—no—an amicability for our past."

"Just because it distinguishes us doesn't mean it's not dead. We get born, then we die. That distinguishes us too."

"So? Atlas," Henryk pleaded for Atlas' third party opinion.

Atlas had had a detached expression since we left the house. He floated his eyes back from a distance beyond Henryk, Simon, Malik, and Kenny, then stared at the ground.

"We make our distractions, then our distractions make us," Atlas concluded vaguely.

"I told you," Simon said.

"What?? You didn't understand."

"I *do* understand, past-tense contender."

"Verdict," Malik announced, "Sy's gotta blow Michelangelo's David and Henny'll suffer amnesia from standing too close to the resulting rock-hard hard-on."

"Everyone's a winner," Atlas tried to joke, breaching the barrier between his wandering mind and the rest of us.

I adjusted my hat and tossed my butt. The move looked tough in the glass. I announced that we would be late. We were only one door down from the stoop where inconspicuous artists smoked and paced in the cool air. They stared at Kenny, then at us. At least I knew what they saw when they looked at me. I touched my hat to make sure it had not moved since its last fixing.

We were at a showing, *W/O MAN: Woman Without the Man*—at a nouveau gallery in the art district. I jumped at the opportunity to cover the art show for the magazine, particularly because I knew Lucy Sparrow was having her first showing.

"You know what I'd like to create?" Sy added as a closing to his argument. "A mirror museum. Where people can see how people have been seeing themselves throughout the ages."

The show, like most things in the art community, was over-priced. Only the snobby could pay the cover charge and not feel ripped off. But how could I be such an arse? Support local art. I had the pin. It was inconsequential if the time you spent to make the money used to appreciate local art was the same time lost from your own artistic pursuits.

"Red or white wine?" an old man in a chequered blazer asked.

"I don't have a glass."

"Glass?" offered a woman in passing with a tray full.

"Red," I turned back to the man.

"Red—Mars," the word embraced the wine splashing into the glass. "Aries is high in the sky tonight."

"Oh yeah? How do you know?"

The man raised an eyebrow humorously.

"Don't you know? All that's in the sky. Don't need the Google for that one."

"Of course."

As he left I pulled out my small black pocket notebook and scribbled in pencil:

pretentious incorrigible elitism ? check!

Despite the man, and that man multiplied, and the numerous dolled up women, most of whom looked far too old for a hip exhibit like this, the gallery itself lacked any pretensions. It was perfectly plain, except for the pieces on the wall and a few sculptures. I had already lost my friends in the crowd, so I walked to the nearest piece.

Confusion is not an emotion but a cultural phenomenon.

"Marvellous, isn't it?"

An over-dressed lady asked me, her bulging eyes telling me that she could not help expressing her feelings to whoever was near.

"Yeah, it is."

"Makes you feel strong. Powerful, almost. Doesn't it?"

"Well..."

"Isn't it marvellous?"

Move on. The next painting was not worth stopping at, but I did. It was just abstract primary colours.

Old shock is now irony of itself, a mockery, like women still feeling the need to have a whole show dedicated for their empowerment.

The next print was a simple black-and-white portrait, but the woman's face raised a rash of emotions. First I hated it because she looked stupid, but that made me sad so I pitied her; then I saw the joy in her carelessness.

Always leave after joy.

Crowds cocooned the next few pieces. I found Kenny alone standing near a pillar.

"Kenny, how're you enjoying your first city art show?" I asked.

"Honest?"

"Yeah. Always."

"I hate it."

"Why?"

"I don't know. That picture over there looks like a pussy. That one's just fucking weird. And other than that, I don't understand the rest of them. But at least I can take my share of the open bar. Maybe I'll understand some of this after some drinks."

I left Kenny with my half-emptied glass of wine and continued.

Something we take for granted in a multicultural urban environment : anybody & everybody's expressionism.

The next painting I went to was across the room. It attracted me that much. Unlike a woman, (and the painting was of a woman), it was easy to approach. Maybe because it did not have legs, or teeth. It was just a close-up of one eye, an eye with its eyelashes plucked. Only one remained. *He Loves Me Not*, the painting introduced itself.

"Hi."

A young lady dressed in grey tones swung her hands in front of her shyly.

"Hello," I smiled.

"You're the first person who's stopped long enough for me to say hi to. So thank you."

"This is yours?"

"Yes."

"This piece pulled me right across the room. I couldn't help myself. I just want to stare back at it. It's just..."

"Please don't say *marvellous*."

"I was going to say beautiful."

"Thanks."

"You know," and I stepped towards the artist, having known the canvas and wanting to know the brush, then the delicate hand that held it, "I'm writing an article about this show. Would I, uh, would I be able to interview you? For the show. About the—"

"Yes. I'd love that. Now?"

"Uh, sure, I guess."

"Okay."

I pulled out my black notebook and flipped passed my observations. I had no questions, but I would not admit that to her.

"What's your name?"

"Adice Bandi."

"Are you from Toronto?"

"Raised, yes. I was born in Lebanon."

"Cool."

"And who is my interviewer?"

"Martin O'Neill. Raised in Mississauga. Born in Ireland."

"So you're no stranger to gunfire either?"

"I wasn't there for long. How old are you?"

"Twenty-three."

"Why do you think it's important that an all-woman's show take place in the modern age?"

Adice blushed, maybe taken aback by my random serious question.

"If my mother had to answer that, she would say it's because men are an oppressive force that will always try to take the teeth out of a woman's chagrin. Men will never make the women's situation appear to be as bad as it is. And that's because they live as they do because of women's labours."

Mother vehement feminist, reactionary to patriarchal society. "Teeth out of woman's chagrin". "Never let it appear as bad as it is".

"So what would you say?"

"I would say it's because someone thought it would be a good idea, and I wanted to show, so I jumped at the opportunity."

Opportunistic. Cute smile.

"Plus some other personal things as well."

Sexually charged.

"Your other piece there is of a nude wearing a hijab, and there's a background of hands grasping at her. What were you thinking when you painted that?"

"That someone would like it. And not only for the exposed aureoles."

"Are those all male hands?"

"Good question. My sister was actually the hand model."

Women clambering at a perfect oppressed image of themselves.

"If the paintbrush wasn't your weapon, what would be?"

"A wet vagina is a force stronger than an AK-47, but I'm too modest to weaponize myself. So probably my modesty would be my weapon."

Modesty as weapon.

"Brilliant. Thanks so much, Adice. Do you think that, uh, I could get your email address? Y'know, just in case I had any other questions?"

"Sure. May I?"

I presented a fresh page in my black notebook, but her hands reached passed the book to my hat, which she took off and reset on my head.

"You looked too arranged before."

She took the notebook from my hands and scribbled her email. I touched the short brim of my toque and resisted readjusting it. I searched the room for a mirror but there were none.

"Thanks, Adice. I'll email you the story once I get it done."

"I'll look for it."

The next piece was a small picture of a hand with a fly smashed in the palm. Another had an iceberg inside a lady's foundation make-up case. There was a time-lapse of a snowman melting. At each new work I turned to look at Adice from it, but after the third one she was gone. When I turned back to the wall of paintings, I was looking at a massive canvas of stucco. Lucy Sparrow stood patiently beside it, having finished her conversation with a small bald gentleman.

"Lucy."

"Martin? Oh my God, I haven't seen you in forever! I knew when I saw Simon and Henryk and Malik that you wouldn't be far. Atlas told me you guys are living together. How have you been?"

We briefly discussed current affairs. The news postings of Facebook. You know, the important things.

"Is Atlas here?" Lucy looked about the crowd animatedly.

"Yeah, he's around. I'll have to let him know where you are."

I knew Atlas had had a crush on Lucy, and I would cover for my brother until the end, until the wedding where he broke down and got so drunk on boxed wine that he played the grand piano in the lobby and admitted he could never provide her with anything she had needed in life anyways.

"I love this."

I pointed to the canvas. I did not understand it, but I figured someone must have.

"I bet you have no idea what it is."

"I know it's stucco. On a canvas."

"How'd you guys hear about this thing?"

"I'm writing an article for the magazine."

"Sweet! Hey, do you think I could do the design for your article?"

"Yeah, absolutely. I mean, I'll have to talk to James and all, but I'm sure he'll be okay with it. He prefers volunteers over our contract designers. For one thing, you're free. But they're not as good as they think."

"I used to think that same way."

"I'm loving this piece. Tell me more."

I flipped passed Adice's email address in my notebook.

"Have you ever just stared at your ceiling?"

"All the time."

"And the stucco becomes a thousand different pictures? That's what this is. Except I pencilled something in underneath, and then blasted the stucco. I think the image of what I drew, and related pictures, arise from it."

You see what you want.

"But then again, I knew what I drew."

"What did you draw?"

"Just look."

"Hey Marty," Kenny slapped my back, liquor heavy on his breath. "Why do artists do so much stuff naked? Would it be weird if I whacked off right now? Or would that be art, too?"

"He's new," I explained to Lucy.

"Nice to meet you," she greeted the surly cowboy.

"Bet you can't ride a bull with that skirt."

"Probably not. Mind you, I've never tried."

"Hey Kenny, I think they announced last call."

"Shit, I'd shake hands ladybird, but I'll need both fists for this."

"You're such a gentleman Kenny."

"Thank you, sir."

"I wonder where Atlas is at?" I said before Lucy could ask any questions.

Lucy smiled helplessly and a man slipped beside me to shake her hand. He was a manager of something relevant. I stepped back to let Lucy pimp herself out, as we would all have to do at some point.

In the past you just had to convince someone your art was good. Now you just have to convince someone's wallet. Sad Lucy :(

And WHAT did she draw?

I found Simon dragging Kenny to the door. We found Atlas alone outside, balancing on the curb.

"We have to get this cowboy back to the ranch," Simon said.

"Let's walk home naked! And then hang ourselves on a wall!" Kenny shouted.

"Where'd you go?" I asked Atlas as we lagged behind the group.

"I saw you talking to Adice," he said.

"Yeah. Do you know her?"

"Nope."

"I think I'll dream about her tonight. Hey, Lucy was asking about you. Isn't that weird?"

"I gave Adice the name and number of your editor, man. I think he'd like her designs. Maybe she could design your story."

"What the fuck!" Simon broke our conversation.

Kenny leaned into a recessed doorway, vomiting loudly. I took the opportunity to break out a cigarette. As I smoked I caught our reflections on the fabric shop's storefront glass across the street. In it I could see my friends but could not see myself. It would've been too vain to move the three or four steps to catch a glimpse of myself, so I turned away from the image.

"You want this puke for your mirror museum?" Henryk asked Simon.

"I bet he'll learn not to drink so much on an empty stomach," Malik said.

"I really doubt that."

I stepped towards my friends, rechecking the glass. I saw Simon. Malik. Henryk. Atlas. A taxi stopped at the curb and asked us if we needed a ride. Henryk declined. While Kenny caught his breath on his knees I pulled out my black notebook, looking for Adice's email. An excited warmth reached me as the taxi pulled away, it made me want to see her handwriting. But I just stopped at the first page I opened to.

Because it told me what I already knew—and now I would be able to tell someone.

You see what you want.

Stucco constellation
pointing the way home through
self-imposed visions.

I WILL BE YOUR SAVIOUR IF YOU WILL BE MINE
[Simon Arcan]

"The problem with any modern movement is that the government is a giant wet blanket that wants to keep things cool, you see. As soon as something gets out of control, or if it provides any opportunity for taxation, they regulate it. They pass laws that act as consensus even if they're not. They will start martial law if they have to. Only the Quebeçois had the balls to push them that far."

The Tomboy touched Hugh Min's arm. It calmed him and stopped his rant. He sat back on the sofa and rubbed his chin while Tomboy complimented our lack of television. Atlas sat lazily on the sofa, but it was a poised laziness. He was alert. There were strangers in our home.

I lead half of the 'Pataphysician collective from their tiny dorm rooms to our expanded townhouse. The Unreverend Hugh Min—he had named himself, I just called him the Man for short—and the Tomboy dragged the Indie Twin. He looked bored, though I noticed he regularly did, regardless of where he was or what he was doing.

"And the solution?" I asked.

"To do it for free," Hugh said.

"For free?"

"That's the only way. It'll happen, on the grand scale, eventually. But we can jump the gun. BANG!"

"Hugh..." the Tomboy sighed.

"So you want five sheets of LSD for free?" Atlas clarified.

I watched Atlas as he rubbed his chin, mimicking the Man. He considered Hugh's lofty proposal. The three 'Pataphysicians gave him a moment to absorb Hugh's long rant. In the meantime, the Tomboy complimented our mismatched garbage-picked lamps.

The deal was simple, but all simple questions had complicated answers. Atlas and Henryk had access to massive amounts of psychedelics, especially acid, courtesy of the Oz. They could easily pass a shopping list to Oz and give him a week to synthesize any chemicals. But for *free*— that was a different request altogether.

Atlas responded quietly, straight to Hugh and partially to me:

"Let's not make the decision right now. Let's wait on it. Maybe we can rummage something up, or think of something else."

"Deal. So, thus, forewith, and what all—I present to you, ladies and woman, Absinthe."

Hugh pulled the bottle from the pack at his feet. The Tomboy's face lit up as soon as she saw the electric green liquid. I shifted forward in my seat and reached out for the bottle. Hugh passed it to me and I ran my finger over the gold-foiled label.

Pour toujours, pour maintenant[82], it read in loopy script.

"Straight up, from France," I reported.

"What do we need?" Atlas asked.

"Shot glasses. Enough for everybody. And sugar. And a spoon. A lighter, too."

"Are we shooting up?"

"Shooting up to the moon. Do you have hole-in-the-roof insurance?"

"Naw, the insurance man scared us enough with their bullshit statistics about fire and flood, hurricanes and armageddon," I said.

"All the important things," Tomboy sarcasted.

Atlas retrieved the necessary items and laid them in front of Hugh. Atlas returned to his

---

[82] ***Pour toujours, pour maintenant*** — (*French*) For always, for now

armchair and watched the ceremonious way Hugh lined up the shotglasses and smoothly poured the drink. He added sugar and fire to each one. The Tomboy urged us all to crowd the table, so that our arms radiated from the line of glasses.

"This is the most important part," Hugh said.

Tomboy called and Hugh responded.

"*One, two...*"

"*Here, do!*"

They lifted their glasses and Atlas and I rushed to catch up. The liquor stung as soon as it hit my lips. From there it rinsed my mouth with a liquorice sweetness, then raged down my throat. I coughed and placed the glass carefully on the table to join the other five.

"Fuck. Don't light a match," Atlas rasped.

For the next shot the five of us were more synchronized. By the third Martin had come back home, the cold trailing him from the blustery winter outside. He happily joined us. By the fourth shot the second bottle was cracked, and Henryk came back home. Atlas got up and animatedly introduced his esteemed colleague Dr. Henryk Zdicz. Damn, Atlas became so awkward when he was drunk. He was no good at being funny. His jokes didn't even draw a laugh from Hugh Min.

Hugh just stuck his hand out and asked if Henryk wanted a drink. Henryk shook his head and asked Atlas what price they asked for. The mood suddenly dulled again.

"Not much, man."

"Really? That bad?" Henryk asked.

"No, man. Literally nothing. Like nothing's nothing."

"What?"

"For free, man."

Henryk lowered his head in thought.

"Hey, my brother, listen, I thought maybe if you heard what we were trying to do you would appreciate the significance of the insignificant amount."

Hugh pitched his idea to Henryk again, with more conviction than before. Henryk watched in silence, with bags under his eyes from the late class and the long transit ride home. He sighed to himself while Hugh spoke.

"That's why free is the way to be. I'm telling you: free music; free books; free love; free paint; free movies; free shoes; free flights. People would be begging to be free for that."

"No, see, what you're talking about is a serious psychedelic hammer that you want to slip to unprepared strangers," Atlas countered, now bold after the Absinthe.

"Yeah," Henryk nodded. "Hugh what you're talking about is cool in theory, but I just don't think it's a good idea. A lot of people might freak out. I even freaked out my first time and I thought I was well-prepared."

"How about if we just ask people? Or like, just make it available to the hip circles?" I suggested.

"No, we're going for the systemic circles. The whole blood flow. If you start just bringing in anybody who wants to trip for tripping's sake, then all you get is a lot of bums who want to get high and lose their minds."

"I thought you were all about ceremony for ceremony's sake," Atlas mumbled.

"I'm not. And even if I was, that's not why we want to do this."

"See what I think is this," Atlas sat forward in his chair, direct in his drunkenness. "That the body is a vessel for an essential energy, and this energy's like water, and in fact, water might be one facet of it. You can't cloud people's energy with something like this. It has to be done at different times for different people. And be warranted, man. The water just goes where it goes, it flows predictably and conveniently, it swerves down mountains and shit, then it gets evaporated, condensed, then falls again. Now if you catch that water in a dam, or in a sewer system, now you've taken a lot of water out of that cycle. Do y'know what I'm saying? Or am I rambling?" Atlas asked this last question to Henryk, who nodded.

"I totally dig the metaphor, my friend, but if people show up to this thing in the Don Valley, without any ads or posters or anything, then wouldn't that water just be naturally draining into that watershed?"

Atlas shrugged, irritated that his metaphor was used again him. Henryk yawned and sat up to appear more awake.

"Maybe you guys should try to find your chems somewhere else," Henryk said. "I just don't think we're down for it. We don't sell. We trade, sometimes. But we don't give away."

Hugh forgot about his offer and asked Henryk if he'd like a shot. This time Henryk took it, settled in his confident reproach.

Small niches began to settle among the alcohol warmed lips. Henryk and Atlas got talking with Hugh—one out of curiosity and the other out of skepticism. Simon tried to get the Indie Twin to jam with him but he confessed that he couldn't play any instruments.

"Anybody can bang a fucking tambourine," Simon said.

"Not me. Even my heartbeat is irregular," he shrugged.

"You can at least bang a tambourine."

"Only if I could do it doggystyle."

"Fuck this kid."

Henryk had turned to the Tomboy. She kind of looked like that cute Philomena chick he'd brought over a few times. I thought that might've sparked his sudden interest. Except this Tomboy had no interest in forests, so it might not have worked out.

I turned back to Atlas' conversation with Hugh. He was lively, amplified by the alcohol and wormwood circulating through his body.

"Naw man, now what you got there is ceremony for ceremony's—"

"Exactly."

"But how's it's opposite anything more than a reaction?"

"Because that's exactly what it is."

"Then how's it any better?"

"So, Hugh, you say you're a SubGenius," Martin said to break the deadlock. "How come I've never heard of these SubGenuis? How many of you are there?"

"Who knows. I don't know. Don't really care."

"Is it some kind of cult?"

"The SubGenuis[83]," Hugh Min began, his fingers pointing matter-of-factly at Martin's face, "Are a group begun by a man in the fifties who believed everything was bullshit. You see, he thought the Church was bullshit, so he created his own, where everybody was a priest and could teach whatever they wanted. The government got wise when these guys were getting loads of members because priests get tax deductions. Everybody wanted in, and the government loves its tax base. That's when it all went downhill. Or uphill. I don't know, but we're on some kind of slope."

"Do you have any literature?" Martin asked.

"No."

"Sounds confusing."

"What isn't? This is just an accepted confusion. A beautiful confusion."

I lost interest in the confusion and eavesdropped on Henryk and Tomboy's conversation.

"Maybe you should start being mean to me," said Henryk.

"On purpose?" Tomboy asked.

---

[83] ***SubGenuis*** — (*Name*) A parodic religion created by J.R. "Bob" Dobbs in the 1950's; he is the smiley pipe-smoker on the self-titled Sublime album

"I'm just starting to like you, so you should bitch me off so I don't..."

"Don't what?"

"I dunno."

"Want to fuck me? Want to fall in love? Want to whack off to me?"

"I dunno. Somewhere between those."

"It seems weird you wouldn't want those things."

"It's not that."

"Then it might be beyond me."

Then Atlas got everyone's attention—which he often couldn't do. He stood in the middle of the room and waved his arms thoughtfully.

"Alright, alright," he said. "Just because I don't understand what you're trying to do doesn't mean that I won't allow other people to try to understand. Let's give him the 'cid, Henny. But just as long as Simon and Henryk's band get to play the show. And my friend Claire gets to perform spoken word."

"Yes!" Hugh stood from the sofa excitedly. "You got it man. That's it. You understand. You say you don't, but you totally do."

You got it, Man—but
why does my understanding
feel so damn useless?

THE GREY MOVEMENT
[Henryk Zdicz]

The first thing I noticed about the three-storey downtown home was that the hedges that once bordered the fence had been trimmed right down to sad little stems. A robin hopped between them, its head cocked, asking the same question I would, before Simon slapped my chest.

"I bet this place will smell like cat piss."

"I say mouldy kitchen," I said.

"If we know anything about Kaya," Atlas pondered, "It'll probably be ganja."

Simon, Atlas, Claire and I squeezed four abreast on the cracked sidewalk. A hum emanated from the home. It was getting late but the sun faked a summer metabolism. The hedge's stems made shadows that darkened the yellowing lawn. I didn't notice I had been left behind on the sidewalk until Claire called out to me. She looked at the lawn, then maternally smiled back at me.

"They could use a women's touch."

"Or a fucking heart."

To be honest, I was already in a shitty mood because Mama reminded me yesterday over the phone that it was my grandfather's birthday today. Which was fine, because dziadek had been dead since I was about eight. It was just the reminder of dziadek's life that bothered me.

So under Atlas' orders I tried to stay in the moment as much as I could.

The house was cramped and surprisingly smelled like nothing. There was muffled music disjointedly shouting to me from all over the house. Atlas had told me they were into experimental art, and Claire had tried to explain their last visit, but it hardly did the scene any justice. As soon as I found Atlas standing beside a tall Pakistani man with an afro, a guy stepped in front of me.

"Heiney for your thoughts?"

He pointed the mouth of a bottle of Heineken beer to my lips. I didn't understand so I laughed, and he didn't understand so he tried to stick the bottle in my mouth. I nearly gagged. He backed up and I grabbed the bottle just before it tipped away from my lips. I took a swig and returned the gift to the strange toad-looking guy.

"Your thoughts?" he badgered.

"My thoughts?"

"Heiney for your thoughts! Your thoughts?"

"Uh...that was fucking weird?"

"*Weeerd*," he croaked, then bounded away.

"I just had the strangest encounter," I told Atlas.

"Henryk, man, this is Kaya."

We shook hands and Kaya remarked that I must have met Thom. Thom was not strange, he was just an absurdist poet.

Dziadek had told me that before the war he and his friends had been pranksters. But after you heard the sound of blood trickling out of a bullet wound, you suddenly realized there was not much to laugh about.

Atlas touched my shoulder and gazed into my eyes. I apologized. Somehow my friend knew I had slipped into reverie. Something in his gaze told me that he knew forgetting would be a difficult task.

Simon and Claire had already vanished into one of the many rooms in the old house. There were people everywhere. I was surprised at how many people Kaya had invited for the ratio of available space. He tried to ask me where I went to school, but he was swept away by a drunk couple before I could answer. Then, before I understood how or why, I was slowly pushed along too.

My grandfather wouldn't have been so easily pushed. Dziadek had inherited heroism from his forefathers, each and every one decorated either in combat or in politics. Name a European conflict and it is likely that a Zdicz was involved. My great-grandfather, Aloysius Zdicz, lead a victorious battalion against the Germans in the First World

War, but died of dysentery when my grandfather was young. The people in Gdansk, where dziadek grew up, believed that Aloysius lived on in the young boy's soul. So when the Nazis moved eastward into Poland, Gdansk naturally turned to my dziadek for protection. He organized an army, rallying every fighter the city had to offer. Dziadek never spoke much of this battle, but I always thought that he must've believed that he could win.

"Hey bro, c'mon, let's see what this shit's all about," Atlas said to me.

We had taken a handful of mushrooms with Claire at her room in Kensington Market before we left for the party, and Atlas' pupils were already reaching the edge of his irises. I found my legs again and forced myself through the crowd behind Atlas.

A new act was in the middle of their set in the first floor living room. A man was bent over the inner-workings of some complicated electronic instrument. Pliers twisted and his head shook as the old 1940's television set in front of him contorted and shattered to ambient music provided by a guy who was carefully playing with the controls of a weird soundboard. He nodded his head whenever it pleased him and bit his lip when it didn't.

The television flickered scenes at random. Some were unrecognizable, some grotesque, some simply absurd. But some were all three of these things—they made me shudder. Tanks climbing over trenches and craters, the Luftwaffe in angular formations shitting out tubular bombs—I completely zoned out. The images invaded my mind.

Dziadek never spoke about the Gdansk battle, but he openly lamented its aftermath. My grandmother was missing, the rest of his family dead or captured. The city was in shambles, and only a few hardcore members of his troupe survived. Out of ideas and ashamed, they gathered all the supplies they could and escaped into the safety of the marshes.

Simon grabbed me by the arm. He rushed me to another room, a front room on the third floor. It was a dark olive green, trimmed with maroon baseboards. Who lived here? Sy had an elevated seat for us on a desk. There were four lamps that a haggard man set up before he turned off the lights in the room.

Three lights were positioned near the head of his set-up, which included a keyboard and two boxes of electronics I didn't recognize. The lights began to twirl as he played with a few knobs on a small box. He continued to switch buttons, turn knobs, and a hum rose. It flickered. Another button pushed—an abstract drum kit going bananas—then he turned to the keyboard.

The intro dizzied me. The worst part was that his entire performance was an intro. A lot of suspense going nowhere. All foreplay. It was very misleading. Annoying, even. It was still an art, and it was done to a tee. If irritating was what he was trying to capture, then he did it perfectly and made his point clearly.

At the end I asked Sy what the purpose of this music was. A stereo played tinny music between the sets and made me feel like we slipped into a low-budget movie.

"*Iknat[84]*," he said.

"What the fuck?"

"Iknat," Sy restated.

"What? What're you saying? I think I'm fucked. Did you say *Iknat*?"

"Yeah, man, Iknat."

"What?!" I restated. "Are your ears ringing as bad as mine?"

"I know nothing about that."

"I know nothing about…" I repeated to myself.

---

[84] ***Iknat*** — (*Simonism*) Acronym: I Know Nothing About That

"I may've made that up just now."

"Is that from something?"

"I dunno."

"Iknat."

Sy laughed and left the room. I stayed, hypnotized by the twirling lights. With the obscure acronym on my lips I walked through the upstairs rooms, looking for something that was constantly escaping me. The ubiquitous sounds were absolutely dissociating me from focus. I stumbled into a bathroom and pissed. I washed my hands and face in the sink. The cool water exhilarated and calmed me simultaneously. I left the water dripping on my face. I was feeling so hot I figured that the water would dry off soon enough.

I peered up to the mirror and searched my face. When I played with *dziadek*'s loose elbow skin as a child, he would point to his wrinkles and tell me he got them in the Polish marshes. It wasn't until later that he told me how he forged raids against the Nazis from the bush like an animal. I asked him once, in an excited fit, unaware of the intensity of my question, if he had ever killed someone. Dziadek said that all Zdiczs in history have either killed a man or saved a man's life, but that either way, they were all doing the right thing.

There was a tumult of knocks at the door. I opened it and a half-naked couple nearly fell onto me. The man let go of the girl and started unbuckling his belt. The girl turned to me with a smile, and her nipples grazed my raised forearm. She asked an unvoiced question with her raised eyebrow. I left the room, closed the door, stumbled down the stairs and bumped into Atlas.

"Hey, Atlas, where are you going?" I asked in a rush.

"You alright, man?" he asked.

"Yeah. Cool, bro, I'm cool. Where are you going? I feel like I'm lost in this house maze."

"No doubt. I think the architect was going mad when he designed this place. I'm heading to the kitchen, man. Someone passed an invite to a session, so..."

I followed Atlas to the kitchen. Claire was already there. The green pastel walls, stacked newspapers and blinding bare lightbulb overhead made the space look tighter than it already was. Noises poured from every orifice the house could offer, even from completely solid, usually quiet objects. The bare bulb was naked as ever. In this room, conversation prevailed. Claire had captured the attention of the room. As she spoke her voice seemed to spin the room, pulling the corners round and round. She was the centre of a preternatural merry-go-round.

She was in full stride, in a tumbling stream-of-consciousness. Claire was in her zone. This was what she loved most. Even though the listeners were geared up to criticize her, she loved the confrontation, the intellectual battleground. I could see it in between her long sentences. A smile peeked through her metaphors.

"It's like walking into an ocean. You dabble up to your ankles, and you're curious about how far you can go. You step slowly up to your waist, and once it's just over your waist, you're like, 'might as well go all the way'. So you keep going, keep going up to your neck, but you can't control the ocean's swells, you can't predict when the waves are going to go right over your head. And they will."

"But we *float* in the ocean," Kaya proposed.

"True enough, but the riptide pulls you out further and further it doesn't matter if you float or not. It gets exhausting to swim out. You get stranded. Plenty of people drown that way."

"Mm-hmm," Kaya agreed sultrily, tipping his head left to right, still unsure.

"So we have a choice to get out, but we have to want to be dry, right? And we can't just waste time.

We can't wait until it's sunny enough to dry off naturally. Then we need towels."

"So what're the towels?" I asked, completely unaware about what Claire was even talking about.

Claire lifted empty palms and shrugged.

While we exchanged stories about the rooms in the house Kaya and Atlas each rolled joints. People came in and out of the kitchen for drinks but nobody stayed. While we smoked the two joints in rotation we talked casually, logically, emotionally— so unlike the experimental madness that the rest of the house hosted. Kaya was an intellectual before an artist, and an artist before a philosopher. I could see how Kaya was Atlas' only friend from his brief university career.

Kaya announced that his roommate was starting a set that he needed to see, so he left us. Claire said she felt re-energized by the smoke and wanted to wander again. Claire was as brave as any of us could be. Even completely zonked out she was prepared for anything. She could take joy in anything.

My heart felt warm. I felt her joy. I felt love. Not that clingy institution of love, but the pure chemical reaction sparked by the comfort of surrounding yourself with people you vibed with. I reached across the table and held Atlas' shoulder.

"You feeling good, brother?" he asked.

"I'm so glad we know Claire."

"I bet your grandson will have a hard time forgetting your stories about Claire, and us, and these times."

"I have to say that this is probably the best place for me to be. How else could I stay in the moment better than in a nuthouse like this?"

"Naw, man," Atlas said, moving to a more comfortable seat beside me, where he could lean against the wall. "This fringe art is as out-of-the-moment as war memories."

I disagreed, and would've started a friendly debate, but three guys walked into the room loudly looking for beer. They officially ended our conversation when they all sat at the table.

There was a bearded man, a shaved-headed man, and a fat kid who breathed heavily upon sitting.

"How's it going, boys?" Beard asked.

The man was drunk. The three of them smelled like a smashed liquor cabinet.

"Just fine, man. What are you guys saying?" Atlas responded.

"Fucking fantastic!" Beard said. "Good music, good people, good shit. Get a good drunk on and fuck yeah. See which one of these bitches is drunk enough to suck a dick."

"Right on," Atlas said.

He rolled his eyes to me while the three guys high-fived. I shook my head. We both thought that they would move on soon.

"So what's your story?" asked Beard.

"Me?" I asked.

"Sure. You. What's your deal?"

"Uh, well, I dunno. I'm just a student."

"What're you studying?"

"Environmental sciences."

"Huh—fuck that shit," said Gut.

"What?"

"If you're wasting your time trying to get trees to poke through concrete you got a losing battle, my friend," Beard said.

It bothered me that he called me friend. Especially in his gravelly tone. It sounded like his voice crackled through his throat. He scratched his chest and played with a bottle opener.

"I don't think that's exactly what I'm—"

"David Suzuki is a fucking liar. He gets kickbacks from oil companies, logging companies, whoever. Then he tells the rest of us to live greener. Like he's a champion for the greater good. Hey,

Matt," Beard called out to a passer-by, "You're an asshole 'cause you don't recycle."

"Ah!" Kaya exclaimed, casually coming back into the kitchen for the bottle opener twirling in Beard's hands. "Henryk, right? I see you've met the Grey Movement."

"The Grey Movement," I repeated, trying to make the words belittle the confrontational bearded man who snatched the bottle opener back from Kaya.

"Kind of like the Green Movement. But more human," Beard clarified.

"What do you do?"

"What everybody else does," Gut said.

"We helped put this show on. For the cutting edge of music. We have to push music to its frontiers. Too much music these days is trying to find something new, but it gets caught doing re-runs. And the ones that are doing new things, they're forced to play menial venues like this."

"But we give them a place," Baldie spoke for the first time.

"We also disseminate info about the truth of the so-called Green Movement."

"*So-called?*" I asked.

Dziadek survived in the Partisan underground resistance for four years. Then he told me about how they were infiltrated by a spy who tipped off the Nazis to their movements. They were ambushed. Only a dozen of his troupe survived. They were transported to the nearest city. There they were interrogated individually. When dziadek was asked if he was a Jew, he said yes, though he had been christened as a Roman Catholic. He told me he lied because he knew the Nazis had been jailing Jews. Dziadek thought if he could find his way into the Jewish prison there would be enough manpower to stage a coup. So from his dozen comrades, he alone was put on a jammed train car headed for a concentration camp.

"Yeah. *So-called*," Beard repeated. "I take it you understand that already, but you're too proud to admit it. But look, nature has natural disturbances. Worms and badgers tear up the earth for their own needs, and birds move twigs around to make nests, and bison trample and eat away the plains."

"And that doesn't count earthquakes, volcanoes, hurricanes, blizzards, tornadoes…" Gut added.

"Right. The whole Green Movement, or whatever you call it, begins with an assumption that humans are not a natural entity on this planet. Why are our actions anymore unnatural than a bison's?"

"Because ours are for excess. Animals' actions are out of necessity. Bison need to eat and migrate to survive. We don't need mp3 players to survive."

I wouldn't have said anything, but their impedance on the kitchen's peace bothered me.

"Why not? Isn't that where evolution has brought us?"

"Not really."

I hadn't expected this barrage. It was discomforting, especially because Atlas stayed quiet. The smell of stale tobacco wafted into the room, and I heard Kaya shouting *no cigarettes!*

"Yeah, check it out," Beard said, pointing behind him to the mini Christmas tree on top of the fridge. "We think the environmentally-friendly alternative to the traditional go-chop-your-tree-down-in-the-forest—because we think that'll wreck the forest,"—Beard spoke animatedly, waving his arms, but the beer steady in his hand—"We think the tree-hugger alternative is a plastic tree. Like plastic hasn't done any damage?"

"Maybe the whole idea of Christmas is the thing doing damage?" I asked inquisitively.

I looked at Atlas. He nodded along, encouraging me.

"But the idea of Christmas, the whole religion and morality about it—that's wholly human," Beard countered. "It's natural, and it's part of how we survive. So what if it can outcompete the forest? Maybe trees should evolve to look uglier so we don't want them in our houses."

Dziadek told me little about the concentration camps. But I knew from history class all the details of what really went on. The most he would say to any one was that the men were sick, and none of them were strong enough to fight, so he realized his bust out of that hell wouldn't happen. He told me little anecdotes when he was distracted, or driving, or trying to nap. Once, he told me about the boy rabbis—the young Jewish men who made it their burden to continue their faith in the Nazi's vortex. These rabbis could rouse the last drip of strength from the masses, but they used it to have the workers doing overtime with joy. That bothered dziadek. He said it was on one of those days that he realized he was going to die.

"*I* don't want a tree in my house," I said.

"Who really does?" Gut said. "Give me a clean house!"

"Okay dude, if you want to get psychological with it, then cool. I'm just saying that it's more about science than suspicion. But psychologically, humanity shows its narcissism by wanting to influence every metre of earth. That's what builds our cities. But what's so wrong with leaving some untouched earth? What's so scary about having to leave something without our imprint?" I asked.

I picked up a warm bottle of beer that had been on the table since we got there and took a deep swig from it. I focused on the bitter, dank taste. Then I looked Beard in the eye. I made a move to get up from the table.

"Yeah, and anyways, man, you and I both know that there's no such thing as human nature."

I thought it was weird that Atlas said that, but he pushed me out of the kitchen before anything could follow from it. We snaked through rooms, and I eventually lost Atlas. There was a dark room on the top floor, quiet before the music started, and mostly empty.

I sat in a bean bag chair through a whole musical set. A man, too old to be considered anyone's friend, was kneeled over a microphone while random people within the room played instruments at their leisure. There was no rhyme. No reason. The man's vocals were no different. After twenty minutes the musicians tired and lay their borrowed instruments beside the man, who summed up his performance over a xylophone melody.

"*Over and around the under…*

Ankles over ears we sunder…
Shenanigans dragging our peels…
In between the last sign's lines….
Synchronous with the denial….
The denial."

The extension cord was unceremoniously unplugged. I checked out the room for the first time since I got in. Simon was in an armchair nearby, sitting upside down in it. I crawled over and placed my face to his nose.

"Are you done here?" I asked.

"Aww, am I dead?"

"No, you're still alive."

"Then lessgo!"

Simon rolled to his feet and started out of the room. I followed him, almost frantic. The house felt so small. Only two could pass abreast in the widest areas. There were definitely too many people here. I grabbed Simon's shoulder and pushed him into a room when I saw Atlas in it.

"Atlas, man, what are you saying?"

"I thought we were leaving," Atlas said.

"Me too."

"Lessgo!"

Simon led, going nowhere. We winded down an endless corridor of stairs. It was hard to figure out whether Kaya had painted every wall a different colour, or if I was just delirious. It was then that I realized that I'd left my orange juice in the refrigerator. I slapped the wall and called for a stop, but no one heard me. I turned around anyway and backtracked to the kitchen. The Grey Movement were still perched at the table, except that they had overtaken our wall seats. I ignored them, beelining for the fridge.

I found my o.j. promptly, it was front and centre. On my way out I couldn't help but look at the Grey Movement—especially Beard. He was staring at me. I noticed how blue his eyes were. They were sharp, there was barely any pupil. I gave the boys my peace on the way out, but Beard reached over the door way, trying to block me.

"No, wait, buddy, wait up. Look, you like your orange juice wrapped the same way I do. In plastic. And all juice. Yeah, dude. Fuck nature's orange creation. We can do it much better."

Dziadek never mentioned much about camp life, except that it was hard. *Hard*. The word sounded hard in his mouth. He worked for more than a year in the lager. He was one of the tortured few who could keep healthy. But then, one morning, the Nazi guards seemed nervous, and they called all the inmates to the showers. Everybody knew what that meant. They weren't stupid. No one was stupid enough to not recognize that nobody showered, and that those who did, didn't come back. At the remote showering facility the Nazis corralled the prisoners, but not before the sound of Allied jet planes rose in the sky like an ominous gasp. Minutes later there was shooting at the fence line, and minutes after that the Allied soldiers marched into the lager, welcomed by the fallen Nazi soldiers. Dziadek said it was the happiest day of his life.

I noticed the game these three Grey chums played. Everyone who came to this party, I finally noticed, had come to play a *part*. So that led some to fuck around with televisions; some others with music, playing shamelessly like they're on grand tour; and some just came with an agenda.

"Look," I moved Beard's barrier and continued out the door, "You can do your thing, and I'll do mine. Let's just leave it at that."

"Lame!" Beard shouted to my back.

I was so glad that was over. I slapped down the steps without focus, walked into Atlas, and burst onto the street. The air calmed me down a little, but I must've been noticeably stressed because Claire sung to me.

"Who were those assholes in the kitchen?" Simon asked me.

"I don't know. Never got their names, actually. They call themselves the Grey Movement."

"The Grey Movement? Sounds like a lot of shades of indistinction. Hey, let's cut through the park. There's another subway station this way."

We ignored the paved path and cut across the darkened park. I walked quietly behind everyone, still obsessing over the Grey trio. I let Simon take my role as navigator. I didn't pay attention to his route.

"Oh fuck," he said, stopping abruptly. "Naw, this isn't it. Wrong way."

"I'm glad you took all those turns so we could get disoriented," Atlas said sarcastically.

I recognized where we were. I felt sober, almost alert after my escape from the house, even though the mushrooms had full reign.

"You guys..." I sighed. "It's this way. We're far from any subway stations. You suburban bastard," I teased Simon.

"Oh, go plant a tree," Simon mocked Beard's gravelly voice.

"I think I will."

After we got out of the subway and emerged into the suburbs, I felt drained. Atlas drove, and I sat shotgun. The streetlights passed by, orange-headed soldiers guarding the streets from night.

There must've been something terrifying in the night sky. Something that made busy city-dwellers tremble enough to set up these relentless lights. I closed my eyes, but I could still see the orange hues through my eyelids. Atlas nudged me. He told me not to sleep, and I told him I wasn't trying to.

"I'm just drained, dude."

"Me too. The avant-garde makes me feel sick," Atlas said.

"I wasn't exactly in the mind-space to get fucked with tonight."

"I know what you mean, bro. Jeanne texted me tonight. Five times, man."

"What about?"

"Saying I'm distant. Like, implying that I just wanted to use her for some self-righteous purpose. Revenge, sorrow, I don't know what, man. I'm just trying to not get hurt. I want to leave with my heart intact."

"That's what I should've said to those Grey bastards. I just want to leave with my logic intact. I've made my decision about being on the earth's side, right? I don't want to have to defend it for someone else's sake. I felt like I was their fucking entertainment."

"If that's the case, karma will repay you for that."

"Then it'll repay you doubly. You have a right to protect yourself. Especially since you know her track record."

"Maybe she's right."

"At least she's literally distant enough to not have any awkward interactions. For me, these identical houses are mocking me as much as the Grey Movement was. Because they *are* the Grey Movement. This is what they were talking about. The only remnant of what they tore over are these manicured parks and the subdued greenbelts."

"Man, just because it's a movement doesn't mean it's right. Or necessary. Besides, we can't fret about our prison here. Prisons begin and end in the mind. I think we take advantage of what they give us, and we never forget the original wilderness. Right? The Valley is our second home. We use their greenbelts to break their rigid drug laws. We have our own movement. The only difference is that ours is breaking against the traditional, and theirs is supporting it. That's how suppression works—they make you think you're wrong by using the status quo as a weapon."

"Damn, man, you should've kept on with philosophy."

"Fuck that. Besides, this is just stuff I picked up from Claire."

"Do you believe it?"

"Yeah man, of course. Or else I wouldn't have said it."

We grooved to the music for the rest of the way home. I unlocked Unit 3E's door and headed straight for my room. I got undressed for bed, then stood at my window. From my narrow view of the world I could see four walls that didn't form a room. I literally laughed out loud. Then I went to sleep and didn't wake up until I had forgotten all about the night before.

> Dressed in grey, the city
> builds the prison in which
> it is prisoner.

~~DRUGS~~ COINCIDENCE RUNS EVERYTHING AROUND ME
[Simon Arcan]

"*Namgrants*[85]. The whole lot of them."

"What? Are you reading for a Tennessee Williams play?" I asked.

---

[85] *Namgrants / Immigrunts* — (*English*) Slang for immigrant...possibly...made up from an obnoxious caricature...

"Tennessee who? No, look. Down hole there, in the construction vests. I guess they don't work at night or else no one would see them."

I could never tell if Kenny was ignorant of his racism, or if he did it to playfully aggravate me. Kenny had cooled down the cowboy thing, especially when we were in the city. No cowboy hat anymore, and some days he opted for his sneakers that he laced clunking spurs to. That was cool, I had to give my man props for that. But he wouldn't part with his over-sized belt buckle, or his tucked-in shirt. I think he thought it made women think to look at his crotch more often.

"I say we pay 'em a penny-a-piece and have a corporate lunch," Kenny smiled crookedly.

"Chill out there, Mr. Moneybags."

"Why don't we get a beer before our lecture?"

"Because it's one in the afternoon."

"It'll warm us up. Let's stop here, they have pints of Big Rock. Big Rock is an awesome beer. Best beer in Canada, easily. Made in Alberta, of course."

"Dude you fucking fell asleep last time we drank before class. You're not exactly a proactive drunk."

"C'mon, one beer. When's the last time you ever really said no to an offering of drugs?"

"I'm not worried about me, man, I'm worried you can't hold your shit together."

Kenny had no interest to hear my complaint because he had already turned towards the pub door.

Although Kenny probably drove a pick-up truck all his life, he probably never drove hitch-hikers in the back of it—his mentality was more like, you all get your own trucks and follow along behind me if you want to go this way.

So I started up my truck and ducked into the dark bar.

Inside there were a few occupied tables, and some good open ones by the window, but Kenny went straight to the bar. The waitress was already pouring his pint of Big Rock. I sat on the stool next to him and asked for the same. The waitress asked for ID, which I reluctantly handed over while Kenny laughed and pointed out the obvious fact that he hadn't been ID'd.

"Simon. Hmm. Cute," the waitress handed back the card.

"Damnit Sy, how the hell do you do it?"

"What are you talking about?"

"Didn't you just hear her?" Kenny whispered, even though she was in full earshot.

"She's just working her tip, guy," I said more discreetly.

We drank the first half of our pints in silence. Kenny watched commercials on TV, then stared behind the bar when the show came back on. I tried to people watch, which was awkward from the linear bar. There was one man with a ten-o'clock shadow and a ragged baseball cap who nursed a dark pint beside an empty one. He caught me looking and laughed, as if he had just finished a joke.

"Hey Charla, is it going to rain today?"

The bartender washed a glass, staring out the faraway window.

"I don't think so."

"Charla," the man explained, turning to me, "Has accurately predicted the weather everyday I've known her. Everyday!"

"I heard a man on the radio who does the same thing," I said.

"No, no, she doesn't listen to the news or anything. Tell him, Charla."

"Whatever, Herman. It's not that big of a deal. Coincidence," she noted, looking to me.

"Coincidence? I run my life on coincidence," I said.

"I've sat at this bar every morning for the past four months," the man started, poking his finger in my direction. "Four months, and I know because that's how long I've been out of a job. I just walked in one morning and they said fuck off, basically, so I packed my stuff and came to this bar. And I've done it every day since. Those bastards propped me up with everything they had: my name plate, my sharp business cards, all that crap, and they just took out the poles and unpropped me one morning, just out of the blue."

The radio played a Neil Young song over the muted TV, and Kenny hummed along. Charla moved farther down the bar, looking busy, probably tired of Herman's self-pity.

"But I say—if there are people like Charla here who know how things are going to turn out, like how she can see if it's going to rain or not, then at least I know that it's just me. It's me, and everyone else is fine. That makes it okay."

Herman swallowed the last of his beer in one fell swoop of his elbow.

"So my question to you, son, is: *is it going to rain?* Charla! Is it going to rain this afternoon?"

"Herman, I told you, it won't. Don't you have that appointment to get to?"

"Oh yeah. Yeah, I do. Look at her. *Look* at her. She's got it. Got it all! I'll see you tomorrow Charla. And you, you take it easy son. Make it okay for me."

"What in the hell was all that shit?" Kenny asked with a grin.

"Sorry about Herman, he's just a regular," Charla managed an embarrassed yet unfrazzled smile.

"Naw, not even the slightest problem. Sad dude," I said.

"Yeah, he's miserable. But the only thing he does to help himself is spend his dwindling money here. He was in investment banking or something. Then, you know, it all went downhill and he did too."

"That's too bad."

"Same thing happened to my mom," Kenny said. "She was making lots in real estate in Calgary. All those beautiful high-end condos that you can see the Rockies from, real crisp on a clear day, she sold those like hotcakes. Then it all went to shit, and Alberta pretty much got screwed from its riches."

"I tried to tell him to get on, you know, to move on," Charla continued on our conversation, ignoring Kenny's remark. He already started humming again.

"I try to help him when I can, but I mean the guy has to get over it and make something of himself."

"I guess he never had time to pack himself into that box of his."

"Probably not. I do like seeing him in the mornings. At least I know he hasn't jumped off a building."

"My uncle's ranch-hand jumped off the quonset one fall," Kenny interjected. "He just couldn't take the fact that the summer was over. He'd wasted all his money on whiskey and women. Good thing to waste your money on, though, he was a smart man."

"He seems to think highly of you," I said to Charla.

She shrugged, then excused herself and got something out of her purse. She turned her back to us so we wouldn't see her swallow pills from her palm. She continued her work. While she replaced the pour spouts on the liquor bottles she glanced into the mirror a few times, but not to look at us or behind us. She looked at herself each time, pausing once to touch up her mascara and lipstick.

We finished our beer and I laid the cash on the table, leaving Charla a large tip. Sometimes I wanted to play the deliverer of good karma. Sometimes I wished I could be that way all the time.

"How 'bout a bottle of beer for the road, misses?" Kenny asked as we stood.

"You can't walk around with open liquor, guy. Plus we got class."

"How 'bout you just give it to us closed?"

"I can't. Law. I can't lose my job," Charla shrugged.

"Let's get out of here. We're going to be late. Peace out Charla. Keep the change."

"Thanks," Charla smiled meekly.

"How 'bout we stop by a liquor store?" Kenny asked me.

"No way you're drooling on my shoulder again. No fucking way that you're dragging your heels and leaching off my notes."

Kenny quieted down in the fresh air. He stuck some chew into his mouth and spat periodically. I noticed that I moved with a quicker gait than Kenny, who skipped to keep up.

People smoked in every available crevice along the street. Some stood under awnings and some in the middle of the sidewalk. Many had earphones— same as the pedestrians on the street with mini-concertos going on between their ears. Then I noticed how many people had coffees in their hands.

Cups addicted to their filling. Mouths addicted to their thirsts.

We passed a homeless man tucked between two bas-relief pillars. His arms shook, addicted to unseen syringes. I stopped feeling concerned about Kenny's thirst. I didn't even stop him when he stepped into the LC before the subway and picked up a mickey. I stayed outside, watching people pass. Most were worse off than me, and the ones that were supposedly better off were the worst. They were addicted to their cars, which were addicted to fuel. They were addicted to their indoors, their carpets, their gilded door locks. A woman passed with a cigarette, and I asked if I could have one. She considered me for a second, then passed me her pack. I took one and lit it with her borrowed lighter. When I handed the lighter back I smiled, but the woman had been smiling the whole time.

A woman addicted to surprising herself.

Luckily Kenny came back before I stopped making sense.

"Got some Southern Comfort. Easy to drink straight."

"Whatever."

"You don't have to, but I got a shot in here for you, to quell your thirst."

When Kenny said thirst I noticed the metallic taste in my mouth—my cells addicted to chemical reactions. They were exchanging energy in massive amounts, always interacting. Kenny slapped my back and pointed to the subway entrance, proud that he finally was familiar with the part of the city we frequented. Downstairs the titillations of a fiddle grew until we saw the frail man commanding the instrument between his chin and fist. A man addicted to music. The ticket man took our tickets without even looking at us. A man addicted to boredom.

The platform was quiet for the time of day. Kenny and I stood in polite succession from the other sporadic passengers. In the echo of the tunnel Kenny spoke quietly and cracked the mickey.

"I love this next lecture. Even if it's early," he gulped a swig. "It's awesome. I feel learned after it."

Kenny sighed, then put the mickey into his jacket's inside pocket.

"What are you up to tonight?" he asked.

"I dunno. Same shit as always, I guess."

"Hey, do you know where Martin got those horse tranqs from?"

"You mean ketamine?"

"Yeah. Where'd he get it from?"

"A dealer. Like everyone else."

"Do you think he'd be able to get more?"

"That's the whole concept of dealing, so yeah. Why, do you want some of that shit?"

"I think it'd make for a good time tonight."

"Don't tell me that you were exposed to ketamine in Alberta, but not fucking good whole-hearted ganja."

"I'm no drug addict. Although cocaine was cheaper than weed, from what I heard. But I never touched any of that shit."

"Well, I don't think you should be tripping on ketamine either."

"Why not? How are *you* getting all authoritative on me?" Kenny laughed.

"I'm not. I'm just saying that I won't be the middle man between you and K, dude."

"If I don't get it from you then I'll get it from Marty."

"Do what you need to do."

The subway pulled up and we scurried to the doors. Kenny squeezed himself in front of an elderly Asian woman to get in, then swung between seats to get to a free one. I followed, but only after the woman who gasped at Kenny's rude entry found her seat.

"Okay, Mister Straight-edge. Since when do you draw lines between good and bad? Where do *you* draw the line between a good drug and a bad drug?" Kenny questioned.

"I guess, where you draw the line between an immigrant and a Canadian."

Kenny slapped my chest and laughed. I ignored him, but he didn't care.

There were businessmen who sat next to each other, playing on their Crackberries. Other men who couldn't keep their eyes open. There was a couple, completely folded into each other. Beautiful addicts, like any good human. And like any good human, they were probably wrong.

The illusion of
great power is the power
of great illusion

THE DIFFERENCE BETWEEN YOU & ME AND US
[Martin O'Neill]

There were only a few occasions when life seemed so much like a dream that you did something crazy to ground yourself. .

Last week I had a dream that I could fly. And flying was the least important part of the dream. The best part was that I could consciously control how and where I flew, because I was lucid. Claire talked a lot about lucid dreaming, about how it was an indication that you were feeling in control of your life. I hadn't felt in control of my life since I was eleven and learned how to masturbate.

In my notebook I made a little celebratory note about the week's success:

Got published in lit mag.

Got a sweet job offer, post-Glossolalia.

(Got a date with Adice. Desserts post-date.)

I would add that last one in the morning.

Adice Bandi's long brown arms covered my chest. She was so warm her skin vibrated with her warmth. I knew every curve and sinuous nook of her body. My cock was curled close to her pussy, both damp from the repeated sex.

Unknowing sex. The best kind. It started like an accident. Adice and I went out for dinner at the sheesha lounge between our houses. Since the last time I seen her at the gallery, she had dyed her hair a scarlet red. Matched with her Persian tan and green eyes, she looked like an Irish gypsy.

Her hands and feet were decorated with faded henna tattoos, the remnants of her sister's recent wedding.

She moved her latticed hand to my chest.

"I can feel your heart," she said.

"What's it saying?"

"It's pounding. I think it wants out."

Of course it did. How could I ever want to be anywhere other than here? Of course my heart needed out, it had a tome that it would recite for Adice. It wanted to feel her hands and carry her soft feet.

And I could have said all this to Adice, except that a massive doubt stood in the way of my tachycardiac heart.

"Do you mind if I smoke?"

"It's your room," she said.

"I usually don't smoke in here, but I'm willing to make an exception."

"What else are you willing to make?"

"You," I laughed, reaching for the cigarettes and stopping to loom over her.

Adice poked me, so I poked her, and I forgot about my itch for a cigarette.

I drank from her lips, big gulps that tried to swallow her. She stopped, and I continued nibbling her neck. If I had any real conception of time, any linear momento from my past, then I would've never stopped measuring her with my mouth. I would've never given into my arm's fatigue, and I would've never lay back down beside her.

But I did. We stared into each others eyes.

"My grandmother always told me that you could see the face of God in beauty, and that when you saw it, you were on the right path."

She stroked my face. My bristles made a rough buzz under her fingers.

"She was a Sufi. They call it *ihsan*[86]—that sensation of beauty and goodness in all things. Observing beauty was a mystical experience for her."

Adice ran her fingers through my hair, and I tried to imagine seeing a god I didn't believe in in her face. Then she kissed me again, and I closed my eyes, becoming enthralled with her skin, mapping it over and over again with my hands.

I had no capacity for mystical visions. But if my mouth wasn't occupied, I would've told Adice how having sex with her was unlike anything I had ever done. It was different from any drug, any rollercoaster, any breath-taking sunset I had ever seen. After every shared orgasm I had hypnagogic

---

[86] **Ihsan** — (*Arabic*) Islamic term for transcendant beauty

hallucinations in her arms—wild, fleeting daydreams about things I quickly forgot about—scenes replaced by other scenes, first-person narratives replaced by third-person cinematics, replaced by untouchable insights.

So unlike the auto-erotic ejaculations of telematic sex.

When we pulled apart again, we met eyes.

In her deep mahogany eyes I saw Adice with her head wrapped in a black cloth. She continuously unwrapped the cloth, spinning one arm around her head to reveal only more black cloth.

"What does the face of God look like?" I asked naïvely.

"Oh, Martin," she giggled. "I'm not a Sufi. My mother told me my grandmother was paranoid. Isn't that what religious people are, after all?"

I kissed Adice. And this time I didn't let go, because a thread of my linear life broke through, and I suddenly knew that Adice would eventually leave my bed, and I would be left alone again. Alone and without visions. Humanity's story.

And now I had a place in it.

God's face shades the
beauty of fleeting moments—just
stay with me instead.

THE MOSQUITO
[Atlas Sangman]

Mid-morning, the house was quietest. My three Homeboys were out in their respective worlds. Me, I was stuck in mine. My days had become all too predictable. Even my alarm clock was wise to my schedule. After it rang, I turned it off and turned in bed while it watched me with its demonic red eyes, reminding me of my duty. Work, work, work.

That infernal metronome.

I sat up in bed and decided to stretch. I did a short yoga routine, which was harder for me in the morning because my bed was too soft. I considered sleeping on the floor tonight.

Though my arms and legs and pelvis moved repeatedly like they did every session, my mind wandered. I thought about Jeanne, for no better reason than I remembered that I had dreamed about her last night. Couldn't remember how. All I remembered was her smile.

Her smile made me think to months before, months before Jeanne left for Cannes, when we were still immature fledglings of the alternative scene who called no scene home and preferred the society of each other. Jeanne and I walked along the inter-suburb portion of the River for hours. She plucked a handful of wildflowers.

"We should get married," she said.

"But who'll run the service?"

"That bird—who cares?"

I shyed away, answering with the side of my face, making her look at my profile so that maybe she would understand my inadequacy.

"We should get married," she said.

But not because of a church, or out-dated customs, or legal status, or for the vanity of the celebration, but for the sanctity of Love, for the compelling simplicity of Love. The sun shone, Jeanne smiled, and a ray of light twinkled from behind her hair. The flowers in her hands, the sound of gurgling water, my unnecessary laughter—that chimed with the pastoral bird that sang a short riff, watching us from its perch. I stared beyond Jeanne to seriously ponder her offer, until I concluded:

"We don't need marriage."

"Of course not."

Because we were alone together, and the sun shone. There was no need for any of that wrinkling concern over the future.

When Jeanne returned from Cannes enamoured with her paintbrush I understood what she had asked me for.

I went to the window, abdicating my yoga for today. It would do no good if I couldn't focus. I watched what little slice of outdoor life I could. There was so little action that the day could have fooled me into thinking that it never happened. But I knew better. My alarm clock knew better. I would be late if I dawdled much longer.

I paused at my window and bent to the windowsill. There lay a mosquito, crumpled like fine discarded twine. I had noticed it the night before, running again and again into the glass. I had let it be. It was strange—I didn't have a single bite on my body. That mosquito had spent itself trying to find an escape it would never achieve, when it had all the warm-blooded sustenance it needed in easy accessibility.

I cranked open my window and pulled the screen out. I picked up the mosquito by a wing and tossed it out the window. I watched it arc downwards until I lost it in a busy background.

Work. It was time for work, I convinced myself.

I am a cook by
trade, nomad by birthright,
lover by accident.

CHEWED THROUGH
[Henryk Zdicz]

I struggled to admit it, but it was true. The Grey Movement had shook me to my core. I was frazzled by my brief encounter with them. I didn't know how to feel right again.

Sometimes I felt like a rat in this city, but I felt it all the much more now because of that stupid bearded fucker. It was times like these when I wanted to skip school, say screw everything and go back to the mindless grind.

The mindless grind of a rat. I found it weird that we felt the need to eradicate the actual rats infesting the city. It made me uncomfortable.

True, rats carry disease and ruin perfectly fine baked goods. They copulate with miraculous success. I bet if we just fed off the rats like they feed off us now we could over-populate the world and carry our diseases to eliminate competition across the globe. But I bet if we did what we were doing now we would do the same.

The city made me feel like I had a thousand uncovered scabs. The tiny teeth of rabid rats.

But it could've just been me. The dichotomy of my life had recently doubled—a quadropolomy— split between music, school, friends and loneliness. Then each split off within themselves. Music became band and personal exploration, friends became the trusted and the weird, loneliness had seen sadness and pride, and school had become defined by my education in the natural, organic, balanced world, and my applied tutelage, living like a consuming whore who wanted nothing more than to drill more holes to fuck the world over.

That could be why the city put me in a stupor. I was learning about the forests we disappeared to erect our own. Everyday I crossed our urban forest on the same old game trails. Climate control! Streetlights! Plumbing! All a clever parody of what we destroyed.

Everyday I rode the rails. I inhaled the train's fumes with disgust. No wonder all the business men were so hooked on blow—any distraction was valid when our creations crowded us.

Atlas told me about the city's revived rat problem. It was their own fault, but if you asked them, it wasn't. Mostly too much garbage not moved quick enough.

Our leftovers became urban humus—we played the part of decomposers—our anthropocentric re-creation of the ecosystem was that much more complete.

The floor of the subway car was tiled by candid snapshots on the front pages of all the scattered newspapers. It seemed like more people ignored the newspaper than read them. But that was okay, it was the leaf litter in our reformed forest.

The more I learned about the earth, the more the earth knew about me. Or at least I became aware that the earth knew it about me.

That's why I skipped class and rode the subway.

And that's why the rats made me uncomfortable.

There was one stey grey fucker on the subway. Just after morning rush hour. It was just hiding away in a nook under the seats. If it was pregnant, wherever it debarked would be fucked. Or blessed. But who wants luck spilling over the feet of the cooks? That's why Atlas feared the rats, because if they got into his work, he would be fired. And he was becoming very comfortable with his job. It was too good to give up. We couldn't complain.

Symbiosis. Everything in its place—everything to its season.

I didn't mind the rats, though I didn't want to see one on today's ride. I was in no mood.

I wondered what people would do. It was busy, but there would be space to run around. This car could suddenly become very violent.

I wanted to shout *Rat!* and see what happened.

But I wouldn't. Not today.

Instead I stared up at the advertisements. The dreary man over the speaker announced the next stop. Only one stop had passed. Seven more to go. Time snailed on, tearing a rip in the skirted pantyhoses, leaving mucous from the common cold everywhere.

Now I was looking for a rat. I wanted to see it come down the long legs of the girls braving skirts in the late winter freeze.

Now I felt uncomfortable because I associated rats with sex. That was fucked up. I hoped I didn't get an uncontrollable boner before I had to get off. Get off. Don't stop, not yet, six more after this next. Six more. Oh man.

It was inevitable. One of the skirted women looked at me. I watched her in the reflection. I thought I saw a smile but it could've been a scowl. The windows wobble in the subway. So wishy-washy underground. How deep did the tunnels go? Would I still see her smiling if we got buried together?

Great, now necrophilia.

Copulate, young man, and do it well, make her scream. Sex! Everything in the forest fucks. So in our forest, we will fuck.

Fuck, I had three stops to get the boner down. I tried ignoring the lady, but it may have been too late.

But my erection was exactly why we all rode the subway. Why we left our homes at all. All for a primal urge, an instinctual hunger. We were all still hungry past breakfast, hunting the subway tunnels for the moist tender love of a something-year-old who looked hungrier. It was a strict evolutionary survival game that everyone played, even if they didn't know it. These poor people. They just wanted to fuck.

That was who was to became the new natives of the country: all the poor sexless people, who started life bright-eyed and resilient, but ended up haggard and hopeless by the time they made their last RRSP payment.

And we all copiously copulate to no end, just banging like woodpecker bills. Well adapted to senseless sex because we need to reproduce to survive in the wild scary woods of reality. Chiselling the land! Alien slaves to love!

The new native knows nothing besides what's illuminated along the roof of the subway car.

And I saw them so much I could recite them. But I wouldn't, because that would just be murder, I think. And the new natives drew lines, although they weren't moral or spiritual. They were just the same old lines that were drawn in sands all over the world. There was no religion. Drunks! Who wake up munching down bacon and jerking off before going to watch television for Sunday afternoon reclination. That was okay. But it was crazy to go to church. It was crazy to love rats, even if you went to church. We were a collective Tony Montana protecting our stash with our lives—don't fucking touch the coke mountain, rats, or else you'll be numb from the AK-47—the universal weapon of choice, by the way. That or the remote control. Like life from afar. Life with one more stop to go.

I stood and made my way to the door. I knew the last leg of this journey by heart. I surfed along to all the distinctive bumps.

The station doors opened. I stepped to the lit platform—the neat mosaic, the large readable stop name, the yellow line that was supposed to save my life.

For a moment, outside of the car with erratic clicking surrounding me and frantic bodies changing places, I stared down the subway train. Closest to me a punk guy with oversized headphones bobbed onto the car. Through the crowd I saw an old couple wobble together through the doors. Farther yet I saw a woman in a fancy business suit, face tightened from a Sour Puss hangover. At the farthest end I saw a church group orderly boarding the train. The image came clear: I thought the subway looked like a totem pole flipped horizontally. A lazy totem pole. Which way would be up? The way it went or the way it came?

No answer from the train, only a whirl of wind and an empty tunnel. I realized the cannabis lounge wouldn't be opened until eleven, and I had not had breakfast—then I saw a rat scurry along the blackened rails.

"Dirty fuckers," I uttered.

Then I realized something more.

I desperately needed to leave the city's concrete disappointment.

> These natives, they're strange:
> each life carved out for
> the top of the totem pole.

AROUND & AROUND WE GO
[Simon Arcan]

We were hanging out at Malik's, getting mind-fucked in his basement. I'll be straight up with you —we didn't always have a reason to partake in certain ceremonies.

Tunes played from a stereo somewhere around the bend. Malik's basement was shaped like a doughnut. It circled the stairs and the middle supports of the huge house. There was an interior room to the doughnut: the Timbit[87]. That's where we usually hung out, unless there was something specific we were doing other than hanging out. There was a corner for burning, a corner for snorting, and a corner for jamming. The last corner had dusty Christmas boxes stacked in it.

We had rolled in the Timbit room in anticipation of this fine Thursday night. First, we had a nice stash of blow that needed consuming, so we took it to the square glass table with a chessboard in the middle. Pieces stood disarranged on it. Who knows who played chess last. They didn't finish.

Kenny sat back because he was all against drugs. He chugged at a mickey of whiskey and a can of coke.

Martin smoked a cigarette while he meticulously cut the lines. One for each of us. He took his hit and sat back in the big wooden chair for a moment. He pulled on his cigarette. I reminded the man to keep on the move. We all stood and moved a chair to our left, so that the person sitting

---

[87] **Timbit** — (*English*) A Canadian delicacy

in Martin's old chair would be able to take their line. Atlas did his and moved in a swift motion. Henryk cut his further into two lines and took them separately. Then, trying to joke, Kenny sat in Martin's chair.

"I can play with you crazy train conductors too," he said.

He felt around in his sweater pockets, then pulled out a small baggie of ketamine. He let some out of the bag and took up the razor. He started chopping it, looking at us in turn to see if we would react. Martin and Atlas weren't even looking at him, and I just shrugged when he looked at me.

"You guys fuck around with that crack. But me, I just get right to the point—I get where I want to be. Which is nowhere. Exactly nowhere."

Kenny laughed and took the line. He held his nose, complaining about the burn. I pushed him out of the chair, took my line, then licked the table clean. Malik took my place and erased the last line. We all moved slowly to the burning circle in the next corner.

We barely sat. We were all wired. We stood and talked and passed the joint. Kenny sat quietly. He laughed occasionally, but it was always too much or too delayed.

Then Kenny decided to speak, and when he did, I punched him in the face.

"You guys are fucking crazy. Bat shit crazy. I'm getting the hell out of this place. Get me out. Get the door!" Kenny shouted at Malik.

"What's wrong with this guy?" Malik asked.

"To begin with?" I asked. "Well I dunno, bro, but it's probably that he's consumed an eightball of K in the passed few days. Probably some kind of psychosis."

I had to grab Kenny and throw him down on the sofa in the Timbit. The Homeboys followed behind me. We shut the door and circled Kenny. The guy was tripping hard, he looked like he shit his pants.

"Yo, Kenny. Chill out. Here, have some water. Atlas can try to brew you up some tea."

I tried to comfort him, but he was far-gone. He looked like he was trying to stay afloat in a sea. He tried to speak but couldn't say anything. Atlas asked if he should be taken to the hospital. We hoped not.

"I think he's just hit the K-Hole, guy. He's on his way where he needs to be. He'll be back."

I tried to put a positive spin on it. We would check on him in a bit. For now: another line.

One more line.

One line.

Kenny was easier to talk to when we returned. We had also calmed since his outbreak. We thought it must've just been a panic attack.

"Yo, K, what's up? How're you feeling?" I asked.

"Feeling? Huh—that's new."

"I think he's alright."

"Oh I'm alright. I still need to get out of here though. I should go. I need to go."

"Hold up, cowboy. Why do you need to go? Why don't you wait 'til we all go?"

"If you don't let me leave, I'll leave anyway. I'm just telling you."

"There's gotta be reason."

"There's always a reason," Henryk laughed, manic from the line.

"What's the reason Kenny?"

"He's uncomfortable, man, "Atlas said. "He needs to go home. I think he's finally become afraid of us. It was delayed, man, because he never even knew we really existed before."

"Then let the man leave," Henryk confirmed.

"Naw, dude, I have a sneaking suspicion that Kenny has something to say to us. I don't know why. He let something slip, and I want to know what it was," I peered at Kenny.

"I'll tell you why I'm leavin'," Kenny stood shakily in front of me. "It's because I can't hide it anymore. My mom is officially tellin' me I can't hang out here, with you guys. She's really gettin' on my case. She just doesn't approve."

"Doesn't approve? What is this, the fifties?"

"My mother doesn't exactly approve of immigration into this country," Kenny said defiantly.

He regained most of his balance. He stood resolutely in the middle of the Timbit. He looked at all of us in turn. I felt edgy, and I was sure the Homeboys were feeling it too. Kenny looked ready to be violent.

"And where is your mother from?" Henryk asked accusingly.

"Canada."

"She must be Cree, then?" Atlas asked.

"Nope. Canadian."

"Thanks for the clarification. Spill it, Kenneth! Get to your point."

Kenny fell onto the couch and rolled around until he was in a comfortable position. None of us sat.

"My family was successful. We were sittin' real pretty, believe you me. My mom wanted a job to keep herself busy and to make more mad money.

My parents were hungry like that. But then, you see, she found a trick to getting money, something that seemed to make sense. When I first heard it it made sense. She was going to market to new Canadians—the 'namgrants who have no idea what life is really like here. You charge them more than what it actually costs for insurance, houses, cars, whatever else, you charge them more as, like, a processing fee. It was all good 'til a couple smart ones caught on and seeked legal counsel. Then we were fucked. For what? Because my mom had to work double hard to help 'em out? No way. That's why I say fuck you. Fuck you!"

"You asshole!"

I thrashed at his wide chest, but Henryk quickly grabbed me by the shoulders. Kenny staid his ground cradled on the sofa and watched us. Atlas looked calm, so I tried to vibe off that. I sat on the armchair behind me and threw my hands up in the air.

"Alright, man, whatever. You're probably right. Karma will get its man."

"You should fuck off, Kenny," Henryk said. "There is no way I'm wasting my time with you."

"You should go now," Atlas said.

"I'll go, but give me some time, please. I need a minute to catch my breath. I took too much of that shit."

Everybody looked at me. I looked at Malik, who showed how much he cared by shrugging. I nodded slowly, noting that Kenny knew he wasn't wanted here. At least we could make him suffer through guilt.

"Yeah, guy, you can stay here and chill. Take your time. Atlas isn't going to drive you home, though, alright? Yeah so, chill out. I'll be right back —I'm going to take a line and chill."

I left the room, fiending for a line to calm me down. I could at least render the body calm, even if I couldn't steer my anger right now.

GUERILLA TRIBUNAL
[Martin O'Neill]

"Naw, fuck it, I changed my mind," Simon said, crashing back into the room.

He grabbed Kenny by the back of his jacket and pushed him upstairs.

"Lessgo. All of us. C'mon," he instructed the rest of us.

Malik told his mom we were leaving, making sure to grab the van keys on his way out of the kitchen. When he came back Simon had already walked Kenny out of the door. Kenny complained, but was too subdued from the K to put up much resistance. Simon pushed Kenny into the backseat and took shotgun next to Malik.

"To the Valley, my friend," Simon said.

Simon was beyond pissed off—he just sat in the front looking sternly at the road ahead. He itched the sparse growth of his beard thoughtfully with the two fingers that held his cigarette. He almost looked exquisite. Exquisite but grungy. He reminded me of the grainy photos of Castro in the Cuban mountains. Simon even had that same crazy look in his eye.

I was beyond fucked. I had no idea what exactly was going on. But it was a fun ride. I loved to be moving when I was on blow. Malik rocked some loud tunes, and slowly the city lights blinked out to the dark countryside. Orange and blue and orange and blue. There was a full moon that cast an empty silver light on everything. I thought I saw wolf eyes light up in the ditch as we passed, but I was probably just imagining things.

When Malik killed the engine at the Valley trailhead I fully appreciated where we were. I got out of the car first, taking in the sweet spring air. My heart raced. I saw the bridge and started towards it. Half way there Simon told me to come back, we weren't going to be here long. I joined my friends in the tall grass beside the parking lot. Kenny was sitting on the ground, his head almost between his knees. Simon stood over him and faced us.

Simon had given up trying to make sense.

"He fucking played us, guy. I'm not down with the whole redemption thing. Naw, this motherfucker had no qualms with screwing us over. Maybe not *us*. But people like us. How do you think Kenny-cunt's going to think about us when he finally grows up? When he finally gets some balls? He already hates us immigrants because of what we apparently did to his mom. Fuck that. We're going to let Kenny grow a set of balls. In the same way we all grew balls."

Simon pushed Kenny down and stood over him. He pressed his face into Kenny's and launched a furious finger at him.

"You're going to do it like we all did it. You're going to walk home through this strange land. You're going to walk home by yourself. Fuck you."

Moonlight cold, night warm,
footsteps in the dark to count
all the ways back home.

'PATAPHYSICAL HEALTH TEST
[Martin O'Neill]

This is *echt*[88]!

That is what Conrad Hemingway would have said if he was here.

The day had finally come. Simon's friends at the 'Pataphysician's Office put in a lot of work for such a disorganized group. They mobilized all the energy they could on campus. They involved as many groups and individuals as possible to put together their happening in the Don Valley. The campus had probably never seen so much traffic. It was spring, the temperature was warming, the snow was long gone, and I felt it as much as everybody else felt it—there was a ubiquitous feeling of *awakening*.

But that was too cliché. James, my editor, would have shredded that nutgraph.

Simply put, the 'Pataphysician's Office was putting on a show in the cleared portion of the Don Valley which was sanctioned for social events but rarely used. Hugh Min riled up as many of the university's clubs as possible to attend. He had carpenter friends who built a stage free of charge. In front of the stage there was a grassy field bordered

---

[88] ***Echt*** — (*German*) Genuine

by the Don Valley's oaks and elms that were starting to bud. Around the edges of the field Hugh got people from the different clubs to set up shanty booths—mostly blankets hosted by a club member. He had young artists hang pieces from the trees. Weeks before, Simon and Jeanne drafted up hundreds of posters and postcards to leave around the city in the subway, bus stations, cafés, record stores, and anywhere else they thought they would be noticed.

They must have been noticed. Early in the afternoon people already started showing up. They made circles in the grass and smoked joints, drank beer and wine, they laughed and played acoustic guitars. When Hugh showed up at six o'clock he hopped in excitement. He pointed at all the people and pulled his hair. If he had Conrad's German vocabulary, he probably would have also said, *this is echt*!

I was impressed. I convinced James that I would cover the event, which did not have a name or any real press coverage. In fact, it was more of a massive house party. Without a house. Or a party, really. There was nothing really happening at the happening. Hugh did have some bands lined up for after the sun went down, but it was an after-thought more than the main event.

In the late afternoon Hugh manned the *Old Tattered Recipe Book Club*'s vats of chilli, handing out bowl after bowl to munchie friends and strangers. The *Recipe Book Club* ran out of their homemade buns quickly, and someone ran uphill to the campus to fire up the ovens for more.

There was no exchange of money in any way—that was an explicit rule set out by the 'Pataphysician's Office. Some I interviewed thought it would keep people from offering services. A bunch of those people must have made a vow to become more generous though, because by seven-thirty the clubs who had set up shop at the forest's edge had their blankets piled with fruits, munchies, and drinks. The *Official Party Club* had twenty-three bottles of assorted liquor, and they passed out cups like army rations.

In fact, that's what the event already reminded me of. I imagined that in World War II, before the troops headed to the front lines, they had glorious feasts like this one, gorging on food and drink and love.

I tried to ignore my looming anxiety, asking, how soon does the war come?

I tried to scribble everything I could into my notebook:

Wartime lovers saying goodbye—nobody leaving

Conscious Eaters Club blanket a 'vitamin C' haven (bananas, oranges, grapes!)

Girl actually wants to dance with me & there's not even music

Sun goes down, more people fill the small field

I wished I had brought a camera.

Simon and I helped the groups set up their goods. We helped assemblages of neo-hippies lay out their blankets and inflate their beach balls. We shared joints with the friendliest of them. I tried to remember all the exchanged names. I knew I would forget them before long, and they would forget too. We also learned the inventory of intoxicants that our new friends were quick to share: mushrooms, MDMA, alcohol, 2C-b, pot, weed, hash, herb (no shortage of cannabis—that was standard fare at this point).

Between Simon and Hugh the rumour about free LSD spread quickly. Simon tried phoning Atlas and Henryk to see where the acid's bearers were, but they never answered. He figured they were underground, on the subway. Hugh did not fret, he was too excited about the whole night to worry about details, although he spent an hour with the two stoners manning the light board, working with them to figure out the best light arrangement for the stage.

All Light Lets All Heed (Muslim club) giving free hugs for the night—claim to be the night's 'sitter' [censor for mag: they would stay straight-edge, provide stability for those not feeling the groovy vibes]

Seeing their browned skins reminded me of Adice. One of her paintings hung from an oak tree behind the A.L.L.A.H club's tent. I found myself staring at it when my eyes wandered.

Simon naturally gravitated to the pretty girls. He was not ashamed about gloating a little bit about being the event's creator. They asked him for special privileges, like going on stage to dance or whatever, but he toed the 'Pataphysician's line: there were no rules.

No rules, so people gathered periodically on stage, singing accapella. Someone was brilliant enough to have brought a few sets of bongos, and these floated between groups, sparking impromptu jams. Simon made it his mission to unify the segregated groups. One by one he introduced an individual to another, or joined a bongo-slapping group with one plucking their acoustic guitars, and soon enough all the circles of friends grinded together, unlikely cogs running an intangible machine none of them understood. It was around the time that I noticed the moon sitting in the twilight sky that almost everybody who was in attendance joined in an ecstatic rendition of *Wake Up* by the Arcade Fire. I even found myself inharmoniously chanting along to the wordless bridge.

Children, Wake Up! this will probably end up on YouTube somewhere.

After the song ended a few tried to keep the sing-a-long rolling, but they had a hard time finding a common song that everyone knew, so these hardcore musicians became a new circle, fiddling around for the ideal song.

I climbed the hill towards campus. I sat halfway up, turning back on the Don Valley for the view. James would hate this article, I already knew it. Nobody who read about this after the fact would ever really get it. I lit a cigarette, crossed my legs, and smiled uncontrollably.

It was not the marijuana. It was not even the small parachute of MDMA some dude (who looked like the Zig Zag man) passed through my lips. No —this was what I had longed for so long in my life, the one thing that I wanted—the most clearly essential but inexplicably cruel—the fleeting rush of oxytocin—

Remember today. All I want it <u>this.</u>
This was love.

Fleeting like wind,
flowing like water, growing like grass—
Wake up! It's Love.

[Simon Arcan]

I breathed deeply. The air was pungent with spring. The moon was in the sky by late afternoon. Hugh told me that the sun and moon had come to an agreement for the day. They would meet in the sky, because today was above divisions, it was about a pure unity. The man was an idealist. I believed him, so that probably made me an even bigger idealist.

I was super-excited about the night, when the celebrations became unfettered in the dark. The LSD would show up soon, if Atlas and Henryk ever made it. Then there would be a beautiful insanity. Something like what Martin told me, as he came down from the hill, his hands coolly in his pockets but his lips flapping: the night would be like falling in love with life.

After failed attempts at getting Atlas and Henryk on the phone I texted Henryk, and he messaged me that Atlas got home late from work and they would be in the vicinity soon.

There was already a substantial crowd, something neither Hugh or I had anticipated.

Kaya and his trio of experimental musicians played a disorientating song on stage, using a dissected tape player, a synth and a drum kit. The anti-music only hyped me up. It may have given some of the other heads the wrong impression, so I found a couple of other musicians from my political science classes and played sporadic jams that attracted a small crowd.

As the sunlight settled into greens and blues Martin and I lit the dollar store torch lights. We had more than fifty, and they lit up the field nicely. I was lighting a joint with the last one when I peered up the hill and saw Henryk bounding down in long leaps.

"The show begins!" I shouted.

I met him at the bottom, and he opened his backpack to reveal half a dozen water bottles.

"Diluted LSD," he said. "Atlas has more."

He pointed uphill, where Atlas and Claire were slowly descending. I hugged everyone and led the pair to Hugh. He raised his hands and announced their arrival to whoever was nearby. He led them to the table where he had set up a ten gallon jug.

"Is this it?" Hugh asked, pointing to the bottles.

Atlas nodded, wordless since his arrival. Henryk helped him unload the water bottles into the jug, and they stacked cups provided by one of the clubs. Martin tried to take Atlas aside, but Hugh grabbed Atlas' other shoulder.

"This is phantasmagorical! Yeah? How strong is it?" Hugh asked franticly.

He dipped a finger into the mixture and sucked on it. His puckered lips showed it was bitter, and Atlas nodded again.

"How do you want to do this?" Hugh asked. "Line up? Scramble? Survival of the fittest? What?"

"No," Henryk said. "We made tickets. You can hand out these tickets. Everybody gets one. Then we see what we can distribute after that."

"Tickets? The fucking party boys are handing out free liquor by the fistful, and you made tickets?"

"This isn't liquor, man," Atlas finally spoke up.

"Yeah, we aren't here to brain-rape some innocent people," Henryk added.

Claire pulled at my hair and smiled like a child. I held her hand and asked if she was okay. She giggled and nodded. I noticed, on her left cheek, a hand-painted upside-down peace sign inside a crossed out circle.

"I never knew you were against peace," I told her.

"It's *anti*-anti-peace," Hugh pointed out.

"You must be Hugh Min," Claire said, stepping towards the fidgety man. "Or human? I never got that. What's your actual name?"

"Enough with this idle chitter chatter. Let's get these tickets out and around. People!" Hugh shouted. "People! Get your ticket! Take the ride."

Martin rolled his eyes at the poor Hunter S. Thompson reference, but he grabbed a ticket and presented it to Henryk. Henryk poured him a short shot of the clear liquid. Martin gulped it down, then received another hug from Claire.

I picked up a ticket and handed it to Henryk gallantly, of course—the way any gentleman should be when he is accepting a mind alteration.

Hugh was right, the shot was bitter. I chased it with a drink someone had left on the table. With all the chemicals streaming through my veins I figured the acid would kick in quickly.

While I followed Hugh to the stage handing out tickets, Claire walked beside me and watched the groups of people I pointed out: the arts folk, the biology majors, the philosophy freaks.

"You don't need to label these people for me, babe," Claire said.

"I'm not labelling. I'm just sharing knowledge," I said.

"I'll know them if I need to know them."

"Yeah, yeah, *chiquee*, for the rest of us who don't have ESP, or whatever, a nice pre-introduction is helpful."

"I can feel that everyone here's chill. I don't think either of us will need any kind of formality. Besides, who has ESP?"

"How's the acid?"

"Phantasmagorical," she said.

Claire changed pace while she spoke. She paused to think between sentences. As we passed a torch I noticed that her pupils were dilated, almost completely over-taking her mahogany pupils. Soon I would be right where she was.

I swung an arm around her shoulder. She was right, there was no negativity here today. *Anti*-anti-positivity, as Hugh might have put it.

She sat cross-legged at the foot of the stage, staring out at the crowds of people while I helped Hugh align amps and plug in wires. The walk had given me jitters—the pre-trip excitement. I used my tasks to calm myself down. I paid extra attention to the bass set-up. I'd be playing later, and I was excited at playing live on a massive psychedelic trip. The four of us figured we would fuck up, but we would turn the volume way up and hoped no one cared enough to throw shit at us.

Claire walked up behind me, now flanked by Atlas and Henryk.

"Sy, do you need a sound check?"

"I guess we could use one."

"We'll do one. Do you mind?"

"Mind? I don't give a fuck what you do. Hugh won't either. Do your thing."

I left them on stage, wondering what they planned and jealous that they hadn't included me. Henryk picked up a guitar and played with the pedals. Atlas searched the stage until he found a clay drum brought by one of the drumming circles that afternoon. I manned the watercooler with Martin, filling and passing out shots for tickets.

"Sound check," Claire crackled through the microphone. "Sound wreck. Check. Check. We are *Santalaceae Ecstasy*[89]."

The guitar ripped through the ambient silence. Most people turned towards the stage. Some whooped in encouragement. Atlas jumped in with a simple drum beat, and Claire hummed into the microphone. She worked a pedal that flanged the vocal mic. People in line paused to listen to the enchanting rhythm, so I stopped handing out shots. Martin scribbled some more in his little black book.

---

[89] ***Santalaceae*** — (*Latin*) The Sandalwood Family of plants

Claire had an amazing voice that she rarely made public. She looked perfectly at peace, slithering behind the microphone stand. That made my night—even if it all went to hell, this made it worth it. To have a person find joy in something you found joy in—that was friendship for me. I pulled out my pipe, loaded it, and smoked while I watched my friends surprise me.

The song ended after Claire skipped around the stage, bashing different drums and cymbals to the beat. People clapped and hooted. I continued serving drinks.

"Some of those lines sounded familiar," Martin said. "From the *Tibetan Book of the Dead*, I think."

"Makes sense," I said. "Man, Claire is blasted on this shit, I'm sure the three of them were already tripping out at the house."

"Sounds like a good time, then."

Henryk and Atlas took over the table again, so Martin and I got to wander. There had been a flush of people who must've rushed from the campus plateau when they heard music. It was insane. Hugh wished that this night would be significant, but I wasn't optomistic enough to see his vision. But now I could start to doubt my cynicism. Good old *anti*-anti-optimism.

Insane. I lost Martin in the crowd, but I found Claire sipping a smoothie prepared by the *Conscious Eaters* club. We walked together as the Punk Twin's band, *Omphaloskepsis for Dummies*[90], began their three chord punk progression.

"Punk rock," Claire ruminated. "Would you like some of my smoothie? It's delicious. It tastes like the colour orange. But it's purple. Here, try some."

"Want to smoke a joint?" I asked.

"Of course."

I led Claire up the hill, where we could watch the Don Valley's proceedings in relative calm. Couples were scattered across the hill, cuddling or making out. I lit the pre-rolled joint and handed it to Claire, who took long hits from it. The smoke curled around her raven hair. I watched it wisp into the purple sky.

"I heard what happened to Kenny," Claire said between tokes. "The disingenuous can only stay that way for so long."

"Why be disingenuous at all?"

I asked rhetorically, and was glad Claire understood that, because the pronunciation of that shitbag's name made my stomach growl. I had to

---

[90] ***Omphaloskepsis*** — (*Greek*) Contemplation of one's own belly-button

stay positive—the LSD would only magnify whatever I gave it to magnify.

"Why be anything at all?" Claire asked.

"That's what I'm saying."

"But you don't."

"Naw, I'm passed that, I guess. If I was still like that, I wouldn't have been part of this event. Look, there's people being *open*. Like, where do you see that anymore?"

"Between two people on a hillside."

After laughter we paused, considering the scene below us. Claire laid back on the hill, propped up on her elbows, and stared over the people. Since I woke up that morning I'd been on the move, organizing, setting up, and coordinating. There wasn't a minute to sit down. Finally this hill gave me rest—even after making me sweat earlier that afternoon carrying equipment up and down it earlier in the day. Finally I could rest, and I wished I hadn't.

Anxiety overcame me. Inexplicable as it was, it swung my heartbeat against my chest. All the things that could go wrong—plus all the things that could go right but still be unacceptable, or unnecessary, or —I flinched out of my panicked thoughts as Claire nudged me to take the joint. I looked at her and felt warm again. Aglow, even. And I never said aglow. Claire met my eyes and moved close to my face.

"If you believed half of what you say, you'd kiss me right now."

"What do you mean?" I asked, half playing the fool, and half insulted about whatever she insinuated.

Claire leaned back on her elbows and took the joint from my fingers.

"What's punk, Sy? You know how people always ask that? What is punk rock?"

"If chamber music is the music of the soul, and folk is the music of the heart, then punk is the music of the gut."

"I thought you'd say energy."

"Energy drives the soul, heart, and gut, so..."

"So you're right."

The phrase struck my heartbeat into its anxious fervour again.

"Calm down, baby. Simon. Chill out. There's nothing wrong right now."

Claire put her hand on my chest and tried to guide my diaphragm with slow movements.

"I'm okay. I'm okay," I said, brushing her hand off of me.

"You're freaking out."

"What? No I'm not."

"You're panicking."

I looked into Claire's eyes and saw how clear her pupil's abyss was. There was nothing to hide from Claire. If there was going to be any chance of calming myself down, I would have to acknowledge that.

"I'm afraid."

"And you want to bring this fear to everyone else?"

My fear was rooted in simple things—but once feared, anything became complicated. Easiest way to explain it was that I was afraid that Atlas and Henryk were right, that this was a bad idea that looked good in the mind's eye, but would quickly degrade once fully materialized.

"No. I don't want to scare people. Of course not. I'm not an animal. I really want to do something good for people. I do. But what? I thought I knew. Fuck. I don't want this to be it. If it goes all fucked up, y'know?"

Claire nodded patiently and waited until I rested my head in my hands.

"You know this will only turn out the way you want it to," she said.

"I need to go for a walk."

"Where are you going?"

I wanted to tell her not to follow me. Instead I stood and walked away.

"Can I come with you?" Claire called out.

I didn't answer. My silence would speak for itself. If I said anything, it would've been vague anyway. I would've said something like, *Come if you're* anti-*anti-confusion*.

I walked towards the dark forest of the Don Valley, away from the distorted noise and the twitchy firelight.

I wasn't sure where I was going, and while I would never admit it to Henryk or Atlas, I had never explored the Don Valley much, so I didn't know where to go. At least—

"You don't know where you're going."

I felt Claire's hand before I heard her voice. I jumped at her touch and whipped around to face her. In the dark I could only see ambient light reflect off her eyeballs.

"Come, there's a log up this way."

Claire led me blindly through the forest. I masked my face from the twigs Claire avoided, and stopped when my shins met the log. We sat down and basked in the silence of our stillness. The sound from the stage faintly reached us. Being draped in darkness felt peaceful, especially after the panic I had felt on the hill.

There was a warm breeze coming through the trees which pushed my hair playfully. Claire leaned her head into my shoulder. She was warm, and her weight calmed me more.

"Sy, did I ever tell you about the accident?"

"What accident?"

"When I was twelve, I was driving from Montréal to Toronto with my parents. We were moving. There was a drunk man in an SUV. He crashed into us, head-on. He came over the median and hit us."

"What? Shit. I guess you're alright, though, since you're here."

"I broke four ribs. My parents each had some broken bones. And scarred memories, too."

"Claire..." I sang, thinking I heard her sobbing.

"I'm okay about it, Sy. It's been too long for me to fret about it anymore. But this is the weird part that still gets to me."

I sat upright in the dark, my eyes adjusting enough to pick out her vague form.

"The reason we were moving was because we'd been referred to a Toronto psychologist."

"For what?"

"For me. Sy, I knew the car was going to hit us. I saw it happen before it happened. And I could've prevented it."

"You knew? I guess you are pretty intuitive with all that ESP shit—"

"No, that's the thing. I didn't have any of my...sensitivities...before the crash. But I used to see sporadic instances of the future. Now it's different. After the accident we never ended up seeing the psychologist, but we stayed in Toronto."

"Well, I'm glad you came. But have you ever thought that maybe you didn't predict the future, but you just saw what was going on in the man's head? Like, you knew he'd crash the car because he was so fucked."

"*Intéressant*[91]. At first, I thought it was something I'd grown out of, like baby teeth. Atlas could never see the future, and he's the only other person I've met who is legitimately like me."

"You're tripping me the fuck out."

I stated the obvious. I was calm, but I was stupefied by the alienness of Claire's ability— stupefication, something the supernatural naturally brought.

"Let's say you're right—" Claire said.

This time the word didn't prick me like before. I leaned forward towards Claire's silhouette and relished in the budding debate. I could see Claire

---

[91] ***Intéressant*** — (*French*) Interesting

talking with her hands. She still moved slowly, stunned by the LSD. I thought she looked like a forest nymph who grew up in the city and lost a touch of her ethereality.

"Let's say you're right and I knew all along what the man was thinking versus what he was going to do. You could say, then, that thoughts have consequences."

"Obviously."

"Obviously. And if you're panicking, don't you think that's only going to have consequences? Like, on the same people you want to help?"

"I guess..." I said, being coy so her moral wouldn't make my nerves look so obvious and witless.

"You know it. We should go back. Henryk needs us."

"You're doing your mind-reading stuff."

"If I see anything, it's only what people want me to see, Sy."

"Yeah, yeah, I'm sure. I have to play soon anyways. Let's go."

Claire guided me through the forest, giggling the whole way. Still in the dark, I grabbed her arm and stopped her.

"Hey, if there's any chance that you can see the future...is tonight going to be a car crash?"

"I can seriously say that I have no idea."

"Can I still get that kiss?"

"No."

"C'mon, I need it to calm me down."

"Haha! Sy, you *are* the car crash."

"Life as a car crash," I said, as much to the trees as to Claire. "Loss of bones and old virgin sensitivities."

"Nice haiku."

As we came out of the forest, back into the open field, I lit a cigarette. The warm breeze picked up, swaying the trees. It made Claire fall gently into me. We fell into a bush. The cigarette feel into my hair, tickling my scalp.

> Fiending wind: smoking
> as much of my cigarette
> as I am—it longs—

[Henryk Zdicz]

As soon as I saw Simon emerge from the treeline with Claire, I left Atlas at the water cooler and rushed towards him.

"Hey, what the hell, man?" I said. "We have to play in, like, fifteen minutes."

"I know. I'm good to go."

"Claire, how's it going?"

Claire had taken three of the strongest hits off the sheet of LSD, and I had taken to being her sitter, since neither Atlas nor I dropped any acid.

"Beautiful, Henryk. Me and Simon took a little stroll through the woods."

"You should stay in the light. Don't go running off. I don't want to have to find you naked in the woods."

"Not if they have anything to say about it."

Claire looked passed me. I followed her gaze to a trio perusing the crowd in pressed black business suits. It took me a second to get a good look at them, but once I did I recognized them right away.

The Grey Movement.

"See, you knew that Henryk was going to need back-up, you called it," Simon held Claire by her shoulders and spoke seriously. "Tell me. Car crash or not?"

"Hey Sy, could you do me a favour?" Henryk asked.

"Yeah. Of course, brother," he said, stepping away from Claire long enough for her to slip away. "Don't let me forget that I have to talk to her before we go on. So, what is it?"

"Could you kick someone out for me?"

"Who? Those Grey fuckers? Banishing someone seems kind of contrary to the whole theme of the night, doesn't it?"

"These guys aren't here for the benefit of the crowd."

"Not for the Benefit of Mr. Kite[92]? Hugh would say no, straight-up. But I gotta look out for Mr. Kite."

I followed Simon to where the Grey Movement bargained for fruits at one of the stands. They were trying to force money into the hands of the people giving them bananas and oranges.

"There a problem here?" Simon asserted himself. "What's going on?"

"This guy's trying to give us money that we don't want. I don't know how to explain it to him any other way," the girl at the fruit blanket said.

"Dude, it's cool you're being all generous and shit, but you can't force money into peoples' hands," Simon said. "Tell you what, I'll take the cash as a donation to the 'Pataphysician's Office."

"Fuck no," Beard stepped towards Simon.

Beard was a head taller than Simon. He spoke into Simon's afro. In their suit pockets, they each

---

[92] Yet another Beatles reference: "For the Benefit of Mr. Kite" off Sgt. Pepper's Lonely Hearts Club Band

had a forty-ounce bottle of beer. The mouth tipped when Beard spoke, splashing Simon.

"Okay, Captain Spilly-Pants, get the fuck up out of here. On behalf of the 'Pataphysicians, I don't want to deal with your shit."

"It's a free country. It's a free campus," Beard said—then he stopped, and caught my eyes. "Oh shit, boys, check it out. It's our tree-lover from Kaya's. Thought we'd find someone like you here."

"Look, man, this isn't a stage for your theatre, or whatever," Henryk said.

"We're just here to enjoy the night, dude. I think you're the one being uptight. Afraid we'll turn some people against you? Nice confidence, it fits you well."

"Maybe you didn't read the fine print," Simon said, unfolding a promo poster from his pocket.

He held it up to Beard's face so he could read it. Beard squinted, but couldn't see anything, so Simon moved the paper closer to his face. When it was within centimetres, Simon pushed the paper into Beard's face.

Beard immediately pushed Simon backwards onto the ground. Standing about the same height as the bearded man, I stood in his way before he could grab Simon again. I told Simon that we were leaving for our set. On our way Simon stopped

Hugh Min and told him about the Grey Movement. Hugh went to meet them, while we met Izzy and Wude on stage.

I slipped on the guitar with my back to the crowd and took a few breaths before turning around. Izzy snapped the drumsticks, then we kicked out the jams.

The show seemed to stretch on forever, but not in a bad way.

I was covered in a therapeutic sweat by the end. I rolled around in the cool grass behind the stage first thing. I wanted to lay in the grass all night, watching the stars migrate, but despite the Don Valley's illusion of wilderness we were still under a thick canopy of light pollution.

That reminded me of the Grey Movement, whom I had forgotten about while on stage. I imagined them mocking me, asking if I had ever seen the Milky Way, or any planet besides Venus. Then they would revel in humanity's great power to redirect all attention back towards ourselves. And that made me sick.

Luckily Atlas found me behind the stage. He joined me on the grass.

"Great set, man."

"Thanks. It felt awesome," I said.

"Yeah, I could feel that. It sounded fantastic."

"Glad that wasn't one-sided."

"The watercooler's empty."

"I didn't think it'd go so quick."

"Me neither. I don't think Hugh knows what he's getting into."

"No, he doesn't know what he's doing. Thank God we saw that coming."

"Yeah, I know, I'm glad we—"

"Henny!" Claire came towards us with her arms raised, hugging the ground with long strides. "I'm tripping out *so* hard, and you blew my mind. I loved it! The sound occupied space, for a moment, and washed over me, like waves. I was standing in the ocean of sound. Oh! We should've set up the tent up! Now it's dark."

"I don't know if we should camp here anymore, Claire."

"Aww. Why not? C'mon, it'll be fun."

"Tell you what. When it's a little warmer we'll go up north and camp for real—not this half-assed backyard camping. We'll do it properly."

"Yeah, Claire, it's wild right now," Atlas said. "Man, I have a feeling this thing's going to get shut down before long. There'll be drunk people everywhere. That's not the wildlife we're looking for, man."

"Partypoopers!" Claire said, and howled in laughter. "It's fine, I'm having a blast. I think I may be stuck in this trip *ad infinitum*. I hope I am. It's heaven. I'm going to go find Simon. He's bugging out. I'm glad he didn't drop any of this LSD. Or else he'd really be loopy. See you guys around!"

"Damn," I said as Claire disappeared. "I meant to ask her if Hugh managed to kick the Grey Movement out."

"I don't think Hugh would."

"He said he would."

"Yeah, but..."

We sat in a few moments of silence, until we heard the next band's amps crackle to life. Atlas produced a joint from behind his ear and asked if I wanted to go for a hike in the woods. I looked up at the sky once more, then followed Atlas between the oaks. We followed a sinuous creek, eventually finding a terrace where we could sit with our backs to the field. Ahead of us the distant din of the Don Valley Parkway; behind us, the electrified indie music. We sat in the dark silence for the first few tokes. Then Atlas cleared his throat, and asked me if he could confide something to me.

"Of course, bro."

"This is weird, but I feel like I need to say it...I keep getting left behind in dreams, man. Like, last night, I had a bunch of dreams, and each one ended the same. In one, I was on a tour bus, and we stopped at this grocery store. I went in to get some food, and when I came out, the bus was gone. In the other, a group of us were told to get to the twelfth floor, and when I got there, nobody was there and nobody came. I worship coincidence as much as anybody, but I don't like the feeling this gives me."

"My friend," I wrapped my arm around Atlas' thin shoulders. "It was just a dream. You won't get left behind. Not with us. We're your brothers, and family doesn't let people just fall off."

"Maybe you won't want it to happen, man, but it will. Listen, let's not trip out over this."

I nodded, but Atlas couldn't see it. I changed the subject to override the awkward emotional funk.

"Claire is flying, eh? She's ripped."

This time Atlas nodded in the dark, and somehow I felt that I had successfully took his mind off his sultry dreams. After a few puffs on the joint Atlas abruptly stood and looked back towards the stage. He patted himself like he couldn't find his keys.

"What's wrong?" I asked.

"Let's get back. I need to find Claire."

I followed Atlas back towards the fire-lit clearing, badgering him the whole way about his suddenness. He didn't answer. He weaved through the crowd, ducking his head around. He broke from the throng and headed towards the treeline again. I think he forgot I was with him. I kept following him anyway. By the edge of the clearing I saw Claire with somebody. Atlas beelined for them. When we were in earshot, I recognized the voice before I recognized the face.

Beard leaned against a tree, looming over Claire's small frame. She squirmed fluidly against the tree, trying to push Beard back while he tried to push into her for a kiss. Atlas interrupted their solitude, grabbing Claire's hand.

"What the fuck, you smelly hippie!" Beard said.

"Blow me," was all Atlas said.

He tried to lead Claire away from Beard, but she leaned her weight back.

"Claire, man, you don't have to let this asshole try to mack you like this."

"No, no, no..." was all Claire said.

"Fuck off," Beard pointed to me.

"I'm not going to let you rape my friend, cunt-rag."

"I ain't rapin' nobody," he said.

Atlas urged Claire away, but she shook her head.

"I can deal for myself," she sputtered. "I'm a big girl. I can handle myself. I can..."

Atlas dropped her hand, and Claire fell back onto the tree. He looked stunned, but only for a moment—he caught me watching him, and he toughened up his expression. He told Beard that he should be careful with her, and Beard laughed in his face. Atlas tried to look gangsterfied as he stomped off, but I could read my best friend: he was utterly destroyed. Claire had just stepped on his brittle heart, and I wasn't sure if I should've been pissed off at Beard or Claire.

I started to walk away, too, but I stopped only a few steps away. Beard had resumed his advances. He slurringly assured her that he had a nine inch dick. He told her that he had his truck parked not too far from the clearing. He asked her to feel his muscles, and assured her that he could carry her.

I turned around. I wasn't in the habit of stopping people from making their own decisions, but I understood LSD and its effects. It gave you the ability to not only realize, but actualize all the possibilities of your consciousness. Quite literally, anything could happen. A vegetarian could eat meat. A wallflower could become the life of the party. A homosexual could find himself lapping up sweet cunt juices. Claire could end up fucking a douchebag. She wouldn't in any other case, but if the possibility presented itself now, it would appear as plausible as fledging wings and learning to fly.

I wouldn't let Claire do that to herself. I wouldn't let her do that to herself, and I wouldn't let her do that to Atlas. She would thank me later.

I marched straight up to Beard and moved him aside. I put my arm around Claire's shoulder and lead her away. Beard put his hand on my shoulder but I shrugged it off. He muttered something about hugging a tree, but I ignored him. Claire looked up to me, cherubic, her pupils engrossed even in the darkness. She asked me where I was parked. I guided her to the A.L.L.A.H tent, and told them she needed water and some Rumi.

If I wasn't so intent on finding Atlas to tell him about my victory; if I wasn't straining my ears to hear a familiar voice; if I didn't throw myself blindly into the crowd; then, maybe, I would've noticed when I was surrounded by the Grey Movement, and I would've been able to throw up my arms before the first fists started to fly.

Small victories like
the defiant sound of skin
slapping against skin.

[Atlas Sangman]

Martin hugged me when I ran into him. He seemed oblivious to the pain I wore plainly on my face. He seemed agitated, but ecstatic. He led me with a beefy arm.

"Atlas, my friend. I know, man, I *know* what you *mean*. I understand."

"What? Martin, man, you're making no sense."

"I get *it*. You know? *It*. I get it."

"Do you need some water or something?"

"You have to lend me the *Tibetan Book of the Dead*. That song tonight, it was from it, wasn't it? You have a copy, right? I remember seeing one in your room. Maybe you and Claire can guide me through it?"

Hearing Claire's name made me bite my lip. The universal gesture for anguish must've been obvious enough for Martin to stop and face me squarely.

"What happened? Where's Claire? Where's Henryk?"

"I don't know, man, I don't..." I trailed off.

Martin jerked his upper body like he was going to shake me, but then he stopped. I'd never seen him so jumpy. He was usually the most docile, even when he was amped up on amphetamines. He pointed over my shoulder. I followed his finger, which targeted a kerfuffle in the centre of a jeering crowd. He said Henryk's name just as I saw Henryk's face surface between jabbing arms, and I ran as quick as Martin did right passed the insensitive on-lookers to pull the assailants off of our friend.

Baldie, whom I only vaguely remembered from Kaya's party, threw a punch in my direction—but he missed and fell to the ground. Martin and I picked Henryk off the ground. He had a nose bleed, but he wasn't too frayed from the beating.

Meanwhile, Simon threw himself at the Grey Movement in a fury, not exactly fighting, but rather erupting all his limbs in random disorder, launching sloppy punches and kicks at the confused trio.

There was a substantial crowd that formed around us, forceful enough in their curiosity that Martin and I couldn't push Henryk through.

Hugh Min managed to make his way through. He stood between the Grey Movement and us, waving his arms.

"What the hell is going on? Simon. Simon says, Simon stop!"

Simon grabbed Hugh. Realizing who he had in his arms, Simon stopped and asked Hugh what he wanted.

"I want you to stop ruining this."

"Ruining what?" Simon asked, breathing hard.

"What's with this fighting? Are we animals? Did we come here to offer a sacrifice to Apollo?"

But Hugh had stopped speaking to Simon, addressing the crowd as a whole.

"Did we come here to revert to our evolutionary past? Or did we come here to move on? Didn't we come here to grow? Yes! The answer is yes! If you didn't know it, if you were mindlessly putting on your shoes earlier today wondering *why am I going to this crazy thing tonight*? that is why. We have come here to ascend. We have come here not to exist in spite of death, but despite death. We have all joined together here, tonight, whether you know it or not, because we're all prepared to die. But not at each others' hands."

With Hugh as the epicentre, a large contingent of the night's revellers listened in awe at his charismatic shouting. He spun while he spoke, addressing no one but being heard by all. Martin looked at me with an eyebrow raised, and I shrugged. It was incredible that Hugh was trying to turn Henryk's beating into something meaningful. We tried to push through the wall of people again, but we were kept in place.

"Be prepared to die. Because that's what the old generations have left us with. And we won't have that. We won't have their death. And that's why we are prepared to die. Not in spite of their ignorance, but despite it. We are all here because each one of us will lead insignificant lives. But little do you know it, we'll each carry a torch of the new light. Of our light. We will turn our backs on money. We will turn our backs on consumerist political systems. The older generations have done everything in their power to fuck the world and leave us with their mess. So, alright, this is our mess. Let's forget their greed, their 'me-first' mentalities, let's forget their consumer-compulsions and take this mess as our own. If there is one lesson we can learn from the previous generations, it's the ability to say *fuck it* in a completely guilt-free way."

By this time, tambourines rang in the crowd, and people cheered Hugh on. He galvanized the whole crowd. They pushed forward, so that Martin and I had to hold Henryk from falling over. I had seen townhall meetings on the reserve, where whole communities were being gentrified for a highway, and I never saw people so titillated. Hugh continued, completely gregarious on account of the blind mob's encouragement.

"So, brothers and sisters: fuck it! Fuck their suits. Fuck their formalities. Fuck their debts. Fuck their mortgages. Fuck their cynicism! Fuck their apathy! Fuck their destruction to our planet. Fuck their reductionism. Fuck their life-support machines. Fuck their pensions. I can't wait to die. Yes, I don't fear death, so I don't need their games that are born and sustained on their utterly desperate fear of death. Our previous generation had one good idea that they screwed up. They used chemicals to unlock their potentials. But they unlocked their egoism. We won't let that happen. That's why we should thank our supporters for their watercooler"—people cheered its mention—"We can thank them for freeing us. We'll all walk away from this, having said *fuck it* to the past, and we can walk into the future to see it the way we want to."

Hugh leapt into the crowd, throwing himself into hugs and all sorts of generous adoration. Martin and I took the opportunity to pull Henryk away from the insane mob. Henryk told us to head for the A.L.L.A.H club's tent, which maintained its calm despite the roar behind us. Claire sat with a crosslegged woman in a hijab. They spoke tenderly to one another, and I felt rude to interrupt. But when Claire saw us she understood it was time to go.

As we parted from the Don Valley, Hugh Min's screechy voice called up after us. He was running towards us. He pointed at Henryk accusingly and asked why we were starting fights. Then he pointed to me, and asked why I hadn't brought more LSD. Henryk shyed away from the man, speechless with a fat lip. Martin kept moving with Claire, they spoke together quietly with heads bowed.

"Now I'm trying to appease drunks with a head full of acid," Hugh said.

"Chill out, man," I said under my breath.

"What? What did you say? Speak up, Inca."

"I said chill the fuck out. You're not on acid. It's all in your mind."

"What do you mean? I had, like, four of those watercooler shots."

"Yeah, and there's a whole river full of those shots in the valley bottom. With a nice touch of sugar and a smidge of salt."

I had to give Hugh credit for being so easy to read. I watched him put together my vague confession. When he finally got it, his eyes lit up and he aimed a fierce finger at me.

"You didn't give us acid at all. You motherfucker! You said you would! Now look at what you've done."

"I haven't done anything, man. It's all you. You've made all of this."

"Thanks a lot, asshole. Thanks for ruining my experiment," Hugh concluded.

"Naw, man, not even," I sighed, getting as close to Hugh as my distrust would allow. "Leary already tried this experiment, man. The Merry Pranksters already tried it. That was their experiment. It's old. If you want to be original, you can tie a dead horse to a post and beat it with a stick. This is our experiment, man. And you proved us wrong. So thank *you*, Hugh Min, thanks. You better get back to your disciples. They're hallucinating, I think."

I threw up a peace sign over my shoulder as I left. I could feel Hugh's arms reach after me in desperation, as if he could really blame me for anything. Inside, he was crying. That poor bastard, he really thought a few micrograms of LSD would start a new revolution. He built this whole night on that preception. And when I pulled that foundation away, when I pulled the tablecloth from under his main course, he saw how utterly plain the table looked, and how unfulfilling that main course actually was.

Oh well. We all learn our lessons. It was just too bad that he was too old to admit he had learned something. So in a small way, I felt guilty that I may have helped to create a bitter old man.

Simon came running up after us, carrying the watercooler. He asked me if there was any more watercooler brew, but I told him he held the last of it. He said he was starting to come down, and I realized that Simon also thought he was tripping.

I broke the news, pointing out that Claire was the only person in this valley who was on LSD. Simon didn't skip a beat.

"I knew it, guy. Of course you couldn't've let Hugh convince you to spike these people. I knew you wouldn't, I knew you knew better. Hey Claire, we were both wrong. No car crash. No car."

The five of us piled into the Sunfire for a quiet ride home. Nobody spoke a word the whole way. When we got home I made Claire my homemade lentil soup (one of her favourites) and brewed a big batch of tea for the homeboys. Henryk cut up the actual remaining tabs of acid and handed them around. We sat in the Studio all night, talking. We didn't waste any time reminiscing over the night. It was over.

By sunrise only Claire and I were still up. We cuddled in view of the sliver of window that showed the eastern sky. Claire didn't apologize about earlier. I didn't expect her to. I wouldn't have accepted her apology. There was only one thing we needed to learn from tonight, but it wasn't that people are free to make choices, for good or ill.

Ours was a lot simpler, which also made it a lot harder to recognize. I fell asleep worrying I would never understand our lesson from tonight.

Morning sun rising,
reminding me of the light
you bring to my life.

MALIGNANT TUMOR
[Simon Arcan]

Cancer is a little bit like the heavy empty weight of black holes in the universe.

I had contemplated that for a minute three years ago. I was flying on mushrooms and home alone. I was lying in bed in the dark, with spacey lounge music seeping out of the speakers over my bed. I closed my eyes—or maybe they were open, it was always hard to tell at this stage of the trip—but either way, I was on the moon. It was a crisp vision. I had to lay flat on the rocky surface beneath me, to stay attached. For a short rotation I saw the earth wax and wane by. The stars were infinite, the galaxies clear. Everything could be seen in that wild space. Then slowly all the stars started to fade away. I saw our own sun grow, and turn red, then explode and consume everything, destroying its own solar system. Then it zapped into a tiny white light, pristine and naïve in the darkness all around it. I tripped immensely, alone in that inferno, watching the sun catch its cancer and pass away like all the other things in the Universe.

I never thought I would have to contemplate that again.

But then again, I never thought I would hear that my best friend Atlas had been kicked out of his house by his manic mother, again.

I never thought Henryk would ask me for help with his homework, but he did when he was frustrated about an essay he had to write last semester.

I never thought Lukasz would ask me to go shopping with him. Especially clothes shopping. I probably should've known better.

I never thought that one day my dad would phone me and not open with a pretentious tone. It was confusing when I had to ask him to repeat himself because he was mumbling his sentences together. After a few attempts he said it.

"Mami's got cancer."

"What?"

"Yes, Simon. And—and it's not a good kind of cancer. Not one they know how to treat. It's some rogue cancer. It's got her, Simon, it's got your mother."

"So what does that mean?"

I found myself even more confused, like what he was saying made no sense. But it did. I understood what was happening.

"Probably a month, a month and a half. They have no way to estimate besides the other sporadic cases. It's strange, no doubt. But...God, Simon, she's in the hospital now."

I asked which one and he gave me directions. I tried to think if it was on a crosstown bus route.

I compulsively cleared my desk. I needed clear space. I stared at the vacuated middle of my desk and breathed slowly.

"Simon? Are you still there? Are you going to go?"

"Yeah. Of course I will."

"We can go together, if you like."

"No. I'll go alone."

"Okay, son."

We shared a silence over the phone, which sounded like a fuzzy whisper.

"She wants to go home. She wants to leave the hospital. I don't think it's a good idea, but the doctors, they're not sure if they know if it's a good idea or not. So...I don't know. What do you think?"

"What do I think?"

"Yes. Should I let her come home?"

"She should probably go back to the *Domincana.*"

I enunciated the country's name like Mami always did.

"The Dominican?"—Dad pronounced it all truncated and curt—"Shit, Simon, she could get sicker."

"I think she'd enjoy it. I'm just saying. You should let her decide, though, right? I mean it makes no difference to me. It's up to Mami as far as I'm concerned."

"Fine. That's fine. Now Simon, when you go to visit, don't rattle her with your complaints about me. Just take it easy, for God's sake. Let's try to remind her that we are a loving family."

"Yeah sure, Dad," I found myself saying it without thinking it. "I'll do that for you."

"Oh, and Simon?"

"Yeah?"

"Maybe you could cut your hair before you go see your mother? I think she'd appreciate that."

"Bye, Dad. I gotta go."

"Call me after you go. Or, you know, visit or something."

"Alright, Dad. I gotta go."

"Fine. Talk to you later. Be good."

I hung up the phone and took some deep breaths. I cried a little bit. It was intense but brief. I ended up on the floor, head down and hands folded in prayer. I wasn't praying, because I knew it was pointless. Because what was happening was what I told everybody was happening: people are a transfer of energy, and, inevitably, everyone's energy transfers.

I knocked one of my textbooks to the ground in misplaced rage.

I paced around the room for a little while. I stared out the window. Nothing. A brick wall.

It was crazy, it was all crazy.

Plus there was going to be so much fucking paper work.

Fuck.

FUCK.

I went to find Atlas, but he wasn't in his room. Of course. He was at work. Just like Mami, always at fucking work.

Henryk was at the library, probably with that Philomena chick.

Fuck fucking. It was all pointless.

Martin was out somewhere, catching a story. I wanted to tell him this news break.

I could've made a YouTube video, because I felt it was the only way I would find somebody to hear me out. To hear why Mami shouldn't go, why she had to stay—and also why I knew she had to go.

I sat on a kitchen barstool and lit up a cigarette. It didn't occur to me that we had never smoked inside. I pulled on the cigarette slowly, comfortably, ashing in a nearby glass. I rubbed my eyes with my palms. I stared at the marble blots on the tiles and thought about nothing. Then I saw the day's newspaper folded on the counter. I grabbed it, unfolded it, ruffled the pages to loosen them. I stared at the headlines but didn't absorb anything. I looked over the photos and the bolded words that caught my eye.

But whatever I looked at looked like cancer. Even the paper looked like cancer—it was a mutated tree—and the ink looked like a mold that seeped into its host tree. I ashed the cigarette on the business section and threw the sports insert on the floor.

Mami moved on, and so will I. It was the way it all went.

I was that same energy. I could waste my energy feeding all these cancers. I could also beat the cancer. So maybe I wouldn't accept the myth of ultimate death—fuck the cancer-ridden horses of the apocalypse—my energy would not be wasted on modernity's frivolous self-destructive pursuits. They will know it is right when they feel it. They might fall or they might follow. And if not, at least I would have dutifully passed on my energy.

I grabbed my coat and two joints. I snorted the last line of blow I had stashed away and grabbed some music for the road.

I waited for the bus going in the opposite direction of where Mami lay. I would see her later. But first, I needed justice. It was time to use my energy for what it was meant to be used for.

Yeah, I seemed just as cryptic to me. I had no idea what I was going to do. All I knew was that I was going to do it.

Free-radical fed
off the termination phase—
¡*iniciación*!93

ONLY THE RIVER KNOWS
[Atlas Sangman]

I stepped out of the car haltingly, in polaroid snapshots—the enclosed comfort of the car interior

---

93 ***Iniciación*** — (*Spanish*) Initiation

popping open to the chirping, squirting, flittering exterior. My feet crunched on gravel, an unfortunate sound. When I used to come here, under the Bridge, the parking lot was typically empty. The occasional old Asian man found the river access and unsuccessfully fished in it. Today was no different. But there was an addition to the familiar scene: Conrad Ernestway's black coupe.

Not that there was anything wrong with that. It was just unexpected. Jeanne invited me over the phone. We didn't speak much, she only told me to meet her under the Bridge. For years the epic arches of the concrete Bridge were a place to escape the busy city operating above.

Small gravel pened onto larger stones, which met angular boulders that braced the shoreline from the rushing river below. North and south of the Bridge a greenbelt snaked along the shallow floodplain that had carried the first settlers through the hilly suburb.

But that was long ago.

I had the impression from our conversation that it was going to be like old times: Jeanne and I and some good herb, listening to the river gush beneath while we lushed like two fireflies above it— endowed in a smoky cacoon, innocent in our exchanges, intimate and incarnal, asymptotic, yet unified in some strange way whose essence was washed downstream.

But that was long ago.

I walked through the willows to the stones. Indeed, Jeanne sat beside the always solemn-looking Conrad. He wore dark sunglasses and smoked a cigarette. Jeanne saw me but didn't call out to me until I was closer.

"Been a while since we held up this Bridge."

"Yeah. I'm surprised it stood for as long as it did," I chuckled to remain unthreatening.

"Hey Atlas," Conrad said quietly.

I shook the man's lean hand because he offered it.

"We've been waiting."

"Yeah, I rolled a nice one just for you," Conrad smiled.

"Damn, man. I spun something too."

"*Fantastique*," Jeanne clicked.

We made small talk while our breaths were occupied. After the fourth or fifth hit I noticed the distant sounds of overpassing cars, and the amplified birdsong. The shrubbery offered up its odours, though Jeanne's perfume wafted and plucked my senses back to another time, a treacherous time that was our past. There was no way to escape it now—the two joints were getting down to their homemade filters, so extra care had to be taken. When we passed the joint our fingers overlapped.

Jeanne mocked the amateur graffitti on one of the Bridge supports and we all laughed. Then she told us of this marvellous stonework on a painted bridge in France, how it was not only architecture, but art—that modern North America did not *create* but *build*—how the city should at least pay real graffiti artists to design patterns on its bridges. Conrad teased, claiming the transformation of rock into concrete was art. From the absence of lackadaisical wit that characterized Conrad over the past few months, I figured he wasn't so upset about their break-up anymore. He could move on. Jeanne had moved on.

But that was long ago.

When Conrad bowed his head to fix a canoeing joint, she guiltily met eyes with me—but the sentiment switched abruptly to a smile with peaked eyebrows, as if asking for some forgiveness— if I was kind, and I was—but Conrad's flattened smile filled in the story. He made sure to mention that they had just had dinner. A date, for lack of a better term.

So this *was* going to be like old times.

I watched Jeanne's reaction while Conrad spoke softly. Her smile was stale. At the corners of her mouth her expression peeled, her cheeks cracked, her forehead fell away. Indeed, Jeanne was sad. There was no doubt.

Conrad excused himself to the willows to piss. Jeanne lit a cigarette, and when we made eye contact she gave a one note laugh. A joyful laugh, a real soulful release. I smiled back. Her dull smile left with Conrad. Jeanne's skin took on a different tone. She bounced when she flicked her ashes. Out of the corner of my eye I thought I saw movement. That tended to happen in this place. The things here, under this Bridge, weren't what they seemed —or, at least, they could be something other than what they were at any other time in any other place.

Martin told me, under this Bridge years ago, that the Celtic Druids believed the Earth deity left places between the material and immaterial worlds, small fractures in the earth where the mystical appeared. Martin couldn't be deluded enough to believe it, even though he was Celtic. It made me wonder why he mentioned it at all. It was strange that in the over-developed suburban refractal this small swath of river had escaped the gluttonness subdivisions—that despite the numerous rivers disappeared and now flowing from basement to basement, this river remained—from a discreet spring in the Niagara Escarpment, through the Valley, to the fringes of the city, passed backyards of costly acreages, then sneakily cutting between strip malls and housing subdivisons, all the way to Lake Ontario. To meet its lover. The eternal Odysseus, doomed to do nothing but return to Penelope.

"Do you remember when we first met?" Jeanne asked suddenly.

"Yeah. It was very random."

"I thought about that recently."

"Oh yeah?"

"I don't think anything so random had ever happened to me like that. And it hasn't since."

"Chaotic."

"Yeah," Jeanne laughed like she was exhausted. "Hey, Jésus and Tori were grabbing some coffees, then they're reaching here as well."

"Cool."

"We'll hang out, just the two of us, sometime. Maybe Friday?"

Conrad crossed the space between us.

"Sure," I said, even though I knew I would be busy.

"Is that Jésus and Tori?" Conrad asked, chinning to the parking lot.

The two appeared through the willows, Tori wringing along his faithful guitar by the neck and Jésus treading the stones with his hands in his pockets.

"Jésus hath risen!" Conrad yelped.

I hugged Jésus because it had been months since I'd seen him. Tori worked with me, so I saw him too often. He sat on the stones below the rest of us strumming the guitar while Jésus procured a long two-pape joint from behind his ear.

Jeanne told another story about a Mediterranean coast cycle tour she took. How after thirteen samples of wine she could hardly find the seat of her bicycle and nearly tumbled away into the sea.

While she spoke I peered over the boulders and imagined falling into the River and being carried like a forsaken leaf to Lake Ontario. No one would notice me, no one would try to save me, no one would scream.

One time, when we were eighteen, Jeanne and I brought two pieces of paper and wrote secret poems on them under a smoked out canopy, then made bulky paper ships that we floated down the river. It didn't feel as corny as it sounded. It was truly a release, even if I'd since forgotten what I'd written. I peered over the boulders again, engaging the River in conversation, asking what it could tell me.

It only bubbled the same song it sung since I first came here.

I turned back to our circle, stammering a giggle-phrase while Tori passed the guitar to Jésus. Jésus played a gentle nocturne. Conrad whistled once he caught the melody. Tori backed Jésus' disembodied voice. I stared at Jeanne, who stared at me, and in the darkening shades of twilight we danced without touching, caressed each other without speaking, confessed something we couldn't commit nor admit in less words than were misspelled in graffitti under that bridge. Her face looked long. The moon waned, early in the sky. The wind picked up, muting the music in hurried sweeps. It pulled at the ends of Jeanne's hair, raising and twisting them. They looked like garland in the echoed streetlight from above.

Jeanne mentioned that it was supposed to rain tonight. Thunderstorms. Jésus slowed the music to its end.

"Rain? Must be Atlas and his rain dance," Conrad said.

"I didn't do any rain dance, man."

"For sure. I just saw you."

Conrad glared at me with the fat sunglasses he refused to remove. I tried not to look at Jeanne. Tori asked if there was a drought dance. Conrad told him he should try. It was all bullshit anyways. I snuck a look at Jeanne over Conrad's turned shoulder. She shrugged imperceptibly, the processed smile held onto her face. Our masquerade dance may have been rainchecked but it was not over. I bowed to my partner. She forgot to bow back. I hugged Jésus again, and made arrangements to meet them on Friday.

The river carries
itself in hushed nocturnes—
an open secret.

ROLL ON RIVER
[Henryk Zdicz]

Paddling is like...
Walking on your hands.

Feeling the river breeze wash over your face is like...
Embracing a lover.

Unlike either of those...meeting at Philomena's house to be briefly lectured about canoe safety by her father, which made my intimate greeting hug with his daughter violate several of his unspoken rules.

Thankfully Philomena had strapped the canoe to her car's roof already, so I didn't have to raise that beast over my head. I would later, and twice is enough in any day. I discovered, through the open garage door, that Philomena's parents argued for fun. Could have been a lack of anything else to talk about, because Philomena was nothing like her parents. Since I opened the door she had been wearing a smile. I wondered if she ever wore anything else.

Paddling is like...
Going nowhere fast.

Running your fingers through the spring run-off water is like...
Combing your fingers through a lover's hair.

Like one of those things...the two hour drive to the escarpment, near where the river began as an inconspicuous seep, all the while apologizing politely for the CD's we hadn't brought.

The escarpment's forest was just beginning to bud. It leant a satisfactory voyeurism into my new vision of the interworkings of an ecosystem. By nine-thirty we were on the water, already wet to the knees. The sun bellowed summer-like through a spring wind.

My oar smacked the side of the canoe—such an amateur. Behind me, *kapitan* Philomena scooped the water in proper J-stroke, silent as a swan. I wanted to watch her graceful movements, but the scene was too astounding, and I was sitting forward, looking off the bow.

Paddling is like...
Being tricked into thinking you have any say in where you go.

Following the runs and riffles of the river is like...
Watching the curves of your lover's body sway rhythmically.

Like both of those things...catching the current so that Philomena only had to keep her oar over the back as a rudder, so I could turn around and we could share our first beer.

The paddle down to Mississauga would take about three hours, and we had the whole day, so we stopped frequently at interesting spots, either to check out a viewpoint and snap photographs, or memoriegraphs, or just sit on the sand closer than we could on the boat. Philomena sat as close as she could to me without sitting on my lap. I leaned into her when we laughed, and she pushed in when she spoke. The wind was blowing east, and I could smell her shampoo on the drafts that whished her hair out of its ponytail. On our third stop, on our third beer, to the hushing of the river, we locked eyes: happy, or serious, or maybe both. I leaned in after Philomena misjudged her own timing. We locked dried lips. Hers were soft and warm. My lips felt mechanical, stony. Philomena ended the kiss, laughed a little bit, then changed the subject.

She brought my attention to the lush forest over the exposed gravel bars of the river shore. Life on the rocks. I kissed Philomena again, so she wouldn't forget what had happened. She ended the kiss again, excused herself to get us new beers. I declined her offer and slid the boat back into the water.

Paddling is like...
Sublimating rough sex through your upper body so the canoe can cut along the helpless dominatrix.

Jumping out of the canoe to skinny dip in a run while Philomena laughs hysterically and gives you shit about nearly tipping the canoe is like...
Watching your lover pass by your house without stopping by.

A little like both of those things...having to convince Philomena to join me in the silty water, all the while hanging on embarrassedly to the tail of the canoe, and her declining until I let go and told her I wasn't going the rest of the way.

I floated around a bend and saw the canoe parked on the sand ahead of me. Dark footprints showed little bare feet toeing towards the shore. There Philomena bobbed in the water, her dark hair slicked back, her shoulders bare, the deceiving breasts almost bared, yet bra'ed by the occluded water. She knew there was no way I would be able to get home if I didn't go with her. She splashed me, so I dove underwater. I wished I could've kept my eyes opened underwater, but it stung. Instead I swam the opposite way.

Philomena was shivering in under five minutes. The water was still cold from the short days. I tried telling her but my lips were too numb from the water. She told me she had enough, turned to get out, then turned back to me. She asked if I was going to swim away, or at least turn around. I told her I wouldn't. Philomena shook her head, laughed and breathed loudly. She started, still crouched in the water, then leaped up and out. Desperately covering herself and shivering, Philomena stopped to see if I was still watching, which I was. She wiggled her hands, to warm them, and shrugged. She asked me if I was going to get out or if I was going to stay shrunken all day. Then she disappeared into the reeds.

I kicked myself out of the water as quick as I could and wiped myself down with my jeans. The midday sun broke through the thin clouds and the shadows darkened. I headed into the reeds, listening for Philomena's movements over my own rustling. I came upon a patch of willows, whose canopy created a small enclave within the riparian area. The grass was matted, probably from bedding deer or moose. There Philomena's body was muted among the shadows. But her mouth was unmistakable—a pale sickle to take me down.

So I bent down to enter under the branches, and Philomena rolled onto her side to meet me. I tried to crawl over on the grass gracefully, but I felt like a clumsy child. She had catkin fuzz in her hair. I met her eyes, pushed in my head. She pursed her lips for my tongue.

Paddling is like...
Losing yourself to something you thought you could overcome, but maybe should have never tried to overcome.

Listening to the leaves bustle in the wind is like...
Hearing ancient songs long lost to human ears, and understanding why we bothered to procreate at all.

Becoming an animal again, full of sex and grass and muscle and hunger, was like both of those things.

Paddle far away,
right into my heart, under
the willow catkins.

FROM THE SPRAWL, MOTHERFUCKER
[Simon Arcan]

You know what? Fuck it.

That's what I said to myself when I woke up this morning.

Before I went to see my mother at the hospital I marched up Bay street with a mission. A vague but pragmatic mission.

See, I learned something in university that was worth more than what the pigeon-holed diploma-heads taught me. But if everybody thought like me, then the universities would probably dissolve, and become free.

Freedom, that was a cliché term I didn't want to use. But I did want to have it. I guess that's why I was on Bay street last week, your Honour.

You keep talking about it like it happened in a different life or something, guy. Don't twist what I did. There was no fucking witch doctor shit going on. I thought you guys were supposed to fucking represent the people?

I'll watch my language if you mind your hearing.

Alright, so what I was going to say was that I didn't know what I was going to do until I did it. When I saw Mr. Moneybaggers, or whoever the fuck he was, when I saw that guy, I knew that was the end of my mission. And, uh, I just proceeded to punch him in the face. I didn't mean to kill him. I didn't know he had a heart condition. Sorry, I didn't research his medical records. There was no pre-meditation. Nothing subliminal. It was really just the punch.

I never carry ID with me! Am I stupid? No, you don't *have* to know who I am. I would let you know if it was pertinent. And yeah, this time was pertinent, so I told the cop. That pig told me I was going to be arrested in a way that sounded like he was going to Rodney King me. I remembered his badge number too, do you want that? I remember it.

Alright, well if I sounded crazy when you arrested me, then it's probably because you're crazy. Probably.

I would bet—solidly, in fact—that you would do the same shit I did if you wouldn't end up in this courtroom being humiliated by you corporate-fat bureaucratic law-farmers who slice-and-dice every fucking thing a person does. You should consider self-help books. I heard there's good money in that.

Are you going to convict me? Like, hundred percent? 'Cause then I'll just tell all, I don't give a fuck. Just tell me before I really fuck myself over. Go ahead. Please.

Thank you, your honour, for the final countdown on my life. It's enlightening. Alright, well straight up, all I did was punch the man in the face. I didn't know who he was, I don't know what he does, I don't give a shit about where his suit came from—

Sorry, your honour, the language. Right.

My dad was subdued over by your system, trying to play by the rules. My mother, just a rape-and-pillage victim, another colonialist wallow on the landscape. My friends, totally fucked over by you guys. Do you know what you do to a regular man on a regular basis? You inflict fear and guilt for things that may be far from both those things. I'm telling you, that's objectable.

Objection! Sustain that.

Well, before you carry me off this podium I would like to say one thing.

You can kill the man

but you only birth a void.
Let me call my mom.

SOCIAL PROPRIOCEPTION
[Atlas Sangman]

I always knew it was going to happen today.
Don't ask me how I knew, I just did.
I saw it all happen, clear as if it was happening that very day…months ago in a *Salvia* vision.

I did everything I needed to do.
I convinced Martin to go after Adice Bandi. He was madly in love with her, but he held himself back because of his perceived inadequacies. The man was brilliant, and I wouldn't be able to save his damaged ego, but at least I could help him recuperate some loss.

Henryk didn't need much pushing to get away with Philomena, especially now that he was having sex again.

I posted Simon's bail and told him to go see his sick mother.

After my friends were finished mourning, they would be able to look back on this day and say that love saved their life.

A cup of cold green tea waited for me in the Studio. I sipped it, then went to the various stash boxes throughout the room. I took out the last of the oxycodone and LSD. Nobody was going to need it anymore.

I took the oxycodone with the green tea and nodded woefully to myself. This was how they needed to find me. It would be a lot easier to understand that I had been too high to save myself than the truth.

That I *was* saving myself.

The oxycodone kicked in quick. I had an empty stomach. I gnawed on the tabs of acid, stolidly awaiting the inevitable.

The phone rang.

I was by the window, watching the clouds, trying to find forms in the overcast sky. I looked to the other side of the room where my phone lay. It was Claire. I couldn't answer. Plus my knees had started to shake as the oxycodone pushed through my bloodstream, and the corners of the room exchanged places with one another as the acid turned on.

A dog barked in someone's backyard. I made eye contact with his small coal eyes and he waved his front paws at me. I shook my head and shooshed him away with the flick of a wrist.

Go, dog, go. You are free again.

The phone rang again.

It was Claire. I knew it, don't ask me how. This time, I reached over and picked up the phone.

"Atlas!"

"Hello?"

"Atlas, what are you doing?!"

"Nothing."

"No. Atlas, you don't have to do this, baby, do you hear me?"

"Yeah, I do. It's gotta be done. So it goes."

"What?"

"I don't know. I saw it. The *Salvia* showed me. It's the way it's supposed to go."

"There's no way it's supposed to go. You know that," Claire said with urgency. "You have a choice, baby. There's always a choice."

"Not this time."

"If you really have any faith that it's all predetermined, then you'd know what I was about to do, and you'd promise me you'd get out of there. But you don't know. All we know is what is, and what's happened. The rest is—"

"What are you going to do, Claire?"

My head was a whirlpool. I couldn't close my eyes because there was too much to see, and I couldn't keep them open because it was too hazy.

Besides Claire's voice, there was a roar. She called my name, but I ignored her because out of the whirlpool of my mind a thin stream reached out and wrapped itself around me. It said, *Maybe I don't want to die.*

I gulped heavily several times and wet my lips. I trembled with excitement and fear.

"I...I love you, Claire."

"Go, Atlas," she said. "Leave."

DREAMS
[Martin O'Neill]

From where I stood on the curb I could see into the den.

This wasn't the way I usually saw our home when I returned from work. Atlas had painted the front door red in the early fall. For feng shui, he said, but also because he liked the colour red. He convinced the superintendent that he would paint all the doors of the complex the same colour for a small rent discount.

I had gone out for dinner with Adice, so I was late coming home. Late enough that twilight was descending, so on any other day, even if I had a clear line of sight into the den, I probably wouldn't have been able to see it. That was where the blue &

red lights came in handy. They flashed repeatedly from the three cop cars and one fire truck parked haphazardly before the row of townhouses. An ambulance blinked its bright stars a little further away.

I pulled myself from a stagnant stupor toward the charred remains of our home. It looked like a charcoal sketch of a warzone. It looked like all the movies made it look. A house on fire is a tragically simple concept to grasp, until it becomes your own house. Then it becomes as easy to handle as a hot iron.

I couldn't believe how stunned I was. I repeated over and over, *the house is gone, the fucking house is gone, the house is fucking gone*, but each time—despite the stunning visual evidence everywhere around me—I couldn't understand one word of the phrase.

House?

Gone?

Is?

"Excuse me, sir, stay back," an officer's mighty palm held back my shoulder, though my body kept advancing.

The police officer moved his bulk in front of me so that I bumped into him. I stared confusedly into his eyes.

"You'll have to stay back."

"That's my house," I said, pointing at the blackened wood that once supported our abode.

"You lived there?"

"Yeah."

"Stevens!" he shouted over my head. "Got one."

"Was anyone inside?" I asked.

"Captain Stevens will be able to help you now."

"Was there?" I badgered. "Was there anyone inside?"

"The Captain will be here shortly."

"But you are right here! Answer me, you fucking asshole. Was there anyone inside the house?"

If I could explain my rage, then I probably wouldn't have truly been in a rage. I pushed the beefy officer's chest, feeling the bullet-proof vest instead of flesh, and I was instantly trapped by clasping arms from behind.

"Calm down, son," said the voice from behind.

"Where are my friends?" I shouted.

"Calm down, or we aren't going to be able to help you, goddamnit."

I struggled, so the officer cuffed me and lay me on the ground with a heavy knee on my spine. He dragged me to his vehicle. The lights flashed blue and red in my face. There was no chance that I was going to slow my breathing like Atlas had taught me to do when I panicked.

"I live here, man, I live in that house and I want to know what happened. Did you find anybody inside?"

My voice quivered, it made me feel like a pussy in front of the tough police officer.

"Okay, come with me."

He uncuffed me and led me to an unmarked car. I followed at a distance. He informed a suited man about my presence before I got there.

"My name is Detective Hadley. Captain Stevens tells me you lived in one of those houses?"

"Yeah."

"Which one?"

"Three-E."

"Three-E? What did you know about your neighbours in Three-G?"

"Three-G? I don't know. They were young like us, I guess, but we never saw them. Like once or twice a month we'd pass in the parking lot."

"We found marijuana in your household."

I felt my face go cold. The confusion around me blacked out for a profound: OH FUCK.

"What? What do you mean?"

I had nothing else to say that wouldn't sound incriminating.

"There was one particularly large stash that we found. We also found a bong. You guys were fans of the weed were you? Do you know if the occupants of Three-G were?"

"Uh..." I laughed, trying to show the cop I wasn't a hardened criminal. "Yeah, I guess. Who isn't a fan? No, no, I don't know if they were. Do you know what happened? Just tell me, man, it's all I want to know right now. Are my friends okay? We can deal with the other stuff later, right? My friends might have been in there."

"Your friends are alright."

"Okay. Thanks..."

"Don't thank me. I didn't do anything. The marijuana probably didn't help the house from burning. Did you ever buy any product off anybody from Three-G or that you believe were associated with Three-G?"

"Are you saying they chopped?"

"Um. Yes. Did they chop?"

A dealing neighbour? Damn. A dealer next-door it would've saved us a lot of time and gas money. The police knew more than we did. Who really had the problem?

"I don't know," I said.

The detective sighed, wiped the corner of one eye and stared behind me to the wreckage.

"Unit Three-G was where the blaze started. They had a dope lab with poor electrical work. These old townhouses...they burn quick, leave nothing once they get started. Luckily Three-F was home and she called it in. We were able to stop the blaze from spreading."

"But my friends are okay."

"We don't know."

"But you said—"

"There are bodies that have yet to be identified. You can come down the morgue to name them."

I tried calling Henryk. I tried calling Simon. I called Atlas. No one answered. They might have been too busy to pick up, it was possible, but they didn't phone back. I watched the firemen carefully disarm the fire and its mess for twenty minutes before I told the detective I would see the bodies.

> What once towered & crowded us
> crumbles & floats away, like
> visions dreamed on sand castle spires.

CODA
[Martin O'Neill]

A week later I stood before the taped-off remains of our old home. It looked so frail.

I lit a cigarette, inhaling thoughtfully.

Atlas was dead. The fire consumed him. It burned from the kitchen up, took him in the studio. The neighbours, whose shanty grow-op had started the electrical fire, already had a long list of felonies they would have to face in court, but Atlas' death was not one of them. He was just another lost casualty, a misfortuned body who was in the wrong place at the wrong time. Just like everything.

But he wasn't alone. Claire was the second body. They were both in the Studio, charred from the blaze. When the firefighters found them, they had to extinguish their skin before carrying them downstairs.

Claire and Atlas, in side-by-side morgue lockers, their faces calm like nothing had happened at all.

Simon was in custody, surely to spend some years in prison. His mother's cancer accelerated its spread while he was on bail. She would probably die before he heard his sentence.

Henryk did not deal with Atlas' passing well. He cried. He cried in Philomena's arms, he cried in Lukasz's arms, he cried in my arms. He wrote his final exams in misery, which was a terrible state in which to prove your capabilities to a removed third party. After his last exam he packed Atlas' Sunfire full of camping gear and drove north with Pilomena. He asked if I wanted to go, but I couldn't leave work. I would have to bear the brunt of a dead friend in the same rut I was in when he was alive.

Adice opened up to me at Atlas' wake, saying that she was ready to be a girlfriend. It was a cheap way to get her to go out with me, but I took it. I understood it would all pass in the end, anyways.

Nihilism was a wonderfully inefficient dressing, but it stemmed the bleeding so well.

I coughed out a lungful of smoke, realizing I had held that first inhalation that whole time.

This was stupid. I threw down my cigarette and crushed it with my shoe. I stared at the scattered tobacco, then back at the house.

Nothing could take back the fire. Nothing could resurrect Atlas or Claire. Nothing I could do could make it better. There was only one thing I could do.

Onward & outward.

Straight ahead.

∞

¡SHOUT OUTS!
[The Homeboys]

[in no particular order, so don't trip]

Atlas Sangman would like to thank...
Marie, Rachel, Shiva, Robin, Dr. Carveth, Mina,
Paola, Reeve & Patty, Rebecca, the Beatles, Jolene,
the Algonquin peoples, Lisa, Natalia, Bob Dylan,
Kerouac, Mike, Buddha,

Simon Arcan would like to thank...
Mississauga!, Peter, Abuela y Abuelo, Dr. Fonseca,
Kat, pussy!, Juan Pablo, Tia, King, Paolo, Albertan
cowboys (especially you, Ryder), Dr. Hoffman, B-
Unit, Arthure, Laura, Marcela, Julian, Courtney,
Stovie, psilocybin, Wade, Uzee, Shannon, Matt,
Ernesto, Daniel,

Martin O'Neill would like to thank...
Darren, Honey, Maki, Tim, Max, Ibi, Brenda,
Karen, Alex, Kaylyn, the Internet, Erin,

Henryk Zdicz would like to thank...
Jason, Andrzej, the Earth, Kerri, Olsen, Dr. Cook,
Amber, Corey, a different Jason, strangers of
Toronto, Kelly, Evan, Chet, Gerasil, Ellie, Lizbet,
National Geographic...

...but most importantly the Homeboys would like to
thank **YOU**,
for making this Universe possible, even if for only a
little while.